The Girl From The Killing Streets

David Hough

www.darkstroke.com

Discover us online:
www.darkstroke.com

Find us on instagram:
www.instagram.com/darkstrokebooks

Include **#darkstroke** in a photo of yourself
holding this book on Instagram and
something nice will happen.

To my grandsons,
Henry and Oliver.

Acknowledgements

I did not get to be a published novelist without the help and encouragement of so many fellow writers. There have been too many to name individually, but I would like to say a big 'thank you' to all those friends I made while attending Della Galton's weekly classes, the Cygnatures Writing Group meetings, the Dunford Novelists' meetings, and the annual Swanwick Writers' Summer School.

When I started work on this novel, I was given valuable feedback by friends who read and commented on the original manuscript. I thank you, all of you. I was delighted when the final manuscript was accepted by Darkstroke and I must thank Laurence for dreaming up the inspiring front cover.

Finally, it would be wrong of me not to mention the people I lived amongst and worked with in Northern Ireland back in the early nineteen seventies. Many have now passed on but, for those who are still alive and who helped me in the difficult days we went through, be assured I have not forgotten you.

About the Author

David Hough was born in Cornwall, England, a distant relative of the historian, Dr A. L. Rowse. Because of his father's work he grew up in the Georgian city of Bath. He began his working life in an accountancy office in London, but quickly changed career to something more demanding. In 1965 he began training as an air traffic controller.

In 1968, at the end of his training, David was posted to Belfast Airport in Northern Ireland. The following year 'the troubles' erupted and David was the Aerodrome Controller on duty when troops were airlifted into the province. Away from work, he mixed with people from both sides of the divide and listened to their stories. It gave him a deeper insight into the grievances behind the violence. He subsequently worked as a civilian controller at a military radar station in Northern Ireland. The violence got worse and, from inside his own home, he saw bombs explode nearby. He was on duty when the radar station was targeted by mob rioting. Thankfully, he had moved on when it was attacked with mortar bombs.

After leaving Ireland, David worked as an Aerodrome Manager and as an Area Controller in Scotland. He then took up a post as an instructor at the UK college of Air Traffic Control. That was when he suffered a heart attack and was prevented from returning to operational ATC. He turned to writing stories as a therapy during his recovery. When he finally retired from Air Traffic Control, he became a full-time writer and has had more than thirty books published.

David now lives with his Irish wife, Fionnuala, on the south coast of England. They have a daughter, two sons and two adorable young grandsons.

The story of The Girl From The Killing Streets owes much to David's experiences in Northern Ireland. The vivid descriptions of life in Belfast in 1972 could have come only from someone who lived there and saw 'the troubles' at first hand.

Readers can learn more about David and his books on his web site at: **www.thenovelsofdavidhough.com**

The Girl From
The Killing Streets

PART ONE

Human life is a learning experience
Death is merely the end of the lesson

Chapter One

September 1980

They were two hundred and fifty feet above sea level, but they stumbled around like half drowned shipwreck survivors on a remote shore. I counted more than a dozen of them: armed soldiers caught in torrential rain at a moorland roadblock a few miles from Armagh city. A line of traffic built up as they examined each car in turn.

What the hell was the problem? Gun-running? A prison escape? Or was this the army's answer to a tip-off about the movement of yet another car bomb? Were the troops told to get their arses up here and watch for a vehicle with a heavily-laden boot? A dead give-away was that: a sagging boot stuffed full of fertiliser bags ready to be soaked in fuel oil. The IRA's bomb of choice.

When I reached the head of the queue, a rain-soaked figure signalled me to wind down my window. Rainwater cascaded off his Gore-Tex waterproofs as he leaned towards me, hugging his self-loading rifle against his chest. He had a young face - too young to be soldiering in a dangerous place like this - and his youthful voice fought against the noise of the downpour.

"Where are you going, sir?"

"Armagh Gaol."

"Why?"

"To interview a prisoner." I pulled my briefcase from the passenger seat, took out a formal letter along with my passport and held them up to the open window. A sudden gust of icy wind washed the rain over them. "This is my letter of permission from the prison governor, and this is my ID."

5

He glanced only briefly at the documents before staring intently at my face. "Where have you come from?"

"Belfast Airport. I flew in from London just an hour or so ago."

"Has anyone stopped you along the way?" His gaze remained tightly focussed on me. He seemed nervous but who wouldn't be in his place?

"Yes, you. Are you expecting trouble here?"

"Maybe. We'll need to look in your boot."

"Okay." I sat back and waited while another soldier opened the boot lid and rummaged inside. He would have found nothing except the spare wheel. After no more than a minute of searching, he slammed the lid shut. The boy beside my window stood back and waved me on. Rain was still cascading from his waterproofs.

"Move along, sir." He sounded utterly pissed off.

Clearly, I wasn't what they were looking for.

"What's your name, soldier?" I asked.

"Why do you want to know?" He sniffed and wiped the rain from his face.

"Curiosity."

He should not have answered my question, but he did. "It's Atkins. Now, move along."

"You're in the wrong war, son. Tommy Atkins belonged in a much earlier conflict."

He shrugged and walked away.

Was I once like that boy soldier? Was I like him back in the days when I lived here in Ulster? Pissed off while the world about me went utterly mad? Maybe so, but I had a wife then, someone who was able to smooth away the jagged nerve edges that remained at the end of each day.

I accelerated past the barrier and flipped on the car radio, not sure which channel it was tuned to. Pop music for the oldies seemed to be the general idea. Buddy Holly, *Raining In My Heart*. Buddy I could take, but the 'rain' theme was just what I didn't need. Not in this downpour. It was followed up with Barry Manilow's *I made it Through the Rain*. I switched it off.

The weather got worse. Ugly black clouds dragged their ragged bottoms low across the bleak landscape. As I came to the outskirts of the city a lightning flash lit up the sky and a thunderclap boomed directly overhead. In that same moment, the hire car's engine missed a beat, ran rough for a few seconds before recovering. Maybe it was warning me to turn round and go home. In this weather I could so easily have been persuaded. More lightning and more thunder followed. The car wheels splashed through floodwater, and the windscreen wipers fought a losing battle. You'd think that God had finally given up on Northern Ireland. Let's face it: He had reason to call it a day here after years of unremitting violence. But I had to keep going because my next book would depend upon what a young woman was prepared to tell me.

Her name was Sorcha Mulveny.

Eight years ago, she had been tried for the murder of a police detective and a police informer. It was an unusual case. At the start of the trial she entered no plea and then, to everyone's surprise, she confessed under cross examination. I remembered it well.

The prosecuting counsel asked her, "What happened when you met Detective Constable Dunlop that night?"

I imagine he was expecting a pack of lies, but what he got must have knocked him for six.

"I killed him." The words came out just like that. No explanation, no excuses, just a confession. She looked so small and insignificant as she stared down at the floor; a lamb in the courtroom slaughterhouse. I had to concentrate hard to hear her.

The prosecutor looked astonished at the unexpected admission. "Would you say that again?" he asked. Maybe he wanted thinking time. Clearly, he hadn't prepared himself for this.

"I killed him," she repeated in a calm, quiet voice. "And I killed Jimmy Fish the next day. I killed them both."

She refused to say any more. In the face of her admission of guilt, the trial ended abruptly, and she was handed a life sentence.

My interest in the case might have gone no further, but Sorcha's confession didn't feel right. The more I thought about it, the more it bothered me. Uneasy thoughts like that had served me well as a journalist, prompting me to look deeper into stories that other hacks accepted at face value. I saw a lot of harrowing court cases in those days, but this one intrigued me more than most. I couldn't understand why the defendant seemed more like a victim than a perpetrator. Was I likely to find answers eight years after the events?

I could try.

That was why I was here.

***

Pounding rain was hammering at the barred windows when I walked into the prison later that morning. Thunder rattled the frames. They used to tell me - when I lived and worked here - that we English are soft because we don't get the sort of weather that turns Irishmen into real men.

They were probably right.

Sorcha instantly stood up to meet me in the interview room. The visible change in her was striking, I saw it straight away. Still in her late twenties, she looked like a middle-aged woman who had endured a hard life. Skin that had once been fresh and flawless was now sallow and lined. Despite that, there was a look of determination about her, something I hadn't seen in court eight years ago. Her clothes still let her down; a well-worn skirt coming apart at the hem, and an off-white blouse that had seen better days. She was allowed to wear her own clothes, but she would probably have looked better in prison issue.

She reached out her left hand to shake mine. Her right elbow had been shattered by a bullet on that terrible day in 1972 and it still gave her trouble. It most likely always would. The atmosphere within the interview room was claustrophobic, tinged with the odour of other people's tobacco smoke, but that was better than the smell of pee and sweat that filled the windowless corridor that led to this part of the prison. Pee and sweat: the more obvious symptoms of fear perhaps?

I had written to Sorcha weeks ago to explain the reason for my proposed visit. It took that long to get her agreement along with permission from the prison governor. With the formalities behind us, we were able to get down to business quite quickly. "You know what I want to hear from you," I said. "There were so many things that never came out at your trial."

"That was eight years ago," she said as she sat down. "I've changed since then. I'm ready to talk now, so I am." Unlike her physical appearance, there was something fresh and vibrant in her voice. "I want to get it all off me chest. I know people will hate me for what I did, but I want to tell youse everything."

"Did you really do what you said at the trial, Sorcha?"

She shrugged. "You can't imagine how guilty I felt, but it wasn't the way people thought."

"What do you mean?"

"It was more complicated."

I still didn't understand, but I asked, "Will you be seeking a review of your case?"

"No. But I want youse to write about it. Tell people what really happened."

The contradiction still didn't make sense, but I let it pass for the moment. If she was innocent, there would be time later to talk about a judicial review.

"What did happen?"

"That's what I'm gonna tell youse."

Some people get irritated by the Ulster habit of making the word 'you' rhyme with 'whose', but I was used to it. I'd lived in the heart of Belfast when my wife was alive, before violence and a very painful loss drove me back to England.

"What brought about this change of heart?" I asked, puzzled by the extent of the transformation.

She thought for a moment or two before replying. "Time

9

and… and the prison chaplain. We've had some long chats, so we have. I never told him what really happened, but I need to tell someone. I'll talk to you instead." She thought for a moment. "'Tis all about guilt, ain't it? Yes, 'tis all about guilt."

"Why didn't you open up fully to your priest?" I asked.

"A priest? Godsakes, I'd not talk to a priest!"

"You no longer believe in your Catholic faith?"

She shook her head fiercely and wiped a trace of dampness from the corner of one eye. "After what they did to me? Took away my... Hell! I've no time for priests. Not now. The chaplain's a Proddy… the Reverend Mayfair. He's a good man, so he is, but I'd rather tell the full story to someone who isn't tied up in religion. I had a belly-full of religion when I was growing up."

"Was that what brought this about? Just those chats with the chaplain?" I was cautiously sceptical.

She sniffed and a trace of colour returned to her cheeks. "There was me official prison visitor as well. We talked a lot… about the guilty feelin's… not what I actually did… just the feelin's… and then I told her about yer letter. That's the one where you said you wanted to hear what actually happened that day."

I gave her an unwise grin at that point. "Did you notice, Sorcha? You can say 'you' when you try."

"Don't criticise me!"

"Sorry." I tried to sound apologetic. "Tell me what your prison visitor said."

She took a moment to calm down before she continued. "She said you could be my opportunity to finally put everythin' to rest. She said it could be good for me to tell youse what really happened. Told me it could bring a sort of personal closure, whatever the truth of it."

Whatever the truth of it.

There it was again, the suggestion that the real story would prove to be an eye-opener. If she was deliberately trying to grab my attention, she was sure as hell succeeding. I tried to curb my impatience.

"These people..." I said. "... the chaplain and the prison visitor, they must have been persuasive."

"'S'pose so. One day I found meself seein' things in a different light, so I did. It brought things home to me. Made me want to clear the air. Made me want to speak about the things I didn't say in court." A forced grin came back to her face. "I remember seeing youse in court back in seventy-two, so I do. Came in every day, so youse did. Every day. I don't know why youse stood out, but youse did. Youse used to stare at me and yet youse looked kinder than the rest of them, as if you felt for me. And youse looked a lot younger then."

I was surprised by the sharpness of her memory, but I made no comment. I was now approaching the forty-year mark and I didn't need remarks about my age from a young woman like Sorcha.

I set my notebook on the table between us and took out my pen. "You don't mind if I start taking notes?"

"Fill yer boots." She drew a deep breath, and then both eyes grew moist again. "They will hate me, won't they? The people who read yer book... they will hate me for what I did?"

I shook my head. "I hope not. From the little I learned at your trial I'd guess that you were a victim of your environment. I suspect you were a victim long before the events of Bloody Friday."

"A victim? Youse mean what the nuns did to me, after the baby...?" She looked away and the lingering dampness in her eyes turned to a trickle of tears. The previous air of determination was gone in an instant. I allowed a moment of silence for her to compose herself. The revelation about a baby surprised me, but this was not the time for me to question the matter. Later, maybe.

When she seemed recovered, I told her, "I suspect that your story goes a lot deeper than most people realise." I injected as much of a tone of compassion as I could muster. She needed compassion like a starving man needed food, probably more, and she'd had precious little of it so far.

"Youse think so?" she mumbled.

"Sure of it. Look, we can delve into the more painful parts of your past some other time, if you prefer. Why don't you start this interview by telling me about what happened that night, the night *before* the bombing? Tell me what actually happened when you came across that policeman, the one who..."

"No!" She suddenly shook her head fiercely and shouted at me. "No! Not that!" Her air of cooperation vanished in an instant, leaving me nonplussed. "I don't wanna talk about that bit yet. Not yet. Why can't you leave it for the time bein'?"

"But you said you'd tell me..."

"Not yet! I ain't ready for that yet!"

I struggled to control my frustration. We hadn't even begun and already I had come upon a brick wall, and I didn't know why. I tried to keep my voice calm. And then that suspicion came back to my mind; the suspicion that told me something about her confession wasn't right. There was far more to her story than anyone had guessed. However, this wasn't the time to force the issue. Patience was going to be important here.

Patience and persistence.

"All right, Sorcha. What about later that night? When the Protestant boy died. Can we talk about that?"

"Suppose so." She sounded more compliant now, as if this act of violence was somehow unlike the killing of the policeman. Her voice was firm, but not so angry. "That wasn't me. I didn't kill him."

"I know. I heard what you said in the trial – what little there was of it. I'd like you to tell me about it in more detail. Make it more personal."

"More personal? You mean; what I was thinkin' at the time."

"Exactly."

"Yes, I suppose that's what I need to tell youse. What was in me head."

"If you're up to talking about it." I tried to inject a tone of encouragement into my voice. "Go back to what happened in the early hours of that morning. The time you were with Fitzpain in that back alley. Tell me exactly what happened."

She wiped at her eyes and she thought about it for a moment. "Youse mean… the moment when the boy had his dick cut off?"

I shuddered. I'd seen the graphic police photographs. "Yes. That's where I might begin the book, so why don't you start there."

"God, what a night that was."

"Tell me about it."

Chapter Two

Friday 21st July 1972
0410 BST

What Sorcha Mulveny saw in the dimly-lit back alley that night wasn't justice. She understood that.

It was mindless retribution.

Bile rose in her throat as she watched Brian Fitzpain castrating a Protestant pervert. He sawed off the boy's penis with a serrated kitchen knife and he was smiling as he did it. It was a cruel, self-satisfied sort of smile, as if he was enjoying himself. With such a grin, he could have been carving a Sunday roast, with his mistress and their five children gathered around the dinner table. Except that he was no longer living with or supporting the poor woman and her children. She was said to be good in bed, but even she couldn't hold on to him all the time.

Sorcha gagged on the bile. She thought she understood Fitzpain better than most people but, just when she imagined she'd seen it all, he would surprise her. He'd show her what further depths he could sink to. He relished administering harsh punishment, much like their parish priest relished buggering young altar boys, but today he was surpassing himself.

She wanted to look away, but guilt made her continue watching; the guilt of knowing she was a party to this butchery, this act of retribution. She shivered yet again, and it wasn't the night air that was getting at her. It was remorse… and fear.

"This bastard won't last long." Fitzpain scowled. "Stupid Proddy wanker."

Sorcha stared at him, aware that his lingering smirk was only a surface image. Underneath it all, he was just an animal carving up another animal, and she had allowed herself to be drawn into it.

God forgive her. Drawn into violence yet again.

She would have crossed herself if she had any remaining faith in the teachings of the Catholic Church, but she had long since fallen out of love with religion... and with Brian Fitzpain. His behaviour was the cruelty of a feral child. Her wickedness was born from fear of retribution if she refused his orders. So, which of them deserved God's forgiveness?

Neither, she guessed.

The smell of bile still lingered in her throat. With her heartbeat thumping like a Lambeg drum, she breathed deeply in an effort to calm her rising panic. Then she wiped a trace of spittle from her mouth.

Damn you, Brian Fitzpain! Damn you to hell.

And where did your family get that name anyway?

"'Tis the pain that fits the crime," he'd often say when he was administering punishment, and then he'd laugh. You were expected to laugh with him. It wasn't an option if you wanted to stay in his good books. And staying in his good books kept you alive.

The boy fought and screamed, but two men held him down. They called themselves the Pain Men: Brian Fitzpain's loyal and dedicated apostles. It was almost like a religion: you believed what the holy Brian and his followers told you. Or, at the very least, you pretended to. When it came to the crunch, you did as they demanded. You hid Republican snipers in your home and you diligently emptied your pockets when the IRA collection plate came round. The alternative didn't bear thinking about.

One of the men thrust a fist into the boy's face to make him shut up. It didn't work. The screaming got even louder. It echoed between the brick walls along the narrow alleyway at the rear of Mafeking Street where drug-stained syringes lay discarded alongside used condoms. Neither social workers nor pious priests were ever seen cleaning up the mess in this ghetto.

The boy's screams must have been heard half a mile away, but no one came to find out what was going on. They dare not. Too many of them had died sticking their noses in where they weren't wanted. They would have been woken up by the boy's cries, but they would know better than to open their doors or windows to investigate.

The grim red-brick terraces were wrapped in semi-darkness.

Not a single curtain twitched.

Not a single door creaked.

Sorcha relaxed her breathing as a measure of self-control returned. The foul smell still filled her nostrils, but the rhythmic thump of her heart began to lessen.

Until the deep boom of an explosion filled the night air.

A red flash silhouetted the line of houses.

Fitzpain looked up. "Not one of ours. It'll be the Loyalist bastards, so it will." He spoke with the offhand manner of someone who had grown used to explosions in the streets of Northern Ireland. It as the behavior of a man who revelled in his own part in the violence, believed in the righteousness of it.

We've got to do it, boys. We've got to blow the place apart. There's no other way.

It was yet another mantra of religious proportions.

The explosion was a car bomb, Sorcha decided. A vehicle loaded with ANFO; a low explosive mixture initiated with a small amount of high explosive. Pure high explosives sounded quite different to anyone used to hearing them repeatedly.

She waited until the night went dark again before she asked, "Are youse sure 'tis one of theirs, Brian? Sounds more like one of ours."

"'Tis not on yer list, is it? Much too early."

"S'pose so." She focussed her mind on the hand-written page he had given her earlier, and she lived again the moment when a man was killed because of it; a peeler. She recalled the look of surprise in his face just before he died.

He was a Catholic, but he went to his God without the last rites; totally unprepared for whatever he met on the other side.

She shivered at the memory and wrapped her arms about herself. The image of the knife in the man's chest came back to her and her shivering intensified.

"What's the matter with youse?" Fitzpain snapped.

"Nothin'."

"Damn you!"

She forced herself to wipe the images from her mind. It was far from easy. Her thoughts came back to the present when an army Saracen armoured personnel carrier rumbled noisily along Ladysmith Road, briefly visible in the streetlight at the end of the alley. That particular light was one of very few left working in this part of Belfast. Most of the junction boxes had been robbed of their timers by thieving IRA electricians. They were re-used in the manufacture of home-made bombs. The last remaining light in Ladysmith Road wouldn't be working much longer because many more bombs were needed if the IRA was to win this war.

As for the troops in the Saracen vehicle, they would most likely be on their way to deal with that last explosion. God help them.

And God rot them all for the mistakes they made here in Ireland.

Bloody Sunday would live long in the memories of the people of Northern Ireland. Long after the last British soldier went home to a comfortable fireside in a cosy English city. Long after the population of Northern Ireland was left to try to sort out its own problems its own way. Try... and fail yet again.

Meanwhile, the Proddy boy's severed penis lay in a pool of blood, dimly lit by that single streetlight. His severed testicles lay nearby. Funny how Protestant dicks and balls looked pretty much like Catholic dicks and balls, Sorcha reflected wryly.

You'd almost think they were the same race.

17

She wouldn't try out that cynical observation on Martin Foster. He wouldn't appreciate it because he was too compassionate and thoughtful for his own good. Naïve as well, but she could forgive that.

He was her impossible dream and she knew that such dreams were never perfect. Never lasted. Sooner or later the cracks had to show. In the meantime, she reluctantly admired the ideal way of life he offered her. Anything else meant facing up to the full extent of the ugliness of her own background. It was easier to pretend innocence and pander to his niceness and his naivety.

After all, she would be dead now, but for him.

Pity he was a Protestant.

A scruffy mongrel wandered out from a back yard, sniffed at the severed penis, pissed over it and ambled away down the alley.

No one commented.

"Now let's put the bastard out of his misery." Fitzpain thrust his knife deep into the rapist's crotch and opened an artery. Blood spurted over his hands and his dirty jeans, but he seemed unfazed by it. He laughed as the fountain of red flooded down over his shoes. "He won't last long now. Don't any of youse ever say I'm a man without an ounce of pity." And he laughed again.

The Pain Men laughed with him.

It was expected.

Sorcha let out a cry of disgust as a splash of red hit the torn and faded jeans she wore. They were not her jeans. Hers were thrown away in a bin outside Brian Fitzpain's place, the bloody evidence following the peeler's death. These jeans had previously been worn by a prostitute.

Ironic in a way, she thought.

She shivered once more as she turned away, remembering that less than half an hour ago the dying boy had tried to seduce her.

Tried, but failed.

In hindsight, she was glad of that. He didn't deserve normal sex, not after what he did to the child. But did he

18

deserve this? God, what an eejit he was, and him barely out of his teens. No older than herself. He should have known better.

She gritted her teeth. The poor wee sod.

She'd done what was expected of her… demanded of her as a matter of loyalty… but what would it achieve? Just one more killing. One more act of bloody revenge. It was at times like this when she wished she's had the courage to go ahead and end it all.

If she had terminated her miserable life a month ago, she would not have been at Brian Fitzpain's rented parlour house last night. But she *was* there. She had been drinking heavily to deaden the impact of the peeler's death. Who else could she turn to at a time like that, even though she blamed him for what happened? That was when word got to them about the rape. An IRA runner called at the front door, a teenager with protruding teeth and a mop of red hair. When the riots started, he would need a hood to cover that hair. It was a dead giveaway.

"There's been a Proddy rape last night," he announced in a shrill, reedy voice. "A poor wee Catholic girl got raped, so she did. Joe Cahill says he wants the guy pulled in and done over."

"Who did it?" Fitzpain asked.

Sorcha stood behind him, a glass of whiskey grasped in one hand, and she heard the boy give the name of Hamish McGovern followed by a brief description.

"And where do we find him?"

"There's a Proddy stag night goin' on right now." The runner's teeth flashed intermittently in the dim hallway light. He gave them the address of an illegal drinking den in a Protestant area. "We think t'was him what did it, but ya'd better make sure before ya do him in. If we're wrong, the Prods will come lookin' for ya."

After the runner had left, Fitzpain looked at Sorcha thoughtfully. Then he said, "Youse'd better do the findin' out, so youse had."

"Not my job," she protested, downing the last of her

whiskey. It stung the back of her throat. Hadn't there been enough violence already? Wasn't she sick of it all?

"Don't bloody argue with me," Fitzpain told her. "Go and find out for sure if it was him."

"Why me?"

"'Cos I'm tellin' youse to!"

"And if I don't?"

"Youse'll regret it. By Christ, youse'll regret it. I'm not doin' youse any favours, Sorcha."

She felt fear then because she knew what he meant. Her only hope was her belief that he would draw a limit. He might have her beaten to within an inch of her life without a moment's regret, but he couldn't kill her. Not that. As the daughter of Barbara Mulveny, she was too close to him. It occurred to her that maybe he'd be doing her a favour if he could kill her. A bullet through the brain would be a quick and painless way out of this shitty life. And it would be ironic if he, of all people, was the one to end her miserable existence. But he couldn't do that, could he? Not to her.

"How do I go about it?" she asked, forcing a small measure of control into her voice. "How do I get him to confess?"

"Use yer wits and yer tits, girl. Ye're no wee innocent with men, are youse? Just get him in a mood to talk."

The inference of what was wanted could not have been clearer. She could almost hear Fitzpain telling her to drop her knickers and give the boy a good time because that would induce him to talk. What boy was going to keep his mouth shut when he'd experienced what Sorcha Mulveny had to offer?

Her mammy was away visiting relatives in Ardglass village, and her sister was on night duty at the Mater Hospital. The way was clear. She relented and approached the boy in the early hours as he stumbled away from the stag night in the Loyalist drinking den; drunk and incapable. She sidled up to him, lured him away from his mates and told him she was one of the future bride's friends. Told him she fancied him. He gave her a whiskey-sodden grin in return. He was too drunk to notice when she led him back to Mafeking Street. Within half an hour he was in her bed, lying on top of her and breathing whiskey fumes over her naked breasts. The sex was rubbish, he couldn't get it fully up, but she wheedled a confession out of him anyway. He told her, in a slurred voice, about how he'd raped a dirty little Fenian. It was revenge for a Prod child killed by an IRA bomb, he said. Of course the poor girl had nothing to do with the bomb, but she was a Fenian and that was guilt enough. His drunken rambling disgusted her, so she persisted in setting him up for the punishment. She bundled the boy into his clothes and led him, still too stoned to protest, through the back yard and into the alley where Fitzpain and his thugs were waiting.

Dawn was not far off by then, but Hamish McGovern would never see it rise. He should have kept his trousers zipped up.

The wee bastard was shitting himself uncontrollably now. The slimy mess mingled with his blood, and the smell lingered.

God, what a stink.

Sorcha waited for the end; anxious to get back to her bed, and yet dreading the nightmares that would mar her sleep. Ahead of her the dirty cobbles were lit by the streetlamp where the alleyway met Ladysmith Road. It was the sort of early morning when no one would show surprise if a mutilated body turned up, dumped in the dirt like a sack of rubbish. What would be a big news story elsewhere was a common enough occurrence in a city that had long since lost all sense of humanity. She flinched instinctively when a police Land Rover sped along the road, a sudden burst of noise that faded just as the boy's screams began to weaken.

She heard Fitzpain laugh and say, "That'll teach 'im. 'Tis justice where it's wanted."

"No it ain't," she muttered. "'Tis revenge."

"Same thing," Fitzpain said.

"No, it's not."

Fitzpain shrugged. "Does it matter? He's got what he

deserves. Taught 'im a lesson, so it has."

"And what's it gonna teach him now he's dead?" She turned back to face the gruesome scene. "D'youse want me to call an ambulance?"

A stupid question.

He was a Loyalist who'd raped a twelve-year-old Catholic girl on her way home from Mass. So what did it matter whether he was carted away in an ambulance or rotted where he lay? Anger boiled inside her, deep fiery anger. Was it because the girl was only twelve, or because she was a Catholic? Round here, either was good enough reason for retribution. Or... Sorcha paused... was it because *she* was the one who set this up? Which was worse, she wondered: setting up a victim, or killing one? And her thoughts carried her back to the earlier killing.

The peeler.

The image of it still held sway inside her head. Still sickened her.

Barrel-chested and tall, Fitzpain stood up. His voice rose like the devil himself climbing out from hell, starting low down and ending a full six foot above the ground.

"Nah! Let him lie there. Teach the rest o' them perverts a lesson, so it will." This time there was a sharper tone in his voice; like the shiny edge of an otherwise grey knife blade. That was him all over, Sorcha thought. His voice was the sharp, shiny edge, and the rest of him was the grey bit. When you got to know him, you soon saw that he was just another middle-aged grey man. Angry, but grey. Receding grey hair, gaunt grey face and rumpled grey clothes. And when you looked deep into his eyes you saw such bitterness that made you wonder who had damaged him in his grey, misty past. His parents? A boy-buggering priest? Or was it a woman who had psychologically maimed him for life? One thing was for sure: other people were now paying the price of that damage. But wasn't that a common motto for all that was wrong around here? Whatever the trouble, someone had to pay.

Someone else.

Like the peeler who had to die because of what he saw!

She shivered again, remembering how the poor bastard lay on the pavement with a knife in his chest. It was Fitzpain's serrated kitchen knife, the same weapon he used here to carve off the rapist's dick. But her fingerprints were on the handle when the peeler died.

She remembered how she had vomited in the gutter.

It was one of the Pain Men who finished off the Proddy boy's punishment. Finn McKenna - the one with the livid scar on his cheek - took Fitzpain's knife and carved a cross on the boy's chest. It was a tribal mark known to everyone who lived in this street. The Cross of Pain, they called it.

Sorcha drew a deep breath, but it didn't achieve much. The reality of her pointless life lived on. As for Brian Fitzpain; making people pay seemed to be what this miserable existence was all about. Retribution for other people's crimes, real or imagined. Mostly imagined, but that was the nature of the man. His imagination was limited to other people's faults and failings.

He wasn't one of the more senior Belfast Provos, more like a piggy-in-the-middle man, the sort who took orders from above and passed them on to the Provisional IRA foot soldiers out on the streets. A killer, nonetheless. A mindless killer who was out on those hate-filled streets last night when the peeler came along.

Sorcha sighed in frustration. She should hate him, really hate him, but she knew the part he had played in her life and that made full-blown hatred so difficult. So she feared him instead.

She focussed on his heavily lined face, keeping her gaze clear of the figure now motionless on the ground. Looking at the boy would remind her of the part she played in this latest killing. Fitzpain was the murderer, but she had been the lure who approached the boy and distracted him... ordered to do it by Fitzpain. And it was Fitzpain who ordered her to approach the peeler as he walked through the Ardoyne.

God forgive her on both counts.

"Can't youse move the boy's body somewhere else?" she asked. "Can't youse dump him on a Proddy estate?"

Fitzpain shook his head. "We'll let the Prods know where to find him. They can come and fetch him and dump him on their own patch."

"What about the police?"

"Jeez, girl! When was the last time youse saw any peelers down this alley?"

"I saw a couple o' British soldiers come down here last week."

"Bastards!"

Sorcha shrugged and took a step back, anxious to get away from the stench.

Fitzpain wiped the knife blade on his already-stained trousers. He looked like he didn't really care if anyone saw the stains. Why should he? Everyone hereabouts would know what it was all about, and who did it. And anyone who grassed on Fitzpain would likely face a similar fate. Even the suspicion of treachery could be enough to get a man killed.

Sorcha bit at her lower lip. "The Prods'll want revenge, Brian."

He stabbed the point of his knife towards her. "No they won't. They'll know what he did and they'll be glad we did the job for them. The wee girl was one of ours. T'was our job to make this bastard pay. The Prods'll know that."

She wasn't convinced. "They'll want to kill one of ours in return. Youse know they will."

"Let 'em try!"

"They will."

They damn well would try. Her conviction was just a matter of common sense and nothing to do with her sleeping with a Protestant this past month or more. Thank God the Pain Men knew nothing about Martin. He wasn't a militant Prod, but that didn't matter. Sleeping with the other side was dangerous enough in these parts. She hoped to God the Provos would never find out.

Fitzpain's voice mellowed slightly at that point. "Never

youse mind what they bastards choose to do. Youse did a good job tonight, Sorcha. Yer daddy would've been proud of youse."

"Oh yeah?" What else could she say? The truth? The man he referred to wasn't her daddy, not her *real* daddy. Brian Fitzpain, of all people, should have known that well enough. Patrick Mulveny was just a faded photograph hidden away at the back of a drawer. A ghost from a distant past. Someone not to be talked about in front of her mammy because he ran out on her before Sorcha was born.

Before she was conceived.

"Yeah. And here's a word of warnin'." Fitzpain edged closer to her. "Stay home the rest of the day. If youse know what's good fer youse, don't even cross yer front doorstep, except to make those phone calls."

"Why?"

"Youse knows why. Just do as ye're told." He tried to say more but his words were drowned by the sudden outbreak of gunfire somewhere nearby.

Sorcha listened. She had grown used to the differences in the noises made by the weapons. This time it was British army SLRs shooting it out against an IRA Sten gun. Nothing new there. A few people would end up dead. By morning friends and relatives would be comforting the widows. The *Belfast Telegraph* might run a paragraph or two, but it wouldn't make a story in any of the national newspapers.

A helicopter approached, the thubba-thubba sound disturbing the sleep of anyone who wasn't already awake and wondering how long the gunfire would continue. Its searchlight illuminated an area a few streets away.

The shooting continued.

It was par for the course.

***

25

September 1980

A loud explosion somewhere near the prison brought our discussion to an end. The door rattled; the bomb was that close. Even the burly warder was momentarily put out. Was this what the waterlogged soldiers at the checkpoint had been on the lookout for? Yet another bomb? Sorcha lapsed into silence while the prison warder went to speak to someone out in the corridor. I tried to ignore the sudden tension and ran a finger over my notes. This was a good start to my research, but there was a lot more to be unearthed, more detail to be discovered behind the raw facts.

I felt a tingle of excitement at the scale the girl's willingness to open up to me but, as before, I deliberately asked no questions about the baby she had referred to. It was easy enough to guess. When I was a newspaper reporter here, I learned all about the horrors inflicted on unmarried pregnant girls in Ireland. The effects of the cruelty stayed with those girls throughout their lives. Maybe she would tell me about it later. I hoped so.

The warder came back into the room and I resumed my questioning. "Sorcha, when you spoke about Fitzpain, you said you knew who he was. What did you mean by that?"

"'Twas what I thought... what I suspected then... at that time. Not now." She gritted her teeth as if suddenly angered by the thought. "I'd discovered the full truth of it by the end of that day and... and t'was more than I bargained for."

"What was the full truth?"

She looked away and lowered her voice. "The truth... the real truth was... shite... me mammy was a whore."

"Meaning?"

"That's all I'm tellin' youse fer now. Don't ask fer anything more. Not yet." She turned back to me abruptly, jutted her chin at me and her eyes radiated defiance.

"None of this came out in court," I said.

She sighed, a deep heart-felt sigh. "Me lawyer knew all about it, but he thought it might turn the jury against me."

"Why?"

"Never mind. It's not important now."

"It could be very important, Sorcha, but we'll talk more about it later." Although I could see that she was getting tired, I had to ask her, "The things you have told me… you don't mind if I put all this into the book?"

She shrugged, a weary gesture. "I wouldn't have told you if I wanted it kept a secret, would I?" She suddenly wiped a hand across her forehead and frowned. "I'm getting' a headache, so I am. Can we stop now? I don't want to talk any more. Not just now."

"You find it emotionally painful?" I had no wish to overstay my welcome. There was so much more I wanted to learn from her.

"Makes me want to cry, so it does," she said. "But youse'll come again? Youse will, won't youse?"

"Of course. We'll have several more chats before we're through."

From the start I had accepted the need for numerous interviews before I had a complete story. Some people think I can get all the information I need for a book from just one interview, but it doesn't work like that. And it certainly wasn't going to work like that with this book.

When I came to leave the prison, a guard warned me that a building in the next street was ablaze. "Take a detour if you're going back through the town," he said. "There might be other bombs. It never stops, does it?"

I wondered once again if the soldiers at the checkpoint were expecting this. Were they looking for a car carrying explosives in the boot? Did the bomber escape their attention? Did the vehicle get through the checkpoint because someone messed up in the torrential rain?

I would probably never know.

It was still raining heavily when I walked out into the dismal daylight, a cold rain that struggled to wipe away the lingering smell of smoke and cordite. An army truck raced past, closely followed by a Land Rover. A bomb disposal squad on its way to defuse yet another device. It was what still counted for normal here.

I was caught in another queue as I drove along that moorland road that brought me here earlier. The blockage seemed to be in the same location, but this time there was much more activity around it. As I came closer, I saw that a bomb had exploded on the far side of the road and the traffic was being directed onto the nearside grass verge to avoid a burned-out Land Rover. I wound down my window when a soldier – an older man – tapped on the glass. He looked tired, war-weary.

"Where are you going, sir?"

"Belfast. Has anyone been killed here?"

"Never mind that, sir. Be careful as you drive past. The grass is muddy."

"Is Private Atkins safe?"

He jerked his head back and frowned. "You know him?"

"He spoke to me when I drove past here earlier. I thought he was too young to be caught up in the Irish Troubles. Should have been in college back home."

The soldier shook his head sadly. "Too many of our lads are in the same boat." He glanced across the road towards the wrecked vehicle. "Atkins was in the Land Rover when it was hit by a mortar bomb."

"I'm really sorry to hear that."

"Drive carefully, sir." He sniffed again as he walked away.

I drove on to Belfast where the atmosphere was no better.

People think Belfast is just one big city, but it isn't. It's two half-cities intermeshed and glued together against the wishes of the people who live there. It's a Protestant, Loyalist half-city which claims to be British although it's technically not a part of Great Britain. And it's a Catholic, Nationalist half-city which would rather be a part of the Irish Republic, provided it could still take advantage of the financial benefits supplied by British taxpayers. I'd learned all this years ago when I married an Irish woman and moved from leafy Surrey to the grim reality of Belfast, trying to make a living as a journalist. Even today, it didn't make any sense to me, and I doubt that it made much sense to the people of Northern Ireland. But, like I said, it was normality to them. There was no sense in it, but they knew nothing else.

When my wife died, I buried her in Belfast because it was her home town. I moved back to England, but the contradictions of Northern Ireland went with me. The grief of losing Annie also went with me, but that's another story. The grief came back to me that rainy day as I drove into Belfast and detoured to the cemetery to visit Annie's final resting place. I was glad of the rain dripping down my cheeks, mingling with the tears when I placed a sodden bunch of flowers beside the tombstone. As I stood beside the grave, the cold Irish rain speared through my body as easily as hot pee through six inches of snow. I was chilled to the core and that made things seem worse than they really were.

Late that day I flew back to Heathrow, took a taxi to my flat in Wimbledon and read through my notes over a heated up ready-meal. They represented a sound start to my investigation, but told me very little about the murders. If Sorcha really was guilty, why did I have those alarm bells ringing inside my head? And if she was innocent, why did she confess? Why did she feel so guilty? I was determined to find out.

Chapter Three

September 1980

The trouble with the Irish Question is that no one really understands what the question is, so what's the point of looking for an answer? That's what my editor used to say when I worked as a reporter for the *Belfast Telegraph*. He taught me the value of cynicism and his teaching stayed with me. Little had changed since then, except that I was now a damn sight more cynical than I once was. But at least I was my own man. Age and experience had taught me to accept nothing at face value. Belfast was behind me, Fleet Street was behind me, but I still had the mind of a sceptical journalist.

Another thing I had learned along the way was the importance of detailed research. In this case, it wasn't just a matter of what actually happened on Bloody Friday, it was also a case of seeing into the minds of people who were there. I was curious about how the RUC conducted their enquiries into those two murders, overloaded as they were by the bombs. Common sense told me I needed to speak to a policeman who had been intimately involved. That was why I made contact with William Evans. I figured that, as a Welshman, he would have a degree of neutrality towards the Northern Irish problems, but I should have taken more care over the effect the Troubles had on his wife, a Belfast woman.

My first meeting with Will was at his home in North Wales. I drove to Llandudno and met Will while his twin girls were at school and his wife was busy shopping. Framed photographs of the two attractive teenagers sat on every flat surface, a sure sign that they were well-loved by their parents. Will was at home because it was one of his off-duty days. He now worked daylight hours manning a duty desk at a rural police station not too far from the town. With the house to ourselves, I sat at the kitchen table and he made us both a mug of coffee. I remembered how drained he had looked when I met him at Sorcha's trial. He seemed more at ease now. You had to look hard to see the residual effects of the damage to his face; lips that drooped marginally too low on one side, and an eye that seemed to be tugged away from its correct focus. The signs were faint, but they would probably go with him to his grave.

He took a whiskey bottle from a cupboard and opened it. "Something to put hairs on your chest?" He aimed the bottle at my coffee.

I put my hand over the mug. "Never touch the stuff, Will."

"Teetotal?"

"Far from it, but I've seen too many lives ruined by whiskey. It's dangerous stuff."

"In that case, don't mind me." He gave me a disbelieving look and added a large helping to his own mug. "I needed it when I was with the RUC. We all did. There wasn't a single desk drawer at the North Castle Street barracks that didn't have at least one bottle hidden away. The bosses knew all about it, and they knew it was what kept us going when the bombing and rioting started."

"But that's all behind you now. Isn't it? Now that you have a normal desk job here in a country at peace."

"Depends on what you mean by 'behind you'. It'll never be fully erased from my mind. Never. I still wake up with nightmares, so do our girls. Milly seems to be the only one coping with the aftermath."

"Your wife is Irish. Is that what helps her?"

"Why should it? Too many Northern Irish people have gone to the dogs because of the Troubles. Too many families torn apart. No, Milly copes these days because she's basically a strong person. She's managed to put the worst of the strain behind her. Nowadays I depend on her." He took a long gulp of whiskey-infused coffee. "Can you believe it? I was the cop who saw it all first hand and yet I now depend on my wife to keep me sane."

I gave him an inquisitive look. "Are you up to telling me more about what happened on Bloody Friday?"

"What can I tell you that you haven't already heard?"

"The human side, Will. Especially the human story behind those murders. I know what was said before Sorcha Mulveny's trial collapsed, but I want to hear and write about the bits that didn't come out in court. As far as the bombing campaign is concerned, I want my readers to know more than just the number of explosions and how many were killed. I want them to understand how it affected people like you. I want to write about the hell you went through."

"You mean… why I still have nightmares?"

"Whatever you can tell me. Lead me through the day, a step at a time. Why don't you start with when you woke up that morning? Was it the beginning of what looked like just another normal day in Belfast?"

"Like hell it was!"

***

Friday 21st July 1972
0545 BST

Detective Sergeant Will Evans had been dreaming. It was a warm, comforting dream filled with memories of the North Wales coast where he grew up. The images floated gently through his head, as if he was watching them while drifting on a calm sea. He saw dreamy depictions of majestic hills, a balmy shore and the stark outlines of ruined castles. And then he found himself amongst the friendly people he had known in his youth.

But it was only a dream.

He was woken abruptly when a bomb exploded. It was his second rude awakening that night. The shock wave hit the house and the windows rattled, but the glass stayed intact. He instantly registered the tonal sound of the detonation. It was a car bomb and it wasn't too far away.

He felt Milly shift in the bed beside him, as if she was trying to hold onto the last vestiges of sleep, and failing. He was about to speak, to reassure her, when a grey mist passed over his eyes and a painful throb struck his forehead.

Not again!

He lay still, knowing it wouldn't last long. It never did. But it annoyed him because he should have done something about it before now. He should have signed himself off sick while the medics investigated the problem. He should have... but he didn't. He dreaded what they might discover, so he did nothing, and the problem arose again and again. And the longer he put up with it, the more difficult it became to take some sort of positive action.

He waited for the mist to subside before he finally spoke. He tried to adopt a jokey tone, but he couldn't.

The words came out as pure bile. "Good morning, Belfast. This is your friendly terrorist wake-up call." His acid sarcasm reflected an in-built bitterness.

"That's not in the least bit funny." Milly groaned and rolled onto her back.

"Sorry." He rubbed away the last of the pain from his forehead.

"That bomb will have woken the girls," Milly said. "Maybe I should check on them."

"Don't bother. They'll be all right. They should be used to it by now."

"Used to it? Our children should be used to it?"

"Sorry."

Will regretted the blasé words as soon as they were uttered. How could he be so callous about the effect a bomb would have upon his twin daughters? He tried to recover his composure with some vague reassurances. "Patsy will jump into Jill's bed and they'll cuddle up and console each other. Give it half an hour and they'll be fine again."

Milly didn't seem to be persuaded. "They shouldn't have

to console one another, Will. And they shouldn't have to put up with the noise of bombs at their age. Bloody Belfast!"

She sat up and pushed aside the bedsheets. Her long, blonde hair streamed down her naked back. She shook her head and the hair shimmered like waves of silk.

"It's your home town, love. Not mine." Another callous remark, instantly regretted.

"And I hate it. Absolutely hate it. You know how it's affecting the girls. Wetting the beds at their age. Ten-year old children shouldn't wet their beds in fear!" She screwed up her round puppy-dog eyes and glared at him.

"Sorry." Will reached out a hand to her. "Let them be, love. They'll be all right. It'll be the only half hour in the day when they won't be fighting and arguing."

"Maybe. Even so..." The sudden anger waned as quickly as it arose. She yawned, let out a long, loud sigh and lay back down in the bed.

Will glanced at the window. His head was now back on an even keel, and the weather forecasters had promised a nice summer's day. Perfect for the ferry crossing to Liverpool and the drive into Wales. He swept his gaze round to the alarm clock. There was plenty of time to load the car. The luggage was already packed and stacked on the lounge floor, so why not enjoy one of the few pleasures left in his life? Already the explosion was fading into the back of his mind.

He held back from saying sorry yet again. Didn't someone somewhere say love means not having to say you're sorry? Not that he believed it, but he did love his wife. Maybe he didn't always show it as well as he should, but he never regretted marrying her.

"Relax, Milly, it's going to be a long journey. Let's have a moment to ourselves." He turned on his side and slid his hand between her legs to gently massage her inner thighs. Lean, healthy thighs connected to a lean, healthy body: the physical beauty of a woman still at the tail end or her twenties. It had been a warm night and they both slept naked.

She sighed with pleasure. All signs of her irritation were put aside for the time being.

"How would you like your breakfast, My Lady?" he asked, injecting a note of desire into his voice.

"Long and hot," she replied, taking up the hint. Her smile told him her annoyance was temporarily on hold. It was a hesitant smile, but a smile nonetheless. "You may serve me now."

"Yes, My Lady." He slid his hand into her bush.

"Oh yes, Boyo... there's a welcome in the hillside," she said, putting on an exaggerated imitation of Will's Welsh accent.

And then a second bomb exploded, closer this time. The thunderous boom echoed through the early morning air. The flash backlit the curtains and, again, the windows rattled.

"Hell!" Will sat up suddenly. "Not now! Can't they even give us peace to..."

"Calm down, Will." Milly sat up beside him. "Tonight we'll have all the peace and quiet we need."

"In the meantime, I suppose that puts an end to...?"

"For the time being."

"I was all ready for it. Rising to the occasion, I was."

She wagged a finger at him as if she was scolding a small child. "You'll just have to be patient, won't you?"

Not long after, they heard gunshots. IRA snipers shooting at soldiers on the prowl, Will guessed. They called them 'duck squads', those army patrols. Sometimes the soldiers died, sometimes it was the IRA attackers who were killed by the return fire. Violent death was a way of life in Belfast.

Will let out a long-exasperated sigh. "I suppose I'd better check on the girls. That last one really was a bit too close for comfort. Dammit!" His frustration increased once more as he clambered out of bed, crossed the room and yanked open the bedroom door.

"Will!"

"What?"

"Put your dressing gown on. The girls will be frightened enough anyway."

***

September 1980

Will paused to add more whiskey to his coffee. He sipped at it before speaking with a sudden hoarseness in his voice. "The doctors told us the girls would forget all about it as they grew older, but that was a load of shit. They didn't forget. It's the same with other kids who've had to live with the bombs and bullets in Northern Ireland. It mentally scars them for life. Have you read about the amount of self-harm Belfast kids do to themselves? Have you?"

I had, but I chose not to voice my opinion. I wanted Will's side of things. "And you, Will? Has it scarred you for life? Or will it all fade in time?"

"Don't ask such a bloody stupid question."

"Okay. Let's move on, shall we? You didn't manage to get away on that holiday you needed. Tell me more about that."

He took a deep breath. "That was when the trouble really started between Milly and me."

***

Friday 21st July 1972
0715 BST

Will ambled down to the kitchen in his dressing gown. Dirty dishes were piled into the sink. They were forgotten in the previous evening's efforts to get the cases packed. He ignored them, put the kettle on and switched on the radio while wiping aside all thoughts of police duty; a duty that wouldn't bother him today.

The BBC radio news caught his attention. Earlier that morning an express train in Spain had run head-on into a local train. Many people were dead and many more injured. He turned off the radio with a heavy jab of his hand. Much as he felt sympathy, he had no wish to hear about people

36

dying. Not when he was looking forward to one whole week of peace.

Milly came down a few minutes later, bursting into the kitchen in a swirl of silken gown and silken hair.

"The girls?" he asked.

"Playing with their dolls."

"Good."

"And arguing."

"Problem solved." He laughed.

Milly gave him a sour look.

He was eating his breakfast at the kitchen table, and Milly was complaining about the noise the twins were making upstairs, when the phone rang. Will wiped a stray milky cornflake from his lips, sidled into the lounge and picked up the receiver. Despite the radio news, and despite the earlier bombs, he was beginning to relax.

"Yes?" He never announced himself on the phone, not until he knew who was calling. It was a habit as ingrained as checking for a mercury tilt switch bomb under his car each morning. Like thousands of other RUC officers, it helped keep him alive.

"Bad news, Will." It was his boss, Detective Chief Inspector Thomas McIlroy at the North Castle Street RUC barracks. His voice was unusually cold. "We need you over here. Now."

Will's relaxed mood withered and died in an instant. "I'm on leave, boss."

"Tough. We need you." The senior detective's tone of voice defied argument. It was not like McIlroy at all. A warning sign.

Will drew a deep breath. Resentment began to course through him, a sudden surge he had difficulty controlling. "But I've got a whole week off. I'm taking the family on holiday."

"Forget it. You're on duty again. There's something up. Something big, and we're two men down. You'll have to cover the rest of the 'early'."

"Is that an order or a request, boss?"

"'Tis a request which you turn down at your peril."

The early shift started at 0700 and continued to 1500, and the ferry to Liverpool left in a little over two hours. Outside, the Evans family car was waiting to be packed.

Will struggled to contain his annoyance. "I don't think you understood me, boss. We're booked on this morning's boat, all the family. We're all geared up and ready to go."

"Sorry. I can't help that." Sorry? McIlroy didn't sound in the least bit sorry. "The family will just have to go ahead without you."

"It's that bad?"

"That bad."

"But it's not an order?"

"I can make it one if you force me to."

"Seems like I have no choice."

"Spot on. I'll come over and collect you in ten minutes or so. Get ready as quick as you can."

Will's hand was shaking as he replaced the receiver and stared out through the lounge window. They had tickets for a crossing to Liverpool, followed by a short drive to his sister's house on the north Welsh coast. And then... peace and quiet away from the bombs and the bullets. A week of relaxation in a land where the Evans family had their ancestral roots. A tremor ran through him. It wasn't fair! It wasn't just him who needed this holiday. Milly and the kids needed to get away at least as much as he did.

"Who was that?" Milly wandered in from the kitchen, her loose gown open at the front. Shielding the girls from overt nudity didn't extend to their mother. She brushed a stray wisp of hair from her face.

Will mumbled his reply, still seething inside. "Inspector McIlroy. They want me back on duty. Something's up."

She froze. The usual mellowness of her voice suddenly faded. "Not now?"

Will dropped his gaze to the floor, unable to confront her. "Yes. Now." He tried to sound firm, but inside he was seething. How could he feel otherwise?

"But..." Milly stared at him dumbly for a few seconds,

her lips trembling, as if she was having difficulty understanding what he was saying. Then she spoke in a low, hoarse tone. "Why? What's up?"

"Dunno. You'll just have to go on ahead without me."

A sharp gasp escaped her mouth before she cried out, "No! You can't do this! We're all booked on the ferry. All of us. We can't just go without you."

"You'll have to." He continued to avoid her gaze. "I'll come and join you as soon as I can."

"No, Will. That's not fair." She stepped up close to him, dragging back his attention and further raising her voice. "Haven't we had enough to put up with already? You've got to tell them! You can't go on duty. Not now!"

He forced himself to look her fully in the eye. "Milly, I have to. There's something afoot and it sounds serious."

Her cheeks were damp now, glistening with tears. "Well, we're not going to Wales without you. No way!"

"But it's best you go on ahead. I'm sorry, love."

"You're sorry? For God's sake! How do you think I feel? I'm sick of this place, sick of all the hatred and bombing. Sick to death of it. And just look at you, Will. You're washed out with stress. Twenty-nine years old and already on the verge of a heart attack. You need this break!"

"I'm stronger than that, Milly," he said with little conviction.

"Don't talk rubbish, Will. It's getting to all of you at North Castle Street. You know it is. Look at you; all pale-faced and washed out. You don't sleep well. And you're still not fully recovered from that knock on the head."

He gave a brief snort. "Don't go on about that. There's not a man in the RUC who hasn't had a knock or a cut from the riot line. It goes with the job."

"You should have seen the doctor about it. You know you should."

"For heaven's sake, Milly! How many times have I told you? Don't go on about it!"

She was partly right, of course, but it wasn't a doctor he needed; it was a week of peace and quiet in a country that wasn't at war with itself. Just one week, that was all, and he would be his old self again.

She glared at him, and he saw that she was hurt by his anger. "If only we could all get away together, even for a week…" Tears now streamed freely down her cheeks. "Even for a week."

He relented, wrapped his arms about her and lowered his voice. "I'll tell them we have to get away tomorrow." He tried to make it sound reassuring, but it wasn't easy.

"Tomorrow might be too late." She sniffled against his dressing gown. "If only we could get away for good. For good, Will! Get away from all this violence, and live in peace."

"But this is where my job is."

"It doesn't have to be." She suddenly pushed herself away from him. "We could move away. You could get a police job in England or Wales."

"Is that what you want?"

"You know damn well it is! I swear to God, Will, I can't take much more of it. Neither can the girls." She drew back her shoulders and wiped at her face. A look of defiance suddenly flickered in her eyes. Her voice rose to a screech, a mental barrier suddenly breeched. "If I have to go on holiday without you, I'll be going for good. I swear to God I will. I won't be coming back. Ever!"

Will was momentarily at a loss for words. What could he possibly say? He went silent hoping she would calm down, hoping this was just a momentary loss of control. Milly suddenly turned away from him, bent her shoulders forward and clasped her hands onto the sideboard. The silence hung in the air for several minutes while her whole body trembled, a sign of soundless weeping.

"Mummy!" The child's cry drew Will's attention to the hall door.

Patsy stood in the opening, clasping her teddy bear and sucking her thumb. She and her sister were too old to be constantly cuddling comfort toys, but they needed them.

Milly straightened up, wiped at her eyes and then ran to

the child and clasped her tight.

"What's happening, Mummy? Why were you shouting just now?"

"It's all right, my love." She turned her head back to Will and her look told him it was far from all right. She glared at him. "I meant what I said, Will. I meant it! We'll wait here until tomorrow. If you don't come with us then, I'm leaving you. For good!"

***

September 1980

Milly arrived home that that point, along with the twins. They were now tall, slim young ladies in school uniforms. Images of their mother at that age, I guessed. I noted instantly how they eyed me warily as they walked into the kitchen, as if they had the same distrust of me as Milly. Their arrival instantly put paid to any hope of continuing the interview with Will.

Milly greeted me with a single staccato grunt, and then she gave me a fierce look as if she suspected me of upsetting Will. Maybe she had a point.

"You've finished your chat." Her words came out more as a firm instruction than a question.

"For the time being," I said.

"Good." She made a point of unpacking her shopping in front of me. I took the hint and put away my notebook.

"We'll talk again another day," Will said as he escorted me to the front door.

"I'm glad she didn't leave you," I kept my voice low.

He gave me a surreptitious smile. "It was touch and go for a while. Then, at the end of the day, she saw how I was in hospital. I think that was what put me back in the driving seat."

"She cares about you, Will."

"I know. I depend upon it." He allowed himself a brief moment of thought. "You know, someone once told me there are four doors out of an RUC policeman's life. They're labelled 'murder', 'suicide', 'nervous breakdown' and 'peaceful retirement'. Do you know what it's like to walk through that last door?"

"No."

"Neither does anyone else."

Chapter Four

October 1980

It was a difficult month in Northern Ireland. Seven Republican prisoners began a hunger-strike in protest at the ending of special category status. The following day Margaret Thatcher announced she would not give in to them because they had been convicted of criminal offences. Tensions in Northern Ireland began to rise even higher than they already were. Rioting in the streets became a daily ritual.

Fully aware that things were getting ever more fraught over there, I nevertheless telephoned the Armagh prison governor to seek permission to interview Sorcha Mulveny again. We had spoken several times before and he seemed to be in tune with my aim in writing the book. This time we had a longer chat, in the course of which he described Sorcha as a model prisoner.

"Not the sort of person you would expect to end up here as a lifer," he said. "She seems to be taking her punishment with a lot of stoicism. Never once has she caused us any trouble."

Was that why he was willing to smooth the formalities of my access to her? Or was he trying to show some leniency in the face of the stand-off between the hunger-strikers and the British government? It was probably not in his remit to discuss her case with me in detail, but I got the impression he had similar reservations to my own about her guilt. I became yet more determined to discover the truth.

The following Sunday I flew from Heathrow to Belfast Aldergrove Airport and checked in at the Europa Hotel in

Great Victoria Street. It had earned itself a reputation for the number of times it was bombed. Not the best way to earn a good reputation, but what the hell? I told myself it would be safe enough if I stayed only a couple of nights. Despite the bombs, the hotel was a popular venue for so many journalists covering the so-called Troubles. There were more of them here than usual, a consequence of the hunger-strike. I knew a few of them from my time on Fleet Street. That was after Annie died, when the Belfast violence lived on and I left Ireland to work in London.

I enjoyed a drink or two with the old hacks the Sunday evening I arrived, catching up on the gossip, as journalists are wont to do. As always, I avoided the whiskey, but my old chums were less particular. The bar did well out of them. A young female reporter from the *Daily Mail* gave me a slobbery kiss and asked me if I was open to offers since my wife died. I was tempted – she was a beautiful twenty something – but common sense prevailed. Besides, I was far too old for her. If Annie had lived, we would now be coming up close to our twentieth anniversary. Twenty years! I had already made a reservation for one person at a quiet restaurant in Wimbledon where I would be able reminisce over the years we were together. Eating alone came a little easier as time passed.

The next morning I hired a car and drove to the prison in Armagh. It was where most women prisoners were held in those days, including Republican criminals. A year ago a prison officer was shot dead and three colleagues were injured during an attack on the prison by the INLA. Foul smells were more prominent on this visit. The Republican women were engaged in yet another dirty protest, smearing their cell walls with menstrual blood.

Sorcha took no part in the protest. She was waiting for me in the interview room and her instant smile told me this was likely to be another productive session. I glanced at the female warder standing behind her: a muscle-bound woman with a piercing gaze and a grim expression. She was the visual epitome of a German death camp guard, and she was probably very good at her job.

"I've been thinking about what I want to tell youse," Sorcha said, getting down to business straight away. "I was remembering what happened that morning after I got home."

My initial response was disappointment as I was anxious to learn more about the murders. Be patient, I told myself as I set out my notebook on the table and tried to sound enthusiastic.

"Your mother was away, as I recall."

"Yeah, but me sister was there, so she was. She'd been on a night shift at the hospital, but she'd come home. Arguing with me as usual."

"Tell me about it, Sorcha."

***

Friday 21st July 1972
0745 BST

"There's blood on yer jeans," Bridie Mulveny said.

Sorcha sniffed. They weren't *her* jeans. Last night, Brian Fitzpain had persuaded a prostitute to hand over some clean clothes on a promise of later payment. The dead peeler's blood had spurted out and stained Sorcha's own clothes, just as it had stained Brian's serrated knife. He'd simply wiped the blade on his trousers. Not all the peeler's blood was removed, but that was him all over. Not an ounce of sense.

It was the young rapist's blood that later stained the borrowed jeans.

God, what a mess! What a bloody mess.

Sorcha shrugged. "I was changin' a tampon." A blatant lie, her period was not due for another week, but no other excuse came immediately to mind. Lies came easily to Sorcha when Bridie was around.

Her sister frowned as if she suspected something sinister was afoot. She seemed to have a knack of suspecting Sorcha of misdeeds, especially in those awkward moments when

45

the younger sister was quietly berating herself for something she'd done wrong.

If it wasn't telepathy, what the hell was it?

Bridie settled herself in front of her breakfast with a look that could have been acceptance or disbelief. She didn't give away her deeper private thoughts too easily. She raised her nose and sniffed loudly before she spoke. "One o' them filthy Prods got cut up and killed last night, so Old Edna told me. Standin' on her doorstep when I got home, she was. Told me she heard the screams. Did youse not hear the noise of it, Sorcha?" Bridie scooped up a spoonful of porridge and shovelled it into her gaping mouth.

"Should I have?" Sorcha averted her gaze and shivered.

It was summer, on the verge of a warm sunny day, and yet the house felt cold; the sort of unearthly cold that crept up the River Lagan on a morning mist and sank deep inside her bones.

"They found the body in the alley. *Our* alley, would youse believe? Someone cut his dick off. They're sayin' he's the same Prod what did the rape. Someone paid him back, so they did." Bridie shovelled more porridge into her mouth, shutting off further comment. She glanced again at her sister's jeans.

Sorcha shrugged. "Good riddance."

"Now they're waitin' for the Prods to come and fetch the body." Yet another spoonful of porridge slid into Bridie's mouth. Her nursing uniform bulged at every seam.

They were they so different, Sorcha reflected. Not like sisters. When she looked in a mirror, she saw her own figure as slim and sensuous as any cat-walk model, but tainted with dull, mousey hair that hung around her shoulders like used dishcloths. Bridie, two years older, was fat and slovenly and gifted with the sort of lovely shiny black hair any model would be proud of.

Did they really have the same daddy? Well, it was an obvious question, wasn't it? Sorcha was pretty certain she knew the answer.

"The Prods can bury their own dead," she muttered.

Bridie sniffed dismissively. "Not that we should care. That one'll be in hell now, just like all them other dirty Prods. Father O'Hanlon says all Protestants go to hell, so they do."

Her voice had a coarse edge and a thick accent that marked her out as a product of a Belfast ghetto. Sorcha hated it and tried to inject a more mellow tone into her own voice, but she was unable to cast aside the worst of her Belfast idiom. She had tried to avoid saying 'youse' when she first knew Martin, but invariably she failed. It proved more difficult than she anticipated. Of late she didn't bother. If only she wasn't the product of such a shitty background.

What the hell did Martin see in her?

"Don't talk such bollocks, Bridie!" Sorcha wiped a hand across her forehead, brushing aside an incipient ache. She had not slept, kept awake by lingering images of the castrated rapist. And the dead peeler. She drained the dregs of her coffee and left the mug on the mantelpiece. Mammy could wash it when she got back from visiting relatives in Ardglass village.

Bridie glanced up. "'Tis true. I heard Father O'Hanlon say so."

Sorcha sniffed and sat down opposite her sister at the tiny, Formica-top table in the in the tiny, grubby parlour room.

What a ridiculous family they were! There had been no father-figure when they were growing up. They had only their mammy, a hate-filled despot who held the family together with harsh words and even harsher opinions.

And what a shitty pair of sisters they were! Bridie was the well-favoured one who brought in a decent wage, while Sorcha was the unemployed, good-for-nothing runt. She hated the way her mammy looked down upon her as if she despised herself for giving birth to such a pitiable offspring. Or did she despise the way her second daughter was conceived?

She never actually said, "I should have drowned you at birth," but the inference was there.

It hurt.

And there were times, like this, when Sorcha regretted not taking that last final step into oblivion.

She said, "Don't talk such bollocks, Bridie! Youse shouldn't believe things like that. 'Tis just O'Hanlon's holy crap." She choked back her next thought. It probably wasn't wise to point out that the priest was a raving poofter. If the rumours were true, he'd buggered half the altar boys at St Winifred's Church. There were even rumours he'd been buggering the new curate. If anyone was going to hell it was Father O'Hanlon.

Bridie wasn't convinced. "Mammy says youse'll end up like them filthy Prods if youse don't go to Mass, Sorcha. Youse'll end up in hell like them."

Sorcha stared past her sister at a faded print of Jesus with his heart exposed. There was a damp patch behind it and the old flowery wallpaper was beginning to peel. It was the sort of image she saw in most of these parlour houses in Mafeking Street. Sorcha saw it as a tired and depressing fairy tale image: homage paid to a human body pump. But her mammy crossed herself in front of it every morning. Was that, she wondered, a sign of a life resigned to simple beliefs that did nothing to answer complex everyday problems? Or was it just habit? She had no firm answer.

Maybe Martin was right in wanting to take her away from this. Wanted her to go to England with him, so he did. She was sorely tempted, so sorely tempted. So why didn't she jump at the chance? So many sensible people had left already; the well-educated and intelligent ones who found it easy to get a new job across the water. Since the Troubles began England had done well out of Northern Ireland's exodus. Why shouldn't she follow the well-worn trail? Fear, that was why. Fear of moving to a land portrayed by Republicans as the closest thing to hell.

She stood up suddenly. She must force herself not to believe the mantra: all Protestants went to hell and so did the English. Why did it bother her that her sister believed such nonsense? She paused. Was it because she had once believed it herself? Not now, of course. She'd long since thrown aside all traces of that stupid brainwashing... or so she told herself. She no longer went anywhere near St Winifred's on any day, let alone Sundays. But something lingered at the back of her mind, an understanding of how stupid she'd once been to allow such ideas into her head. And... as if to confuse the matter... there was just a lingering doubt about whether the priest might have been right after all. That's what brainwashing did too you, she decided. It never let you go. Never really allowed you to think for yourself.

"Youse seein' that secret boyfriend again, are youse?" Bridie's voice cut into the momentary silence.

"Maybe. Maybe not."

"What's he called?"

"Martin."

"Martin as in McGuinness?"

"No. Martin as in Luther." It was the first retort that came into Sorcha's mind, but it was probably stupid.

Bridie put on a sneering tone. "Martin Luther was a Proddy."

"And he was a priest before that." Sorcha jutted her chin. How she resented her sister's sneering. She'd grown up with it and she hated it.

"Don't tell me ye're being fucked by a priest."

"God forbid."

"He probably would. Mammy was askin' when youse're gonna bring yer man home. She wants to see what sort o' person youse're goin' out with."

"Well, she'll just have to want, won't she?"

"Shaggin' youse on the quiet, is he?"

"None o' your business."

"Be more careful this time."

"I always am these days."

"Usin' those filthy rubber things?"

"Why not?"

"It ain't decent."

"Does the job though."

Sorcha looked away. Of course their sex was done on the quiet. It had to be because he was a Protestant. Catholic girls in this part of Belfast, even lapsed Catholics, didn't drop their knickers for Prods. Not if they valued their lives. But Sorcha had broken that golden rule. There were shadowy hotels and bars in the city where they met for a drink without attracting too much attention, but they were careful not to take a room. A hotel room in Belfast meant checking in, showing some form of identification, and hotel registers could be scrutinised. Both the Provisional IRA and the UVF made such checks, searching for evidence to use against people they suspected of colluding with the other side. For sex, Sorcha and Martin went to a flat, rented by his mate, Ivan, in a street off the Shankill Road. They always went at night, when there was less chance of being recognised. It was a dangerous place for anyone from the Catholic Falls area, but she was getting away with it. And he was damn good in bed, was Martin. Tall, dark and incredibly handsome... as well as giving her damn good sex. He gave her orgasms more powerful than any other man had achieved, and something else... he made her feel like she was someone special. That was a whole new experience. At times, he acted... she found it hard to comprehend, but... he acted as if he was actually in love with her. Genuinely in love. And what were her inner feelings towards him? Dear God, that was a place she didn't want to go.

If only he wasn't a Prod.

If only she was as innocent as he seemed to imagine her to be.

And then there was Brian Fitzpain. If ever he found out she had been to bed with a Prod, he would go wild. If she was anyone else, she would be dead meat. No question about it. Other girls had discovered that punishment too late, just before they were tortured and had their throats slit. But she wasn't anyone else. Brian would be mad at her, for sure, but there was no way he could slit her throat. Not with him being who he was.

Bridie finished her breakfast and heaved herself out of her seat, scraping the chair legs across the well-worn lino. "I'm off to me bed, so I am. Takin' the train up to Derry this afternoon. Goin' to see Aunty Aggie. Need some sleep first, though."

And pop some pills, Sorcha thought. Many a morning after a busy night duty, Bridie resorted to sedative drugs. Did she really think no one noticed the signs? Most times she used Valium lifted from the hospital, more pills than were good for her. Hardly surprising. The things her sister would have seen in A&E, God help her!

Bridie didn't often talk about the aftereffects of the bombs and the bullets, but when she did it turned Sorcha's stomach. One boy losing his dick was gruesome enough, but what Bridie saw was violence on a conveyor belt. The television news showed little of the injuries, little of the real damage done to people. The worst of it was edited out from their films. But Bridie Mulveny saw it up close: bodies that might eventually be partially repaired, and minds which would never be the same again. Did it matter whether the victim was maimed by a bomb blast or knee-capped with a Black and Decker? Not much. Kneecapping usually did less physical damage than a bomb, but the psychological effect wasn't much different. The trauma the victims suffered would last the rest of their lives.

Only the ones who died instantly had peace.

"Maybe youse should give up the job," Sorcha once told her.

"And what other work would I get round here?" Bridie had an answer for everything. "It pays well, so what the hell? Anyway, the violence won't stop. Won't ever stop."

"It will one day."

"Bullshit. It won't stop 'cos the next generation feeds on it. And the next one after that. Our lot feed on the Famine and the Easter rising, just like the Prods feed on the Battle o' the Boyne and the Siege of Derry. It just goes on and on." She had raised her voice to a squeal at that point. "Damn it, Sorcha! 'Tis people like me who have to deal with what's

51

left of the victims."

Sorcha was surprised that her sister was able to conjure up such a deep insight. Intuition, mixed with emotional passion. Maybe she was too clever for her own good, and yet her philosophy allowed that all Protestants went to hell. Only in Belfast could such ridiculous contradictions exist. Only in Belfast could the underlying truth give rise to such unqualified hatred.

And Bridie was right. It would never end. For all her protestations, Sorcha saw that clearly.

She waited for the sound of Bridie's bedroom door closing before she hurried up the stairs to her own room. She changed out of her blood-stained jeans and grabbed a coat. As a last-minute thought, she pulled out an envelope from her jeans pocket. Damn! She should have thrown it back in Brian's face. It was just too dangerous, and she wanted nothing to do with it. Could she still off-load it back to him, tell him to make his own warning phone calls to the police? Or would it be better to keep her mouth shut and simply dump the evidence? She couldn't make up her mind. In the meantime, she stuffed it into her coat pocket.

And she would not stay here on her own.

That was when the dustbin lids started banging on the streets outside; a cacophony of noise that was almost a Republican anthem. The local 'mammies' were warning people that British troops were in the offing. And something else was up. Was it a riot, or had the Brits discovered another arms cache?

Don't leave the house, Fitzpain had told her, but not because of this. It was common sense that urged her to stay indoors now, avoid the conflict out in the streets, whatever it was. But common sense rarely held her back these days. As for Fitzpain's warning, that didn't hold her back because she knew the locations that would be bombed this day. It was all there in that envelope. That list. She could avoid the hot spots if she wanted to, so sod you, Brian Fitzpain! And sod the British troops who would have to deal with the bombs! She wasn't going to stay here like a prisoner. Tired though she was, she was going to see Martin.

Her impossible dream.

She couldn't call him. The telephone call box round the corner had been smashed up too many times. No one bothered to repair it now. But she could waylay him when he went for his aunt's morning paper. He did that most days soon after breakfast; bought the paper from a small shop that opened all hours. They could go somewhere for a coffee. It might help wipe away from her mind that lingering memory of the Protestant boy's dick lying in a pool of blood. And the stench of his shit.

And the dead peeler.

She went to the front door, where Mafeking Street was alive with tension. The noise of the banging bin lids was much louder. Old Edna McRostie stood on her doorstep in a dirty wrap-around apron, curlers in her straggly hair, arms folded beneath her ample bosom, a cigarette glued to her lower lip. Her phlegmy cough was getting worse.

A gang of youths was busily painting graffiti on an improvised corrugated iron wall at the barricaded end of the street. The first 'peace walls' went up in 1969. The Mafeking Street barrier was erected a year later, after the end-of-terrace house was fire-bombed and the Kennedy family was killed. Shot by a Loyalist gang. Sorcha looked upon the wall as a hideous monstrosity, a memorial to bigotry and hatred. The more it was daubed with grammatically ignorant racist messages, the more hideous it became. It was intended only as a temporary structure, a barrier to contain the growing violence between Mafeking Street Catholics and the Kimberley Street Protestants.

She hated it.

And yet, like the rest of the residents in both streets, Sorcha had no wish ever to see it removed. Lives depended upon it remaining.

A noisy crowd was gathered at the other end of Mafeking Street, where it joined Ladysmith Road, another Catholic ghetto. Stubble-faced men shouted foul abuse. Youths with scarves wrapped around their faces threw broken paving stones. Sorcha moved out onto the doorstep, but she was unable to see the target around the corner.

"What's happening?" she asked Edna.

"The Brits. They found a car bomb."

"A Loyalist bomb?"

"Hell, no. One of ours."

"What's it doin' here?"

"That eejit, Sean Lenahan, was supposed to hide it before drivin' it up to Ballysillan this mornin'. What did the eejit do? He left it outside his own house all night."

"Why?"

"Pissed out of his fuckin' mind. That's why."

"How was it discovered?"

Edna coughed and spat on the pavement. "Someone grassed on 'im, I reckon."

Ballysillan? Sorcha called to mind the targets she had been given by Fitzpain. Ballysillan was amongst them. So, one bomb could now be wiped from the list, unless there was a spare, a stand-by. And assuming someone else was willing to drive the thing.

"Hope the English don't come searching down her," Edna said. "Hate all those bastards, so I do."

"Youse hidin' something'?"

"Two crates o' petrol bombs. Them's bein' collected tonight."

"Get them moved soon, Edna. If those things catch fire both our houses will go up, so they will. And things is gonna get hot today. Really hot."

"Think so?"

"Know so."

"Youse hidin' anything," the old lady asked.

"There's an Armalite hidden under mammy's bed. Been there a few days now."

"Brian's gun?"

Sorcha nodded. "Yeah."

"They'll be searchin' his own house one o'these days."

"They already have. Found nothin'. Why d'youse think the Armalite's under mammy's bed?"

The Brits would find it if they searched her mammy's house today, she thought, and it would be his fault. Brian's fault. Damn him for taking advantage of an old lady like her mammy.

She took a step forward and then stopped suddenly. Someone was watching her. She focussed on a shadowy figure standing at the rear of the mob. It was Jimmy Fish. That little runt. What was he doing here, and why was he staring at her? He seemed to become suddenly aware he had her attention because he turned away and scurried off along Ladysmith Road, away from the source of the confrontation.

"Bugger him." Sorcha sniffed and walked on.

He was nothing to her anyway.

***

October 1980

"You had a hard life, Sorcha," I said. "So much was stacked against you right from the start. I hope you can see that now… see how your background played a part in the things you did."

She shrugged. "The lawyer tried to make an issue of it at the sentencing, but the judge was only interested in what I actually did."

"I know. I was there. Do you want to tell me more, or would you rather break off here?" I hoped she would take the hint and let me lead her towards the truth behind the murders, but she shook her head and drew a deep sigh.

"Let's call it a day for now. Youse'll come back, won't youse?"

I accepted the disappointment and put away my notebook. "Of course. There's a lot more I want to learn from you."

I drove back to the Europa in Belfast and enjoyed a beer with the hacks now camped out there. They were full of the latest news about the hunger-strikers, but my mind remained focussed on Sorcha Mulveny. I still couldn't figure out what she might have done that day.

55

Chapter Five

October 1980

The next time I interviewed Will Evans I arranged the meeting at a pub in Llandudno. I was wary about the risk of meeting Milly again and I thought he might be more likely to open up to me if he knew we would not be interrupted. I had a scotch whisky lined up waiting for him when he arrived.

"How's the family?" I asked.

He downed half the drink before he replied. "Milly thinks I'm a fool to be talking to you. She says no good will come of it."

"Depends how well the book sells."

"Women don't think like that. You married?"

"I was." I hesitated before adding, "She died four years ago. Cancer."

"I'm sorry."

"She was a good woman. Like you, I married an Irish woman. That's how an Englishman like me came to be working as a reporter in Belfast at the time of Sorcha's trial. That's why I was in court when you gave your evidence."

"And what did you make of my performance?" He emptied his glass and set it down on the bar table with an air of precision.

I laughed coldly. "Too wooden. It was obvious you were holding back on your emotions. Want another whiskey or are you ready to start telling me what really happened that day? What really got to you?"

He sniffed. "We'll talk first and then you can get my glass refilled. Make the next one an Irish whiskey. Not this

Scotch stuff." He gritted his teeth. "Reminds me too much of the violence of the Tartan Gangs in Belfast."

I made no comment on that. It could lead us into awkward territory.

***

Friday 21st July 1972
0820 BST

An unmarked black Ford Cortina drew up outside the house. Will hurried out before it attracted too much attention, not looking behind him for fear of what he might see: Milly glaring at him from the front doorstep.

Detective Chief Inspector Tom McIlroy beckoned him to hurry up.

Will hesitated, pretending to do up his jacket. His anger peaked. To be called in today of all days! Could he defy the voice of authority within the RUC? Could he refuse to go?

He glanced around to see if any of the neighbours were watching.

The Ballymacarrett area was a mixture of Protestants and Catholics and, in some ways, that was good. It showed that not all of Belfast was divided into sectarian ghettos. A lesson for the children, Will thought. But, as Catholics, you could never tell which of your Protestant neighbours was spying on you. That made it a dangerous place to live if you were a Catholic serving in the Royal Ulster Constabulary. Even if you were Welsh. In Belfast, any Catholic peeler was a traitor to his religion, a man fit to be tortured and killed. IRA gunmen made a career out of killing peelers, and the Catholic ones were always first in the line of fire. Will carried his Webley revolver with him everywhere, even to Mass. He had never killed anyone with it, but the threat was always there.

Another gesture from his boss urged Will into the Cortina.

McIlroy, a plain clothes detective in the driver's seat,

57

accelerated away as soon as Will slammed the car door shut. His boss looked pale and drawn this morning. His eyes were bleary, as if he had been deprived of sleep. They made an odd pair, Will thought. He was tall and thin with unruly black hair, while DCI McIlroy was shorter and more solidly built, with a layer of matted grey that carpeted his scalp. The DCI was rapidly approaching his fiftieth birthday, old enough to be Will's father, but there were times when the young detective sergeant was glad to have the support of McIlroy's long experience of police work.

Not today, however.

"Sorted out the family, have you?" The senior man glanced sideways at his passenger. His cheeks were lined from years of stress. This morning the lines were more pronounced.

"Sort of." Will avoided McIlroy's gaze.

"Angry with me, are you?"

"Don't ask. *Sir*."

McIlroy went silent for a moment. Then he jutted his chin and hissed out. "Don't sir me, Will. I've enough problems of my own to contend with. For what it's worth, I had no option but to pull you in because we're two men down. One sick and one dead. Killed last night."

Killed? Yet another peeler killed? Will felt a sudden pang of remorse rise within him. Maybe he had been a bit too quick to show his anger.

"Who was it?"

"Johnny Dunlop. Stabbed in the chest. They found his body in the Ardoyne at daybreak." McIlroy's grey, bushy eyebrows quivered with suppressed anger.

"Oh, God." Will clasped his fists tight. He'd worked with Dunlop, a young fresh-faced detective constable who came from Larne. He was another Catholic peeler, the same age as Will. They tended to stick together whenever possible because they were such a tiny minority in the RUC. Now he was dead. But that was how things went here in Belfast: you got to know and like your mates, drink with them, work easily with them, and then one day you heard they'd been murdered. That was the RUC for you: the highest rate of policemen murdered for any force in the western world. The ones left behind usually found a way of coping with it, often with the help of a whiskey bottle. The alcohol deadened the emotional pain. There was not a desk inside the North Castle Street barracks that didn't harbour a whiskey bottle.

"What happened?" he asked, knowing there was a tremor in his voice.

"Johnny's car was in for service so he was walking home last night. He must have run into an ambush in the Ardoyne. Didn't stand a chance. Knifed through the heart. The uniforms are pulling in some local dickheads to see if we can get the names of the boys that did it. I don't give much for their chances though."

"Who's investigating?"

"The guys at Oldpark CID are taking the lead on this one, but our beloved leader, Detective Superintendent Boyle, wants us to keep our eyes and ears open. Dunlop was one of ours and he thinks we owe it to him to help find whoever did it."

"The Oldpark guys won't want their noses knocked out of joint."

"The beloved leader is squaring it with them."

"The beloved leader… is that meant to be irony, boss?"

"No. Pure odium."

Will blinked. "Why?"

"Don't ask." The tiredness in McIlroy's voice was close to over-spilling.

Will pondered over asking anyway, but decided against it. He lapsed into a minute's silence before he said, "It won't be easy to square things with Oldpark."

"That's our beloved leader's problem. Not ours."

Will pictured the route Johnny Dunlop must have taken. North Castle Street ran between the Loyalist Shankill Road and the Crumlin Road. The fiercely Nationalist Ardoyne area was close by. No peeler should ever walk alone through the Ardoyne and Johnny Dunlop knew that. Maybe, being a plain clothes detective, he thought he would be safe enough, but safety was something no one could rely upon in Belfast. Safety went out of the window back in 1969 when British troops were moved into Ulster. Illusions of safety counted for nothing in a civil war.

"Is that what we're about now? Looking for suspects?" Will's question was softened by the realisation that it could have been him. It could have been any one of them at the North Castle Street barracks. You didn't have to walk alone through the Ardoyne to get yourself killed. It could happen anywhere.

McIlroy shook his head. "No. Something else. There's a Provo operation in the offing. A big one if the reports we're getting are correct. Something to take our minds off Johnny Dunlop." McIlroy turned onto the Sydenham by-pass and headed towards Holywood on the city outskirts. "We don't know what it'll be, or where it'll be, but there's information coming in that's got the top brass on edge, including the Chief Constable. They want more detail."

"So, where are we going now?" Will's voice was returning to normal, his previous anger with McIlroy melting away.

"I've had a call from Jimmy Fish. Says he's got something to tell us. Something very important, so he says. He'll meet us by the shore. Usual place."

Will sank back into his seat and went silent. His mind flipped between the past and the present; between Johnny Dunlop and Jimmy Fish. The young Catholic peeler now dead, and the Republican informer who was very much alive. Eventually, it settled on the present.

Seamus Codd – Jimmy Fish to everyone who knew him – had once worked the fishing boats out of Ardglass Harbour, a largely Nationalist enclave some thirty miles south of Belfast. A year or more ago Jimmy had turned his attention from cannabis to heroin and that made him a danger on any fishing boat. The boat owners understood that, so he never went to sea again. Instead, he slept rough and fed his habit with money he got from being both a police informer and a small-time thief. Jimmy Fish had a history of theft. Twenty years ago he did a twelve month stretch for stealing from a pub. He was what McIlroy laughingly referred to as 'a normal decent criminal', one who stuck mostly to shoplifting and burglary. Republican activity was not his scene, but he had his ear to what went on in Nationalist bars. He could have been banged up for theft many more times, but he was a useful man to have out on the streets. Even a small-time crook had an insight into the depths of Belfast's world of terrorism. There was always a chance that one day he would deliver the really big tip-off, so he stayed free and he stayed on the unofficial payroll of Detective Chief Inspector McIlroy. It had to be McIlroy, Jimmy insisted, because he trusted the DCI to play fair with him. There were two CID men in a secure basement room at North Castle Street barracks who ran most of the covert informants. They also paid them, but they didn't pay Jimmy Fish. McIlroy did.

"If I can't see 'im face to face in the street, I ain't dealing with 'im," Jimmy insisted, and nothing would budge him from that position.

A little way beyond Sydenham aerodrome, McIlroy turned towards the shore, swerved onto an overgrown dirt track and finally pulled up on a patch of waste land. A year ago, Will had been part of a team that discovered the mutilated bodies of two young British soldiers here. They had made the supreme mistake of drinking off-duty in a bar in the Ardoyne. Someone should have told them what Belfast pubs were all about. Their last drinks saw the death of them.

McIlroy kept the engine running as a shadowy figure darted out from behind a crumbling wall, raced towards the car and clambered into the back seat. His chest heaved with the exertion of running. A small, wiry man in his late fifties, Jimmy Fish smelled permanently rancid. He pulled a black beret from his bald head and clasped it in front of him.

"When are you going to wash, Jimmy?" McIlroy sniffed loudly and pointedly.

"When I get a place o' me own, Mr McIlroy." The voice

was unusually squeaky.

"Don't leave it too long." He reached into the glove compartment and pulled out a can of air freshener which he sprayed liberally over the man in the back seat.

Jimmy Fish shrank back. "What did ye do that for, Mr McIlroy?"

"Because you stink, Jimmy. Now, what have you got for me this morning?"

"Somethin' worthwhile, Mr McIlroy." Jimmy Fish jammed his head between the shoulders of the two policemen. Despite the air freshener, the body odour intensified. "'Tis real bad trouble this time, so it is. And it's gonna be a big operation. I swear it is. I heard them talkin' in the bar last night."

"Which bar?"

"Ach, I can't tell ye that, Mr McIlroy. Ye know I can't. They'd kill me. But they was absolutely clear about it. 'Tis gonna be a real big one, so it is."

"Who are they. Who did you see?"

"Can't tell ye that either, Mr McIlroy. But it was one of the IRA's top men."

"Not good enough, Jimmy. Tell us something we can use, or get out of my car!"

McIlroy turned to look out the side window, a trick he used to give the impression of losing patience. He pulled out a cigarette and lit up. The smoke had some small effect on masking the informer's smell.

Will understood the ploy well enough. It was time for him to take over the questioning. He leaned across the seat back to watch the little informer. The blood was draining from the man's pinched face. A cloud hovered around his eyes.

"You've told us nothing useful, Jimmy," Will said calmly. "There's no money in it because there's nothing there we can use."

"It's gotta be worth somethin'," Jimmy Fish muttered. "I got all these bad debts, ye see."

"No, it's worth nothing. Now tell us something useful."

The informer pursed his lips and lapsed into a period of thought that lasted a full thirty seconds. Only the steady purr of the car's engine broke the silence. Then he spoke slowly, measuring his words. "Before them bombs go off, ye'll get lots o' warnin's. Some'll be real and some'll be false. Ye won't know which is which."

Will frowned. "Bombs? You said bombs. Plural. How many, and where?"

"Ach, I swear to God I don't know, Mr Evans. Truly, I don't." The urgency in his voice sounded real. "But 'tis goin' to be somethin' real big. Somethin' ye won't have seen before. 'Tis all because that English government man, Mr Whitelaw, won't give into the IRA's demands."

"You're talking about the breakdown of the ceasefire?"

"They were supposed to be havin' secret talks, so they were, but the talks haven't come to anything, have they, Mr Evans?"

"Not if you listen to IRA gossip, Jimmy."

"Ach, to be sure, 'tis more than gossip, from what I hear. The IRA are on the move good and proper, so they are. And they built up a whole stockpile of bombs in the ceasefire."

Will shook his head, his mind now focussing on the possibility that the interview might be getting onto more solid ground. A stockpile of bombs: that was always a risk in the course of the ceasefire… which had already ended.

He spoke firmly. "We're pretty good at guessing which warnings we can trust, and which are hoaxes."

The little man leaned forward again. "That's 'cos most o' them hoax calls come from kids who don't know the right code words. This'll be different. This time the bombers themselves'll be out to fool ye. Ye'll have to believe every call, and ye won't have the men to cope with it. Ye'll get all the blame 'cos ye won't be able to cope. That's what I heard them sayin'."

"Which bombers? And who's masterminding this attack?"

Jimmy Fish lowered his voice to a hoarse whisper. "Ye know well enough who's who in charge of the Provos'

Belfast brigade, Mr Evans. Ye know that as well as I do."

"The top man?"

Fish looked away and kept his voice low. "I heard them say 'tis the man with the Thompson sub-machine gun who's gonna be in charge on the streets."

"McGuinness?"

"Ach, 'twas ye who said that, not me, Mr Evans. But the final say will have to come from higher up. The very top. 'Tis gonna be that big."

McIlroy suddenly swung round in his seat and grimaced at Will. He nodded to indicate he would take back control of the questioning. "And you heard all this in a bar, Jimmy, but you won't tell us which bar."

Fish turned to face the senior policeman and twisted his beret in his lean, tremulous hands. "Honestly, Mr McIlroy, if it got out that t'was me what grassed about this one, I'd be dead before nightfall."

"How does this information help us?"

"Ye mustn't be too quick to react to every call ye gets, even if it sounds real. Ye'll need to think about every call as it comes in. And ye'll need the army to back up the peelers on the streets. As many troops as ye can get hold of. Ye'll need to warn them now to be ready when it all starts."

"And when will it start?"

"Today."

"Today? That's all you can tell us?"

"It's as much as I dare tell ye. But 'tis enough, ain't it? Worth the money?"

McIlroy sighed. "All right, Jimmy. I believe you." He pulled an envelope from an inside pocket and held it in the divide between them. "Don't spend it all on drugs. Get yourself a decent meal."

"Ach, ye keeps on tellin' me that, Mr McIlroy." The little man's eyes lit up and he reached for the money, but McIlroy held on to it a little longer.

"And you keep ignoring me, Jimmy."

Fish tugged at the envelope. "I'm clean now. Honest, I am."

"As clean as sheet of used bog paper." The policeman kept his grip on the money. "One more question. What's the word on the streets about the murder of Detective Constable Dunlop?"

Fish looked thoughtful for a few seconds. "Ach, well now. There's some serious stories goin' about that one, fer sure there is. I could tell ye somethin', Mr McIlroy, but…" He chewed at his lower lip. "… but it would be worth a few more pounds, so it would."

"Talk, Jimmy."

"Another twenty, Mr McIlroy. I owe this money, ye see."

"No."

"Ten, then. Just another ten."

"All right. Ten and no more." McIlroy released his hold on the envelope and pulled out his wallet. He drew out a single ten-pound note and held it in front of the informer's face. "Now talk, Jimmy."

"Ach, so difficult this is, Mr McIlroy. So difficult. The thing is… I'd be grassin' on a sort of relative. If ye know what I mean."

"Come on, Jimmy. When were you ever slow to tell on anyone? For ten pounds, give me a name."

"Can't do that. Can't grass on a sort of relative, even one like this. Me conscience wouldn't let me. But I can tell ye this… ye're good at diggin' up names, ain't ye, Mr McIlroy? Ye're good at doin' the diggin' and findin' out fer yerself." He adopted a coy expression. "I'm not givin' ye a name, but I reckon ye can ferret around a bit and come up with somethin'. Someone… sort of related."

"A relative, you say?"

"A *sort of* relative. That's as much as I'm sayin' and 'tis worth the ten, so 'tis. Do the diggin' and work it out fer yerself, Mr McIlroy. But I ain't givin' away any names. Me conscience is clear on that."

"As clear as the shit on your boots, Jimmy."

McIlroy nodded and released his grip on the note. Within seconds the informer had exited the car fast. Maybe he thought the policeman would change his mind.

When he was gone, McIlroy and Will sat regarding one another.

"Who do you think he was referring to, boss?" Will said. "Which of his devious relatives would have reason to kill Johnny Dunlop?"

"Fitzpain. It has to be him. And I wouldn't put it past him, Will. Sad bastard that he is."

McIlroy put the car into gear and drove off with a squeal of rubber on the rough ground. He stared straight ahead and spoke calmly as if weighing up the evidence with a measure of care. "Jimmy Fish and Fitzpain are cousins. They grew up in that same village; Ardglass. Time was the Codd family and the Fitzpains were thick as thieves. They fell out years ago, but that's history. If it was Fitzpain who killed Dunlop and I was in Jimmy Fish's shoes, I'd also be very wary of naming him outright."

"Nothing he's said will stand up in court."

"Right. But the more I think about it, the more I'd like to get Fitzpain into an interview room. I think Jimmy Fish may have given us a useful tip-off despite his reticence over a name. Something we can keep in mind for future use. He's probably earned the price of a meal."

"He'll spend it on drugs."

"His choice."

Will thought about it. "We'd better report this straight away, boss. After that, it'll be up to either Superintendent Boyle or the Oldpark guys to decide whether or not they want to talk to Fitzpain. My feeling is they'll want something more positive first, something that can be conclusively pinned on him before they haul him in."

"You're probably right. In the meantime, the bomb is more important, and we don't know where it'll be planted," McIlroy said.

"Bombs, boss. Jimmy said bombs. Plural."

"You're right, Will. Plural it is. If that bit of information is correct, we're in for yet another hell of a day." He rammed his foot down on the accelerator as he turned back onto the main road. "One hell of a day."

Will settled back into silence.

Bombs.

Plural.

Bombs meant dead bodies, mutilated bodies, grieving families. Yet more anguish and misery in a province overloaded with anguish and misery. Will's thoughts wandered. Riots, mortar bomb attacks, car bombs, IRA ambushes. Was it any wonder the RUC had not only the highest murder rate, but also the highest rate of suicides amongst any police force in Europe? Overworked policemen who couldn't take any more of it.

Maybe Milly was right.

Maybe it was past the time he should have been thinking of getting out. More than just thinking about it. And then his vision blurred again for a few seconds.

That damn knock on the head!

***

October 1980

I bought Will another double whiskey, a Jameson this time. He downed it in one and rose from his seat.

"Going already, Will?" I asked. I had many questions running round inside my head and hoped he would be able to give me some clear answers.

"I promised Milly I wouldn't stay more than an hour." He glanced at his watch. "She'll be getting dinner ready. Give me a call in a few days and we'll talk again. You'll have other interviews lined up in the meantime?"

"I'm seeing Martin Foster the day after tomorrow."

"Oh yes? Where does he live now?"

"He's still in Belfast. Never did join the army. I'll be seeing Sorcha again while I'm over there. It makes sense to see them both on the same visit."

"The Mulveny girl? Good luck with that one. I doubt they'll ever let her out of prison."

"Maybe. Maybe not. She's changing, Will. I've seen the

signs of it."

He shook his head. "She's too devious by far. Don't get taken in by her." He didn't look back as he walked away.

Chapter Six

October 1980

Martin never left Northern Ireland. Instead, he took a clerical job with a firm of accountants before he married his cousin. I thought he was right to steer clear of the army, but foolish to stay in Belfast. However, it was his life. I called on him at the house his aunt had once owned. She was now five years dead and Martin lived there with his wife, Emily. They had one daughter who was now four years old. As I entered the house, she stood close beside her mother, staring at me through big, round eyes.

Martin had aged noticeably since I last saw him, at the trial. He had grown a moustache and his hair was prematurely grey. He was dressed in faded jeans and a tartan shirt that might have given the wrong impression in some parts of the city. He wore an air of suspicion to begin with, as if he was unsure of my motivations in writing the book. Emily must have been equally suspicious because she eyed me warily. She said little, made a pot of tea and then she left Martin and me to talk in the small front parlour room. It had a claustrophobic air about it, as if the dead aunt was still there; a ghost lording over life in her absence.

"You have a nice family," I said as a way of breaking the ice. "Are you happy now, Martin?"

"How can anyone be happy as long as the Troubles continue?" It sounded like a deliberately evasive reply.

"You decided against moving to England."

"Emily persuaded me to stay,"

I waited for further explanation, but none came, so I asked, "Did you ever contact Sorcha after the trial?" It was time to give the discussion some positive direction.

He nodded but kept his gaze away from me, as if he was afraid I might question his actions. "I wrote to her soon after she began her sentence. She wrote back and told me not to get in touch with her again."

"Did you do as she said?"

"No." He looked up and his voice took on an angry tone. "I wrote again and again. She never replied to any of those letters. I tried to arrange a prison visit, but she refused to see me."

"But you still think about her?"

"What do you think? It's been eight years now since Bloody Friday, and barely a day goes by when I don't think about her. Emily understands that. She's a great comfort to me. I don't know what would have become of me without her support."

I took a moment to consider my next words. "You understand what I want to learn from you?"

"The Bloody Friday bombs? That's all in the past. It no longer bothers me." A slight tremor in one hand gave the lie to his words. How could anyone in Belfast assert that it was 'all in the past'?

I kept my voice unruffled. "Not specifically the bombs, Martin. I've already gathered enough information about the bombs. What I want to know is how that day affected you and Sorcha."

"You want more of the personal angle?" His voice was steadily growing calmer.

"Exactly. The things that never came to light in court. Are you willing to talk about that?"

He shrugged. "When you phoned me, I said I'd tell you everything."

"Okay. Why don't you begin with the moment you first saw Sorcha on that Friday morning?"

"Don't you want to know how we first met?"

"Of course, but I want to write that part of the story from Sorcha's viewpoint. I don't mean to be rude, Martin, but this is more her story than yours."

"Because she ended up with a life sentence?" There was a new hint of acrimony in his voice. The past bothered him still, despite his denial.

"No. Because the story all comes together through her. She's the only one who can never be cut from the final manuscript. So, begin with what happened that Friday morning when you met her. Tell me all you can remember."

"Everything?"

"Everything."

***

Friday 21st July 1972
0855 BST

Aunt Judy was unusually quiet that summer morning. Martin understood why, and he made an effort not to draw attention to himself. It was because of his father's brother, Uncle Alfred Foster. He had been a corporal in the British army, a proud young Belfast man who was newly-wed when he was sent off to fight in the Korean War. Alfred Foster spent just one week with his bride, Judy, and they never saw one another again. He was killed exactly twenty years ago: the 21st July 1952. Aunt Judy never really got over the loss of her husband. She probably never would, Martin figured, even though she now lived near the heart of another war, one that was playing out on the streets of her home city.

And more young Belfast men were dying.

Martin escaped the heavy silence at the breakfast table and shut himself in his bedroom. He had a letter to post, one he did not want Aunt Judy to know about; not until it was too late for her to do anything about it. It was his application to join the army. An office job, not a fighting job. He could never bring himself to lift a rifle and shoot another human. However, he was old enough to enlist; nineteen last March, and he didn't need Aunt Judy's consent. But he was unemployed and that irked him.

He sat at a small table beside the bedroom window and

stared out at the neighbours who were on their way to work. There were fewer of them than there had been before the Troubles began. He envied the younger men who had beaten the odds and managed to get employment in a city at war. He wasn't any sort of layabout, he told himself. He had 'A' level certificates, and hard work didn't put him off. A career in accountancy would be his first choice, but he just couldn't find a Belfast company willing to give him a chance, a step on the ladder. He had tried and tried again, but the political and religious divisions didn't make the interviews any easier. He couldn't always be sure of the interviewer's affiliations.

They always began with the same question: "What school did you go to?" It was a recognised code for the unspoken question; are you a Catholic or a Protestant? Give the wrong answer and the interview was terminated there and then. Half of his answers had been wrong. Well, it seemed like the army might give him a better chance, and he was anxious to take advantage. A chance of a job and a chance to escape from Belfast.

He sealed the envelope, licked a stamp and fixed it to the front. Then he slipped the application into his coat pocket. As he did so, he detected one of Aunt Judy's church collection envelopes. She insisted he contribute to the Reverend Ian's church even if he never entered the building. Martin humoured her. It saved a lot of bother.

The letter with his application form would go into the post box at the end of the street, outside the shops. One of the few boxes that had not been vandalised or repainted Republican green as an act of IRA defiance.

Oddly, it wasn't Uncle Alfred he had in mind as he tip-toed down the stairs; it was his parents; killed in a motor accident when he was still at primary school. What would they think about him becoming a soldier? He hoped they would have understood had they been still alive, even if they didn't fully approve. Not after what happened to Alfred.

His other worry was Sorcha, and that was even more of a

problem.

He was at the foot of the stairs when the front door opened and his cousin, Emily, came in. A quiet, seventeen-year-old with a constantly friendly smile, she daily helped Aunt Judy with her housework. Tall for her age and pliantly slender, she paused inside the door and gave Martin a querying expression. Her full lips were pursed, almost as if she expected a kiss.

Martin put a finger to his own lips and nodded towards the dining room. "Aunt Judy is in one of her silent moods," he explained softly.

Emily gave a nod of understanding. "You think I should come back later, Martin? Mammy says there's a lot of tidying up to be done in here. And the bedclothes to be changed."

Martin never liked to see the girl used this way, almost as if she was an unpaid skivvy. He replied in whispered tones. "Your choice, but this is no way for you to be using your school holiday. You should be out enjoying yourself with your friends."

"Mammy says I have to help in here."

"Well, don't stay too long. These silent moods can be tiring."

"Do you have to go?" She adopted a wistful expression, as if she was disappointed to see him leaving.

"Yes. Sorry. Something important."

"Something or someone?"

"Don't be so suspicious, Emily."

He hurried on out of the house before her sad look could unnerve him.

Harold Street, a branch off the Crumlin Road, was almost empty when Martin posted the letter. The paper shop was equally quiet when he strode in to buy Aunt Judy's newspaper. The few early customers had gone to their workplaces. Later customers, the ones with no work to go to, were likely still in their beds. Martin bought a *Daily Express* and studied the front page as he left. *MPs Split*, said the banner headline. He had no interest in that division, whatever it was.

He was back in the Crumlin Road, idly turning the page when Sorcha ran out from an alleyway and fell into step beside him. She grinned at him with eyes that were brown and playful. She didn't kiss him. There was no telling who might be watching: Republican or Loyalist.

"I didn't see you coming." He smiled as he closed up the paper and stuck it under one arm. He hadn't expected to see her today, but she could be just what he needed after Aunt Judy's silent behaviour. She wasn't wearing her new clothes, the clothes she bought on the day they first met. Instead, she wore a white tee shirt that was moulded around well-formed breasts, a denim mini skirt that only just hid her panties and a lightweight cotton jacket that only just reached to her slim waist. He glanced down at her long, shapely bare legs and felt a tingle of pleasure. Sex oozed from her body like sweat from an athlete, but far more welcome.

"Did youse do it, Martin? Did youse post yer application?" She sounded worried as she slipped a hand into his. It felt warm, comforting, unlike her hesitant voice.

He nodded. "Posted it a few minutes ago. Too late to back out now."

She bit at her lower lip before replying. "Can we have a wee while together?" Something in her voice spoke of a deep concern.

"You want to go to Ivan's flat?" He pictured her naked body writhing on top of him and was unable to suppress a sudden grin. Was this the moment for an unexpected stroke of good fortune to come his way? It was a good job she was a lapsed Catholic, he reflected, because they had worked their way through one whole lot of condoms in the past month. And it was a good job Aunt Judy had no idea he was sleeping with a Catholic. Aunt Judy was a regular worshipper at Ian Paisley's Free Presbyterian Church, where Catholicism was an ugly word. It wasn't the nearest Presbyterian Church, but it was the most appealing to Aunt Judy.

"You should come and listen to the Reverend Ian," his aunt often told him. "He's a true believer in the teachings of Jesus. And it saddens me that you no longer attend any church."

"Religion no longer means anything to me, Aunt," he would tell her.

In truth he had turned away from the Presbyterian church because of its overriding message of gloom and doom. Even a friendly game of football on Sunday was a moral sin. The descendants of Scottish settlers had, it seemed, brought their dour religious lifestyle to Ireland with them and then ramped it up until it was beyond Martin's liking. At least the Catholics made some effort to enjoy their lives.

"But the Reverend Ian's voice is the word of God, Martin," his aunt told him.

"In that case I wish God wouldn't shout at us, Aunt."

She had a well-practiced way of shaking her head sadly. "You're a wicked sinner, Martin. What have I done wrong for you to end up like this?"

Thank God she knew nothing of Sorcha Mulveny. He couldn't even mention her name in the house. It was a dead giveaway. There were no Protestants in Northern Ireland called Sorcha.

As he walked beside her, Martin's thoughts intensified. Out of bed, she was an attractive young girl: an island of beauty caught up in in a sea of ugliness. She was not a complete innocent, that was obvious, but neither was he. There had been other girls, Protestant girls, but none of them had appealed to him so much as Sorcha. Likely, she had secrets hidden in her past, but he didn't care. No one was wholly pure in this damned city. In bed, she was a powerhouse of sexual emotion. She had an uncanny way of leaning her head back and crying out, "Yes, yes!" just at the moment he ejaculated inside her. It was her Eureka moment, she told him, the recurring discovery of the ultimate orgasm, the one that had so long eluded her with other bedmates. It also heralded his certainty that he would never want to have sex with anyone else. Protestant or Catholic, what did religion matter when they were so good in bed together? It would matter even less if she would go with him to England. He could marry a Catholic in England and who would care? Their lives would not be at risk.

He gave her a brief inquisitive glance, a look designed to display his sexual need. To his disappointment she seemed unwilling to respond to it, even before she spoke.

"'Tis not sex I need right now, Martin. I just want to spend a while wi' youse. The thing is… we need to talk. Can we go somewhere for a coffee? Somewhere safe, where we can just be together and talk."

He looked away to hide his initial frustration. "There's a café just along the road here. It opens early."

"A Prod café? I said somewhere safe."

At that moment he saw an expression of fear invade her eyes. Why? Did she really think she'd be shot for going into a café on this part of the Crumlin Road? Or was he the one who was being thoughtless? He replied with an air of resignation. "You've come with me to Ivan's flat many times over the past month, and Ivan's a Protestant like me."

"After dark," she said. "We went there after dark. Not in broad daylight. I wouldn't walk into a Protestant house in daylight. Someone would see me, fer sure."

He snorted loudly. "You're in a Protestant area now, Sorcha. Everything round here is Protestant, until we get a mile further down the road. You know what it's like down by the Oldpark Road. Down there, they might as well put up a notice: No Prods allowed here on pain of death."

She hissed back through gritted teeth. "I told you! I'm not going into a Protestant house or a Protestant café in broad daylight." The look of fear never left her eyes. "I'd feel safer if we go that mile farther down the road. Are youse too scared to come wi' me?"

Martin stared hard at her, wondering if she was serious. It was the first time he had seen her so frightened.

"We don't all go around killing Catholics before breakfast," he snapped before he could stop himself.

Her gaze fell away in the light of his hard stare, but her

voice remained firm. "Youse are scared of comin' with me, aren't youse? D'youse think they'll roast youse alive in retribution for Bloody Sunday. Do youse?"

"I had nothing to do with that."

"And I wouldn't be here if youse had."

She had delivered a deliberate taunt, but he was not going to show cowardice in the face of a girl who gave him such a good time in bed. He was made of better stuff than that. He jutted his chin defiantly. "All right we'll walk on and you can choose where we get the coffee."

"Glad you can see sense at last." Her voice lightened and he detected an easing in her stride. "Get rid of that English newspaper first, will youse. They don't like English newspapers in the Oldpark Road."

"They don't like anything English down there," he replied, and dropped the paper into a hedge. Whoever found it could have a free read this morning.

They walked on down the Crumlin Road, past the outskirts of the Ardoyne area, until they came to a junction. Had they carried on another hundred yards they would have come to the Crumlin Road Gaol and the Mater Hospital. Over the years, the gaol had held numerous IRA men, including de Valera. The Belfast courthouse, where many a terrorist had been sentenced, stood directly opposite it. In 1942 a nineteen-year old IRA man called Tom Williams was hanged in the goal for killing an RUC officer. Martin glanced down the road towards the edifice and reflected that the staunchly Republican Oldpark residents would still remember Tom Williams with favour, but they would have little thought for the policeman he killed. Was he wise to follow Sorcha here?

As he and Sorcha turned into Oldpark Road, a sudden burst of gunfire drew them both to a halt. It seemed to come from several streets away, deeper into the ghetto. They looked at one another and waited for a return of fire. There was none so they shrugged and walked on.

"Is this more comfortable for you, Sorcha? Do you think you'll be safe from attack now?" Martin asked, unable to hide the irony in his voice. His doubts about his own safety now began to hit home. Too many innocent Protestants had died because they strayed into the wrong areas, and the Ardoyne was very much a 'wrong area' for a Protestant. And that gunfire had been only a few streets away.

"Are youse laughing at me?" she snapped angrily.

He turned and grinned as a way of covering his own unease. "Of course I am. Now, where are we going?"

"We're in the Bone, so we keep walkin'." She pointed ahead. "There's a small hotel along here where they know me. I do some wee jobs for them sometimes, so I do. Washin' dishes and the like. We can get a cup of coffee there. And we can talk."

"Why d'you Catholics call it the Bone?" he asked, wondering if her reply would be fact or legend.

She replied easily, as if everyone should know the answer. "The Bone... the Marrowbone... Marylebone."

"You think the 'bone' comes from Marylebone?"

"'Tis true. 'Tis because of Marie Le Bone. Mary the Good, in French. That's where it comes from." She spread her hands to show her certainty. "Funny how the English called a London railway station Marylebone after Mary the Good, and we call this part of the Ardoyne after her."

"Really?" He held back from expressing his thoughts. His original question had been rhetorical because he had read that the London Marylebone came from the church of St Mary at the Bourne. *Bourne* was the old English word for a stream. But Sorcha came from a world of myth and legend that was often at odds with reality, a world in which St Patrick cast out all the snakes from Ireland. If they stayed together in Belfast it was inevitable that disagreements like this would come between them. They would find themselves arguing about so many deeply entrenched opinions, especially religious opinions. Prudence and the joy of her naked body told him to keep that day at bay for as long as possible... until he could persuade her to join him in England. It would be their only real hope of staying together.

Sorcha seemed unaware of his reservations. "They say there used to be a shrine to Marie Le Bone somewhere round here, so there was." She paused before asking, "What's it to youse anyway?"

"Nothing." He should have known better than to ask. He had no wish for an argument right now.

His regrets at venturing into the Nationalist area began to mount. The evidence of rioting was here for all to see: the bullet marks on the walls and the distorted tarmac where cars had been incinerated. His attention was drawn to a burned-out car abandoned on a patch of waste ground. Beyond it, Provisional IRA graffiti adorned a gable wall. In Loyalist areas the most common wall art was 'Bugger the pope'. Here it was 'Fuk the qeen'. The only thing Martin deduced from it was the marginally higher standard of literacy on the Loyalist side of the divide. The standard of ignorance and bigotry was about equal.

A shop directly opposite had been torched. The windows and doors of the next two houses were boarded up. Bricks from a recent riot littered the pavement nearby where a group of unruly children played noisily. They stopped their game to stare at Martin, a face that would be unknown here. Distrust of strangers was the norm to these children. He turned his head away and another gable mural met his gaze. A giant painting of Provo killers proudly parading their Armalite AR-18 rifles, the 'widowmakers'. The hooded heads and the lethal weapons looked down threateningly onto the dirty streets. We rule here and don't you forget it, they seemed to say. Martin suppressed a gulp and gritted his teeth.

Surely England could never be anything like this.

If the Green Hills Hotel in Oldpark Road had a star rating it would have been on the minus side of zero. It was nothing more than cheap lodgings on the first floor above a terrace of run-down red-brick shops. A faded sign at street level was falling loose from its mountings. Sultry youths loitered nearby and watched Martin and Sorcha with expressions of wariness. A trail of smoke drifted from what looked like cigarettes, but were not cigarettes. The lingering smell was not nicotine.

"Ignore them," Sorcha said, and she led the way up a narrow flight of stairs to a dim reception area. An elderly, white-haired woman in a drab grey dress sat behind a desk, busily knitting. She had a pair of scissors in one hand, snipping away at the woollen ends in a newly-darned man's sock. She eyed Martin suspiciously. He knew the look. It said 'who the hell are you' without a single word being spoken. He glanced around as a way of avoiding her gaze. A crucifix hung on one wall. A print of Jesus with his heart exposed hung on another. He looked for an image of Mary the Good, but saw none. The whole place stank of animal urine, but there was no sign of a cat or a dog. He looked back at the old lady, wondering if the smell came from her. The knitting continued.

"Youse're abroad early, Sorcha," the woman muttered, never taking her gaze from Martin. The way she peered at him with her small, beady eyes made him feel he was still being interrogated. He flinched, knowing that suspicion of strangers was an everyday part of life in any Belfast ghetto. They learned it from birth.

He wondered what she would say or do if she knew who he was. Hatred of Protestants and the English wasn't solely because of Bloody Sunday, although that fiasco played a major part in it. It went all the way back to the famine, the plantation, the various Irish risings and beyond. He understood that, and he understood how the stories evolved with their telling, like Chinese whispers, until they became a version of Irish history that was considerably at odds with Irish history.

He resolved to keep his mouth shut as long as possible.

"Can we have a couple of coffees, Maggie?" Sorcha put on a casual air. "Me and me cousin are parched."

"Yer cousin?" The old lady's voice held an air of doubt. The scissors hung in the air as if she was about to turn them onto Martin.

Sorcha relied firmly. "Aye. He's visitin' from Derry. Is

that okay?"

"Ach, well…" The old woman put aside her knitting and stood up slowly, rubbing at her bent back. She moaned as she shuffled away.

"We'll sit in here." Sorcha pointed to a tiny sitting room. She leaned closer to him and whispered. "If anyone asks, ye're called Patrick. D'ye hear me? Martin sounds too Proddy for this area."

"Martin McGuinness isn't a Protestant."

"That's different."

"Why?"

"It just is."

Martin shrugged and followed her into the room. A small window was open, letting in the street sounds and a welcome breath of air.

"Aunt Judy would kill me if she knew where I am now," he said.

"Better she kills youse than the Provos." Sorcha indicated him to sit on an old, well-worn two-seater settee. She nestled beside him, grasped his hand and asked in a low voice, "Are youse really gonna go to England?"

"Yes."

"I've never been there. Have youse?"

"No, but I'm sure it's the right thing to do. And 'tis my own choice."

"You're quite sure? They say 'tis a terrible place for us Irish."

"Who says that?"

"Everyone."

"Republican nonsense. Anyway, I made up my mind a long time ago." He spoke quietly, wary of the old lady in the reception area overhearing him. "I just never got round to actually doing something about it. Thought I could put it off and live here for a few more years, but it isn't working out. I've no job and it's not like a proper home here, is it? Not with IRA bombs going off day after day."

"But, England…?"

He paused. "My dad was English, did you know that?"

81

"No." She gave him a surprised look, released his hand and shrank back.

"It's true," he said. "He came from somewhere down in the south of England. Moved to Belfast after he married my mum and got a job in the shipyard. She was Belfast Irish through and through, was my mum. So I'm told."

"'Tis not just England that worries me, Martin. Maybe I could cope with that if I tried. 'Tis more the thought of youse joinin' the British army an' maybe gettin' sent back here to kill innocent Irish people." A sharp element of hostility crept into her voice.

"The people the army go after are not innocent, Sorcha," he said, struggling to keep calm.

"They were on Bloody Sunday."

"Maybe, maybe not. It was all a tragic mistake," he snorted loudly.

"Innocent people died," she pointed out.

"Innocent people on both sides have died in the Troubles, Sorcha. Don't forget that." Then he remembered where he was and dropped his voice back to a whisper. "'Tis bloody unfair. The IRA go out onto the streets with the deliberate aim of bombing and killing innocents and your people say nothing about it. The army makes a stupid mistake and you're all up in arms."

"That's not true. It was such a terrible thing to happen, everyone should be up in arms about it. But let's not argue." She looked around in case anyone was close enough to hear. "Please, Martin, let's not argue. Not here."

"You started it." He wished now she hadn't brought him here.

"What about yer aunt?" she asked. "Will she mind youse goin' to England?"

"I doubt it." He thought for a few seconds, his anger slow to dissipate. How much should he tell her? How much should he explain? The icy looks that had followed him through his adolescent years? The beatings when he was a child? In the event, he said, "I know Aunt Judy deserves credit for taking me in after my parents died, but she's never been like a real mum. It always felt like she had to do it from duty rather than family love. Maybe she just wasn't cut out for motherhood. Or maybe it's because she never got over losing my uncle. I'll thank her before I go, but I suspect she'll be glad to see the back of me."

"And youse think England will be better than Belfast?" Sorcha said.

He laughed lightly. "Come off it, Sorcha. Right now any place is going to be better than Belfast." He put an arm about her shoulders. "The question is; would you be willing to come with me?"

"Live in England?"

"Yes. With me."

A telephone rang in the background, but he ignored it.

"Why?" she asked. "Why do you want me of all people to go with you? Why me?"

"Because I don't want to lose you." He wanted to say how much he loved her, but he sensed it was too soon. He would be asking too much commitment from her before they were both sure. They had known one another little more than a month, and her reservations were obvious.

She went into a short period of silent thought before she spoke again. "If youse don't want to lose me, don't join the army."

"I must." He cast a hand towards the window. "There's nothing for me out there. I must get a job and quickly. The army is one obvious choice. With luck I'll get sent to Germany."

"You wouldn't have said that in 1940."

"I wasn't alive in 1940 and I don't live in the past... unlike some." He gave her a hard look and wondered if she would pick up his meaning. Belfast was full of people who lived in the past. The 1916 rising was only yesterday. The famine was the day before.

She turned her gaze away from him. "Youse'll have to go where the army sends youse. Youse could be sent back here."

"I'm not going to enlist as a foot soldier. I've an A level

in maths and I want to join the admin branch... accountancy... book-keeping... something similar."

"Paying wages?"

"Whatever's on offer. I'll tell them it's in their best interests not to send me back here. I need to get away from all that's going on here... or go mad. So... will you come with me?"

"I don't know," she said. "And that's the truth. If it was just England... maybe. But with youse in the army... I don't know."

They both went silent when the old woman brought in a tray set out with two coffee mugs, milk and sugar. She put it down on a small, low table in front of them. She didn't speak until she stood back and eyed the two of them warily. "Brian's on the lookout fer youse, Sorcha. He phoned me a few minutes ago. Askin' if I knew where youse were." Her voice turned screechy, as rough as fingernails dragged down a blackboard.

Martin felt Sorcha suddenly grow tense alongside him.

"Why? What does he want?" she said.

"Dunno. None o' my business, is it? But he's on his way over here."

Sorcha stood up suddenly. "Oh, shit!"

***

October 1980

"What happened when Sorcha came face-to-face with that man?" I asked.

"I don't know. She made me leave."

"But you saw him?"

"Only briefly, just as I was going. You'll have to ask her what went on between them. You'll be seeing her, will you?"

"I've arranged a visit this afternoon. I wanted to use that meeting to ask her about how you two first met. Now you've given me another topic to explore."

The door opened and the child strode in. She stood beside her father's seat and glared directly at me. The big round eyes held no hint of welcome. "Mummy says it's time you went."

Chapter Seven

October 1980

My mind was filled with yet more questions as I drove to Armagh, questions I needed to ask Sorcha. She was waiting for me in the prison interview room, leaning forward on a metal and plastic chair, her elbows on the bare table, as if she was anxious to get on with the meeting. One eye was badly bruised.

"What happened?" I asked even before I sat down.

She shrugged. "I refused to be part of the latest dirty protest. Don't ask any more about it."

I didn't need to ask. I understood. The Republican women in Armagh gaol had a reputation for being every bit as ruthless as their male counterparts. 'Join us or suffer' was an instruction as persuasive as any religious dogma, but Sorcha was not persuaded. Whatever my concerns, however, there was nothing I could do to help her.

The same burly female warder stood against the wall behind her. I took a seat at the opposite side of the plain wooden table and pulled out my notebook. I began by telling her I had met with Martin that morning.

"How is he?" she asked, her interest peaking. "Is he happy?"

"He seems to be coping with life in his own way. He still lives in Belfast and he's married now."

A frown flittered across her face. "He's married? I suppose I should have expected that."

"What more do you want me to tell you?"

She shook her head forcibly. "Nothing. Nothing more. I don't want to know about his life without me. Only that he's happy. And you did say he's happy?"

That wasn't what I said, but I let it pass. I understood her feelings. "In that case, let's go back to the past... let's talk again about what happened eight years ago. Martin told me that you went to a small hotel in the Bone area and Fitzpain came to see you there. Do you remember that?"

"Yes."

"What happened?"

"The police came along..."

"No, Sorcha." I put up a hand to stop her. "Start at the beginning. Tell me the story from the moment you heard Fitzpain was on his way to see you. And Sorcha..."

"Yes?"

"Tell me more about your feelings for Martin. You did have strong feelings for him, didn't you?"

"Feelings?" She looked away. One hand wiped slowly across her bruised eye. "Of course I had feelings. I loved him. And he saved me life, so he did."

"Really?" I shuddered. "You hinted at that once before. Tell me about it."

***

Friday 21st July 1972
0930 BST

A cold fear clutched at Sorcha in that dirty little hotel. She put a hand to her forehead and tried to steady her breathing. Martin was staring up at her, as if something was seriously wrong. Of course something was wrong, but she couldn't tell him what it was.

He opened his mouth to speak, but she waved a hand furiously at him. "Don't say anythin', Martin! Not now."

She turned away. Damn that eejit, Brian Fitzpain. How the hell was she going to explain this to Martin? Was this how their relationship would end? She'd kept so many secrets from him. He didn't even know where she lived, except that it was in a Nationalist area. God help him if he genuinely believed she was a simple, innocent Catholic girl stuck in the wrong place. Surely no one could spend so much intimate time with her and still believe that. If only it was true though. Or... if only she could keep the truth from him forever. But she couldn't. Certainly not if Brian Fitzpain found them together.

Did it matter?

Yes, it mattered because Martin was the only man to have demonstrated that he cared about her. That was the essence of her problem. He was the only one who didn't look down on her as nought but a means of exciting sex. With him it was more than just a detached moment of sexual release. It was a prolonged moment of love that left her emotionally sated. Maybe there were others, Catholics who could do that for her. Maybe she just hadn't yet met such a man. So why did she have to fall for him of all people, a decent-minded Prod? Why did she have to fall in love with a man who was one of Catholic Ireland's hated enemies?

She had been to bed with many men from her own side of the divide and most of them gave her little or no physical satisfaction. Alcohol-sozzled kisses, fumbling hands and dicks that went limp within seconds of entry. Sometimes before entry. A surfeit of Guinness and whiskey had that effect. They claimed she was amazing in bed, regardless of their own performance, but what was the use of that? She cast her mind back. Until she was fourteen, she knew nothing but constant sneers and condemnation. Useless at school, useless at home, useless anywhere. She was a nobody. And then she discovered there was one thing she could do well.

"By God, ye're a damn good shag, Sorcha," men and boys would tell her. "The best around here." And then she would feel a sense of elation because she was acknowledged to be better than other women. Better at something. In her own mind, she was recognised as having status within the community. Was that why she allowed herself to be seduced by men for whom she secretly harboured revulsion? How would Martin react when he discovered she'd been to bed with several Provisional IRA killers? Not Fitzpain, of course. How could she possibly give in to him, with him being who he was? But there had been others.

She wasn't a prostitute. She never took money for sex, but she gave away her body too often in return for that admiration and sense of achievement. It might have gone on like that if Brian Fitzpain had not pointed out the obvious. "Don't fool yerself, girl. They all laugh at youse behind yer back. They laugh at youse because ye're a wee whore. A good-for-nothin' bitch with a pretty face. That's all ye'll ever be, so get used to it."

At first she refused to believe him, but the truth could not be so easily ignored. In time her opinion of herself changed. He was right, of course he was. Why hadn't she seen it so clearly before? She wasn't clever like Bridie. She wasn't gifted with words and ideas. She was useless, except for what she had in her knickers. The revelation led her into a period of intense depression. She would never be anything more than a cheap whore living in a ghetto of hatred, bigotry and violence, so what was the point of going on? Inevitably, the obvious answer came to her and she accepted it. Better to end her life now, before she sank even further into the gutter. Suicide was the only realistic answer. So she gathered together the tools.

And then she met Martin.

He was different. He behaved like a gentleman. He showed her what real love was all about. He offered her a way out of her problem. A much better way than the one she had been planning when she met him. Could she go away to England with him? The prospect was so tempting.

They first met little more than a month ago. It was that critical Saturday morning when she had been shopping in the city centre, buying clothes for the last time. She chose carefully: a smart new pleated skirt, a new white blouse, a new comfortable bra and frilly panties. She had the pills and the booze stashed away in her bedside cabinet, and she would end it all that night. When the end came she would look good, like she never had before. She was determined on that. None of the worn old clothes that made her look so dowdy, so cheap. No, when her body was found she would be looking pretty, as a girl should look. That was how they would bury her, and that was how they would remember her; looking attractive. Not that she could afford to buy the clothes, but she had some cash in her purse, money she had stolen from her mammy's rent tin. It didn't matter. She would be dead before mammy found out.

She was leaving the shop on Royal Avenue when she tripped on a dislodged paving slab and fell, knocking her head on the ground. The man just ahead of her turned at her sudden cry for help.

"Oh God! What happened?" She felt dizzy, struggling to sit up.

"You fell." He grasped her hand, pulling her into a seated position.

"Stupid thing to do." Her vision began to stabilise.

"Blame the pavement." His voice was soft, mellow.

She looked up at the man and saw that he was young, no older than herself. He wore a dark blazer and grey flared trousers and his flowery pink shirt was open at the neck. His hair was long, like David Essex, and his smiling eyes seemed to bore into her with some sort of pleasure.

"I must look like a damned fool," she said.

"No. You look quite delightful. Just a touch unlucky."

"Fuck me," she said without thinking. No one had complimented her like that before.

He laughed. "That's a very tempting offer, but shouldn't we get to know one another first."

There was blood on her face. He wiped at it with a clean handkerchief and then eased her to her feet. The dizziness persisted so he led her into the café next door and bought her a cup of coffee. He stayed with her until her senses returned to normal, chatting easily in that smooth, well-educated voice. He offered to see her home, but she refused. She had no idea which side of the divide he came from, but he promised to meet her again the next day. A gentleman who was willing to see her again, without a hint of wanting sex! Not then. A surge of excitement rose inside her. So she put off her thoughts of suicide. For the time being.

That night she dreamed of a change in her fortunes, hoping he would keep his promise. He did. He took her to a restaurant in Royal Avenue for lunch, and they talked until long after the meal was finished. When they parted, he gave her a phone number for her to contact him. She hid the fact her mammy couldn't afford a phone. Instead she called him the following day from a call box in the city centre. The boxes near Mafeking Street had all been vandalised long ago.

It had been such a simple, harmless beginning, but it had become very dangerous as it continued. A few days... almost a week... passed before she went to bed with him. And it was so different to all the sex she had known before. He gave her beautiful orgasms and kindness in equal good measure. It was his thoughtful attention and the wonderful sex that persuaded her to hold off indefinitely from ending her life, and that was the worst part of it. As long as she continued living she had to carry on with those other things, the hateful things that blighted her existence; the things she had never revealed to him.

Would a life in England be the answer to it all?

Well, the question wouldn't arise if Brian Fitzpain found them together. They would never get to England. He would kill Martin the moment he discovered he was a Prod. And he was on his way here.

She waited until old Maggie had left the room before she hissed, "Youse had better get out of this place, Martin. Now!"

"Why? What's the matter?" He stood up slowly, puzzlement etched across his face.

He reached out to her, but she pushed him away. "There's someone on his way over here and he doesn't like Prods. Just do as I say, Martin. Get out now before he sees youse."

Martin stepped back. "He's coming to see you: that's what the old lady said. Why? What's going on?"

Sorcha grabbed at his arm and pushed him towards the door. "Don't ask questions. There isn't time to explain. Just go. I'll phone youse later."

She ushered him out into the reception area in time to hear heavy footsteps in the stairwell. Oh, God, the bastard was here already! She hissed at Martin in a low voice. "Go, now. And don't even look at me." She thrust him away from her.

"But…"

"Go, I said."

He was at the far side of the reception area, beside the old lady's desk, when Fitzpain reached the top of the stairs. The Provo's face was filled with a look of thunder. He gave Martin only a cursory glance before he gestured Sorcha to follow him into the sitting room. She glanced back to see Martin leaving. God, what he must be thinking now!

Fitzpain pushed her back against the settee, jabbing at her chest. "I told youse to stay home, youse stupid bitch!"

She forced a defiant tone into her voice. "Didn't see why I should."

"The bombs, youse stupid fool! The bombs. Anyway, maybe it's as well youse did bugger off because they're onto youse, Sorcha. Damn youse! The UVF are searchin' fer youse. Mad Mac McKinnon himself."

"Why?"

"Can't youse guess? Youse lured one o' their people last night and youse delivered him up fer execution."

"But 'twas youse what killed him, Brian. Not me."

"And youse were seen, Sorcha. I wasn't. One of his mates followed youse to yer house. Did youse not realise? If youse has any sense youse'll not go back home. Not now. Get out o' Belfast fer a while. Until things calm down."

"Where? Where should I go?"

"How the hell should I know? And why should I care? Wherever youse goes, it won't be fer long. Youse knows damned well there's something much bigger gonna take their attention pretty damn soon."

"But…" She turned away as Maggie came scurrying into

the reception area from the kitchen.

"Stop arguin', youse two! Youse were seen comin' in here, Brian!" Maggie pushed Fitzpain towards a small window overlooking the street. "Look! 'Tis that eejit out there."

Sorcha eased herself into a position alongside Fitzpain and peered through the glass. A shifty-looking figure in a dirty raincoat lurked beside a telephone box at the far side of the road. He took a long drag on a cigarette and then stared up at the window.

"Shite!" Fitzpain slammed a fist hard on the sill. "'Tis Jimmy Fish. An' the bastard's spyin' on us, so he is."

"Why should he do that?" Sorcha asked.

"How should I know? But he damn well is spyin' on us. Damn him to hell!"

Sorcha stared down at Jimmy Fish. She knew well enough that the Codd family and the Fitzpains were related through a mish-mash of intermarriage within Ardglass village. But what was the runt up to now? There were rumours about Jimmy Fish, rumours about where he got his money, but no proof. As she watched, the devious bastard glanced back along the road to where something had caught his attention. Whatever he saw, it caused him to pull his beret down over his forehead and scamper away in the opposite direction. Seconds later a police Land Rover screeched to a halt outside the building. Two burly RUC policemen, armed with assault rifles, jumped from the back of the vehicle and headed towards the hotel. Body armour covered their dark green uniforms.

"Shite! They're comin' here!" Fitzpain turned and ran towards the stairs. He stopped suddenly. The thump of heavy feet warned that the RUC men were already inside the building.

A deep, loud voice bellowed, "Police! Stay where you are!"

Fitzpain pulled a knife from his coat and pointed it towards the stairwell. "Don't come any further," he shouted. "I'm armed and I'll kill youse."

The same deep voice called back. "Don't be foolish, whoever you are. Let's do this quietly." The policeman climbed slowly into view. His rifle was aimed directly at Fitzpain's heart, never wavering from its aim. He paused at the top step. "Oh? So, it's you, Fitzpain. We wondered if you'd be tied up in this."

Fitzpain kept his knife pointed at the policeman. "What d'youse want?"

"It looks like we're after *you*, man. Been butchering a peeler, have you?"

Sorcha felt her heart thump. The peeler who died last night: that was what this was all about. Would they want her as well? Did they know about the part she played in Fitzpain's foul deeds?

But the peeler seemed uninterested in her. He looked around at the two women, showing surprising calmness for such a confrontation. "Sorry about this, ladies. I mean no trouble to either of you, so please move back."

"I told youse, I'll kill youse." Fitzpain still held his knife at arm's length, but his hands were shaking. His face had turned ashen. Had the policeman noticed that? Was that why he seemed so composed?

"Be sensible, man." The policeman took a step forward as another uniformed RUC officer came up the stairs behind him. Then he spoke with the sort of formality that said he was simply doing another day's work. "Brian Fitzpain, I am arresting you for the murder of Detective Constable John Dunlop…"

"I fuckin' didn't!"

"That's for someone else to judge. Just come quietly."

"Do as he says, Brian," Sorcha said. "They'll kill youse fer sure if you don't put the knife away."

Fitzpain let out a long resigned sigh. He snorted at the policeman, "All right. No need fer youse to read the riot act over me. And youse can put yer gun down." He lowered his weapon arm and turned towards Maggie and Sorcha. "'Tis the work of Jimmy Fish, fer sure. That little runt'll have to pay for this. I swear to God, he'll have to pay. D'youse hear me!"

Sorcha looked towards Maggie and saw her nod almost imperceptibly. The message was clear. Jimmy Fish had crossed a line in the sand, and he had to die. Maggie's face indicated she would willingly act on the threat. What else could she do but try to avenge Brian Fitzpain's arrest? Vengeance was in their blood... all of them.

***

October 1980

I must have interrupted Sorcha too many times in the telling of this incident. I certainly butted in with numerous questions regarding that first meeting with Martin. It was crucial to the book and I wanted as much detail as she could recall. However, my interjections took up time and that was the problem.

"The old lady... Maggie... she was never called to give evidence in court," I said.

"No. After I changed me plea to guilty there was no need. I confessed to both killings and that was the end of it." She turned her head away as she spoke. It was the only time in that interview when she appeared evasive, as if something was left unsaid. That was my opportunity, my opening into what happened at the time of those murders.

I was about to question Sorcha when the burly warder stepped forward and tapped at her watch to indicate my interview was at an end. I cursed her under my breath.

"Just a few minutes more," I begged her.

"Not a chance."

I stood up slowly, curbing that sense of frustration. "I'll write to you when I get home, Sorcha, and we'll fix up another interview."

"Soon?" She seemed eager to continue with the process, as if it gave her some sort of emotional release to be able to talk to me.

"As soon as I can find the time to come back over here.

95

And I'll want to talk to Martin again, as well as you. I need to know more about your relationship with him. How did things pan out between you and him after this incident?"

"Badly." It was the last thing she said before she was led away.

Chapter Eight

November 1980

I spent the next two weeks in my study at home in Wimbledon, working on my manuscript. Some days I spent ten hours at my typewriter, drafting and redrafting until I was satisfied I had created an accurate picture of what I had learned so far. I'm not a fast writer and I try to get as much as possible into a coherent form at that first draft. That took time, and it saw my waste bin often filled with screwed up paper in the course of one day. I am sure my account was accurate, but I worried that it gave such a bad impression of Belfast. Would that impression change as the story progressed? Would I find some saving grace in the two half-cities? Even then, I had little hope, but I was determined to stay true to what I experienced. As a writer I was duty bound to describe the world as I saw it. Anything else was a personal falsehood.

I wrote to Sorcha, inviting her to write back with an account of her next meeting with Martin. On a whim, I also penned a letter to Martin asking him if he would like to write back, telling me his side of their next meeting. I had a suspicion I might get different versions of the event. I wanted more face-to-face interviews, and I would have to knuckle down to them sooner or later, but flying over to Belfast was expensive and I was living on a small advance from my publisher. My bank account was running down fast, so I planned my next visit to Northern Ireland nearer Christmas.

At the beginning of November I drove over to North Wales to meet Will Evans. I checked into a hotel in

Llandudno and invited Will round for a drink in the bar after dinner. I wanted to know how the police investigations were progressing on that fateful morning. He seemed easier in his mind this time, launching into his account as soon as I bought his first whiskey.

***

Friday 21st July 1972
1000 BST

An air of tension had settled over the North Castle Street RUC barracks when Will and McIlroy arrived there. It was due to more than just the killing of Detective Constable Johnny Dunlop. Something big was looming.

McIlroy went off to brief Detective Superintendent Boyle about the informer's warnings while Will made his way to their office to write a brief report. It was a working office: untidy enough to show that things happened here, but not so untidy as to impede the business of crime detection. The two desks were set at right angles to each other, giving the two occupants the chance to discuss cases without being confrontational. Will took the seat at his own desk, with his back to the single window. McIlroy's desk had the advantage of an oblique view of the world outside, but he was the senior man. Will left the office door open and the hubbub of police work added a noisy backdrop to his report-writing.

Already, stories were coming in about a mutilated body discovered by the army in a Nationalist area; a young man with his penis cut off. A cross cut into his chest told them it was a tribal matter. The incident added little to the general air of expectancy because they all knew it was yet another brutal Provisional IRA punishment. Nothing new. One day they might discover why he was mutilated. They might even discover who did it, and who dreamed up the idea of a cross cut into the chest. Or they might not. There had been so many brutal killings in Northern Ireland this year, and many

98

of those that occurred in Nationalist areas were never reported to the police. Even so, the clear-up rate was nothing to write home about.

"What did the 'super' say about Jimmy Fish's bomb warnings?" Will asked when McIlroy returned to their office.

"Not a lot. There's not enough solid evidence. We know that something is in the air, but we still don't know what or when. I got a rocket for not giving Jimmy Fish the hard treatment to find out more."

"That's a bit unfair."

"Boyle is trying to show me who's boss around here."

"What's the point? Jimmy Fish wasn't going to say any more, whatever threats you used."

McIlroy scowled. "Probably not, but our beloved leader had to stand up on his hind legs and make his point."

Sensing his boss's growing antagonism towards the Superintendent, Will changed the subject. "Did you tell him that Johnny Dunlop might have been killed by one of Jimmy Fish's relatives?"

"Yes. Like me, he thinks it was Fitzpain who did it. He's got a fixation on that villain."

"Haven't we all?"

Will was fetching himself and McIlroy a mug of coffee when news came in about the arrest of Brian Fitzpain in Oldpark Road. The IRA man was now on his way to the Castlereagh Holding Centre in east Belfast. It was the most secure police building within the province.

"Fitzpain in custody? Is that coincidence?" McIlroy said, nodding to the ceiling. "Or is someone up there listening to our prayers?"

"Just plain old good luck, boss. And the Super will be pleased about it. He may want to do the interview himself."

"If the Oldpark guys agree to it."

"Superintendent Boyle will get his way. He always does."

"I hope not. I want in on this one. And I may even have a lever." McIlroy avoided Will's gaze, as if he was hiding something. He took a single sip at his coffee. "In fact, I think it's time for me to talk to our beloved leader again, Will. You'd better come with me to back me up."

"Do you need back-up, boss?"

"I might need you to hold me in check. You could greet him with a charming Welsh smile and see if it has any effect. It might soften him up a bit."

"*Iechyd da* and hope he opens his whiskey bottle? You've got to be joking."

"It's no joking matter."

The rest of the coffee was put aside to go cold while Will trailed behind McIlroy to the office of Superintendent Boyle. They were met with a sour expression as they entered the office. Compared with their own, this one had an antiseptic air about it. Apart from the few papers on Boyle's desk, there was nothing casual on show: no family photographs to remind the Detective Superintendent of his life away from North Castle Street, and no small ornaments to create even an impression of a homely atmosphere. It was, Will thought, almost sterile.

"What now, McIlroy?" Boyle had been writing, a fountain pen firmly grasped in his podgy hand. He carefully replaced the cap and set down the pen on his blotting pad.

Will held back while McIlroy came straight to the point. "We heard that Fitzpain has been arrested."

There was no 'sir' in his opening gambit. That puzzled Will. He knew his boss to be a stickler for protocol in most situations, but something was seriously wrong here.

"That's none of your business, McIlroy. What do you want?"

Boyle looked in no mood for polite conversation. Malice filled his voice. Whatever it was between these two, it was not one-sided. They stared at each other for a few seconds like gladiators in a Roman arena, each weighing up the other.

Something is very wrong here.

McIlroy broke the brief silence. "I told you earlier. We think he's the one who killed Johnny Dunlop."

"Of course you do. We all do. It's got the bastard's fingerprints all over it. So, have we got any new evidence against him?"

"No. Nothing new." McIlroy became insistent. "It's just as I said before. We had a hint from Jimmy Fish. A sort of relative, he said."

"A hint is all you have, McIlroy. Codd gave us no name. Nothing solid." Boyle sounded sceptical, and more than that. He sounded vexed. "Based on what we have at the moment, no one can charge him with anything. Taking him in was a waste of time and resources."

"Fitzpain is related to Jimmy Fish. It has to be him." McIlroy's hands were gripped tight. Will saw them clutched together behind the DCI's back. Something was bugging him and it wasn't just the matter of Fitzpain. "How did he come to be picked up? Do we know?"

Boyle ran his tongue across his upper lip while he considered his reply. "There was a tip off. Someone phoned in and said we would find Dunlop's killer in a hotel in the Oldpark Road. No name was given, but the man the uniforms found was Fitzpain. It didn't take them more than a couple of seconds to make two and two equal four."

"The call came to us and not Oldpark?" McIlroy said. "Why us? Doesn't that make you suspicious?"

"No. It would have been one of our own informants, obviously; someone who knows how badly we want to pin a murder on Fitzpain."

"Someone like Jimmy Fish." McIlroy leaned forward over Boyle's desk and stabbed a forefinger on the blotting pad. The threatening behaviour was getting out of hand.

Will wanted to intervene, lower the temperature, but he knew well enough he must not. Whatever it was, it wasn't his fight.

McIlroy continued in a gravelly voice. "Will you do something for us? Me and Will Evans."

"Depends. What exactly do you want?" Boyle gave him an inquisitive look. His underlying anger was poorly hidden.

"Let me be first to interview him."

"Why? This is not your investigation."

"Call it professional pride, if you like. We all know he's in the frame for God-knows-how-many past killings. I might be able to get something on one of our outstanding cases. Can you clear it with the Oldpark CID?"

"Give me one good reason why I should let you do the interview. Just one good reason, McIlroy."

The DCI lowered his voice to a harsh hiss. He stared into Boyle's face, defying him. "You know damn well why. Still in your bed, is she? Waiting for you to get back in there with her, is she?"

Boyle jerked back in the swivel chair behind his desk. He didn't reply immediately, using the time to light a cigarette. His face looked thunderous while he composed his response.

Will waited, tensed by this sudden revelation. The enormity of the situation shocked him.

Eventually, Boyle spoke. His manner showed capitulation. "Normally, I'd kick your arse for that, McIlroy, but this time I'm going to let you have your way. I'm going to call in a personal favour with Oldpark CID and ask them to let you and Evans do the interview. And don't imagine I'm doing this as a sop to you. I don't do favours to anyone in this place."

"We had noticed." The harshness was still there in McIlroy's voice, but he stepped back, accepting that he had already won this fight.

Boyle quickly recovered his composure. "Any more cheek from you and you'll be out there pounding the beat with the troops. I'm doing this because I think you may be onto something useful." It was a climb-down pure and simple.

"Of course we are."

"As it happens we're all up to our eyes in these stories of a major bomb attack and Oldpark will be too." It was a lame excuse, Will realised. Boyle was still fighting his way out of an embarrassing situation, and losing his grip. "Even the

Chief Constable is worried by what may be about to happen. I'm expecting a call from his office any time now."

McIlroy nodded towards a thick buff folder lying on the desk. "The background on Fitzpain?"

"Probably not as up to date as it ought to be. I blame you footsloggers for that." Boyle pushed it towards the DCI. "Take it with you."

At a nod from his boss, Will stepped forward and picked up the file. It was an untidy dossier compiled over many years. The front label was well-worn.

Boyle ran a hand across his balding scalp. "He's a hard nut, McIlroy. You really think you can get anything useful out of him?"

"We'll have a damn good try."

"All right. I'll speak to Oldpark and then I'll give them a call at Castlereagh and tell them to hold Fitzpain until you get there." He stood up and ushered the two detectives to the door. He kept his gaze clear of both of them. "Keep the rough treatment within limits, eh? We don't want any more hospital admissions."

"We'll try. But sometimes we have to protect ourselves."

"You know what I'm saying, McIlroy. Keep within the limits."

"We'll do our best."

"Fair enough."

"We'll get on with it, then."

McIlroy wore a hard expression as he led Will back to their office. He made no attempt to elaborate on the acrimony between himself and Boyle. Instead, he sat behind his desk and took the buff-coloured file from Will. He opened it at the first page, glanced down at the precis of information and took a minute to digest it. He made no attempt to read beyond that one page. Then he passed the file back to Will. The information was brief but telling.

CHARACTER OUTLINE

Name:
Brian Patrick Fitzpain

Born:
Ardglass, Co Down. 7th October 1928.

Parents:
Margaret O'Driscoll and Seamus Fitzpain. His parents married in March 1927. The child was taken into care July 1940 to November 1944 because of his father's physical abuse. The father died December 1950.

Schools:
St Ignatious Primary School
Holy Trinity Secondary School
Expelled aged fifteen when charged with violence and alcohol offences.

Employment:
Fishing from Ardglass 1945 to 1951.
No further recorded employment. Believed to have been engaged in cross-border smuggling.

Marital status:
He married Eilish O'Leary in August 1950.
Separated since 1951.
He has subsequently lived on-and-off with a prostitute with whom he has five children.

Criminal record:
He was accused of raping a married woman, in January 1951.
The charge was dismissed when the victim refused to testify.
He was gaoled from February 1951 to February 1953 for a series of violent drunken sexual assaults on young women.

He was gaoled again from 1958 to 1963 for firearms offences.

He joined the IRA in May 1963.

He moved over to the Provisional IRA in December 1969. He is known to lead a small punishment cell known as the Pain Men. The cell consists of Fitzpain, Finn McKenna and Padraig Maginnis.

While Will scrutinized the information, McIlroy pulled thoughtfully at his chin. "This is a guy who's in the frame for at least fifteen brutal murders, and yet we can't pin a single one on him. Alibis pour out of his mouth like spit, and intimidated witnesses obediently line the streets to his house."

Will shrugged. "He can't go on forever."

"Wanna bet? You can study the rest of that report later. It's time we were on our way."

"Okay. Tally ho, boss."

McIlroy shot him a fierce frown. "This isn't going to be one of your English fox hunts."

"Welsh fox hunts."

"Whatever."

"One question: what was the favour Boyle owed you? It was pretty clear he owed you something on account. And he was doing his best to hide something." Will phrased the question as if he hadn't understood the hidden agenda. In truth, he would have been stupid not to pick up the underlying message. He was curious enough to want to know more, but he didn't want to embarrass his boss. Well, not too much.

"Don't ask." McIlroy looked away.

"Personal?"

"Very personal, so shut up."

Will blinked. This was so unlike his boss.

He said, "Fair enough," and tried to avoid McIlroy's stern expression.

At first, they drove in silence to the Castlereagh Holding Centre in east Belfast. The streets looked normal for a

Friday morning. Normal for Belfast. Heavily armed troops manned the barriers protecting the shopping areas. More troops patrolled amongst the shoppers, and the odd military vehicle rumbled past, but there were no big signs saying an unprecedented atrocity was about to happen here. Reality was brought to bear by the number of military helicopters on criss-crossing routes over the city, as well as the occasional distant gunshots.

"You think we've drawn lucky this morning?" Will asked as they raced closer to the holding centre.

"I'd lay money on Fitzpain being the killer, Will. Apart from that, I feel like a bit of exercise."

"Is that what this is all about? Is that the real reason why you wanted this interview?"

"It might just the sort of distraction I need to get me into a better mood."

"Do you need that, boss? Do you need something to improve your mood?"

McIlroy choked loudly and then spoke in a tremulous voice. "She left me, Will. After all these years, she left me two days ago. She packed a few cases and she walked out, and she took our daughter with her." He stared straight ahead as if unable to face his junior.

"You mean…? Your wife and…"

"Boyle."

"I'm sorry to hear that." The tension that had been tainting the air at North Castle Street suddenly became markedly clearer. Will had never met his boss's wife but he knew she was ten years younger than Tom. Was that the problem? A younger woman who wasn't averse to spreading her favours around? A superintendent who was easily taken in?

Curiosity made him ask, "What's she like, boss. Your missus?"

A loud snort preceded McIlroy's reply. "What's she like? I'll tell you what she's like, Will. She has this T-shirt with big red writing across her breast. It says *Down below is even better*. She flaunts it in front of other men because she

106

knows it gets up my nose. An obscene T-shirt! I ask you. That's what she's like. Mind you, she always was that way inclined, even before we were married."

"So why did you marry her?"

"Because there was a time when down below really was even better." He let out a long sigh. "Let's leave it at that for the moment. I may decide to relieve my feelings on that bastard of an IRA murderer."

"Better you take it out on him rather than the Super. Boyle could have you disciplined."

"And risk the whole thing going public? Have the Chief Constable learn that Boyle is shagging my wife? I don't think he'd want that. But you're right. Better I take it out on Fitzpain."

Will felt a sudden burst of resentment. This wasn't the way to handle things. "That's what this is all about, isn't it? You know you'll get nothing out of Fitzpain, nothing at all, but you need to take out your anger on someone."

"Of course I'll get nothing out of him, and I'll have to let him go, but at least let me enjoy the experience of putting the wind up the bastard."

"Is that fair?"

"Shut up, Will. Fitzpain can take what's coming to him. He's no innocent."

Will knew exactly what he meant. McIlroy was well-built, six foot four, a judo black belt and a keen heavyweight boxer. He would know how to hold his own if an interview got rough. Interviews often got rough at Castlereagh. Both Republican and Loyalist suspects sometimes had to be taken to the Mater Hospital.

"Looks like Jimmy Fish might have come good on both counts this morning," Will said, suddenly anxious to change the subject and moderate the anger.

He called to mind their office where McIlroy had a series of black and white photographs pinned to the wall. The top one showed Seamus Twomey, the bookie's runner who was the Provisional IRA's Belfast Brigade Commander. It was a good quality photo taken at a Sinn Fein conference by an undercover agent. He was shown wearing a grim expression that could have been interpreted as determination. Looking at the picture, Will could see why they called him Thumper because of his short temper and his habit of thumping his fist on the table in any argument. Farther down the wall came the middlemen, the links between the Provisional IRA's hierarchy and the ground troops; hard men like Brian Fitzpain. McIlroy had long complained about how much he wanted to pin something conclusive on Fitzpain.

"Is there anything personal in this?" Will asked as they drew close to the holding centre. "Not your argument with the Super. I mean your interest in Fitzpain."

"You could say that." McIlroy took a red light at speed, narrowly avoiding a bus. "One of my cousins was killed by an IRA bomb two years ago. Rumours say Fitzpain was involved."

"Proof?" Will asked.

"Of course not. When do we ever get proof? You know as well as I do that rumour is all we ever have to go on until someone blows the whistle. Well, this time the whistle may have been blown by Jimmy Fish."

"A hint of a whistle. I hope Jimmy's right."

"I'm counting on it." McIlroy finally slowed the car as they came in sight of the holding centre. He pulled up outside the sangar where their identity cards were checked before the gate was opened. The RUC fortress was a large brick building enclosed in a wire mesh shield.

"This is where we either get lucky or we go home in tears," McIlroy said as he switched off the engine.

Anticipation filled Will's head as they passed through further security and hurried into the building. Would Jimmy Fish's tip-off prove reliable?

"Your visitor's down in the cells," they were told by the custody sergeant when they reported at the front desk.

"Behaving like…?" McIlroy asked. It was always useful to get an idea of the suspect's state of mind and behaviour before confronting him.

"Like he's the king of the shitehouse," the sergeant said.

"He probably knows you'll get nothing out of him."

McIlroy grinned. "Oh, dear. What a pity to disappoint him."

Will had been inside the holding centre only twice before, but he had never been actively engaged in an interrogation there. This could be his crunch moment. How would he react when faced with the man believed to have killed Johnny Dunlop? Would he be able to cope if things got rough? He knew well enough that the gloves came off often in here.

McIlroy took him to one side before they went any further. "This is not going to be an easy interview, Will. It's almost certain I'll need to use a bit of slap and tickle on this one, and none too gently. You're a good man and you're a Catholic, so I'm giving you the chance to stand aside now if you choose."

"Because I'm a Catholic?"

"So is Fitzpain. In theory."

"How rough will it get?" Will asked. Indecision filled his mind.

"I'll use whatever's needed to try to get the truth out of the bastard."

"He's unlikely to crack."

"You're right. He's a ruthless killer, we both know that, and it looks almost certain he killed John Dunlop. And whatever I do he'll deny everything and walk free. That's a foregone conclusion. And then he'll kill again. I don't want that to happen, but it's the likely outcome. So I'll give him a bit of slap and tickle to ease my mind." He paused. "It's up to you, Will. Do you want to continue… or wait in the canteen?"

"I'll stick with you."

McIlroy nodded. "Remember that I gave you a choice."

Will gritted his teeth. His reservations were strong, but he wanted to see Fitzpain put away, for John Dunlop's sake as well as for the other policemen he was certain Fitzpain had killed. He readied himself mentally.

He had seen Provisional IRA killers brought in for

questioning at North Castle Street; men and women. Some, the weaker ones, would literally shit their pants even before the interrogations began. They were easily disposed of. Others, the hardened criminals, tried to brazen it out with blatantly offensive behaviour. One man pulled out his dick and pissed across the interview table. Another, a twenty stone woman with the menacing stance of a Nazi concentration camp guard, spat in Will's face before pulling up her skirt and masturbating herself. It was her way of saying, "You can't fuck around with me!"

It was funny, Will thought, that the IRA brain didn't seem to function quite like a human brain. It took him and McIlroy several days to wear down that woman with intense interrogation. Eventually, she admitted to planting a bomb in a Loyalist pub, killing six innocent people. But this interrogation was going to outclass anything he had yet witnessed, and he knew that some physical force would be needed if Fitzpain was to be persuaded to talk.

They signed in, surrendered their weapons and were given name badges. Then they were taken by the custody sergeant down a long green corridor where an overhead fluorescent light flickered like a Morse signal light. Finally down the stairs to the basement where Fitzpain was held. A foul smell greeted them, emanating from the line of occupied cells. It indicated an unholy mixture of fear and defiance. The fearful prisoners would talk, and the defiant ones would not.

Fitzpain glared at them as they approached. He jabbed a finger at Will and hissed through the bars. "So, 'tis youse, Detective Evans! Ye're a Welsh turncoat, a traitor, so youse are. I know where youse lives, an' all. Know where youse goes to church, so I do. Youse'll pay for this!"

"That's a threat you might regret," Will replied easily. But, behind the façade, he feared for his family. Yet again, he recalled Milly's threat to leave and never come back to Belfast. Maybe she was right. The idea grew more powerful in his mind.

"Two nice little girls, youse got, Detective Evans. And

yer missus has a nice pair o' tits on 'er, so she has." Fitzpain continued to show no fear. "Youse better tell yer wife and kids to watch their backs. They'll be dead meat one day soon."

Fitzpain's eyes blazed with hatred.

"Enough of that!" The custody sergeant unlocked the cell door and gestured the prisoner out. "You'd better shut your foul mouth, Fitzpain. Threats like that will get you nowhere in here."

But the threats continued as they escorted him upstairs to a windowless interview room.

"He's all yours and good luck, sir," the custody sergeant said. He walked away and a uniformed constable arrived to stand guard by the door while Fitzpain slumped down onto a hard chair in front of the solitary table.

His manner was pure defiance. "I want to see a solicitor."

"Request refused." McIlroy set down his heavy bulk directly opposite him. Will took a seat alongside the senior officer, ready to take notes.

Fitzpain remained adamant. "You can't refuse me."

McIlroy stared at him with an impassive expression. "I can and you know it. Prevention of Terrorism Act. You're not in some prissy English country village police station now. This isn't something out of a Miss Marple book. This is real life and you're in Belfast in the middle of a civil war. The rules are different here. You'll get exactly what we give you."

"Which is?"

"My fist in your face if you give me one more ounce of trouble."

"Damn youse to hell!" Fitzpain leaned across the table and stabbed a finger at McIlroy. "I know where youse lives Detective McIlroy. Youse'd better watch yer back in future. Especially yer missus."

"Meaning?" McIlroy hissed through teeth tightly gritted.

"Fancy going to yer missus's funeral, do youse? I can arrange it."

McIlroy sighed long and deep. He turned to the

constable. "Would you please go along to the canteen to get me a cup of tea?"

The constable nodded and left. He would know the score well enough. No witnesses for what happened next.

When the door slammed shut behind the constable, McIlroy stretched his left arm across the table and grabbed at Fitzpain's hand. Without a word he suddenly dragged the IRA man towards him. The detective's eyes blazed for a moment and then his right arm swung between the two men with such speed that Will was taken by surprise.

Fitzpain shrieked loudly when McIlroy's fist smashed into him. He jerked himself free and slid backwards, clasping both hands to his face.

"Bastard!" Blood trickled from his nose and his lips.

Will shrank back in alarm. His vision suddenly blurred, and he wobbled in his seat. The sounds within the room became muted, as if he was hearing through a blanket. He grabbed at the table to steady himself. Damn! The knock-on-the-head trouble again.

"You all right?" McIlroy's voice broke through the muffling.

"Yeah. Of course." He tried to sound sure of himself. He wiped at his eyes. The scene swam back into focus. The sounds sharpened.

"Right." McIlroy drew himself upright in his seat and scowled at Fitzpain. "Now let's get down to business. Where were you between nine o'clock and midnight last night?"

"Piss off." Fitzpain ran one hand across his blooded lips, testing the damage.

"Oh dear. The message hasn't sunk in, has it?" McIlroy turned towards Will. "Shall I knock his teeth out, or will you?"

Will shivered, wondering if he should have taken the offer to back out from this interrogation. He told himself he could not show any compassion towards the IRA man. Any sign of weakness would only give Fitzpain the upper hand. He understood that well enough, but the desire to be somewhere else now held a firm place inside his head.

"You're doing well enough without any help from me," he said and hoped he sounded assured in his assessment.

"I think I can do even better," his boss said. He leaned forward grabbed again at Fitzpain's wrist and pulled sharply until the terrorist was sprawled across the table. Then he delivered a karate 'leopard blow' to the soft area of the man's inner arm.

Fitzpain squealed in pain. "Bastard!"

McIlroy kept hold of his wrist, squeezing it tightly. "Want me to do that again, do you? Tell me how you killed Constable Dunlop last night."

"'Twasn't me, damn youse! I didn't kill the bastard."

"We've an informant who says you did."

"He's lying!"

"So, who did it?" McIlroy squeezed tighter. "Tell me before I break your bones."

"Piss off!"

McIlroy gritted his teeth. "Detective Constable Dunlop was stabbed in the chest and you're quite adept with a knife, aren't you? You know how to kill with a blade, don't you?"

"But I didn't kill 'im. I didn't kill the peeler."

"So, who did it? You'd better stop lying because I'm giving you just one last chance, Fitzpain. Then there's gonna be one helluva loud snap as I break your arm."

"I don't know who knifed him! I told youse I wasn't there when he was killed. And that's the truth!"

Will studied the Provo man's face. "If you're lying..."

"I'm not lying. A knife youse says? I'd gladly shake the hand of whoever did that."

"Whose hand would you shake? Give me a name."

"Father Christmas."

"Try again, Fitzpain."

"Mrs Christmas. I'd shake her hand 'cos she knows I done nothing'."

"You *did* nothing."

"See, even you agree."

"All right. That's enough for now."

113

The door opened and the constable entered with a cup of tea which he placed in on the table. McIlroy picked up the cup, sipped at it and then gestured to the officer. "Tell the custody sergeant to take this man back to the cell. Let him stew for a while."

It all seemed so inconclusive, no admission of guilt and no clues about who might have been involved in the murder. Will felt cheated, but he said nothing until they left the building.

"What now, Boss?" They stood beside McIlroy's car.

McIlroy pulled out a packet of cigarettes and lit up. "We let him stew for a while, like I said. So, what did you learn from that?" He offered the pack to Will.

Will thought deeply as he lit a cigarette. He let out a long stream of smoke before he replied. "Nothing positive. He wasn't going to confess."

McIlroy looked pensive. "Of course he wasn't going to confess... never was going to... and we'd have to find more evidence before we could charge him." He gave a sudden cold laugh. "But I enjoyed putting a bit of fear into him."

"Jimmy Fish suggested he did it," Will said as they finally got into the car.

His cigarette had a good few puffs left in it, but McIlroy threw it away through the open car window and started the engine. "Maybe Jimmy's mistaken, or maybe he's been lying to us. But Fitzpain is giving nothing away and we'll not pin this one on him without more evidence. And we're not going to find that evidence while we're sitting in the room talking to him, are we? We'll let him cool down a bit and think about his evil life. Then I'll have to let him go."

"With the agreement of the Oldpark guys."

"They'll agree. They know the score."

The car was now racing back through the city.

"There's no other way of dealing with Fitzpain?" It was the first time Will had seen McIlroy give up so quickly in a line of investigation. What was wrong with him? Was the trouble with his wife affecting his judgement?

McIlroy shrugged. "I told you before we started that

114

letting him go was on the cards. Dammit! We don't have the evidence, Will!"

"He must have done it!" Will sensed a moment of pure exasperation. Intuition told him Fitzpain was the killer and his intuition rarely let him down.

"Don't argue with me." The stern look on McIlroy's face said more than his words.

"But we can charge him with something, surely. How about being a member of the IRA?"

"On what evidence? If it went to court, Sinn Fein would provide him with a tame lawyer who'd prove beyond doubt that Brian Fitzpain is more saintly than the Pope himself. Keeping him locked up is a waste of time, effort and money."

"It keeps him off the streets."

"And it also inspires his thugs to carry out more killings in protest. It's counter-productive."

Will searched desperately for an answer, even though he instinctively knew his boss was right. Actual guilt didn't come into it, conclusive proof did.

"Maybe he was using his natural cunning," he argued.

"He'd have to be a good actor."

"Maybe he is. Maybe that's his strong point."

"No, Will. To charge him right now would be a waste of police resources, and we ain't got much of that left."

"If he's not guilty, why would Jimmy Fish lie to us?" Will said. He still wasn't convinced.

McIlroy shrugged as he opened up the throttle and swerved in front of a black taxi. "Maybe Jimmy hates Fitzpain for some reason we know nothing about. Maybe he wants him taken down in revenge for something personal. I reckon we need to speak to Jimmy Fish again."

"A hard bit of talking?"

"Something like that."

***

November 1980

"Did they really use that sort of rough stuff at Castlereagh?" I asked. I knew the answer but it was worth asking to get Will's take on it.

"Of course. It was the only thing that worked. But some people won't like to hear that. And they won't like me for telling you."

"You're out of Belfast now, Will, but I take your point. I'll need DCI McIlroy's say-so before it goes in the final draft."

"And my say-so as well. Whistleblowers are bad news anywhere."

"Do you care?"

He sniffed and grinned. "S'pose not. Not nowadays. Aw shit! Put it in the book anyway. Are you going to buy me another drink, or am I going to go home cold sober?"

I bought him another Irish whiskey. He was making no effort to end the interview and I figured I still had a lot to learn. "What happened when you got back to North Castle Street?" I asked.

"We had a bit of thinking to do, me and McIlroy."

"What about Sorcha Mulveny? Did she enter into your thinking?"

"No. She wasn't yet on our radar."

***

Friday 21st July 1972
1030 BST

It had been a disappointing end to the interview at Castlereagh, Will thought, as he and McIlroy drove through the city traffic. They lapsed into in silence. Nothing more was discussed until they got back to North Castle Street.

"Coffee upstairs, Will," McIlroy said firmly as they walked into the building.

"I could make us a coffee in the office, boss."

"No. Too easy for us to be summoned to the presence of our beloved leader. We'll pop upstairs."

They sat at a small table in the canteen with their hot drinks in front of them. A hum of voices filled the room as they each quietly thought about the interview. Will had grown used to those periods of silence when they ran through what they might, or might not have learned. He saw it as a way of locking their brains into isolation cells for a while. Usually it was productive, but not today. For the moment, no one took any notice of them. It was a day when the other peelers had their own problems.

Eventually, McIlroy drained the dregs his coffee in one gulp. "Any new thoughts, Will?"

"Nothing we haven't already been over."

"Right. In that case it's time for me to see our beloved leader again and let him know the score so far. But first there's something I have to do. And you know what that is? I'm going to clear it with Oldpark and then I'm going to tell the boys at Castlereagh they can release Fitzpain."

Will sniffed loudly. He had been expecting it, but he felt a need to add one last word of dissent. "Do you really need to? He threatened us, both of us, and our families. We could keep him a bit longer on the grounds of those threats."

"They were empty words. They meant very little. He knows well enough that any physical attack on our families will lead us directly to him. And then I'd really get rough with him and so would a few other coppers. He probably wouldn't come out of it in one piece. He knows that."

"He had a knife when he was arrested."

"So? If we locked up every dickhead in Belfast with a knife we'd run out of cells within the hour." McIlroy jerked his heavy bulk upright and drew a deep breath. "Go and get yourself another coffee, Will."

While his boss was gone, Will bought a doughnut as well as a second coffee and nibbled at it alone at the small table beside a window covered with wire mesh. Outside, the rest of Belfast life drifted by in a haze of unreality. It was a city that did not rightly belong inside the United Kingdom. It belonged in some distant world of crazy people who had yet to learn the meaning of growing up.

Will's thoughts drifted away to Milly and the children. In the light of Fitzpain's threats, would they be safe? Did he not have a duty now to see his family protected from Republican violence? And… the thought loomed large in his mind… was Milly unquestionably right? The best defence against any personal attack was the width of the Irish Sea between Northern Ireland and Wales.

"I thought you were on annual leave." A young female constable sat down opposite him. Artificially blonde, with a slim waist and breasts like melons, Maisie O'Hare had a grin like a wolf about to devour a lamb. She rattled her teacup on the table between them.

"Pulled in for duty at the last minute," Will said.

"Instead of…?"

"Instead of taking the wife and family to Wales for a week."

"What does your wife say about that?" Her voice had that musical lilt that said she was born south of the border. A Protestant born in a Catholic country. Was religion the reason she had migrated north? She leaned towards him so that her breasts hung over the table, tantalisingly close.

"She isn't amused," Will said.

The girl's grin widened. "Let her go on her own. I could easily warm the cockles of your heart while she's away."

"It's not my heart you're after, is it, Maisie?"

"Not unless you keep your heart in your underpants." She wrapped her hands around her teacup and stared at him across the rim.

"I'd be dead if Milly found out."

"If you died in my bed, you'd go with a smile on your face."

"Thanks for the offer, but…"

"But the answer is no?"

"Sorry."

"No, you're not sorry at all. At least your boss didn't refuse me."

118

"DCI McIlroy?" Will blinked in surprise.

"DCI McIlroy. Who else do you work for? And why do you think his wife has walked out on him?"

"I don't believe it."

"You're too naïve, Will Evans." She stood up, gathered up her cup and saucer and shook her head. "And you're too honest for your own good. In this life it doesn't do to be honest." She walked away, wiggling her bottom as she went.

Maybe she was right, he thought, but he would never do it, whatever the rights or wrongs. Milly might walk away from him, but he would never be the first to break the marital bond. It just wasn't in him. Nothing to do with Catholic dogma. He loved her too much.

He was still brooding over his problems when McIlroy came hurrying back. "Get your coat on Will. It's time to go. Jimmy Fish wants to see us again."

"Why?"

"Not sure. He phoned the front desk. Wouldn't give a name, but who else would ask for us in person? It's Jimmy. He said he had something important for us. Something about us barking up the wrong tree, but it was still worth a few extra pounds."

"Barking up the wrong tree? That doesn't make sense."

"So we must talk to him. He said he'll be at the usual café until we get there."

"Having a meal at our expense."

"He'll get no more money from me until he gives us the truth. And I mean the *real* truth." McIlroy looked puzzled. "I wonder what he meant about us barking up the wrong tree."

Will downed the last of his coffee. "Something to do with Fitzpain?"

"Most likely. The sooner we confront him the better. If he does have something important for us, something about Fitzpain, it may turn out that I've made a mistake."

"Mistake?"

"I told Castlereagh to release Fitzpain before I went in to

see Boyle. If Jimmy Fish has fresh information, I may have been a bit premature. Fitzpain will be out there on the streets right now, and he'll be hopping mad because of that interview. He'll be wondering who put the finger on him being at that hotel. He may even know who it was. You know what, Will? I think we need to get to Jimmy Fish before he does."

***

Friday 21st July 1972
1050 BST

The Royal Victoria Hospital fronted onto the both the Falls Road and the Grosvenor Road. The small Corner Cafe habitually used by Jimmy Fish was on the Falls Road, fifty yards down from the RVH. McIlroy parked in the hospital grounds knowing it would be safer there than on the main road. He signed in at the hospital reception desk and then the two men crossed over to the far side of the road. An armed soldier watched them approach.

"Something's up," Will said. He scanned around, looking for signs of trouble. The Falls area was a notorious hotbed of Republican activity. No policeman or soldier ever came here alone.

An army Land Rover stood at the roadside outside the café, its lights flashing. A grey Land Rover, a police vehicle, was parked beyond it. Another young soldier blocked their way as they came closer. McIlroy flashed his warrant card and Will followed suit.

"What's happened here, Soldier?" McIlroy asked.

"A murder, sir. One of the customers has been killed." He looked unsure of himself, as well he might, Will thought. What would any young Englishman make of the complexities of the Irish Troubles? No wonder they made so many mistakes.

"We need to see this." The DCI shook his head as he moved on. "You thinking what I'm thinking, Will?"

"Jimmy Fish?"

"Could be. Maybe he's ratted on the IRA just once too often." He turned back to the soldier. "A male customer, was it?"

"Yes, sir. On the floor in there." He pointed to the café.

"How was he killed?"

"Knife through the heart, sir."

McIlroy gave Will a knowing look. "Just like Johnny Dunlop. Could be significant."

Inside the café a lot was happening. A uniformed sergeant and a female constable were talking to an elderly and distraught woman seated in a plastic chair beside a plastic-covered table. A cup of hot tea steamed in front of her. A man in civilian clothes was examining the body on the floor; forensics looking for fingerprints. Another uniform was taking photographs. The body of Jimmy Fish was sprawled in a pool of blood.

Will felt no sense of surprise.

The uniformed sergeant spoke to McIlroy. He indicated the elderly woman. "This is the owner. She's in a bit of a state. Never had any trouble like this before now, so she says."

"Maybe not a murder like this, but trouble around here is common enough." McIlroy cut in with a curt reply.

"Nothing at all, she says."

"Take that with a pinch of salt, Sergeant. In this part of Belfast no one gets away with a peaceful life. You should know that."

"Just going by what she's told me. She looks genuine to me, sir." The uniform kept his attention focussed on the Detective Chief Inspector.

"Looks can be deceptive. Let me speak to her. What's her name?"

"Mrs Moira Mullins. A widow lady."

McIlroy waved aside the female officer and knelt beside the café owner. "Mrs Mullins, I am Detective Chief Inspector McIlroy. I'd be grateful if you could go over again exactly what happened here."

The woman put a handkerchief to her nose and blew hard. "I told them already."

"Tell me."

"I was in the kitchen when I heard someone come in. Then I heard a crash. When I came out here I saw the body. Him…" she pointed at the figure on the floor.

"A crash? That was all you heard?"

"A crash and then… then a voice and… and a cry of pain."

"A man's voice?"

She nodded. "It was *him* what spoke. The one what died. He said some name, then he said, 'Not you too. Not you too.' That's what he said." She wiped again at her nose. "It didn't sound right, though."

"What didn't sound right?"

"I don't know. But it didn't sound right."

"What name did he say?"

"I'm not sure. Couldn't really make it out properly. Fitz… something maybe."

McIlroy looked up at Will. "Not you too? Why would he say that? Who do you think he saw?"

Will replied with a positive note. "Fitzpain, boss. He must have come straight here after he was released. He'd have had time. It's gotta be him. Jimmy Fish must have known his killer and who else could it be but Fitzpain?"

"Did you say Fitzpain?" Mrs Mullins interrupted. "Now I come to think of it, there was some mention of that name: Fitzpain. At least, I think so. I may be wrong, of course."

McIlroy nodded and spoke again to the café owner. "Mrs Mullins, did you see anyone else? Anyone at all."

"No. No one. Whoever did it was gone when I came in here."

"I see. Did you speak to the victim before the killing? Did he say anything to you?"

She sniffed and wiped at her nose. "Nothing important. Just sat there with his cup of tea saying he'd done some sort of bad thing and he needed some money. He said someone would give him some money when they got here. But that was all."

"He did a bad thing? What did he do?" Will asked.

"He didn't say."

"That was all? He'd done something bad and someone would give him some money?"

"When they got here."

McIlroy grabbed Will's arm and drew him away from the woman. "He got money from me this morning. What else could he tell us and expect yet more money?"

Will shrugged. "Barking up the wrong tree. That's what you said earlier, boss. Jimmy reckons we're barking up the wrong tree. That must be what he wanted to explain to us. He was waiting for you to arrive and give him some more money in return for him explaining why we've got things wrong."

"What was he going to tell us? That's the big question, isn't it?"

"Or maybe he's already given the police some valuable information and he wanted paid for it. But he wouldn't have expected to be paid like this." Will looked around the room and tried to imagine what happened here. "But let's not forget the one name Mrs Mullins heard, boss. Fitzpain."

"A name she thought she heard, Will. *Thought* she heard."

"And what about that, boss?" Will pointed to a clear plastic bag lying on the table beside the body. It contained money. "What do you make of that?"

"Thirty sixpences," McIlroy said. "The murderer will have left it. Thirty pieces of silver. The payment for betrayal."

***

November 1980

Will glanced at his watch and stood up suddenly. "Shit. It's after eleven. Milly will be getting herself in a mood by now. Better be going."

"She worries about you?"

"More than you'd imagine. She's got reason, I suppose."

"I'm sorry to hear that." I finished my drink and stood up beside him. "I appreciate what you've told me, Will. It puts a lot of things in perspective."

He tapped me on the arm. "Remember what I said. Be careful about what you write in your book. I still have a career in the police."

"You'll just have to trust me."

"Maybe. But I'd like to see your manuscript before you go into print."

"Fair enough. When can we meet again?"

He thought for a moment. "Leave it a while. Milly doesn't like me doing this. She says it leaves me drained for days afterwards. I tell her it's the memory of that Belfast experience that gets to me, not you, but she isn't convinced. I'll give you a call when I'm ready to talk again."

Chapter Nine

November 1980

It was late in the month when two important letters arrived on the same day. The coincidence made me wonder if someone in the 'other life' was manipulating my investigation. One letter was from Sorcha and the other was from Martin Foster.

Sorcha wrote in a semi-literate scrawl which left me feeling frustrated. There was something important in it, but the inner truth was elusive. I couldn't be certain of the meaning behind the scrappily-written words. I replied to her the same day, asking for more detail as well as an explanation for some of her unintelligible comments.

In contrast, Martin's letter was immediately fluent and revealing. It was relatively short, but it explained how he and Sorcha came to disagreement. I put aside Sorcha's letter and began to make my own notes based upon Martin's account of what happened that fateful morning. I was keen to draw the story back to Sorcha, and Martin's skill with words helped enormously. It didn't take me long to turn the written words into a vivid mental image of what happened next. I could picture the two of them inside my head.

***

Friday 21st July 1972
1045 BST

The phone rang ten minutes after Martin got home. It was Sorcha. She sounded breathless, as if she had been running. He was glad Emily and Aunt Judy were out in the garden, unable to overhear the conversation.

"Martin, I'm sorry I had to make youse leave like that. I'll explain if youse'll let me. Will youse meet me somewhere?"

He didn't immediately answer the question. Doubts were forming and growing inside his head. After a moment or two he replied, "What have you been doing? Why are you out of breath?"

"Something I had to do. Nothing youse need worry about. Will youse meet me?"

He thought about it for a few more seconds. "Where are you calling from?"

"The City centre. The only place I could find a phone that works."

"All right, Sorcha. Meet me outside the library in Royal Avenue. We'll go for a walk. And if we stop for coffee, I'll choose the location this time."

"I'm sorry, Martin. I really am."

He wanted to ask questions. In particular, he wanted open and honest answers, but he was afraid of what those answers might lead to. So he put down the receiver slowly, silently wondering. There was something about Sorcha he had failed to see. What was it? It wasn't her previous sex life. He could probably overlook any minor sexual indiscretion. At least, he thought he could. No, what angered him now was the suspicion that she wasn't just an innocent Catholic girl. She had somehow crossed that grey barrier between innocence and guilt. The man he had seen at the hotel was bad news, he was sure of that. A paramilitary maybe. If he was right, Sorcha had been leading him on this past month. He wanted to know exactly what other dubious characters she was mixed up with. His doubts about her began to multiply, and doubts that multiplied became more than just doubts. They became serious warnings.

"Was that the phone, Martin?" Emily came back into the house through the kitchen.

"Something's cropped up," he said. "I have to go out again. How are things with Aunt Judy?"

"Still not saying any more than she has to." The girl

126

glanced towards the window. Outside, the aunt was sitting in a deck chair, sipping at a cup of tea.

"I'm sorry I can't stay to help you."

She looked at him with an odd sort of puzzled expression. "Are you in trouble, Martin?"

"Of course not. Why do you ask?"

"Just a feeling. You can talk to me if you need to."

He tried hard to raise a smile of reassurance. "Stop worrying yourself, Emily. I'm fine."

A twinge of guilt hit him as he left the house and hurried away to the city centre. Lying to his aunt was one thing, but lying to Emily was a step too far. He would have to find some way of confiding in her without revealing everything.

Almost an impossible task.

There was no other city centre in the UK like Belfast. Huge metal barriers were erected across the road and the pavements. A sign read: Army Control Ahead. Armed soldiers and police manned the gates giving access to the shopping area. On the corner by Burtons Tailoring shop, Martin was stopped and searched by uniformed civilian searchers before being allowed through the access gate. A soldier, standing guard, asked for some sort of ID. Martin showed his driving licence. More soldiers stopped cars nearby and checked the boots for bombs. He knew what they were searching for: fertiliser and fuel oil, bomb-making ingredients found on so many farms in a province that was littered with remote farms. The two ingredients made a cheap but effective explosive device called ANFO. Pack the car boot with the fertiliser, soak it with fuel oil and add a high explosive initiator. You needed to really load up the car, which could be a bit of a giveaway if the boot sagged, but if you got away with it you could make one hell of a bang when it went off. What made the whole thing even more effective was the amount of shrapnel you got from an exploding car. The petrol tank made things even more lethal. The car bomb was the IRA's weapon of choice.

Damn them all to hell!

Once through the barrier, Martin's thoughts focussed

more firmly on Sorcha. Was she tied up with the people who made these bombs? It wasn't a foregone conclusion; there were many decent Catholics in Northern Ireland who had no truck with the militants, but the incident at the hotel this morning continued to trouble him.

His mood grew darker as he walked on along a street where people seemed to accept the privations as an everyday part of life. God help them. His acceptance was long gone and now he wanted out. And... dear God... he was no longer certain he wanted Sorcha to leave Belfast with him. He had to get the truth from her.

She was already waiting outside the library, and something was very wrong; he saw it immediately in her eyes. She ran towards him, wrapped her arms about him and laid her head against his chest. He couldn't bring himself to reciprocate by putting his arms about her.

She didn't seem to notice. "Oh, Martin, thank God youse came!"

"I said I would." He still made no attempt to give her a comforting hug.

"There's a café just down the road here. Let's talk, Martin."

"No. We can talk here."

She took a step back. A frown crossed her face and her voice began to tremble. "Youse're angry with me."

"I want to know what the hell is going on. Who was that man at the hotel?"

"That man...?"

"You know who I mean."

"He's just someone I know. He hates Protestants and..."

"Hates Protestants? Who was he?"

She lowered her gaze to the ground. He was unable to see her expression but he doubted it would be a friendly one. "His name is Brian Fitzpain."

"Fitzpain? Him? I've heard that name before. Read it in the paper. Provisional IRA, isn't he?"

"Yes."

"And he knows you?" It was as he thought, and yet he

desperately wanted her to give him some sort of logical excuse, a reason why he should not condemn her. But he knew, deep down, it was a forlorn wish. "You've been hiding things from me, haven't you, Sorcha? You're tied in with the IRA and you've been hiding it from me."

"It's not like that, honestly." She continued staring at the ground.

"Really? What is it like?"

Tears now began to course down her cheeks, and she brushed at them with the flat of a hand. "It wasn't my fault. What happened at the hotel wasn't my fault."

"Not your fault? Why do I somehow doubt that?" She was trying to wriggle out of something and that made him even angrier.

"Someone else…"

"Don't start that nonsense with me! It's so easy isn't it, Sorcha. So easy to blame it all on someone else. I hear it all the time, especially from your lot. It's all the fault of the English. It's all the fault of the Prods. It's all the fault of the British government. That's all I seem to hear: it's anyone's fault except your own."

"Youse think we're to blame? Us… me?"

Shoppers were beginning to take notice of them, but he carried on anyway. "You're guilty of something, Sorcha. I don't know what the hell it is, but it makes me all the more determined to pack up and leave this Godforsaken place."

"Pack up and leave? Leave without me? Is that what youse're sayin' now? Without me?"

He paused. Was he ready to make that final split? He wasn't sure. "We're born to be enemies, Sorcha. You know that, and nothing we do can ever change that."

"Enemies? Is that what we are? Youse and me?"

"We live on opposite sides of the divide. You can't deny it. And I want no more of it. I can't change what Northern Ireland is… what it's become… but I can change my life. I can get out and be something different. I can do that, and I will do it. What about you, Sorcha? What are you going to do?"

129

"What d'youse want me to do?"

"For a start, you can come clean, tell me what you've been up to? Or are you going to carry on protecting your IRA friends?"

"They're not my friends." She was beginning to get angry now; he could see it in her tear-stained eyes and the downward curve of her lips.

But her anger wasn't going to distract him. He had to speak his mind. "You're linked to them in some way. I don't know how, but I know now that you are."

Tears were streaming down her face. Genuine tears. "Oh, Martin. God help me, I just don't know what to do. Youse'll have to give me time."

He shook his head. "No. There's no time left, Sorcha. I'm going to leave Belfast as soon as I can. If you can't make up your mind, you can stay here and carry on suffering here."

He turned and began walking away.

"Martin!" she called after him.

But he never looked back.

***

November 1980

The letter ended abruptly, as if Martin had exhausted himself by recalling that acrimonious meeting with Sorcha. It left me anxious to discover *her* side of the story. How did she react to the apparent break-up?

A week passed before I received another letter from Sorcha. It began with a short scrawl telling me she had asked a friend to put her words onto paper. The following pages were written in a far more legible hand. The sentences were grammatically constructed, a clue that the writer was translating Sorcha's verbal dialogue from Ulster dialect into a coherent English form. I guessed this was the work of either the chaplain or the prison visitor, more likely the prison visitor. I was ready to give her full credit for her efforts. As a well-educated Irish woman, she had a perfect grasp of English grammar and the English language.

The letter encapsulated what I had already learned from Martin but, as I hoped, it also told me what Sorcha did after the break-up. I read it twice before I took out my notebook and began to construct the next section of my manuscript. Some of it was easy to describe, but I occasionally had to use my imagination to create a totally convincing picture. It's called journalistic licence.

***

Friday 21st July 1972
1110 BST

Sorcha sniffled and wiped the tears from her cheeks. Within the past twenty-four hours she'd done things she sorely regretted and the guilt sat heavily with her. Each step along that evil path took her further into a state of depression. But she'd been forced to do what she did. She just had to do it. It was a matter of them or her. Life or death. Brian Fitzpain would hold back from killing her, but others might not. Self-preservation existed on a level she had never before imagined.

And now she had lost Martin because of it.

She shivered. Oh, God, what a mess! She had queered her pitch with him, upset him of all people. And she could think of no obvious way of putting things right. An apology? She hated apologies. No one ever apologised to her for all the harm they had done to her over the years, so why should she be the one to say sorry? What would it achieve anyway? And yet she could think of no other way out of her guilt.

She walked back towards the Royal Avenue security checkpoint with a dull pain throbbing above her brow. So many people had come out on this bright, warm morning. God help them, they didn't know what was about to happen. At the far end of the street the grand edifice of Belfast City Hall looked down benignly upon a war zone; a place of violence that had no logic and no conceivable end. The city centre was neither Protestant nor Catholic but that didn't stop terrorist gangs from delivering bombs to shops and businesses. Innocent people died as a result, but the bombs continued.

A sudden loud noise startled Sorcha. She looked back to see a mob rampaging down the middle of the street. A Tartan gang. A Loyalist mob of fifty or more young hooligans screaming foul anti-Catholic abuse.

"Taigs out! Taigs out!"

The shoppers shrank back from them in terror.

"Shite!" Sorcha let out a sudden cry of anger. It would not have been heard by those fifty or more thugs with hardly a working brain cell between them. Their vulgar cries obliterated everything.

The Tartan Gangs came from a violent Loyalist sub-culture within Northern Ireland, a reaction to increasing Republican violence. It had come into prominence in that hot summer of 1972, modelling itself on the gang violence already endemic in Glasgow. *Look at us*, it said to the world, *we know how to hit back at those Fenian murderers*. And the world looked on with growing horror.

You never knew what those hooligans would do, so Sorcha hurriedly squeezed herself into a shop doorway, along with a group of equally frightened shoppers. She glanced around at them and saw nothing, but abject fear reflected in their faces. Were they Catholics or Protestants? It was impossible to tell. A lawless Tartan mob had no respect for anyone who dared face up to them. If any of the shoppers spoke, their words went unheard.

The obscene chants continued. "Taigs out! Fuck the Pope! No surrender!" They might as well have been Nazi brutes invading a pre-war Jewish ghetto. Blind hatred, it seemed, knew no national or religious boundaries.

The gang swaggered on down the street until armed soldiers on both sides of the road moved in to funnel them through a huge metal security gate and out of the shopping area. The noise slowly abated, the chanting faded into the

132

distance. Then the shoppers began to disperse. A sense of relief began to filter through the air. Within minutes the incident was apparently forgotten, just another spot of bother in a city that had far more to worry about. A city that had grown used to mindless bigotry. Grown used to it? They almost accepted it as normal! Just another wee spot of bother.

Sorcha walked on, but her own problems returned to haunt her.

Another fifty yards along, a British soldier stood in the middle of the pavement. Was she expected to walk around him? He looked young, too young to be caught up in a war he could not be expected to understand. Remove his uniform and you'd probably find a kid not long out of school. A Protestant probably, an English churchgoer who had sat in the same class as his Catholic mates at his non-sectarian English school. They probably played together with no thought of religion or segregation. How could he possibly understand this place?

She stopped just an arm's length from him.

"You'd be better employed locking up those Loyalist thugs," she said. "They frighten me."

"Me too, Miss." His smooth voice enhanced the truth in his words.

"What are you doing here, Soldier?" she asked. She hadn't intended to confront him; the words came from somewhere deep inside her mind, too deep to merit thought and reason.

"Looking for signs of trouble, Miss," he replied in a muted Southern English accent.

"Like the trouble those Tartan boys cause?"

"Yeah. Like them wild Protestants. That's why I'm standing here in the middle of Belfast, an obvious target for an IRA bullet. Ironic, isn't it? Can't win, can we?"

She drew back her shoulders and squared up to him. She could think of sharp replies as well as him. "I didn't mean what are you doing here in the street. I meant what are you doing here in my country?"

"Keeping the peace, Miss."

"Really?"

"Well… trying to. Trouble is, we're piggy-in-the-middle, aren't we? Both sides hate us. Both sides are willing to shoot at us."

"So, go home."

"Wish I could, Miss. Wish I could. But someone has to try to keep the peace… keep the warring tribes from each other's throats."

"Warring tribes?" Was that how the British saw them? Warring tribes?

"Figure of speech, Miss," the soldier said easily.

Anger welled up inside her because he was calmly arguing back, and she didn't like that. He should be looking ashamed of what he and his fellow soldiers were doing here, but he wasn't. He was unnervingly self-confident.

She replied indignantly. "You talk of peace. What peace? You think we have peace here? You call this *peace*? You're only making things worse here, so why don't you go back home to your own country? Go back home to England."

"Just doing my job here, Miss." He smiled and winked at her. Not a flirting wink, but an I-know-what-I'm-doing wink. "Besides, the way I see it, Northern Ireland is a part of my country. Part of the United Kingdom. Don't like to see it torn apart like this."

She was surprised he could reply in such positive terms. "So you've come here to put us in our place by shooting us?"

"Not you, Miss. Wouldn't shoot at you. Only the terrorists."

"But you shot at us on Bloody Sunday, didn't you?"

"Were you there, Miss?"

"No."

"Neither was I. So I didn't shoot at you. Wouldn't dream of shooting at a nice young girl like you."

"Don't be so facetious! Bloody Sunday was a massacre. A British massacre."

"You're right, Miss. It was a mistake, something that got

well out of control. And a sad day, it was too. The Paras ran amok. They were out of control. The rest of us would never have wanted anything like that to happen."

"Why? Why did it happen?"

He looked at her with a calm expression that unnerved her. "It happened because that sort of mistake happens in every conflict, Miss. My father was a soldier in the Second World War, and he saw some of the appalling atrocities committed by the German and Japanese armies. He was in Palestine in 1948 and he saw the bodies of hundreds of civilians slaughtered by Moshe Dayan's Israeli army. In 1962 there was a massacre in Paris when the police shot dead hundreds of Algerian protestors. Same thing, Miss. In any violent conflict innocents get killed."

"But it's all wrong!" Anger infested her voice.

"Of course it's wrong, Miss, but it happens. Bloody Sunday wasn't meant to happen and we're sorry it did happen. It was Amritsar all over again."

"Amritsar. What the hell is Amritsar?"

"Where, not what, Miss. It's a place in India. In 1919 British troops opened fire on a peaceful gathering of unarmed Indians. Many died. We should have learned from that, but it seems we didn't." He looked up and down the street, as if checking that he was not acting out of turn. No army officers were about to reprimand him for chatting to a local girl. His voice remained irritatingly calm. "Interesting though, isn't it? Bloody Sunday wasn't meant to happen and people like me sincerely regret it. And yet, back in February the IRA bombed Aldershot Barracks in England, and that *was* meant to happen. People *were* meant to die that day. And the IRA show no regret. There are some who are glad they killed English people."

"Army people," she said, hoping she was right. "The ones who died. They were all British soldiers."

"Not true, Miss. They were mostly civilians; female cleaners just earning a living. Innocent civilians massacred by the IRA. Blown to bits. And there was a Catholic priest amongst the dead. Are you a Catholic, Miss?"

She nodded silently.

"Are you saddened by what the IRA's done, here and in England?" he asked. He stared at her now, silently demanding an answer.

She struggled to find a response that would satisfy her own feelings. Of course she was saddened by the bombing and shooting, deeply saddened, and she was equally saddened by her part in it. But how could she put that into words without giving in to this pip-squeak of a British soldier? The longer she was left without a convincing argument, the more she hated him.

"Damn you!" she snapped.

He stared back at her with barely a flinch, as if he was silently forgiving her for her angry words. And it was his calmness that unnerved her.

She turned and walked away, wondering if the young soldier was still watching her. When she had gone one hundred yards she stopped and looked back. He was still there, standing in the middle of the pavement, eyeing her with a look that suggested sympathy.

How dare he! How dare he show sympathy for her in her own country, her own city!

She walked on.

She put one hand into the pocket of her jeans and clasped that envelope with its telling list. The British would soon discover what Irish people could do when the chips were down. They would be caught up in it when... She stopped dead in the street once again and ran her free hand across her brow. *Dear God*, what was she thinking? Such thoughts belonged to Brian Fitzpain. Not her! Her heartbeat began to increase as she remembered what was about to happen here in Belfast. This very day. More bombs. More killing.

She breathed deeply and forced herself to think carefully. Not an easy thing to do. Her anger slowly dissipated because that pip-squeak soldier was right, although she could never admit it to anyone like him. Too many innocent people had suffered and died already, and more were going to suffer and die before this day was ended.

And she had written evidence of what was to happen.

She had to get rid of it. She dared not be found with it in her possession. It could lead to her arrest. Last night she had seen Fitzpain holding half a dozen of those white envelopes, each containing a list of the planned bomb locations. He gave her one, told her what to do, and told her to keep her mouth shut until it came time to phone in a few hoax warnings.

That was when the peeler came upon them.

Another shiver ran through her. She remembered seeing the shock in the peeler's eyes as he died. He raped no one, and he went to his God with his dick intact, but she saw him die. She saw the life drain from him just as she saw the life drain from young Hamish McGovern. One Catholic victim and one Protestant. An even score.

And she had played a part in both murders.

And then a dark cloud suddenly enveloped her mind and her mental alarm bells began to clang like the bells of hell. It was her Colonel Nicholson moment. Just like it was in the film. She'd seen it several times and that one scene stayed with her. Nicholson standing on the small beach beside the River Kwai. The realisation that the bridge had to be blown. The look of horror on his face as the truth of what he'd done sank in.

The awful question: *What have I done*?

Now it was her turn to ask the same question. *Oh God, what have I done?* And the truth was almost too much to bear.

The realisation.

The bells clanging.

The guilt.

What have I done… and what am I now going to do with that list?

She squeezed her eyes tight shut, but her anguish refused to go away. The list of bomb location. The murders. The argument with Martin.

What have I done?

She breathed deeply when she opened her eyes. After a

moment of panic, she pulled out the envelope from her coat pocket and opened it. Inside was a single sheet of paper which she slowly removed. Her hands trembled as she scanned down the list.

Smithfield Bus Station
Brookvale Hotel
York Road Railway Station
Crumlin Road
Oxford Street Bus Station
Ulster Bank, Limestone Road
Botanic Avenue Railway Station
Queen Elizabeth Bridge
Ferry terminus, Donegall Quay
Garmoyle Street
M2 motorway bridge, Bellevue
Upper Lisburn Road
Salisbury Avenue
Windsor Park
Donegall Street
Stewartstown Road
Shops, Cavehill Road
Railway line near Lisburn Road
Grosvenor Road
Albert Bridge
Sydenham By-pass
Ballysillan

It was all madness, of course, just like the madness in that film. But life in Belfast was just one long story of madness. Many had died, and many more would die today: men, women and children who dreamed of nothing more than an unattainable peaceful life. Some would die instantly, and some would suffer a lingering death, and all would be the sad victims of a senseless war. A war she hated.

She thrust the list back into her coat pocket.

Was it within her ability to stop any of it? Yes. She had the list so she could contact the RUC and warn them about the whole damned plan. It might help her conscience and it would surely save lives, but it would also get her killed. Tortured and killed. If only she had the courage to call the Confidential Line. *What the hell!* She was in too deeply to become an informant. Look at Jimmy Fish; he was an informant and he had to die because of it.

Oh, God, Martin, what have I done? What am I to do about it?

Maybe she could warn the victims. Perhaps she could go to these places and warn the innocent bystanders. Tell them to get out of the way. Would that be enough to assuage her guilt? And, by God, she was feeling guilt already. In truth, she didn't know if it would help anyone, but she would do it anyway. It was the decision of an instant. Nothing that had been deeply considered and carefully planned. Just a sudden idea that wouldn't let go.

She couldn't hope to get to every bomb location, there were too many, but she could do her utmost to try to save the lives of as many innocent people as possible. Where would she begin? Where would most people be gathered? A bus station or a railway station perhaps? Yes, of course. Both were on the list of targets. She scanned the list again. What about the Smithfield bus station as a starter? Yes, she'd go there before the bombing began. The decision, once made, became even more solid in her mind. It might even give her a lever with which to square things between Martin and herself. A small hope, but the only one she had.

As she walked on her thoughts strayed once more. She recalled the young soldier's expression. His youthful face seemed to hold back feelings of sadness at what was happening on the streets of Northern Ireland. Isolated snatches of their conversation returned.

"What are you doing in my country?" she had asked him.

"Keeping the peace, Miss."

"What peace? You think we have peace here?"

Of course they didn't have peace. It was a stupid thing to say.

This is what we are; two savage tribes at each other's

throats.

How dare anyone talk about peace! And it came to her then that the violence she so abhorred was not the soldier's perceived violence.

It was her own.

On an impulse, she turned and hurried back along the road. She was drawn back unwillingly, pulled along by her own conscience, shackled to a long rope that was being coiled in, step by step. She wished she could shake it off; pretend she had never met the young English soldier who was putting his life on the line because her fellow countrymen could not live in peace. Why should she feel such pangs of conscience after all the dreadful things the English had done to Ireland over so many years? The years... that was her problem, she realised. Most of what the English did to merit such resentment was in the past; long past. What the people of Belfast were doing was the now.

And she was a part of it.

They were, she thought, like an old married couple; the English and the Irish nations. Long ago they had been brought together through a badly arranged marriage, a marriage that had gone hopelessly wrong from the start. Neither side had made an effort to keep the peace, which is probably why it came to an acrimonious divorce. Now, the children of the marriage were at each other's throats, both sides wanting control of the disputed remains of the estate. Sharing it was no longer an option.

It was an all-or-nothing civil war.

The young soldier had not moved away. He was still standing in the middle of the pavement, his rifle pointed at the ground, his face impassive as if this was something normal.

She called out to him as she drew near. "Soldier!"

"Miss?" He turned to face her.

She stopped beside him. "Tell me something truthfully. Will you do that? Will you speak the truth?"

He looked puzzled. "What do you want to know, Miss?"

"Does it frighten you, being here in Belfast?"

He nodded. "Too right it does. Scares the shits out of me."

"What is it that frightens you? The bombs? The shooting? The sight of all this?" She swung her hand across the scene before them.

He adopted a thoughtful expression for a few seconds. "It's partly all of that, Miss. But you want to know what really scares the hell out of me?"

"Tell me."

"The people, Miss. The people here scare me. I never know which one of them is going to throw a bomb at me or shoot at me. I see them walking down the street here, looking for all the world like they're out for a nice day's shopping, and I know that one day one of them is going to try to kill me."

"Do you understand why they would kill you, Soldier?"

"Yes, Miss. It's because they hate me. They hate me because I'm English. They hate one another until they're ready to kill one another. And then they hate me. That's what scares the hell out of me, Miss. Never known such hatred until I came here."

He was right, he would never have come across anything like this, and the truth hit her hard. She wished she had not asked the question because the answer was far too painful.

***

November 1980

The letter came to an abrupt end. Even after a second and third reading it left me breathless. The writer had captured Sorcha's feelings and emotions in perfect clarity. The images in my mind refused to fade for some time afterwards. The account was the work of a natural-born writer and that impressed me. I read the letter yet again and then I wondered if I might get to meet this competent letter writer when I next ventured over to Northern Ireland.

141

Chapter Ten

Early December 1980

I received a phone call from Will Evans one Friday evening. He told me he would be in London the following week, attending a seminar on Irish terrorism.

"The Met are organising it," he said. "It's their show, but they think I might have some useful input."

"Reckon they're right, Will."

"Would you like to meet me one evening?" he went on. "I could tell you about a breakthrough we had in our investigations on the day of the Bloody Friday bombs. It was when the name Sorcha Mulveny first cropped up and we began to wonder about her. I thought it might be important to you."

"Too right it'll be important." I instantly became keen to hear about it. "Would you be free on Monday?"

"Could be?"

"Get a tube train out to Wimbledon. I'll meet you at the station and take you out for a meal at a rather nice pub."

"Make it about six o'clock," he said.

"You're on."

In the event he arrived a few minutes early. Over the course of the meal he told me how Sorcha came to the attention of himself and McIlroy.

***

Friday 21st July 1972
1115 BST

North Castle Street RUC barracks was even busier when Will and McIlroy returned. The front desk was littered with official papers and Billy McRee, the duty sergeant looked tired and harassed, even though the morning was not yet ended.

McIlroy walked straight past him, but Will stopped to speak. McRee handed him a foolscap sheet of type-written paper.

"You know he was released," he said with a disapproving tone. "That IRA man, Fitzpain. He was set free from Castlereagh."

"We know," Will replied. "What have we got here?"

"First report from the men who picked up Fitzpain at the hotel. Thought you might want to read it… even though he's got off scot free." The disdain in his voice was clearly evident.

McIlroy paused in mid-stride, turned and took a step back. "Is there anything important in it?" He ignored McRee's inferred criticism.

"Not that I could detect, sir. Just a statement of what happened when they went in and made the arrest."

"Anything about the informant?"

"No, sir. The uniform branch wouldn't have known who the informant was."

"So there's nothing new in it?" McIlroy took a dismissive tone. "In that case, my sergeant can deal with it." He walked on.

Will scanned through the brief account of the arrest. A single sentence noted that 'information had been received by telephone,' but there was no mention of Jimmy Fish being the informant. The following text highlighted the date, time and place of the arrest and noted that Fitzpain had been armed with a knife when the arrest took place. There was mention of two women being present at the hotel, along with a brief description and an address for one. The other was simply listed as the hotel manager residing at the hotel address. Yet more lazy report-writing. Would they never learn to record *everything*, especially names? The arresting guys must have dismissed the manager as unimportant. According to the report, neither woman was directly involved in what happened. They were just onlookers.

Will followed McIlroy to their office and filed away the paper in a green cabinet.

The senior officer removed his pistol holster, but he didn't bother to sit down. "I'm, going to see Boyle to report on where we've got to. Go and get yourself a coffee, Will."

"Okay, boss."

Will ignored the instruction. When McIlroy was gone from the room, he sat contemplating their next move. Coffee and the admin work could wait. Something about Fitzpain's arrest niggled in his mind. After a few minutes, he recovered the report and went back to Sergeant McRee at the duty desk. He waved the sheet of paper in front of him.

"Who took the message from the informant?" he asked.

The duty sergeant still looked harassed. His desk was still overloaded with documents. "I did."

"Not the guys downstairs?" Most informants were run by two CID men who worked in a locked room in the basement, and calls were usually made direct to them. The call that went directly to the front desk was, Will decided, a clue to the identity of the informant.

"No."

"What exactly was the message?"

The sergeant sighed and stood back from the desk. "It was a man who called. He gave the code word, *Phoenix*, so I knew it was probably genuine. He asked to speak to either you or DCI McIlroy. I said you were not here. He went a bit hesitant at that point, as if he was about to ring off. I said I'd put him through to the confidential line, but he said no. Then he agreed to speak to me."

"No name given, obviously."

"Of course not. He said… let me think… he said we should go to the Green Hills Hotel in Oldpark Road and we'd find the murderer of Mr Dunlop. I distinctly remember he called him *Mr* Dunlop. Not Constable Dunlop."

"Anything you can recall about the voice?"

McRee shrugged. "Uneducated. Ye instead of you. He said ye'll find the murderer when ye gets there. But that's not exactly an uncommon mode of speech in Belfast, is it?"

"Ye'll find the murderer?" Will could easily imagine Jimmy Fish using those words. "And you said he didn't give a name?"

"Well, he wouldn't, would he? I asked, of course, but he said it was more than his life was worth to give a name. That's what he said. More than his life's worth."

"And the uniform guys went to the hotel on the basis of that call?"

"Yes. And they picked up Fitzpain."

"And when the informant called the second time? Later, after Fitzpain was arrested. It was the same man, was it?"

"Near as I could tell, yes."

"What exactly did he say that time?"

"He said, 'Tell Mr McIlroy and Mr Evans they're barking up the wrong tree.' Those were his very words."

"Barking up the wrong tree?"

"Right."

"Nothing more?"

"Only that he wanted to see you and DCI McIlroy again."

"Again? That's another pretty good clue to his identity. We've only seen one informant this morning."

"That's what he said: it had to be you two. Oh, and he said he'd want more money, but I was careful not to report that. Thought Superintendent Boyle might not like the sound of it." The duty sergeant adopted a thoughtful expression and rummaged through the papers on his desk. "There is one interesting thing though, Will."

"Yes?"

McRee pulled out a sheet of paper and laid it flat in front of Will. "This is a copy of the report on that lad who was found dead with his dick cut off. Look at the place where he was found. The alley behind Mafeking Street. That's Nationalist territory and we now know that he was a Protestant. So, why was he there? Not exactly his home

145

ground, is it? Now look at the address of the girl who was at the hotel where Fitzpain was picked up. Mafeking Street. Mean anything, do you think?"

Will looked again at the paper in his hand. It held the information that two women were present at the hotel. One was the hotel manager, but no name was given. Will studied the information on the other woman.

Name: Sorcha Mulveny. Age: twenty. Address: 23 Mafeking Street.

That was important. She lived close to where the boy was killed during the night, and she had been seen in the company of Brian Fitzpain at the Green Hills Hotel this morning.

"There's something else, Will." McRee stabbed a finger at the paper on the desk in front of him. "Look at the report on the killing. The poor wee lad had a cross carved on his chest. That's interesting, don't you think?"

"In what way?"

"Well, there's long been a story going around about how it's Fitzpain's men who sometimes carve a cross on their victims. Nothing we can positively pin on them, of course. But, if there's anything in it, Fitzpain and the girl may be linked in more ways than one."

Will nodded. It was a tenuous connection, but a connection nonetheless. "Thanks, mate. I owe you one. Can I take the report on the killing?"

"Sure. It's a Xerox copy."

McIlroy was in the office when Will returned. He was seated at his desk, quietly smoking. A nicotine-infused cloud hung over him like a portent of gloom. Somewhere outside, a car backfired... or was it a gunshot? Whatever it was, it didn't draw the DCI from his deep thoughts.

Will went to the window. "Must've been a car backfiring. No sign of shooting out there."

McIlroy ignored the comment. "I think I should tell you, Will, that I've been talking to Boyle about your domestic problem. Trying to get your leave reinstated."

"And?" Will turned away from the window and stood by

his boss's desk.

"No joy yet. He's a hard bastard, is that man. Doesn't back down easily. But you can leave it with me. I'll keep on trying." He suddenly sat up straight and stubbed out his cigarette. "Wales, you were going to, wasn't it?"

"Conwy. Visiting my sister. I grew up there, you know." He cast his thoughts back to those idyllic days of his childhood. They seemed so remote now.

"So how come you married a Belfast girl?"

"We met at Swansea University. We were both studying law."

"She could have studied that in Belfast."

"She preferred not to. Safer in Wales."

McIlroy waved a forefinger at him. "You should have stayed in Wales, Will. It would have been a lot healthier for you. Both of you."

He shrugged. "Would have done, but when we decided to get married her mother was widowed, unwell and living alone over here. Milly felt responsible for her, so I looked for a job in Belfast. She's dead now, but we're still here. At first the RUC was all I could get into. Jobs don't grow on trees over here. Not if you're a left footer."

"And now you're stuck with it."

"Maybe."

"A Catholic in the RUC is not exactly a healthy job placement, but I'm sure you've worked that one out already."

"And been warned about it many times, boss. But where I come from a man's religion is nothing to do with his job. Unless he's a priest. Besides, I'm a Welsh Catholic, not an Irish one."

"There's a difference?"

"Like shamrocks and leeks. They're both plants but you'd not normally cook shamrocks with your dinner."

McIlroy gave him a wry grin. "An astute observation. Why do you stick it here, Will? Why don't you do as your missus says and go back to Wales?"

Will took a moment to compose his reply, wondering

how far to take the subject. "Look around you, boss. It seems to me that your tiny bit of planet earth is dying on its feet. I figure you need people like me to help cut out the bad bits."

"Like a butcher carving up a disease-ridden cow?"

"Like a dying man needs a surgical team to cut out the cancers that are killing him."

"So you have a sense of purpose. Is that all there is to it?"

"Cutting out the bad bits requires an element of skill. That makes me feel useful. I reckon I'm doing something good here."

"Why do we need a Welshman to help us? We've got our own butchers on the force."

Will laughed; a dull lifeless laugh that had no heart. "Because you Irish peelers are not getting the results you need. You cut out one bad bit and two more spring up in its place."

"Cheeky bastard! I'll write that into your annual report."

It was time, Will decided, to change the subject. He put the arresting officer's report on his boss's desk, directly in front of him. "Look at this, boss. See this name, Sorcha Mulveny."

"Mulveny?" McIlroy gave Will a curious look. "I've heard that name before. Not Sorcha. The name I heard was Barbara Mulveny. Never met her, or had cause to bring her in, but the name sticks in my memory because it was associated with Fitzpain somewhere or other. Can't remember where."

"What was the connection?" Will asked.

"No idea. It wasn't important at the time, but the name stuck in my mind. You know how these things happen. Anyway, Sorcha is a common enough Catholic name."

"Well, I think we now have some evidence that the young Sorcha Mulveny is linked in with Fitzpain."

"Why do you say that?"

Will counted off on his fingers. "First of all, she was there at the hotel when Fitzpain was lifted. Why? What was she doing there? No one thought to ask her. A stupid oversight. Like forgetting to ask the hotel manager's name. Secondly, look at her address: Mafeking Street. I spoke to Sergeant McRee and he got out this report on the boy who had his dick cut off."

He placed that report in front of McIlroy.

"The lad was found in an alley right behind that same street: Mafeking Street. And the people who did that dirty deed cut a cross in the boy's chest. It seems that's an indication it might have been Fitzpain's thugs. Or even Fitzpain himself. I definitely think there's a connection."

McIlroy scratched at his cheek. "Interesting, but it doesn't actually prove anything."

"No, but I have this intuition about the whole set-up."

"Intuition?"

"Yes. The first time I joined forces with you, you told me always to trust my intuition. Well, it's rattling my doorknob now. I reckon it might be worth speaking to the girl."

"You think she might be able to tell us something?"

"It's possible. At the very least I think we ought to take a sniff around that address, boss. You never know; we might come across a nasty smell."

"Nasty smells are common in that area." McIlroy stood up and walked to a large map on the far wall. "Mafeking Street? Isn't that just off Ladysmith Road?" He stabbed a finger at it. "Yes, just as I thought."

"Is that significant?"

"I don't know, Will. Maybe not, but then again... I overheard the uniforms talking about a ready-made car bomb found in Ladysmith Road this morning."

"It was defused, I hope."

"I'm sure the army did their job."

"Those boys don't get paid enough. One other thing, boss."

"Yes?"

"Do you remember? When Fitzpain was lifted, he was armed with a knife."

"He's always armed with a knife. His sort go nowhere without a knife. Or a gun."

"It should have been confiscated. Maybe it's still at Castlereagh. Has it been compared with Johnny Dunlop's knife wounds? Or the marks on the lad who had his dick cut off."

McIlroy frowned. "I don't know. I'll make a note to check on it when we get back."

"Back from?"

"Mafeking Street."

***

Friday 21st July 1972
1145 BST

"We'll take a Land Rover," McIlroy said as they walked out of the barracks building. "I don't want to risk the Cortina being knocked about. You know what those Republican areas are like. They can smell a cop car a mile off."

"The Land Rover could be even more conspicuous," Will pointed out.

"Yeah, but the RUC can foot the bill for any damage, and I'll still have a car to drive home in. If you can call it a home now."

Will risked asking, "She's really gone, is she, boss?"

"Like I said, moved out two days ago. Shacked up with Boyle." His voice trembled. "Let's not talk about it."

The vehicle they were allocated was an older Land Rover with only very basic protection. Will looked at it with a feeling of discomfort. "We should have been given one of the newer ones," he said as he made the routine check underneath for a mercury tilt switch bomb. "They're much safer, and they're made in Wales."

McIlroy didn't seem concerned. "I don't plan on driving into a riot. This will do."

Will made no reply, but he was hesitant as he climbed aboard. The rear was lined with nothing more than hardboard. His sense of unease began to grow.

The overlying atmosphere worried him as they drove into

the Republican ghetto in the vicinity of Mafeking Street. It wasn't just the physical evidence of the everyday sectarian divisions; the graffiti and the boarded-up houses. He was used to that. Something more sinister held sway here, but his intuition wasn't sharp enough to pinpoint the source of the problem. He pulled out his pistol and checked it was fully loaded, something he hated doing because he could never sure whether he could bring himself to shoot someone with it. The vital test had never arisen.

McIlroy stopped the Land Rover in Ladysmith Road at the junction with Mafeking Street. Nearby, a battered old Ford was being loaded onto a trailer. Armed police and troops held a tight cordon around the operation while a mob of sullen youths watched from a distance.

"The hostile Apaches are surrounding the wagon train," Will noted.

McIlroy sniffed. "Or is it Baden-Powell being besieged at Mafeking?"

"I reckon Baden-Powell would have had us scouting around the edges before venturing too far into these streets." Will laughed. "How do you want to play this, boss?"

"Cautiously. I'll start by talking to that uniform sergeant." He pointed to a tall policeman standing in the company of an army officer. "If nothing else, they can keep an eye on the Land Rover while we scout around."

Will waited with the vehicle while McIlroy spoke to the uniformed sergeant. He came back with a serious expression.

"Five hundred pounds of ANFO in the boot of that car. Would have spoiled the day for some unlucky people. They've got the car's owner so maybe they'll get some clues about today's campaign."

"One bomb accounted for, but how many to go?"

"God knows."

"Remember what Jimmy Fish told us. Bombs. Plural."

"Plural can mean anything from two to dozens, Will. Fancy a game of guess the number?" There was nothing light-hearted in his tone of voice.

They walked along Mafeking Street, picking their way along a pavement strewn with bricks from a previous riot. A corrugated iron copy of the Berlin wall blocked off the far end of the street. Will shook his head sadly. They called it a 'peace line' but peace was a misnomer here. It was a battle line in a civil war.

At number 23, halfway along the street, McIlroy rapped loudly on a battered wooden front door. A thin, dowdily-dressed woman in her mid-fifties eased it open and peered out at them. She wore a wrap-around apron and her straggly hair was tied up in a dirty headscarf.

"Waddya want?" Her voice was coarse and prickly.

"Mrs Mulveny?"

"Yeah."

"Barbara Mulveny?"

"So what?"

McIlroy gave Will a knowing look and Will guessed what was going through his mind. If this woman was Sorcha's mother, and if she was the Barbara Mulveny he had once heard about, there had to be a common connection with Fitzpain.

He held up his warrant card. "DCI McIlroy. North Castle Street CID. And this is DS Evans. May we speak with you?"

"Piss off." The woman leaned further out and peered up and down the street, as if frightened someone might see the police on her doorstep.

McIlroy put his foot in the door as she made to close it. "We need to ask you about your daughter, Sorcha."

"What about 'er?" She did not deny being Sorcha's mother. Will mentally filed away the clue.

"Is she at home?"

"No."

"Where was she last night?"

The woman looked away. "Here. Where the hell d'youse think she was?"

"Was she here all night?"

"Of course she was."

"You would swear to that?"

"Of course. So would any mother. Youse think I don't care about 'er? Well, I do care!" She stabbed a finger at him, anger oozing from every pore. Or was it guilt?

"Why do you say that Mrs Mulveny?" McIlroy took a step back in the face of the woman's aggression.

"Why don't youse piss off." This time the woman managed to slam the door shut.

McIlroy was quick to react. He banged on the door and shouted, "Open up, Mrs Mulveny or I shall be forced to bring in some people who will break it down. They'd follow up with a full house search. You wouldn't want that, would you?"

The door opened again, a little wider this time.

"What the hell d'youse want now?" The voice was less belligerent this time. Aggression replaced by fear. What did she fear? A broken door or a house search?

"We want to talk to you, Mrs Mulveny. Do you mind if we come inside?" McIlroy was already halfway through the door opening as he spoke. Will followed in his wake.

The old lady backed away from McIlroy as if he was a bulldozer and she was a mound of earth in its way. She seemed to have got the message that nothing was going to stop him.

"In here, shall we?" He ushered her into a tiny parlour room off the narrow hallway. The room was typical of the Belfast terraces: damp, claustrophobic, with the same wallpaper Noah used to line the ark. Even the dank smell could have come from the biblical times. The front window let in a minimal amount of light, making Barbara Mulveny seem no more than a shadowy outline.

She made no effort to stop McIlroy. All her reserves of bluster and resentment seemed to have been washed away. The DCI had her just where he wanted her.

"Now, let's repeat the formalities. I am DCI McIlroy and this is DS Evans. You're not going to offer us a cup of tea, are you?"

"No."

153

"I thought not. We want to talk to you about your daughter, Sorcha." McIlroy stood in the middle of the room squeezed between a small, sunken-seated sofa and a battered armchair. Nevertheless, he dominated the dismal scene with his presence.

"What about Sorcha?" the woman asked, her gaze darting between the two policemen.

"Where was she last night?"

Barbara Mulveny hunched her back and wrapped her spindly arms about herself. "Dunno. I wasn't here. Didn't get home 'till this mornin'."

Will noted that McIlroy didn't follow up on the change in the woman's story. Instead, the DCI laughed coldly and said, "Really? A night on the tiles at your age, Mrs Mulveny?"

"Piss off."

"Where were you?"

"Visitin' relatives in Ardglass. What's that got to do with you?"

"You know that a boy was killed in your back alley?" Will said. He knew by experience when to join in with his boss's enquiries.

"Youse're not Irish," the woman snorted. Some of her hostility made a brief comeback. Will didn't expect it to last, but he countered it by thrusting out his jaw.

"Welsh," he said.

"Get back to yer own country."

"I might just do that. Now, about the lad who was killed…"

"Filthy Prod."

"Murder is murder, Mrs Mulveny, whatever the religion. And we have to investigate it."

"So piss off and investigate."

McIlroy nodded to Will and took back the lead in the questioning. "That's exactly why we're here, Mrs Mulveny. Tell me what you know about a man called Brian Fitzpain. You do know him, don't you?"

"Him? What about him?"

154

"When did you last see him?"

"Dunno." She looked down at her feet, as if the answer might be floating on the linoleum floor.

"How long have you known him?"

"Since we was kids."

"So, you've known him most of your life? Well, well?" McIlroy canted his head to one side. Will recognised it as his boss's way of letting her know he was taking careful note of her answers.

"So what?" She took a step back and looked up. Her face began to pale.

"He was seen at a hotel in Oldpark Road this morning. Your daughter, Sorcha was also there. So tell me what the connection is between them."

"Connection? Ain't no connection between them two."

"Really? Who else lives here, Mrs Mulveny? Apart from you and Sorcha," McIlroy asked.

"Just Bridie. She's me eldest."

"I see. So let's see what we have so far. You live here with your two daughters. And we have ascertained that you know Brian Fitzpain. What about Seamus Codd? What do you know of him?"

"Jimmy Fish?"

"Yes. Him."

"Don't know nothin'."

Even as she spoke, a strange look appeared in her face. Will noted it and gave McIlroy a brief nod. Once again, the woman was frightened of something. Why? What was it about the mention of Jimmy Fish that brought on her anxiety?

"Let's get back to your daughter, Bridie. Where is she now?" McIlroy asked.

"She's off visitin'. Youse can't talk to her 'cos she's off to Derry for a few days."

"Very well. But we shall need to speak to her. Maybe we should come back when both of your daughters are at home."

"Why? What d'youse want with 'em?"

Will watched her intently. There it was again, that look of fear. Fear of what the two daughters might say, maybe? Or was there a series of connections here somewhere? Sorcha and Bridie, Fitzpain and Fish.

McIlroy didn't answer the question. He turned to leave. "We'll be in touch again, Mrs Mulveny. Tell your daughters we'll be wanting to speak to them, will you? Both of them."

He led the way from the house while the old lady remained in the parlour room.

Will pulled the front door shut behind them.

Standing on the pavement, McIlroy paused and asked, "Well? What do you make of that, Will?"

"Not exactly mother love, is it? Despite what she says. I think we may be wasting our time here. We'll get nothing from her. It's the girl, Sorcha, we need to speak to, and maybe the other one as well. Do you think either of them is here, hiding from us?"

"Probably not. And we're not going to do a house search right now." McIlroy stared back at the closed front door. "Why do you think she bristled when the name of Jimmy Fish came up? I'm a bit suspicious on that count."

"There's something fishy there, that's for sure, boss."

"All the more reason for us to speak to Bridie Mulveny as well as Sorcha."

"Boss, it's pretty clear now that this must be the Barbara Mulveny you mentioned earlier. What more do you know about her?"

"Bugger all that's of any use, Will. But I'll ask a few more questions in due course." The DCI looked up and down the street. "I've a nasty feeling in the water about that woman. A classic Belfast mammy, the sort that rule their kids' lives with a rod of iron. If I was her offspring, I'd be very wary of her."

"Not your typical Mother Theresa."

"And lies come as natural from her as mother's milk. First she tells us her daughter, Sorcha, was at home all last night, and then she admits she wasn't here anyway. Away visiting, she said."

"Natural liars are better at it than that, boss."

"Probably. In the meantime, Will, look that way."

McIlroy gestured towards the corrugated iron wall at the end of the street where a gang of youths was gathered. Some were lounging with hunched shoulders, puffing on joints, while others were scrawling obscene graffiti on the barricade. The 'B' Specials would have gone in there without hesitation and sorted them out in seconds, Will reflected, but that side of the RUC had been disbanded. Too rough and tough for the average street layabout, so they had to go. Their anti-Catholic bias had also been a problem.

"I can smell the dope they're smoking from here," Will said.

"We're being watched and that means trouble. Let's get out of here while we can. We'll try finding those Mulveny girls another time."

"A sound idea, boss."

They kept an eye on the youths as they backed away to the end of the street. McIlroy thanked the soldiers at the road junction when they recovered the Land Rover, but he double checked for a bomb beneath the vehicle anyway. It was a habit and a good one. None of the soldiers looked too happy, but when did a British squaddie look happy on the streets of Belfast? Will sympathised with them.

He felt some relief as they drove away along Ladysmith Road, between more depressing red-brick terraces. Two lines of dismal homes staring at each other across a miserable street. There were few people out on the road, but curtains twitched as they passed. A police Land Rover here was as welcome as a Jew in Mecca.

They were halfway along the next street when a hidden gunman opened fire.

"Jesus!" Will cried as he ducked down.

The sudden bark of the gun was accompanied by holes exploding across the upper edge of the windscreen. Bullets ripped through the top of the cab and out through the roof. The gunman was aiming from low down.

"You hit?" McIlroy rammed his foot to the floor, the

157

engine roared and the Land Rover raced on down the road, zig-zagging from side to side to make the target more difficult. Bullets were now hitting the side of the vehicle.

At first Will dared not raise his head to look for the sniper. "I'm okay, boss. Just get us out of here." He continued to crouch low in his seat and pulled out his pistol.

"Stay down!" McIlroy shouted.

Will said nothing. A few moments passed before he raised his head and risked a peek over the dashboard. More bullets erupted through vehicle, exiting behind the two occupants. Ahead, a figure appeared at an open doorway. He lit a petrol bomb and sent it arching through the air. It burst into flames on the road a few yards in front of the vehicle. Will grabbed his seat tightly as McIlroy swung the Land Rover around the flaming missile.

"Bloody hell!"

"Hold tight, Will."

More bullets hit the rear of the Land Rover as McIlroy raced on and swung round a corner on two wheels. He rounded another corner and then slowed down.

"Welcome to Belfast," he wheezed.

"Bugger Belfast." Will felt a shudder of alarm run through him and then his sight began to blur. His head ached. That damned knock on the skull. He leaned back in his seat and waited for the moment to pass.

"You all right?" McIlroy asked. The Land Rover was passing out of the ghetto area now, but he didn't look round.

"Give me a minute. Just a minute."

"Reckon we both need some recovery time, and a slug of something hard when we get back, eh?"

"If you say so, boss."

What Will needed most was peace and quiet and he wouldn't find that anywhere in this area. The image of a tranquil Welsh shoreline flashed through his mind. Water lapping on soft sand. Milly beside him, holding his hand. The girls playing happily nearby. He'd be on his way there now if it hadn't been for this damned Irish civil war.

When he was sufficiently recovered, he reported the

attack on the radio net and began to relax. They were relatively safe now and neither of them was injured. Thank God for that. His headache eased away as they drove on down the road, putting space between themselves and Mafeking Street.

Five minutes later they met a roadblock just half a mile from the Antrim road. Cars were backed up in both directions. Drivers had left their vehicles and were milling around in disarray. Another police Land Rover was at the heart of the obstruction; a blue Ford van parked sideways across the road.

"Damn. Just what we need right now," Will complained.

A uniformed police sergeant strode towards them, an older officer with the look of one who had seen it all before and wasn't going to be panicked this time. He shook his head as he came near and peered in at Will and McIlroy.

"You guys been fighting a war or something?" He pointed to the bullet holes.

"Moths eating the furniture," McIlroy said. "No one hurt. What's going on here?"

"An abandoned van. We've given it a quick check over. The back doors are locked, but there's nothing obviously wrong. Probably stolen and left here to make us tremble with fear. My constable is about to move it."

"A quick check isn't enough. You'd better wait until the army take a look at it," McIlroy said.

"No. It would take too long. There's already a big tailback in both directions. Should be safe enough…"

A loud boom filled the air.

The van exploded, torn apart amidst a burst of flame and a sudden shockwave. Will shook in his seat as the Land Rover rocked against the blast. The police sergeant was blown to the ground. Long cracks appeared in the Land Rover's front windscreen where it had been weakened by the earlier attack. Ahead of them, Will saw the top of the van opened up like a tin of beans.

For some moments the blast was followed by silence. Then pandemonium broke loose. Will staggered from the

Land Rover and took in a scene of panic. Some of the drivers standing in the road had been bowled over by the explosion. Some were injured. The cars closest to the van were clearly damaged. Bodies lay beside the wrecked van. A mother clasping a child ran screaming from the scene. A young girl in a bloodied mini dress staggered between the cars, weeping loudly. An elderly man stood in the midst of the mayhem and stared into the distance, his face displaying his total lack of comprehension of what had happened.

"Call in for help, boss." Will shouted at McIlroy who was still inside the Land Rover, staring ahead as if he also was in shock.

Shock? They were all in shock.

Will made his way towards the front of the line of vehicles. Each one was more damaged than the one behind. The air smelt of cordite, blood and petrol leaking from damaged cars. That worried him. Flames were licking angrily from the wrecked van.

At first he was able to reassure the people who were left standing, asking them to help others who had been bowled over. But the victims at the front of the queue were in need of serious medical help. As he passed between two cars, a woman grabbed him with one hand. She was bathed in blood. Young or old, he had no idea. She was trying to say something to him, but no words came from her mouth. One arm hung loose, as if it was almost severed from her body. He put out his hands to help her, easing her to the ground.

"Take it easy now. We'll have help in a minute."

He used whatever comforting words he could think of. He would have to do something about that arm, he realised. Staunch the flow of blood. Use a tourniquet, if he could find something suitable. There were others nearby also needing help, crying out for help, but he could do nothing for them while attending to the woman.

The distant sound of sirens alerted him to approaching emergency vehicles. Thank God! He couldn't cope with all this alone.

And then the grey mist descended again, and his mind

went blank. The last thing he remembered was falling to the ground.

***

Early December 1980

"That knock on the head playing up again?" I said.

"That and the stress of the job making things worse. I was too stupid to see it." The pub was almost empty. When Will stopped talking, the room seemed to go silent, adding an eerie emphasis to his description of the car bomb.

"You recovered from it?"

"After a few minutes. Before McIlroy got to see what happened."

I saw how pale his face had become. "Enough talking?" I asked.

"Enough for now. Can we leave it there?" He spoke in a quiet voice. "I don't want to go into any more of this tonight."

"Too many bad memories?"

"What the hell do you think?"

"I don't think I could bring myself to do the things you did, Will. You're a brave man."

"Am I? I'm not so sure." He shook his head. "McIlroy once told me that life is a death sentence, so we may as well get used to it. You can check out now in a blaze of glory, doing what's right. Or you can wait until you're old and decrepit and slide away as a dribbling, incontinent mess. Take your choice."

"You set yourself up for a blaze of glory?"

"No. I put all that out of my mind and simply did my job. You know what I'd like now... before I leave this pub?"

I nodded, went to the bar and bought him another double whiskey. I figured he needed it... probably deserved it.

"One more question, Will," I said when I handed him the drink. "Do you think Sorcha Mulveny really did kill those two men?"

"Why do you ask me now?"

"Because I still have my doubts. Right at the start I asked her outright if she did it and she said, 'You can't imagine how guilty I felt.' How guilty she *felt*, not how guilty she *was*. And she said it wasn't how people thought."

"She confessed," he said in a somewhat dismissive tone.

"That's an evasive reply, Will."

"It's the only one I can come up with. Is that what your book is all about? Your doubts about who murdered those two men?"

"No. Not at all. The book is about the suffering people went through that day. And I ask myself, what sort of suffering would make a woman confess to something she didn't do?"

"*If* she didn't do it."

"Yes. *If* she didn't do it."

Chapter Eleven

December 1980

The memory of Will Foster's words came back to me on an early morning flight into Belfast's Aldergrove Airport. I was getting much closer to the personal tragedies of Bloody Friday now and I had to steel myself for some dramatic accounts. It didn't seem to matter that I had been in Belfast when the Bloody Friday bombing began, a reporter on the *Belfast Telegraph*. I think my boss must have had my best interests at heart that day. He probably felt sorry for me in some ways; an Englishman from the Home Counties trying to make some sort of sense out of Northern Ireland. How could it possibly make sense to an Englishman? Irish people blowing up part of Ireland, killing Irish people, all in the name of bringing Irish people together? Was I mad, or were they?

"Stay here in the office with me, English," my editor said. He always called me English, but with no trace of rancour.

"I should be out there reporting what's happening," I protested.

"No. It's not your battle and I don't want you getting hurt because of Irish hatred. I'll need someone at the end of the phone line as the reports come in, and I'm nominating you for the job. Your family will thank me for it one day."

Because of him, I never left the newsroom while the city was torn apart and people died. Eight years later I still had thankful memories of the way he tried to protect me from the full impact of those IRA bombs. He at least had a sense of compassion.

My next task was to find out from Sorcha more about how she survived that dreadful day.

I checked in at the Europa Hotel in Belfast and called for a taxi to take me to Armagh. It was an expensive ride, but I excused it by telling myself the cost would be set against my taxable income when the book was published. A weak excuse, but I had vivid memories of that first rain-soaked journey to Armagh on the day Private Atkins died. The weather was just as bad today. As before, I was interrogated at the prison, frisked and then shown to the interview room where Sorcha was waiting for me. The eye that had been bruised was now fully back to normal, and she had another woman seated alongside her.

"This is Susan Miller," she said. She gestured to an attractive, dark-haired woman in her thirties, dressed in a green trouser suit. The clean neatness of her clothes gave her fine features and slender figure a strange look of calm authority. She had that enigmatic Irish look about her, a look that reminded me very much of Annie. She would have looked perfect as Sorcha's solicitor, but I instinctively knew she was not.

"Prison visitor." Susan Miller stood up and offered me a firm handshake.

"And letter writer," I replied.

"It did the trick?" When she smiled her eyes seemed to glow. They reminded me of Annie's eyes; alert and yet filled with good humour.

"Perfectly," I said as I sat down opposite the two women and took out my notebook. "Your literary skills do you credit. You deserve my utmost thanks."

Sorcha leaned forward and clasped her hands on the table. "I thought it would help if youse met Susan, in case I ask her to write another letter for me."

"Good thinking, Sorcha." I spent a few minutes in general chit-chat aiming to get both of them relaxed before I asked, "Have you been preparing yourself to tell me the next part of your story?"

"Depends. Where d'youse want me to start?"

I gave a quick thought to the murders, and then decided not to press home that subject just yet. There would be a more opportune time later. "Where you left off in the letter. What did you do after your argument with Martin?"

"I went for something to eat," she said.

***

Friday 21st July 1972
1145 BST

Sorcha was still determined to warn people away from the bombs, but first she needed to eat. There was time before the bombing began. Using the last of her cash, she bought herself a sandwich and a large cup of coffee in Anderson and McCauley's in Donegall Place. She needed the caffeine to counter the effects of a night without sleep. The restaurant was busy, men and women laden with shopping bags, taking the opportunity of lunch in one of the city's best-known stores.

She nibbled at the sandwich and then put it aside, less than half eaten. Her hunger faded behind her sadness. Yet again she had made a mess of things. Screwed up her life. Would Martin give her another chance, an opportunity to redeem herself? It seemed unlikely. So what options were left open to her? Maybe she would have to resurrect those pills and a bottle of vodka, put an end to things once and for all. It was a solution, a viable solution, but it seemed less attractive now that she had experienced what Martin had to offer. If only she could heal the rift between them.

In the meantime, what would Brian Fitzpain have to say if he found out about her relationship with a Protestant? He wouldn't kill her, of course he wouldn't, but he would make her suffer. He enjoyed making people suffer. He was good at it.

It was ironic that she would once have done the same to

him, given half a chance. She could even have put an end to his life, given the right excuse. But not now. She couldn't bring herself to do that now. It was all a matter of who he was.

She remembered the day he had been sitting in the parlour room in Mafeking Street with her mother, drinking tea and chatting. And something odd happened. Something passed between the two of them, a knowing look; an expression of understanding. They knew something she did not, and it annoyed her.

Later, when she got him on his own, she confronted him.

"Brian, how well did youse know me mammy back in those days when youse was fishin' in Ardglass?"

"What're youse getting' at?" he snapped back.

"Just what I said. How well did youse know her? Did youse…" She couldn't bring herself to finish the question.

"Did I fuck her?"

"Well? Did youse?"

"None o' yer business."

"I'll take that as a yes. Did youse make her pregnant? Well? Did youse?"

"Shut up!" He jabbed a fist at her face. "I'll make youse sorry if youse don't keep yer big mouth shut. Just see if I don't!"

If that wasn't a confession, she didn't know what was. Didn't it confirm what she'd long believed? But she'd have one more try to get an outright admission. This time she'd use a different approach. "Why did me daddy walk out on her? Was it because of youse?"

He thought for a few seconds and then turned to leave. "I told youse to shut yer mouth! But I'll tell youse this, Sorcha. Yer mammy was no better than youse in those days. Yer daddy wasn't the only one to fuck her. Now, don't ask any more questions or I'll take me hand to youse good and proper."

She long remembered that confrontation in detail. It wasn't conclusive, didn't give her clear cut answers, but she was confident she now knew the truth. And that was why

166

she could never kill Fitzpain. Because of who she believed he was.

Neither, she thought, could he ever kill her.

She finished her coffee and pushed the mug away. Damn the man! The connection between them was the reason she had taken the credit for something she didn't do, the reason she had shown herself willing to protect someone close to him. When word got back to him... when he learned what she had done within the past hour he would have to look favourably on her. He just had to. She felt sure he would allow her to leave Ireland with Martin and neither of them would ever come to harm at his hand.

Because of what she claimed to have done.

She looked around the restaurant at a sea of faces and brought her thoughts back to the coming action. There was not a sign of trouble here in the restaurant: no antagonism or discontent. Not yet. She shook her head in despair. They would soon learn.

Just look at them!

Middle-aged, grey-haired men and women, glad of a moment away from the horrors of their sectarian ghettos. Young men wearing flared trousers and long hair in the belief it made them look cool. Young girls in mini-skirts and high heels, showing their thighs almost up to their panties.

They were sitting close to one another in the same room, and yet they had no idea who they shared this place with. There were Catholics and Protestants in here, eating together, enjoying a meal in close proximity with one another and it meant nothing to them. And yet, outside of here, they would keep to their own streets, they would send their children to their segregated schools and they would never dream of attending the same church. In here, no one gave a shit who was sitting near them. Why couldn't it be like this everywhere in Belfast?

She slid a hand into her coat pocket and her fingers curled around the list. That list! She drew it out and stared at it. It was written evidence of what was going to happen. She could take this to the police now and they would be prepared. Knowing exactly where the bombs would be placed, they could be ready to stop the whole damned thing. Lives would be saved. Yes, she could do this now. The evidence was here in her hands. She could act to stop this madness.

Except that she couldn't.

Her treachery would get back to the IRA and they would come looking for her. She would be killed. Brutally tortured and killed. Her mutilated body would be buried on some remote Irish moorland. No, she could not do it. She slid the list back into her pocket and felt a shiver run through her. She had the means to stop the inevitable deaths, but she could not do it.

She closed her eyes and asked herself the question, was she wrong to think only of her own life when others were sure to die? Could she really just walk away and pretend it was nothing to do with her?

When she opened her eyes again, she was jolted back into reality. She instantly recognised two men sitting barely ten feet away from her. They were staring at her, and there was the answer to her question. The curse of the Troubles was very much alive in here and she could not walk away because she was a part of it. She had seen pictures of these two in the newspapers and on the television local news. "Bad Boy" Georgie Blair and "Mad Mac" Calum McKinnon. There could be few people in Northern Ireland who didn't know who they were: well-known members of the Protestant Ulster Volunteer Force. They were mindless butchers, the sort who actually enjoyed killing Catholics, and they were here, staring at her with evil intent.

She tried to act as if they meant nothing to her, until Mad Mac approached her with a glaring expression of pure hatred. He stood beside her, leaned forward and placed his two thick hands knuckle-down on the table in front of her.

"We've been followin' ya. We know who ya're, Sorcha Mulveny. We knows what ya did to poor wee Hammy McGovern. And we're gonna get ya fer it."

"Piss off," she hissed back. She felt far from the self-confidence she pretended.

"Don't act clever with me, girl. We knows! And yer gonna pay the price."

Sorcha nodded towards an armed policeman buying coffee at the counter. "Why don't youse go and tell him what youse plan to do?"

Mad Mac ignored the policeman. He leaned closer to Sorcha and hissed between clenched teeth. "Ya'd better watch yer back from here on, Mulveny. Don't go down any dark alleys on yer own 'cos we'll be lookin' for the chance to cut ya to bits. Ya're gonna be dead meat before this day's out."

She growled back at him. "Lay one finger on me and I have friends who'll leave you screamin' in pain."

"Pain? Ya mean the Pain Men. Them pillocks! Don't make me laugh. Ya've been warned, Mulveny. We knows where ya lives and we're gonna come fer ya and the rest o' the Mulveny family. None o' ya bastards are gonna be safe now."

He jerked himself upright at that point, while a figure in dark green uniform came up to the table.

"Any trouble here, Miss?" the policeman asked. Then he paused and said, "Don't I know you? Yes, of course I do. It's Sorcha Mulveny."

Sorcha gasped as she recognised him. Mickey Murphy; a sturdily-built policeman with wide, honest eyes and a constant grin. He'd grown up in Ladysmith Road. They'd played together as kids. More than that, they'd been close to one another. Very close. What on earth was he doing in the uniform of a Belfast peeler?

He must have recognised the UVF man as well, but that was no surprise. Every policeman in Belfast had Mad Mac's image constantly in mind.

"There's no trouble here, Officer," Mad Mac backed away. It didn't do for a Loyalist to make a fuss in front of an armed peeler in a public place, and McKinnon must have known it. His violence was reserved for riot lines and dark corners on dark nights.

"On your way, McKinnon," Murphy said. It was an instruction, not a question.

"Just leaving, Officer."

Sorcha smiled icily at Mad Mac as he backed away, and she told herself to keep a careful watch behind her today. Her life would depend upon it. Dear God, was this the sort of existence she was fated to accept if she stayed here in Ireland, always looking over her shoulder, always expecting the worst?

"No friend of yours, I take it." It was a rhetorical question. Mickey Murphy took an empty seat at her table and set down his coffee mug.

"They threaten any Catholics they come across. You know that, Mickey. How come you're a peeler now?"

"'Tis a job, so 'tis. And it pays well. But what about you? I ain't seen you in two or three years. Or is it longer? What are you up to now?"

"Not a lot, Mickey." She suddenly felt uncomfortable. Not just because she was talking to a peeler, but because this particular one knew so much about her. Dammit, he'd bedded her when they were teenage kids with nothing better to do. Bedded her and spent the rest of the month praying for her next period to come on.

It didn't.

When it was all over, they never spoke about it again. What was not said then, remained unsaid.

Did he remember that? Of course he did.

"Not married, I see." He nodded to her left hand, devoid of rings.

"No."

It was an unkind observation in the circumstances, and it left her feeling uneasy. She hurriedly finished the last of her coffee and made to leave. Better to go now than risk him raking up the past at this late date. Then she remembered the list, still in her pocket. This was her opportunity to show it to a policeman. Her opportunity to help stop the bombings. But she couldn't do it. She couldn't risk the torture and killing. It was bad enough to be threatened with

170

death by those Loyalists, but what the IRA would do to her would be worse. The torture would be too much for her to even think about.

She forced a small smile to her face. "Look, 'tis nice to see youse again, Mickey, but I have to go. People I gotta see."

"So soon?"

"Sorry." She stood up. "Like I said, there's people I promised to meet."

"We must get together again, Sorcha. I always did have a soft spot for you."

It was more than a soft spot, Mickey! God forgive you!

"We'll do that," she said, but she knew they wouldn't. How could she possibly meet up with him again, even if he wasn't one of the hated peelers? How could she meet up with him and live easily amongst the residents of Mafeking Street? They all knew what happened. Pretended they didn't, but they did.

So she walked away.

Her fear now was for the Loyalist thugs who had somehow discovered her part in the emasculation and killing of Hamish McGovern. They would be waiting for her to leave the store, those two. Waiting for a chance to kill her. Well, they wouldn't get her today. Not today. She had a better idea in mind as she made her way out of the restaurant. A simple idea that could save her from a brutal death.

At the restaurant entrance, she turned and gave a final wave to Mickey Murphy. He looked back at her with puzzlement spread across his face.

The UVF men had left first, smiling at her as they walked away. They were, she decided, too confident of their ability to find her in some quiet spot where they could murder her. Well, she could outwit them on that score, just see if she could. A change of clothes would do the trick.

The shop was busy, so she mingled with the crowd while making her way to the ladies wear department. She had no more money with her, but in such a multitude it wasn't difficult to get away without paying. She knew the tricks, had done it before without being caught. Shoplifting was an accepted practice for the residents of Mafeking Street and Sorcha had learned the tactics well.

Taking her time so as not to draw attention to herself, she selected a long, green dress and took it to the fitting room. One other girl was there, admiring herself in the mirror. Her painted face tried to say she was about Sorcha's age, but her body was years past its best. She was stripped down to just her underwear and holding a brand-new dress in front of herself. Her outer clothes were draped over a chair: well-worn jeans that were torn along the seams, and a dirty blouse that would have looked at home in a dustbin. Her legs were painfully thin and her breasts looked shrivelled within her bra. You don't look like you can afford that dress, Sorcha thought, but she said nothing. If the girl aimed to steal the dress, who was she to criticise? Besides, what was wrong with pretending you can look like a film star, even when you're as poor as a church mouse?

She turned away from the girl and stripped off her outer clothes and her underwear, everything except her shoes. Who the hell was going to see her naked except the other girl? Nevertheless, she was hurried in the way she tried on the new dress. It was perfect – clinging to her figure like a second skin, emphasising her slim waist. And not a pantie-line in sight. More importantly, it made her look so different to the Sorcha Mulveny who had come in wearing the denim skirt and white tee shirt. She ran her hands down her front, noticing how her breasts looked more rounded without the bra. Could she feel confident enough to walk around in public without it? This was, after all, an age when girls everywhere were discarding or burning their bras. It seemed to cause the other girl in the fitting room no problem.

What the hell? She would do it.

She hung up her discarded clothes and walked confidently towards the door. It was warm enough to be walking around in so little, and it felt strangely exciting to be wearing nothing but the dress and her shoes. Something she had never before done in public. She glanced back and saw that the other girl was now watching her intently, almost mesmerised.

"You've forgotten your old clothes," the girl called to her. Her mousey hair fell forward, partly obscuring her eyes.

"Don't need them," Sorcha said.

"You're not going to leave them behind, are you?"

"Why not?"

The girl reached out for the skirt and ran a hand across the denim. She sounded surprised. "You mean you really don't want these?"

"No."

"Can I have them?"

"Help yourself."

Giving them away wasn't what she had intended, but it might help her plan. Yes, it would help her in a way the other girl would never understand. And it would enable the poor girl to leave the store without being tainted as a thief.

Sorcha took a step away, and then she stopped abruptly when an idea came to her. She turned and faced the other girl. "Youse can have me clothes if youse'll rumble fer me."

"You gonna steal that dress?"

"Aye."

"Okay, give me a moment." The girl put on Sorcha's clothes and smoothed them down over her thin figure. "I'm ready now. Give me a minute." She grinned as she walked out of the room.

Sorcha waited until she heard raised angry voices out in the store. She peeped around the fitting room door. The girl was arguing with a security guard and a floorwalker was hurrying towards the altercation. Shoppers stopped to watch the fracas. No one was looking in Sorcha's direction. It was a classic act of deception. Smoke and mirrors.

Sorcha smiled to herself as she left the fitting room and strolled out into the mass of women milling around on the shop floor. Theft wasn't so difficult when you knew what to do, and the other girl clearly knew the routine was well as her. Dressed in Sorcha's clothes she was putting up a rare

173

old act of aggression. And wouldn't it be amusing if, as Sorcha now expected, the two UVF men followed the wrong girl out of the shop? She imagined the looks on their faces when they discovered their mistake. She was almost inclined to laugh.

***

December 1980

"Did you steal other things in those days?" I asked.

She sniffed. "We all did. Youse lived here once. Youse know that stealin' and cheatin' is a way of life in the ghettos."

I knew it so I changed the subject. "Do you want to tell me more about the pregnancy?" I asked.

"No. Not now." Sorcha stood up suddenly, clearly agitated. I didn't understand why, she had raised the matter of her own accord.

"It could be important, Sorcha."

"Another time. I'll tell you another time. Not now." She turned away and gestured to the warder. "I want go now."

I watched silently as the warder escorted Sorcha from the interview room. I was left with only the prison visitor. We sat and looked at one another.

"How much of this story do you know?" I asked her.

"Less than you, I imagine."

"What do you make of that admission of a pregnancy?"

"I've seen the same pain in other Irish girls. It hurts more than you might realise." She stood up and gathered together her handbag and coat. "In Sorcha's case, it hurts more than I had realised until now."

"She's not a bad girl," I said. "I suspect she's not a killer."

"Because?"

"Intuition."

On the face of it we had covered so little ground but, in reality, we had moved forward in Sorcha's search for a way out of her predicament. More importantly, I was now getting a much firmer picture of her early life in Belfast. The revelation of an unwanted pregnancy continued to puzzle me as we walked back down the pee-smelling corridor, but an earlier hint had served to mask any sense of shock. Besides, it wasn't by any means a rare problem in Catholic Ireland. The effect that pregnancy had upon Sorcha was something I was determined to learn later.

And then there was Susan Miller. She reminded me so much of Annie, and that affected me in a way that felt both uncomfortable and, at the same time, exciting. It was a contradiction I could not explain. Not then.

As we were leaving the prison, I asked her to join me for lunch at a restaurant in Armagh city. My heart leapt when she accepted and I should have been wary of that. I had long ago decided there would be no other special woman in my life.

"Sorcha told me your wife died," she said after we had ordered our food. "I know it may be a painful subject for you, but I thought you ought to know what I've been told."

"We were married for sixteen years," I said, wondering why I had told her that. I quickly added, "We married young."

"It was cancer, so Sorcha said."

"Breast cancer."

"You miss her a lot?"

"You'll never know how much."

She put a hand over mine. "I'm sorry, but I felt I ought to raise the subject before we talk about other things. So we both know where we stand. Now let's talk about this book you're writing. What prompted you to write about Bloody Friday? Why not Bloody Sunday?"

I thought for a few moments. "I suppose it was because Bloody Friday more closely epitomizes all that's wrong with Northern Ireland. Bloody Sunday was a mistake. A damn stupid and irresponsible mistake, and there are people who should be held to account for it. But Bloody Friday was a different matter altogether. It wasn't a mistake. It was a deliberate attempt to intimidate and kill innocent people, and that murderous hatred is right at the heart of all that's happened here. I remember seeing the images of Bloody Friday on the television news that evening. Bits of human body being shovelled into plastic bags. Did you see it, Susan, on your television? Did you see the bodies being bundled into bags?"

"Yes." She stared at me with something approaching alarm, as if she suddenly realized she had stirred up something dangerous by her question. How does an Irish woman feel about stirring up the emotions of an Englishman? It occurred to me that she had been assessing me on the basis of my past rather than my nationality. That was not the norm in Northern Ireland.

"It sickened me." I was aware my voice was growing louder as I spoke, but I couldn't help it. "These were innocent people going about their lawful business, killed because of the deep hatred that pervades this place. I can't wipe those images from my mind. I need to write about them."

She studied me thoughtfully. "You sound like a man with a conscience. But the killing wasn't any of your doing."

"Of course it wasn't my doing. I was in the *Belfast Telegraph* news office that day, taking reports of the bombs as they came in. But I went out into the streets in the aftermath, when the bombing had ended, and I spoke to people who went through the horror of it. I saw the effect it had on them. I saw their pain while it was still raw inside their heads, and I wasn't able to do anything to help them."

She withdrew her hand and leaned back in her seat. "I was briefly living in England at the time, working over there. I saw the same television news reports, but it didn't affect me the same way. Revulsion, yes, but not the lasting pain you feel."

"This book will be my catharsis," I said. I didn't want to question her true feelings about Irish violence. Not then.

"I hope it works," she said.

I took a deep, calming breath. "Tell me about your day

job." I said, anxious to change the subject.

"Counselling." She ran the tip of her tongue across her upper lip. "I help people get over traumas. There's a big need for it here in Belfast."

"I can believe that. It must be a satisfying job."

She shook her head. "I wouldn't call it that. I see too many emotionally and psychologically damaged people, and there are some I can never help. No, there's nothing satisfying in seeing the real victims of this endless violence, even when I can help them."

"But you do help some of them. You just said so."

"That's the whole point, isn't it? I wish there was no need for it."

"You've helped Sorcha," I suggested.

"Not in the way you're probably thinking. I'm not a forensic psychologist. Prison visiting is something I do as a sideline. Sorcha hasn't opened up her heart to me, or told me why she killed those men – if she really did kill them - and I don't press the matter. Mostly, I try to play the part of a friend. I think she has a real need for friends."

I had no answer to that, so I turned to more agreeable matters and I began to enjoy Susan's company. In some ways it was almost like being with Annie again. Most of the time we seemed to understand each other without having to labour the explanations.

At the end of the meal she drove me to the cemetery in Belfast and I showed her Annie's grave. We didn't stay long but I was glad she was there, listening while I told her how it had been for Annie and me. Then we drove back to my hotel. When I said goodbye to her, I harboured a fierce hope that I would hear more from this prison visitor. In the meantime, I needed to ready myself to talk to Martin Foster the next day.

In my room I turned on the television news to hear that John Lennon had been shot in New York. Another mindless killing.

Chapter Twelve

December 1980

The next day I telephoned Martin and asked him to meet me for lunch. I thought it might be easier for both him and his wife, Emily, if I did not turn up at their house. We got down to business over a very palatable meal in the hotel restaurant. I made a note to ensure the receipt went straight onto my tax return as a legitimate expense.

"You said in court that you witnessed a riot and you thought Sorcha was caught up in it," I said to him when the food was served. "I have the gist of it, so how about you now tell me what happened in detail."

"You really are going into this affair with a fine toothcomb, aren't you?" he said.

"That's what journalism is all about. You find out everything in general and then sift out the bits that are important enough to warrant a deeper examination."

"And you won't incriminate me in any way?"

I grinned. "A policeman called Will Evans has the same reservations. You didn't kill anyone, did you?"

"Of course not."

"Well then, be quite sure, Martin, that I will not incriminate you. I just want to know the truth. All of it."

"You heard what was said in court."

"Yes. And I wonder just how much was not said."

***

Friday 21st July 1972
1205 BST

On his way home, Martin walked into a riot. He turned a corner at the junction of the Shankill Road and North Castle Street and there it was. A Loyalist riot. He had heard no gunfire as he approached the area so - at first - he wasn't unduly worried; he'd seen too many riots in Belfast to get himself into an immediate panic. That level of alarm was reserved for when the serious shooting began. This incident was almost normality.

Brick-and-petrol-bomb riots sprang up all over the city on a daily basis, like fast-growing weeds in a derelict garden. One minute there was no sign of trouble and then the whole area was aflame with feral insurgents baying for blood. Humanity went out the window to be replaced by callous violence. Some riots were spontaneous. Many, especially Republican riots, were planned right down to the cast list. Which Belfast mammies would shield the hidden gunmen? Which schoolchildren would distract the troops with a salvo of bricks while the snipers got into position? Often, it was a well-orchestrated drama.

Sometimes the disturbances blew themselves out in an hour or two. Sometimes they went on for days. There was no apparent logic for predicting how any one of them would pan out. There would be a concocted excuse for this particular Loyalist riot; a police raid on a UVF house maybe? Whatever the excuse was, it would have been forgotten by now. Once started, Belfast violence became self-perpetuating, growing out of an in-built anger that defied all reason.

The noise continued; exploding petrol bombs, bricks bouncing across the road, cars set on fire, loud voices raised in rage and resentment. An orchestrated symphony of civil war.

The army riot squad stood well back from the mob, watching without interfering, deflecting any hurled missiles with their shields. The police were lined up behind the army, also watching without getting drawn into battle. Let the buggers tire themselves out seemed to be the tactic in use here, one which had worked well elsewhere. You didn't need to be a soldier or peeler to understand the tactics in Belfast. It was all on regular display.

One of the soldiers turned to look at Martin. He looked like a youngster, eighteen or nineteen years old, maybe. He must have been a recent arrival here because his eyes expressed his sense of horror. What on earth would he make of this outpouring of pure undiluted hatred? Would he have any understanding of why a Loyalist mob was attacking them? They were supposed to be loyal to Britain, weren't they? Wasn't that why they called themselves Loyalists? And yet they would kill a British soldier without a moment's hesitation if the excuse arose. And if this young man was killed what would his English parents in their neat and tidy English villa in their quiet leafy suburban street make of it? What would their polite English vicar be able to say to them that would make any sense in the face of this madness?

Turn back and face the mob, soldier, and try to make some sense of it. If you can do that maybe you will be better able to ensure something like this never happens in your own country.

Martin breathed hard and tried to suppress the shame he felt for the behaviour of his fellow countrymen... his Loyalist fellow countrymen. Nothing could excuse such raw odium.

He was about to walk on when he saw one of the rioters stumble and fall. It was a young woman wearing a short denim skirt, a white tee shirt and a short coat. The girl's head was turned away from him, but he had no doubts about who it was. In those clothes it had to be Sorcha. What the hell was she doing here? Why in God's name was she caught up amongst a Loyalist mob?

"Sorcha!" The cry erupted from his lips as he ran closer to the police line.

A uniformed policeman in riot gear, standing well behind the army front line, turned and put out a hand to stop him. "Stay back. You could get hurt if you're not careful."

Martin pointed to the girl, now sprawled face-down on

the ground. "I know who that girl is," he said. "She's not one of them. She shouldn't be there."

"Nothing you can do about it," the policeman said firmly. "Keep away. Look, she's getting to her feet. Can't be hurt too badly."

The girl staggered away from the front line of the rioting mob, heading towards a brick wall daubed with graffiti. *Death to the IRA. Fuck the Pope. Taigs out!* Someone from round here, it seemed, was able to spell.

The girl was looking back at the rioters, her face partially hidden by the mousy hair flapping around her cheeks. No one made any attempt to stop her as she continued along a pavement that skirted the fringes of the trouble.

"She's obviously had enough," the policeman said. "She's getting out. Coming our way too."

Sure enough, the girl lurched closer towards the security line. She reached the end of the confrontation, well clear of the bricks and petrol bombs that formed the centrepiece of the skirmish. Martin felt a surge of relief; he had every expectation that she would be able to continue to safety.

And then a gunshot rang out.

He felt his blood run cold as the girl threw up her arms and fell to the ground.

"Oh God, no!"

He wanted to run to her, but the policeman grabbed at his arm and held him back. A loud cry erupted from his mouth, but he had no control over his words. They were stifled back inside his throat.

Something - he wasn't sure what - made him switch his focus back to the mob and a figure in the background. Just a hazy image of a man holding a rifle. He knew enough about terrorist weaponry to know it would be an M1 Garand rifle of World War Two vintage. Belfast gunman had easy access to those rifles. That was no surprise. But the man... it was that UVF thug.

Mad Mac McKinnon!

Martin had seen his photographs in the paper and on the local television news. The figure melted back into the heart of the mob, which swarmed around him, forming a protective screen. Why would he want to kill Sorcha?

Martin looked again at the victim, lying on the ground in a pool of blood. He put a hand to his racing heart and tried to speak, but couldn't. Sorcha! Only a short while ago, he had turned his back on her and now she was shot, probably dead. A terrible bleakness filled his thoughts and the noise of the baying mob faded into the background. All he heard was the muffled noise of a loud wind in his ears. The sound of his blood pressure raised to danger level.

Dear Sorcha! There was no way he could tell her he was sorry. For all the anger he had shown towards her, he was now very sorry.

The army officer in charge must have given a new order because two men moved up from the rear and began firing rubber bullets. The sound was unlike the sound of ordinary gunfire. Each shot made a fuller, rounder noise. The soldiers aimed at the feet of the rioters and the long, black bullets bounced between their legs, bruising and paining as they flew. Under cover of the firing, a four-man snatch squad moved forward, two men in body armour holding riot shields, and two more sheltering behind them. They grabbed the fallen figure and dragged her back to the cover of their own line. There were no more gunshots from the rioters, but petrol bombs were now aimed towards the men who had recovered the girl. Her death was, seemingly, not enough to satisfy the mob mentality.

Martin pushed aside the policeman beside him and ran to where the girl now lay, immediately behind the army line. She was face-up on the ground, an army medic already bending over her, and Martin saw instantly that it was not Sorcha.

Thank God, it wasn't her!

"Is she…?" he asked.

"Shot through the heart," the medic said. "Didn't stand a chance."

The policeman came up behind them. He caught Martin's arm again. "You said you know who she is."

"No. Not her. That's not her," he said sadly. How could he be anything but sad at the death of a young girl, someone who should have had a whole lifetime ahead of her? "I thought I knew who it was, but I was wrong. It's not her."

The policeman seemed far less emotional. "Too bad. It's a fair bet one or more of the rioters will know who she is, but they're not going to tell us, are they?"

Martin took a step back and tried to think logically. Why was the girl wearing Sorcha's clothes? Because, sure as hell, they really were her clothes.

"Wherever you are, and whatever you're doing, I hope to God you're safe, Sorcha," he muttered.

"Maybe she's got some identification on her." The policeman rifled through her pockets and pulled out a sheet of paper. He studied it for a few seconds. "What the hell is this all about? A list of places in Belfast. Not a tourist, is she? We don't get many tourists over here." After a moment he folded it and put it in his pocket. "I'll report this when I get back to base."

***

Friday 21st July 1972
1225 BST

Emily Foster was still at Aunt Judy's house when Martin finally walked in the front door. She was busy at the kitchen sink, a diminutive figure in a light summer dress that emphasised her slender teenage figure, washing dishes that had probably not been touched since the previous day.

"Where's Aunt Judy?" he asked.

Emily glanced back over a shoulder. "She went to the shops to get some bread. She wanted to make sandwiches for lunch. She should have been back by now."

He stood beside her, knowing full well that their aunt would have done little if any of the tasks that needed doing around the house. "Have you been working hard here all morning?"

"There were things needed doing, Martin." She pulled her hands from the water, wiped at them with a tea towel and turned to face him. "You look pale. Are you not feeling well?"

He didn't answer the question because he was not sure exactly what was wrong with him. Was it self-recrimination? Was it anger from the discovery that Sorcha was not as innocent as he had once imagined? Or, most likely, was it the residual feeling of horror that came from seeing a girl shot dead and thinking it was Sorcha?

He picked up the kettle and asked, "Would you like a mug of coffee?"

"Sure. And there's biscuits in the biscuit tin." A pause and then, "What's worrying you? Something is, isn't it?"

"Something rather personal."

"Is it the girl you've been seeing?"

He looked up suddenly. "You know about that?"

"I may be younger than you, Martin, but I'm not stupid. I've seen you sneaking off time and again, and I've watched from my bedroom window and seen you come home late. It has to be a girl."

"Female logic." He tried to rustle up a grin.

"I'm right, aren't I? There is someone. Do you want to talk about it?"

Of course he did, and there was no one else he would rather talk to than Emily. But would she understand? Would she be prepared to keep his secret: that he had been to bed with a Catholic?

He poured hot water into two mugs of coffee granules. He knew she liked milk and sugar. In fact he knew more about Emily than he knew about any other girl, including Sorcha. She was, he sometimes thought, like a kid sister; a sister he could be at ease with. Someone who understood him.

They sat at the kitchen table. "There is someone, Emily. And I've been very naïve. Utterly stupid, in fact. I thought she was different to other girls. I thought I was in love with her. And now…"

184

"And now…?"

"I don't know. The thing is… she's a Catholic."

A look of surprise crossed Emily's face. She grabbed at her mug and it rattled on the place mat. "Oh God, Martin. That could be a real problem. You know what Aunt Judy says about Catholics."

Yes, he knew well enough. The Reverend Ian's condemnation of Catholic ideology made a big impact on Aunt Judy. "There's more to it than that. This girl lives in a Nationalist area and I think she may be mixed up with some bad people."

"IRA?"

"Might be."

"Are you sure about that?"

"No. How can I be sure? But it seems possible."

"Find out for sure, Martin. Don't condemn her until you're absolutely sure. You may have made a mistake." She sipped at her coffee. "What's her name?"

"Sorcha. Sorcha Mulveny."

"A sure-fire Catholic name. How did you meet her?"

He was glad now that he finally had someone to talk to, someone who would at least try to understand. He told her about the time Sorcha tripped and fell on the pavement in Royal Avenue. He told her how he had taken her to a café for a cup of coffee to help her. The more he talked, the easier it became, easier to unburden his secrets.

"After that first meeting, we just seemed to click together," he said. "We got on so well together."

"Have you slept with her?" The question came from Emily unexpectedly. She watched him carefully over the lip of her mug.

He curled his hands around his own mug and stared down into the steaming coffee. "Yes."

"I see."

When he looked up, he saw that she had lowered her gaze and he thought he detected a look of sadness in her face. "Are you cross?" he asked.

"Your life is your own, Martin," she said.

"She wasn't the first," he replied.

"I know that. Your first was Marjorie Cummins, but that was never going to come to anything. She wasn't right for you. Too pushy by far. There were other girls as well, weren't there? Other girls who weren't right for you. This girl, Sorcha Mulveny, must have come well down the list, but it looks like you might have made yet another mistake. You really are a one for getting mixed up with the wrong girls, Martin."

"Stupid?"

"Utterly."

He couldn't argue with that. "How will I ever know if she really is wrong for me?" he said.

"Talk to her, Martin. You have to talk to her and find out the truth about her. That's all I can advise."

"That's the problem. I don't know where she is. I thought I saw her on the way home. Mixed up in a riot. It was a girl wearing the same clothes, but it wasn't Sorcha." He decided to say nothing about the shooting. Emily didn't need to know about that.

"Well, you'd better go and find her, hadn't you?"

"I suppose so. And what about you, Emily? Will this affect our friendship?"

She set down her mug hand. "Martin Foster, you know damned well I've been in love with you since we were both small kids. Nothing has changed and nothing will change until the day you marry. And most likely it won't be to me. At least I'm sensible enough to see that."

"Thank you," he said.

"Now go and find that girl and talk to her. Find out the truth, Martin, once and for all."

She was right, of course, he would have to go back out there and find Sorcha, make his peace with her and get to the truth behind her life. Then he pictured again the image of the girl in Sorcha's clothes. What was going on? Maybe the police would know something.

It was worth asking.

December 1980

Martin didn't touch alcohol, so it was left to me to finish the bottle of wine I'd ordered. Another cost that would go down as a legitimate expense on my tax return.

"So you went out looking for her," I said. "I presume you found her?"

"Eventually. But the bombs were exploding by then. You know that she was caught up in those explosions?"

"Yes. I heard her testimony in court, but I've still to learn the detail of what happened to her. It affected her badly, didn't it?"

He nodded. "She saw people killed, saw the bodies... there was one killing in particular... a young woman with a baby...did she tell you about that?"

"Not yet." We were running ahead of the story here and I wasn't yet ready to delve into what Sorcha saw. I wanted to hear all of that directly from her.

It was, however, clearly a problem in Martin's thoughts. "It upset me when she told me about it, but... what could I do? It wasn't my problem..."

Not his problem? He must have realised that his words carried no conviction. I sensed that he wanted to say more, but he knew how most English people regarded the Ulster violence and he was wary of getting into an argument with me. It was the only way to avoid facing the truth. The more honest Ulster Irish sometimes did that, in those odd moments when the truth became too much to bear. They told us outsiders what they thought we wanted to hear, and then told each other something a little more acceptable to their own ears. Maybe it was something we all did when the facts became too painful.

"Sorcha will tell me about it in time," I said.

Martin pushed his plate away from him and glanced at his watch. He'd eaten only half the meal. "I'd better be going now. I promised Emily I wouldn't stay more than an hour."

"She worries about you?" I was disappointed at ending the conversation there. I had more questions to ask about his experience of the run-up to the bombings.

"Far too much," he said, and the look on his face told me she was right to worry. Eight years had passed and it was so obvious that he was still affected by what happened on Bloody Friday.

Chapter Thirteen

December 1980

It was raining heavily, and the forecast looked bad for the next few days, so I cancelled my planned drive over to Wales. Instead, I telephoned Will Evans one Friday evening. Milly and the girls were at the cinema and Will was preparing to go out to his local pub, but he'd give me half an hour of his time.

It wasn't much but I aimed to make the most of it.

"Tell me what happened after that car bomb. The one you came so close to."

* * *

Friday 21st July 1972
1255 BST

Will and McIlroy had to take a detour on the way back to their police barracks to avoid the Shankill riot. Will was exhausted as they strode past the North Castle Street front desk area. He wasn't physically hurt… well not too much… but he was mentally washed out.

The duty sergeant tried to intercept them, but McIlroy brushed him aside.

"The Superintendent wants…" the sergeant began.

"He can bloody well want!" McIlroy snapped and led Will on along the corridor to their office.

"We could go straight to the canteen for a coffee," Will said.

"Bugger that. We need something stronger." McIlroy

pulled open the office door with a force born out of raw resentment.

Will followed him in and slammed the office door behind them. The DCI grabbed a bottle of whiskey and two glasses from a desk drawer. They each downed the first glass in one go. The next ones went down slower. Will felt marginally better as the alcohol began to take effect. His breath would be tainted when he got home, and Milly wouldn't like that, but it was a small price to pay.

McIlroy's face was pale and his eyes had taken on a spasmodic tic. He put his feet up on his desk, but he was far from at ease. Then his phone rang. He put down his glass with a look of annoyance and picked up the receiver. His irritation continued to show on his face as he listened and made the occasional 'yes, I understand' reply. He silently mouthed the word 'Boyle' to Will and scowled. There was no use of the word 'sir' and that still bothered Will. His boss was suffering because of their senior officer and there was nothing he could do about it.

McIlroy finished by saying, "I'll tell him straight away."

"That was our beloved leader," he said when he put down the receiver. He picked up his glass, drained it and refilled it.

"And what news did he have for us, boss?" Will waited expectantly. He had a notion something important was coming. After a few silent of seconds, he added, "Why didn't you tell him what happened to us out there in the jungle?"

"Later, Will. When I feel calmer. It always helps to make reports of that ilk when you've calmed down." The DCI studied the amber liquid and then took another deep gulp. Finally, he said, "In the meantime I have some good news and some bad news from our beloved leader. The good news is that your annual leave will be reinstated with effect from tomorrow morning. You and the family can bugger off to Wales."

Will let out a sigh of relief. "And the bad news?"

"Too many informants are coming up with the same story

as Jimmy Fish. There really is something big in the offing, so we're both on compulsory overtime until this evening. We should know by then what it's all about."

The damper came down on Will's mood. "Damn. Milly will be furious if I'm late home."

"It isn't your doing, Will. She can't blame you. Give her a call and tell her the good news first."

"And when she hears the bad news she'll have more ammunition to harp on about us getting out of Ireland for good. And she'll be right."

"You think so?"

"It was my decision to carry on working here. I went against her better judgement. Maybe I was wrong all along. Maybe I've been unkind to my wife and daughters. Maybe I should call in at the church on the way home."

"A lot of 'maybes', Will."

"Maybe that's why I should go to confession."

McIlroy gave a short, cold chuckle. "Wrong solution, Will. You Catholics spend too much time confessing to your priests. You know what I say? I say that if you do wrong you should say sorry to the person you hurt, not your priest. Tell Milly you're sorry, Will. Tell her... not your priest. Make it up to her as best you can. Take her to bed as soon as you get home. It's what I would have done with my missus if she hadn't left me."

"You think sex is the answer?" Will took another sip of whiskey.

"For you or me?"

"Either of us, boss."

He shook his head. "Damned if I know."

Will went silent for a full minute. The problem between McIlroy and his wife was none of his business. He was curious about it, wanted to find out how the problem arose, who was really to blame: Boyle or Mrs McIlroy? Or both? But it wasn't his place to ask.

Instead, he said, "Do you remember that film, the one that was in the cinema a while back? Two years ago I think it was. The one where they said love is not having to say you're sorry?"

McIlroy snorted loudly. "Load of bollocks. They got it all wrong, didn't they? Typical Hollywood nonsense. You want my thoughts on it? I reckon love is not doing the things that require you to say sorry. That's what they should have said in the film. Don't do the things that require you to say you're sorry. And if you do go wrong, have the courage to say you're sorry."

Will's thoughts were clouding because of the whiskey, but he saw the sense in his boss's words. Why didn't he see it before? He would have a lot to say to Milly when he got home. He emptied his glass and reached out to the bottle for another refill. "I hadn't thought of it like that. You're a bit of a philosopher, aren't you, boss?"

"Maybe. Or maybe it's the whiskey talking. There's another thing you should know. Something Boyle just told me, about the knife used to kill Johnny Dunlop,"

"Yes?"

"It was a serrated kitchen knife. It could be the same one that was used to take off that boy's dick."

"Could be?"

"Or one very similar. My gut feeling is that the same weapon was probably used."

"And Jimmy Fish? Was the same knife used on him?"

"No. He was knifed with a straight edge, not a serrated one."

"So maybe we have two killers?"

"Or one killer with two knives. Knives are two a penny on the streets around here."

"So are the bombs."

The phone rang again. Will picked it up this time. It was the front desk.

"There's a guy here at the desk, Will. Wants to talk to someone about a missing girl."

"What's his name?"

A brief silence followed while the desk sergeant questioned the visitor. Then he spoke again into the phone. "Says his name is Martin Foster. He thinks the missing girl may be in some sort of trouble. Thinks she may get shot."

"Have we any relevant information?"

"There's news just coming in about a girl who was shot in that riot at the end of the street. No details yet. There's nothing else that fits."

"Okay. Hang on to him. I'll be along straight away." Will slammed down the phone and eased himself to his feet. "Someone at the front desk wants to talk to us about a missing girl. Could be a shooting. You want in on it?"

"Might as well." McIlroy screwed the top back on his whiskey bottle. "You can do the interview and I'll take the notes."

They collected the man from the front desk, took him to an interview room and sat opposite him.

Will introduced himself and McIlroy, and then he asked, "Tell us about your problem."

The young man placed his forearms flat on the desk and clasped his hands together. "It's my girlfriend. I think she may be in danger and I can't find her. I need to know if you have word of any relevant killings in this area in the past few hours."

"You think she may have been killed?" Will said, ignoring the request for information.

"It's possible. There was a girl shot on a riot line. Less than an hour ago. I was there. It wasn't her, but that girl was…"

"Hold on there, will you." Will noticed his boss struggling with his notes. "First, let's get some basic information for our records. Can you just confirm again your name and your address?"

"Martin Foster."

"Address?"

He gave an address in Harold Street.

"And your girlfriend's name is…?

"Sorcha Mulveny."

"Sorcha…?" Will jerked upright in his seat and glanced at McIlroy. "I see. Now, tell us why you think she may be in danger."

"I was about to tell you. The girl I saw was shot in a riot at the end of this street, by the junction with the Shankill Road. She was wearing Sorcha's clothes."

"Similar clothes?"

"No. Not similar. They were Sorcha's clothes." His voice carried a measure of insistence. "That's why I think something bad may have happened to her. That's why I came here."

McIlroy leaned sideways and put a hand on Will's arm. It was a sign he wanted to speak. He drew back his lips and asked, "Martin, why don't you tell us something about Sorcha Mulveny? If we're to help you, we need to know more about her. You said you saw her in a riot."

"I thought it was her because of the clothes she was wearing. But it wasn't her."

"Not her, but it was her clothes?"

"That's right."

McIlroy paused before asking a critical question. "Sorcha is a common Catholic name. I take it you are both Catholics?"

"She is. I'm not."

Will gave McIlroy a knowing look. A mixed match in Belfast: if one side didn't get you, the other would.

"That riot was in a Loyalist area. What would Sorcha be doing there?"

"I don't know. But it's where the other girl was shot. The one who was wearing her clothes."

"I see. And how long have you known Sorcha?"

"A month or so."

McIlroy nodded and went on in an apparently amiable tone that Will recognised as subterfuge, a way of getting the young man to discard any inhibitions. "All right, Martin. Does Sorcha have any connections with any Republican organisations? People who might want to harm her?" He was careful not to mention IRA or INLA.

The young man's eyebrows twitched, as if he was troubled by the question. "I think she has connections with some unsavoury people."

"Such as?"

"There's a man called Fitzpain."

Will tensed. That name again! "What about him?"

"We were at a hotel in Oldpark Road this morning, me and Sorcha. And this man turned up. She told me I had to leave straight away, as soon as he got there."

"I see. And did you leave?"

"Yes."

"So you didn't see what happened between him and Sorcha?"

"No."

"Then what?"

"I met her later in Royal Avenue. We had a row and I haven't seen her since. Then I saw this girl in her clothes… at the riot… and that girl was shot dead. And…"

"Yes?"

Martin's eyes were now burning with ill-controlled fear. "I saw someone with a gun. I thought it was one of those UVF thugs, the one they call Mad Mac McKinnon. But I could have been mistaken."

McIlroy maintained his calm approach. "What happened to McKinnon? If it was him?"

"He lost himself amongst the mob."

"That's the way his sort operate, Martin. And that's when you decided Sorcha could be in real danger? Is that right?"

"Yes." The young man kept his arms firmly on the table, but his fingers were twitching.

"Why would the UVF be after Sorcha Mulveny?"

"I don't know." He stared straight into McIlroy's face, his gaze fixed and unblinking. Will knew instantly he was telling the truth.

"I see," McIlroy continued. "Have you tried the hospitals?"

"All of them. They couldn't help."

"All right, Martin. There's not a lot we can do right now. We certainly don't have any information that will be of help to you, but we will get back to you if we discover anything."

"She's not in trouble with the police, is she?"

"Not that I'm aware of." McIlroy kept a straight face.

"I thought I'd ask because you are policemen."

"An astute observation, Martin." McIlroy rose from his seat to indicate the interview was ended.

Will escorted the young man back to the front desk and reassured him again that they would be in touch if they had any news. He looked distinctly worried as he left the building.

Back in their office, McIlroy planted himself in the chair behind his desk, raised his arms, leaned back and intertwined his hands behind his head. "What do you make of that young man, Will?"

"Naïve."

"I agree. Heading for a disaster if he's not careful," the DCI said. "Meanwhile the Mulveny girl could be in real danger. If McKinnon and the UVF are after her, she's dead meat. But we now know a little bit more about her, especially that she may be mixed up with Republican dissidents."

Will sat in his own chair and studied the few notes his boss had made. "Not a lot we can do about it. What do you think she's done to piss off the UVF?"

"Who knows? Maybe it's because of that lad who had his dick cut off... he was a Protestant, wasn't he? And he was found right behind the Mulveny's house. I have a feeling that Sorcha Mulveny may hold the key to a number of investigations. Not just the lad who ended up with no dick. She could also be involved with the killing of Johnny Dunlop and Jimmy Fish. If she's dead, the vital information will have gone with her. I'd rather like to find her alive."

"And interview her?"

McIlroy replied through gritted teeth. "With a just enough pressure to find out what she really knows." He was still gritting his teeth when the telephone rang again.

He picked up the receiver.

"Yes?" His expression turned to alarm as he listened. "Okay. We'll take the York Road one."

"Trouble?" Will said as the receiver was slammed down.

McIlroy rose quickly from his seat. "Our beloved leader again. The bomb warnings have started. Just two so far: York Road Railway Station and Smithfield Bus Station. Come on, Will. This could be what Jimmy Fish was telling us about."

Will looked at the wall clock. It was now 1345. How much warning had been given? Would they have time to get there before the bomb exploded?

"What about lunch?" he asked.

"Pick up a couple of sandwiches from the canteen on the way out. We may be busy for the rest of the day."

***

December 1980

The half hour had stretched into an hour and I had learned a lot. I thanked will for his time and then I read through the first draft of what would be Part One of the book. The story was coming together well, but something bothered me. The image that emerged from the printed pages was one of horror, and it was going to get worse. Far worse. Was I being fair to the people of Northern Ireland? Was I right to rake over such a terrible day in Irish history? Would it be more helpful if I allowed those events to fade in people's minds?

I put the project aside for twenty-four hours while I thought about it. That I evening I picked up a book at random. It was an analysis of the aftermath of World War Two; a book I had used several times while researching the war. The pages fell open at a chapter on holocaust denial. There was my answer. Horrific events in history were denied to suit a political agenda. That was why it was important for me to record in detail the experiences of Sorcha Mulveny, Martin Foster and Will Evans.

I took a sheet of paper, wrote in big letters, NEVER FORGET, and pinned it to the wall behind my desk.

Then I soldiered on.

Previous books had needed more interviews before I reached this stage, but I had learned from past experience. For this book, I was covering less ground in each interview, but I was covering it more thoroughly. I would never need to go over the same material a second time, but I knew that my next interviews would be harder to conduct.

I had now come to the point where the bombs began to explode.

PART TWO

When killing is a way of life,
who weeps for the dead?

Chapter Fourteen

December 1980

I flew over to Belfast one Sunday evening and booked into the Europa Hotel. The following morning I met Susan Miller in the restaurant at Anderson and McCauley's in Donegall Place. It was a convenient place for us to chat over a cup of coffee before we headed off to the prison in Armagh. She seemed to be pleased to see me. I found myself glancing at her left hand and noticing the absence of both a wedding ring and an engagement ring. It wasn't conclusive, of course, but I made a resolve to try to see more of her.

"The next bit of the story is going to be painful for Sorcha to talk about," I said once we were seated well away from the few other customers. "How do you think she will cope with it?"

Susan gave it a moment's thought, pursing her lips as she did so. "She told me weeks ago that she needs to do this, however difficult it may be. How will she cope? I think a lot will depend upon how you approach the subject."

"Your advice?"

"Just let her talk. Don't interrupt her with questions. Don't try to guide the conversation. Let her find her own path through the mire. If you want to ask anything, wait until the end of the interview. If she clams up at that point you won't have lost much."

"Is this how you conduct your counselling sessions?"

She shook her head. "I'm not here to counsel Sorcha, just to be a friend. But I would also like to help you with *your* problems."

She stared into my eyes and I felt very uncomfortable. "Help *me*? Why?"

"Because I think this book could help you find the sort of inner peace you need. You do need closure, you know."

"Closure?"

"There are demons lurking inside your brain. I've watched you and I've seen the clues. Believe me, you need help." Her voice was clear but gentle, and her eyes radiated an inner conviction, as if she was working on a deep assessment of me.

A sudden jolt of annoyance ran through me. No one had ever before confronted with such candid words. I forced myself to keep calm. "Why do you say that?"

Her gaze never wavered. "Every time you come back to Belfast you remember the life you had here with your wife. You need to move on."

"You think so?"

"I know so."

I blinked in surprise. "You could have misjudged me."

"Possible, but I've a lot of experience seeing such things in others. You still keep the pain inside you. There are moments when I see it in your face and I hear it in your voice."

"And the book will help?"

"It will force you to see pain in others and seek out the reasons. I think that will lead to you face up to your own destructive emotions."

I tried to act as if I wasn't convinced, didn't want to be convinced, but I had an inner feeling she might have been right. And that made me even more uncomfortable.

Shortly afterwards she drove me to the prison. In the event, she was right on one count. I allowed Sorcha to talk uninterrupted and her words quickly took on a force of their own, as if she was desperate to tell all.

***

Friday 21st July 1972
1350 BST

Sorcha approached the Smithfield Bus Station with a measure of trepidation. Could she now do something morally good to make up for the bad things that lay behind her? Could she somehow atone for her sins?

The blue and white buses were operating as usual. Hordes of passengers were coming and going as usual. In fact, everything looked so normal here, she thought, just like any other Friday. But give it another fifteen to twenty minutes and it would all change. There would be carnage here unless these passengers and shoppers could be shepherded away to safety. Could she do the decent thing without being caught?

She paused at the corner of Samuel Street, deep in thought. By now there would be telephone bomb warnings to the police. So many warnings that the police would be completely overwhelmed. How would they determine which were real warnings and which were the hoaxes? The sheer number was all part of the IRA strategy to confuse the peelers and the army. Was that why no attempt had yet been made to clear this bus station? Was this one of the locations where the warnings had been swamped by sheer numbers and overlooked?

She gritted her teeth with a feeling of determination. What could she do here that might save a few lives? Could she go amongst the people and tell them all to get away? Now, quickly, before the first bomb exploded? It was an idea, but who would listen to her? No, she decided, that wouldn't work. She had to get someone else to deliver a warning, someone the shoppers would heed.

Two peelers were patrolling just one hundred yards away. Could she warn them? And almost certainly get herself arrested on the spot? Only someone in on the act would be able to deliver such a warning. The police would have her locked up in double quick time. No, she would have to find someone else to sound the warning. Someone who would not be seen as a bomber.

She turned at the sound of a horn, in time to see a car swerve into an enclosed yard close by the station building. Two pedestrians jumped aside to avoid being knocked down. Shorcha recognised the driver straight away. She had seen him with Fitzpain on several occasions: a short fat man with a squeaky voice. He was reputed to have planted other bombs; bombs which had killed and maimed many innocents. The car disappeared from Sorcha's view. She put a hand to her thumping heart: the Smithfield bomb was now in place. And nothing was being done to get people away. There was little time left. She had to act quickly.

Who would listen to her? Because she was wearing a brand new dress, she no longer looked like the backstreet scrubber she really was. Maybe she could take advantage of that. Maybe she could pass herself off as someone else, someone people would listen to. There was no time left to think about it: she would have to give it a try.

She went into a small café where a dozen or more passengers were taking a last cup of tea before boarding their buses. No one took any notice of her. Of course not; her new appearance would not signify any threat. The muted noise of easy chatter continued to fill the room; the sound of people who had no idea what was about to happen.

Two priests sat near the door. The older one was tall, heavily-built and balding. The younger one was thin, weedy with protruding teeth and a gawky expression. No prizes for guessing who was the senior priest and who was the curate. They had cups of tea in their hands and a plate of biscuits on the table in front of them, and they seemed to be deep in discussion.

It had to be them, Sorcha decided. But who could she pretend to be? There was no time to prevaricate, so she pulled up a chair and sat between them. She tried to adopt the sort of voice a policewoman would adopt. It wasn't easy when she was confronting two priests and she was wearing nothing beneath the dress.

She said, "I want you to listen to me carefully."

Both men stared at her, seemingly taken aback by her audacity. The young, gawky one put down his teacup and it rattled in the saucer. Neither man spoke.

Sorcha continued, still struggling to put on an official-sounding voice. "Youse don't know me, but youse have to believe what I tell youse. A car bomb is going to explode within the next ten minutes or so. It's important to get as many people as possible away from here, but it has to be done without causing alarm."

The older priest frowned at her. "Who are you and what…"

Sorcha held up a hand to stop him in mid flow, her mind working fast as she concocted her story. "Police. CID. There's a couple of our uniformed men just across the road. I want youse to go over there and tell them to start clearing the area. If they don't, people are gonna get killed."

She leaned back in the seat. Damn. Why couldn't she say 'you' instead of youse? The word just wouldn't come out right.

"Why can't you tell them?" the older priest asked.

She glanced around the room before replying. "Because I have to stay here and clear this café, and there are people in here… suspects I'll need to follow when they leave. I can't tell you any more than that. Youse'll have to take my word for it."

The priest sounded deeply suspicious. "Where exactly is the bomb?"

Sorcha pointed. "It's a car bomb and it's already in place, sitting in that yard over there."

"Is this some sort of joke?" He didn't sound convinced.

"No, far from it. God help me, Father, this is deadly serious. Either youse warn them two policemen or people are gonna die here."

"How do you know about this bomb?" the younger priest asked.

"For heaven's sake, stop asking awkward questions. Just do as I say." She stood up. "This really is no joke, I promise

205

you. There's still time to get people away to safety, so go and warn those two men now. I have to stay here if I'm to keep track of possible suspects."

The two priests rose from their seats in unison and the older man pointed a thick forefinger at her. "If this is a joke…"

Sorcha jabbed her clenched fists at her hips. "For Heaven's sake! You must believe me."

"You say you're CID. How can we believe that? You could be one of the bombers."

She lowered her voice to an insistent hiss. "Would I be trying to get people away if I was one of them? For God's sake, don't argue with me. Do it now!"

The severity in her voice must have worked because the men turned towards the door without another word. Leaving behind their tea and their biscuits, they hurried from the café. Sorcha watched them cross the road and confront the two policemen.

She breathed deeply to calm herself. So far, so good.

Now she strode up to the café counter and spoke to a fat, middle-aged woman pouring out cups of tea. She had a cigarette dangling from her mouth.

"Do you have a back door?" Sorcha asked.

"Who wants to know?" The woman didn't even look up.

"Police. Plainclothes CID."

For God's sake don't ask me for a warrant card.

"What are you up to?" The cigarette was glued to the woman's lips as if by magic.

"There's a car bomb across the road. When it goes off it's going to blow in yer windows and cut up yer customers. It may even wreck yer café completely. We need these people out now. The back way."

The woman took a step backwards, the tea pot still in her hand. "Shite!" Despite her shock, the message seemed to have sunk in immediately. Her mouth gaped open and the cigarette fell to the floor.

Sorcha pointed a finger at her. "Do this calmly. We don't want any panic. Ask yer customers to quietly leave their seats and make their way out the back. Tell them to get as far away from the immediate area as they can."

"We ain't had no bombs in here, so we ain't." The woman looked frightened as she came out from behind the counter.

"Speak to the people quietly," Sorcha said, struggling to keep her own nerves under control. "Don't cause any alarm."

But the woman wasn't listening. She hurried out amongst the tables and bellowed with a high-pitched tone. "There's a bomb alert. The p'leece says youse all gotta get out now, so you 'ave. It's across the road, so get out through the back door."

So much for keeping calm, Sorcha thought, as the customers scrambled towards the rear of the room. Voices were raised in alarm and people were elbowing one another aside in their panicky flight. While the woman was shepherding her customers out, Sorcha went back to the priests' table and picked up one of the biscuits. She didn't feel hungry, but it was going begging. Outside, she saw the two policemen directing people away from the bus station.

Her ploy had worked.

She bit into the biscuit and followed the last of the customers from the room. Her hands were shaking as she pulled the rear door shut behind her. The others were quickly dispersing, hurrying away from the bus station. Sorcha followed one group towards West Street. She had done her bit, and now she had to get away.

She pulled up suddenly when she saw the two priests running around a corner from the front of the building. They stopped at the opposite side of the road and turned to face her. The older one pointed towards her.

Then the car bomb exploded.

The blast wave knocked her to the ground. The noise of the explosion followed a fraction of a second later. It deafened her. She lay on her face, vaguely aware that a cloud of dust and debris was falling around her. Some of it landed on top of her. She felt something bump against her back, but she still heard nothing.

It must have been one hell of a bomb.

The thought lingered inside her head to the exclusion of all others.

One hell of a bomb.

She wasn't sure how long she lay there. Neither was she sure what she ought to do. It was all a matter of confusion: the confusion inside her head and the confusion of what was happening around her.

She slowly rose to her feet and her hearing started to return. It began with a loud ringing noise, as if bells were now clanging inside her skull. Her legs wobbled when she was upright. Voices seemed to come from a thousand miles away, slowly growing louder. She put one hand out to a brick wall to brace herself and she looked up to see a pall of black smoke towering over the area. Flames and more smoke curled up from the yard where the car had been planted. Flickering fingers of fire emerged from the bus station building. The smell of burning filled the air.

The confusion continued. She heard other people a little more clearly now: they were screaming and shouting. A mixture or terror and fury. They were in the street around her; a haphazard scene of men and women stumbling over the rubble brought down by the explosion. Some were running away from the station, others were on their knees, crawling. Children were crying. Young girls and old men wept openly, hugging each other for safety as the plume of smoke rose higher above them. One of the priests was helping an old lady who looked injured. Neither of them seemed steady on their feet. A siren sounded nearby, drowning out the clatter of the continuing bells inside Sorcha's head. Police or fire brigade? She couldn't be sure. Her thoughts were still too confused.

Several minutes passed before she thought to examine herself for injuries. There was no sign of blood on her. Her hands were scuffed from where she had fallen, but nothing was broken or cut. Her dress was dirty because of the dust and debris that had fallen on her, but it wasn't torn. She seemed to have come out of the situation reasonably intact.

"Are you all right, Miss?" It was one of the peelers. He gave her a quick glance as he walked past her.

"Yes. I think so." It was all she could think to say.

"Good. Make your way over there and someone will help you." He pointed to where an army ambulance was slowly driving into view. Soldiers were exiting a Bedford truck behind the ambulance. How did they get here so quickly? Had the warning been heeded?

"Thank you," she mumbled.

Sorcha waited until the peeler had moved on before she walked away from the emerging army presence. She had no intention of being examined or questioned by the British military. She hurried round a corner into... which street? She wasn't sure. Her hearing was improving, but her head felt light, as if a dizzy spell was imminent.

She leaned against a wall and waited until her head became clearer. More cogent thought began to creep into her mind. There were so many bombs intended to explode today. Were any others planned to explode near here? She couldn't immediately remember, but the list would tell her and she fumbled to find it in a pocket. Damn! There were no pockets in the dress.

Where the hell was that list?

Then she recalled the fitting room in the store. The list of bomb locations was still in her coat pocket; the pocket of the coat she had given away to the other girl.

Shite!

She stood at the corner and looked back, and she saw injured people being helped into an army ambulance. One young girl... a child... was carried on a stretcher. Her face was covered in blood. She clasped a teddy bear to her. A woman... probably her mother... staggered along beside her, sobbing piteously. Half her dress was torn away. Blood dripped down her exposed skin.

Sorcha felt a sudden physical pain run through her, as if her heart was struggling to leave her body. She clasped a hand tightly to her chest.

She hadn't done enough. She should have stopped all of this!

***

December 1980

"What happened next?" I asked.

Sorcha put her hands flat on the table and stared down at them. "Can I have a glass of water?" She turned to the burly warder standing behind her. "Please. Me throat is so dry, so it is."

The woman went to the door and spoke to someone outside in the corridor. She returned to her patch by the wall and the room went eerily silent until another warder entered with a glass of water. Sorcha drank it in one long gulp.

"Are you up to carrying on?" Susan asked.

Tears began to stream down Sorcha's cheeks. "'Tis the memory of it. The horror, the people running round in a daze, the blood..." She clasped her face in her hands and sobbed. "Oh, God! I can see it all again... just like it was..."

Susan turned to me. "We must stop here. She can't take any more today."

She was right.

"That's enough, Sorcha," I said as I patted her hand. "You've done well to get all this out in the open. Let's finish it another day." I told her I would visit her again, and then the warder led her away, still weeping. The room seemed eerily quiet in the aftermath.

"She's been bottling all that up inside her head all these years," I said.

Susan nodded. "But it's coming out now. That's a good start."

I left the prison with Susan. My head was still filled with the images Sorcha had conjured up, painful images that refused to go away. We went to lunch together at a restaurant in Armagh, but our conversation was stilted to begin with. I think we were both reminiscing on what Sorcha had told us.

"She's not all bad," Susan said, caressing her hands around a coffee cup as she began to open up. "She wanted to help people, wanted to save lives. She probably did save a few lives. We must give her credit for that."

I nodded. "She once asked me if people would hate her when they read the book. I told her I hoped not because she was a victim of her environment."

"Did she understand that?"

"I don't know. But I believe it."

I flew back to London late that evening, still emotionally charged by Sorcha's experience. How could I possibly translate what I saw and heard into meaningful words printed on a page? And I knew full well there was worse to come.

Chapter Fifteen

December 1980

It was coming up to Christmas when I drove over to Llandudno. Heavy rain made the roads slippery and ragged-bottom clouds dragged across the top of Great Orme, but festive lights were strung up in Mostyn Street and along the promenade. Despite the rain, there was a seasonal atmosphere and the shops were lively with Christmas trade. I arrived around lunch time, had a quick snack in a small café, and then drove to Will's house. Milly was again out shopping and Will told me we would have at least an hour to talk. I figured we might need longer.

We settled down in the kitchen with steaming mugs of coffee and Will pointedly topped up his mug with Irish whiskey. "It's the bombs you'll want to talk about now," he said. "This is a crucial part of your book, isn't it?"

"It was a crucial part of your life," I told him. "So, tell me about it in your own words."

***

Friday 21st July 1972
1415 BST

Two bombs exploded. They sounded little different to most of the other bombs that had blighted Belfast in the past three years, but Will and McIlroy knew this was the start of something really big.

They had been warned.

They heard the distant explosions as they drove towards the York Road railway station. The police radio told them one was at Smithfield bus station and the other at Brookvale Avenue.

"Bombs," Will said. "Plural. Just like Jimmy Fish said. How many more?"

"Which of us is going to ask the IRA?" McIlroy pressed his foot down and the car sped through a red light. "They're not likely to give us a detailed breakdown, are they?"

"Confusion," Will said. "That's what Jimmy Fish wanted us to know. There'll be so many warnings we'll be overwhelmed. And we'll get the blame for it afterwards because we won't be able to cope."

The car's police radio came alive with new telephone warnings. Oxford Street Bus Station, Great Victoria Street railway station, Crumlin Road, Liverpool ferry terminus. The list grew by the minute: warnings about the next targets. But which were genuine and which were hoaxes? There was no way of telling. And when were they set to detonate? If they didn't know the order in which the bombs would explode, how could the police prioritise their response?

Will cast a glance at his senior officer at the mention of the ferry terminal. He and his family should have set sail from there by now. They would be out on the Irish Sea, well away from the violence set to wreck the heart of Belfast. They would be safe... but for this campaign of destruction.

McIlroy parked the car in Whitla Street, a little way down from the York Road railway station. The station served the north of Ulster, with the main line running from Belfast up to Ballymena, Coleraine and Londonderry. That was one of Will's dilemmas: Catholics called it Derry, but to the RUC it was Londonderry. Which side of the fence would he fall today? He usually prevaricated.

He glanced up at the clock on the station building tower. It showed exactly twenty minutes past two. Not exactly in the mould of Big Ben's tower in London, but it was a local landmark for anyone from Belfast who didn't possess a watch. With jobs drying up fast, too many people were getting used to seeing their watches in a pawnbroker's window.

The station scene was chaotic as Will and McIlroy strode towards the centre of the activity. The army was struggling to clear passengers from the area. A soldier approached and told them to leave immediately, but they showed him their warrant cards and walked on. In the distance smoke from the other bombs was rising ominously above the city skyline.

"That's DCI McCartney from Grosvenor Road barracks over there." McIlroy pointed to a figure supervising the evacuation of the station building. "Let's see if we can give him a hand."

It was a joint effort. Other policemen from other barracks were busily hastening people from the area. Will recognised Mickey Murphy, another Catholic peeler from Oldpark. Mickey waved at Will and then continued with his task. There was no time to exchange pleasantries. There was serious work to be done here.

DCI McCartney called to them as they approached. "Glad to see you, McIlroy. Can you and your sergeant help with the evacuation? We've asked for more backup, but the Provo buggers are not giving us a chance. Too many warnings. Too many priorities."

"Where's your particular bomb?" McIlroy said. "Have you found it?"

"Yes, we know where it is, and we know what it is. It's in a suitcase left on one of the platforms. The army won't try to defuse it until we've finished clearing the area. They're…"

Then the bomb exploded.

A bright flash and a huge bang.

It was only three minutes after Will and McIlroy arrived.

All three men dropped to the ground under the impact of the explosion's blast wave. A few seconds passed before Will sat up and put his hands to his ears. His hearing was slow to come back on line. He looked around. Smoke billowed out from the station building. Flames licked from the blown-out windows. A huge piece of metal blown out

214

from the canopy roof fell onto the road in front of the station entrance. Shards of broken glass tumbled down in its wake.

McIlroy was first to stagger to his feet. He gave Will a hand, shouting words that were, for the moment, muted and unrecognisable. Will stared at the scene around him as his hearing gradually came back into focus. The crackle of fires within the building burst upon his senses.

Nearby, a young woman was sat on the ground, screaming hysterically. She seemed to be no more than a teenager and her short minidress was ripped down the front. Blood trickled down her breasts. One of her bare legs was bent at an impossible angle. A man crouching beside her slapped at her face in an effort to make her shut up. It didn't work. She screamed even louder. Was she in shock or extreme pain? Probably both, Will decided. Other pedestrians lay prone on the ground, making no effort to move. Were they dead, or badly injured? Impossible to tell.

Will took a step towards the girl, the nearest victim, when a soldier ran up to him and grabbed at his arm. "Get away from here quickly. There may be a second bomb!" He pointed to where other soldiers were directing people into adjacent streets.

"But these people need help," Will protested. "This girl…"

"Leave it to us, mate. We've had a warning of a second bomb."

"But the girl…" Will pointed to where the teenager was still screaming. The man beside her seemed to have given up. He sat on his haunches, his white face staring into the distance.

"We'll deal with it," the soldier insisted.

Will scanned around the scene. The smell of blood filled his nostrils. Beyond the girl, a man lay in a pool of it. One of his arms lay on the ground a few yards away. A woman was spread-eagle on her back. What remained of her face stared up into the smoky sky.

McIlroy grabbed at Will. "We'd better do as the soldier

215

says. Let the army do its job."

Will resisted the move as he dusted down his clothes. "But they'll need help. The army will need us. That's why we're here. To help."

"The army will know what to do here, and they can do it without us. Especially if there is a second bomb..." McIlroy turned to McCartney. "What about you and your men?"

McCartney held back and put a hand to his head. "You're right. I was wrong to involve you. You should both get out of here, right now. No point in you two being killed if there is another bomb, but my men need to see me making some pretence of being in control. God, what a mess!" He turned away and staggered back towards the station. Already his men were mingling with the troops, lending aid where they could. Two officers came up to the screaming girl and bent to her aid. When they tried to lift her, she fainted.

Will and McIlroy followed the directions of an army officer who seemed to be taking charge of evacuating the area. He ordered them into a lane off Whitla Street where they stopped to consider their next move. Their shoes scrunched through the broken glass that littered every road in sight.

"You know what I think, Will?" McIlroy watched as a stream of white-faced people left the station area: men, women and children still in shock. Some were bloodied, some were physically sound while others seemed to be emotionally dead.

"We go back and help, boss?" Will said.

"No. We call in to say we're safe, and then we do what our beloved leader tells us to do."

"We should be helping here," Will protested.

"Doing what, Will? What if we go back and we're killed by a second explosion? The guys back at North Castle Street should have some idea of the bigger picture. Let them decide where we're best employed."

"If you say so, boss." Will suddenly felt tired and then a grey mist crept over him. His head ached and his senses seemed to suddenly switch off. The world around him was just a dim outline of what it ought to be.

"Will! Are you all right?" McIlroy's voice seemed to be coming at him from afar off.

"I'll be okay in a minute." He leaned back against a wall and waited for his senses to return. "Delayed reaction," he said. "Just give me a minute."

"You look like a ghost. I reckon you need a cup of good Irish tea."

Will's vision swam back into focus, rocking from side to side until it settled onto an even keel. "I'm okay, boss. Just a dizzy spell."

"Right. Let's get back to the car and call in."

They walked back to where the car was parked farther along Whitla Street. Broken glass and dust littered the roof, but it seemed to be otherwise undamaged. McIlroy checked underneath for a mercury tilt switch and Semtex. There was none so he switched on the radio which came to life with a constant stream of reports. He waited for a gap in the transmissions, but it was an impossible task. Report followed report, bomb warning after bomb warning.

"We're small beer in this situation, Will. We'll find a telephone and…"

"McIlroy!"

Both men turned at a loud shout behind them.

It was McCartney and he was hurrying towards them. "You'd better come and look at this, guys. One of my men has discovered a body."

McIlroy snapped back. "One body? Haven't you noticed: there are dozens of bodies round here!"

"This one is different."

"Someone killed in the blast?"

"No. Come and see."

He led them further along Whitla Street and then behind the station building to a narrow alley alongside the railway track. A well-built youngish woman lay on her back on a patch of waste ground, her arms stretched out each side. A blood-coloured patch was drawn across her ample chest. A uniform constable was examining the area around the body, but there was no one else at the scene.

"I've asked for back-up to help seal off the site and examine the body, but..." He spread his arms expressively. "It's just one body at a time when we're under a concerted attack. There are too many other bodies. You could help us here."

"Knifed in the chest," Will said. He knelt beside the victim, but held back from touching it. "Any idea who she is?"

"Yes. We found some letters in her handbag. All addressed to someone called Bridie Mulveny."

Will looked up. "Mulveny? Really? And the address?"

"23 Mafeking Street."

"Bloody hell." Will glanced at McIlroy. "We know that address, don't we, boss?"

McCartney turned and pointed to an iron railing alongside the track. "In that case you may be able to tell us something useful. In the meantime... there's something else. Come and look at this."

Will followed the other two policemen to where a sheet of lined writing paper was pinned to a metal post. It fluttered in a light breeze. A message was scrawled on it in an illiterate hand.

We warnd youse so we did Sorsha Mulvny. Weel get al of yer famly Mulvny an weel get yous to.

"All your family..." Will said. "They're out to kill the Mulveny girl's family."

"Mother and sister," McIlroy replied. "This must be the sister. Sorcha Mulveny must have really pissed them off. Whoever they are."

"What should we do now?"

"Someone ought to warn the mother, old hag that she is."

Will put a hand to his forehead and rubbed at it. "Not us, boss. Please, not us. Let's get a message back to base and ask them to deal with it."

McIlroy stared at him. "You okay?"

"Not really."

And the blackness seeped into his brain once again.

***

December 1980

"Do you get any of those attacks these days?" I asked.

"No. That's all sorted now. But the memories of that day... I doubt if that will ever be sorted."

"You're not the only one, Will. Sorcha Mulveny broke down when I last interviewed her. Time doesn't seem to heal anything, does it?"

"I doubt it ever will." He poured more whiskey into his coffee mug. "Do you know how many Belfast peelers...?"

He stopped abruptly when the door opened behind him and Milly strode into the kitchen. She banged her shopping bag onto the table and glared at me. There was no way of avoiding the underlying message.

"Have you finished now?" she snapped.

I glanced at my watch. "I was hoping..."

"Well, don't! Will has had enough for today. I can see it in his face." She picked up his mug. "And you've had enough to drink, Will. Don't pretend it's just coffee. You know what they told you at the hospital."

Will gave me a sad look. "She's right. I think we'd better call it a day for now."

I nodded and stood up. I had a sudden feeling of guilt because I had been so keen to get him to talk. Was I wrong? Was I the cause of something bad? He had been reliving something that was probably better forgotten. And then I remembered again how Sorcha broke down when I asked her to relive her experience. The guilt stayed with me as I left the house and I wondered if I was making a big mistake in writing this book. Whatever the truth, I made myself a promise to phone Will in a couple of weeks. Right or wrong, I had to continue with the project.

Chapter Sixteen

December 1980

As usual, I spent Christmas alone, watching old movies on the television, and reading yet again the Christmas cards Annie and I sent each other in happier days. I set a couple of them on the mantelpiece and it made the room feel warmer, as if she was still around. Was that a mistake? Was Susan right in her assessment of my psychological needs?

I telephoned Will Foster one evening between Christmas and the New Year. By chance and good luck, he was alone. Milly had taken the two girls to a party.

After a few pleasantries, I said, "Can you spare me time to talk?"

"About what?"

"About the next bomb you encountered."

"Oh, that? That was when we came across the girl…"

"Hold on. Start from the beginning, Will."

***

Friday 21st July 1972
1445 BST

DCI McIlroy drove carefully towards the Oxford Street bus station. Will was fully aware he didn't want to go there. Neither of them wanted to go there. Both of them wanted to get back to the North Castle Street barracks and lose themselves in a whiskey bottle, but orders were orders.

McIlroy had left it to Will to find a working telephone and call Superintendent Boyle. Someone would have to call on Barbara Mulveny and tell her about the death of her daughter. It would normally be a WPC who would break the news to the woman, but Will warned the senior officer that Mafeking Street was probably a no-go area for any female RUC officer today. A couple of uniform men would have to suffice... if they could get through the barricades. An army back-up would be wise, if one could be spared. Which was unlikely.

Detective Superintendent Boyle agreed to try to find two uniformed officers. He ended the call by ordering McIlroy and Will to proceed to the Oxford Street bus station.

"The bomb warnings are the priority right now, Evans," he said.

"And when we get there, sir?" Will had responded.

"Use your intelligence. What little you and McIlroy have between you."

Will passed on the message in full and waited for McIlroy to make an insubordinate comment, but none was forthcoming. Maybe he was too tired to find something rude to say about the senior officer.

So they headed towards Oxford Street bus station.

Will recognised his boss's tension and tried to direct the conversation onto something positive. "Do you remember, boss, this morning you said something about the Codds and the Fitzpains in Ardglass village. You said something came between the families."

"Rumour, Will. Just rumour. Nothing you can rely on."

"What sort of rumour?"

"The old, old story. Two men and one woman. So they say. I can't confirm or deny it."

"And the woman was?"

"I never found out for certain. Didn't need to look into the matter until now. Made a few enquiries though."

"You didn't tell me."

"I'm telling you now. Barbara Mulveny lived in Ardglass with her husband, Pat Mulveny. Nineteen fifties. Before they split up. Does that sound relevant?"

"Any idea why they split up?"

"Have a guess, Will."

"She was playing fast and loose with someone else?"

"So the stories go. Two another men, if the rumours bear fruit."

"Two of them?"

Will shook his head in disbelief. Such sexual promiscuity didn't fit in with the image of the Barbara Mulveny they had seen earlier, but she would have been twenty years younger then. If the rumours were true, time had not been kind to her.

"You know what they say about the sexual prowess of us Irishmen, Will."

"You go at it like rabbits, you mean? You do it all night long…"

"… and we still have enough left in us to wank over the wife's corn flakes in the morning."

"Yes, I've heard it often enough, boss. Crude and unkind. Never saw the funny side of it. Who were the men involved, do you think?"

"Again, nothing conclusive, but what families do we know who came from Ardglass?"

"Apart from the Codds and the Fitzpains?"

"Let's stick with them, shall we? We now know that Sorcha, the offspring of Barbara Mulveny, is somehow linked to Brian Fitzpain. Makes you wonder, doesn't it?"

"You think Fitzpain and Barbara Mulveny were…"

"Don't assume anything, Will. We shall need to find out for sure in due course."

Will lapsed into silence. What did it all mean?

McIlroy parked the black Cortina half a mile from the bus station. "We were lucky the car didn't get too badly damaged last time. I don't want to take any risks this time. We'll walk from here."

In the distance, smoke from previous bombs billowed up into the sky and settled over the city like a malignant plague. Belfast was dying on its feet. Another distant explosion rumbled across the city as they walked. More smoke billowed upwards.

People were moving fast along the Oxford Street

pavement, mostly away from the station, some walking and some running. But, ahead of them, a crowd was hurrying towards the main building.

"Don't like the look of that," McIlroy said. "The bomb could be inside."

"Something's very wrong here," Will replied as he and McIlroy began to quicken their pace. They were within one hundred years of the station when a young woman ran past them.

They heard her call out, "Sorcha! Sorcha Mulveny!"

"Did you hear that, boss? Did you hear the name?"

"I heard it, Will."

They turned to see the young woman run towards another woman. This one was wearing a long, green dress that might have been glamourous in a different environment. It fitted her like a second skin.

"Could that be her?" McIlroy said. "Could that be the Sorcha Mulveny we're looking for?"

As he spoke, a military Land Rover raced past. They heard a squeal of brakes as it pulled up at the station.

And then the bomb exploded.

***

December 1980 / January 1981

Milly arrived home at that point and Will had to terminate the call. I was left wondering what happened next, but decided against calling him again for fear of causing more trouble with his wife. It was like waiting for the next episode of a cliff-hanger television serial.

I used odd moments over the remaining holiday period to bring my manuscript up to date, but I deliberately waited until after the New Year before I arranged any more physical interviews. It seemed prudent to let the trauma of my previous meetings die down.

About a week into January I took an afternoon flight to Belfast, with arrangements to see both Martin and Sorcha

223

the following day: Martin in the morning and Sorcha in the afternoon. I also harboured a secret sense of pleasure at the prospect of seeing Susan Miller again.

On a whim, I had phoned Susan that morning and asked her to accompany me to the prison. When she readily agreed I asked her join me for dinner at the hotel that evening. She said yes straight away. Something clicked inside of me then, the sort of feeling I knew when Annie was alive and we made a special occasion of something unimportant, just for the hell of it.

Susan came to the hotel dressed in a smart green jacket and skirt with a white blouse that fastened tight around her neck. An emerald brooch glistened on her jacket. A gold locket hung against her breast.

"I assume this is by way of a business meeting," she said as she sat down at the table, but the sparkle in her eyes told me she was probably happy to accept it as a date.

"I thought we might go over tomorrow's interview with Sorcha. I'm seeing Martin Foster in the morning and I'm hoping he might throw up some topics I can use with Sorcha in the afternoon."

"And you want me there to hold Sorcha's hand if things go wrong. Is that it?" There was a light tinkle in her voice, as if she was playing games with me.

I winked at her. "I reckon you're probably pretty good at holding people's hands in difficult circumstances."

She went silent until the wine waiter had served us before she asked, "Who held your hand when your wife died?"

I hadn't expected that sort of question. I sipped at the wine as a defensive move before I replied. "No one. I coped with things. I'm still coping. Coping well."

She gave me a look that suggested disbelief. "Does the emotional pain still affect you at times?"

"Why do you ask?"

"Curiosity. Why are you writing this book? Is it a form of catharsis? Or is there some other reason?"

"Catharsis?" I avoided her smile. It was too intoxicating. "I know what you're thinking, but Annie is my past. I got over it."

"Sometimes, people try to cover up their own emotional discomfort by immersing themselves in someone else's agony. Something even more painful. The bigger pain hides the lesser one."

"Belfast isn't my pain," I pointed out.

"Oh, but it is." She leaned forward and smiled again in a way that shook me to the core. "Belfast is where Annie was born, grew up and met you. It's where the two of you enjoyed your lives together. It's where you lost her, and I don't think you've ever got over it. I saw that when we were at the graveside. I think you come back here time and again, exploring other people's traumas, because you're still trying to wipe out your long-lasting grief. Exploring other people's pain is your way of coping."

I was stunned into silence for a few seconds before I replied. "No one has ever said that to me before."

"It's time someone did."

"You make it sound like I need help."

"You do. Am I upsetting you?"

"A little."

"Then let's change the subject. Would you like me to stay the night?"

I blinked in astonishment. "We hardly know one another, Susan."

"Agreed. So we need to do something about it."

"Why?"

"Because you need me."

***

During the night I awoke with a start. I had been dreaming; troublesome dreams of Annie and me. Dreams that had their origins in the past, and refused to go away. Images of Annie the day we were told there was no cure. Annie in pain as the cancer progressed. Me in the hospital, holding her hand when the end was close. The minister reading a eulogy over her coffin. The empty house in the days that followed.

They were not 'bad' dreams, not the sort of dreams that would bring me out in a sweat and leave me gasping for breath. How could they be bad when Annie was there? 'Troublesome' was a better description. Memories of a difficult time. These dreams had come to me often since Annie died, and I had learned to cope with them. That was what I told myself: I had learned to cope.

Full consciousness came to me with the sound of a gunshot out in the city. It wasn't too close and there was no answering blast. I reached out a hand for my wristwatch and my fingers passed over the smooth skin of a naked arm. I felt Susan shift in the bed beside me.

"You were dreaming," she said. A sliver of moonlight passed between curtains that were not fully drawn together. It illuminated her face.

"Oh, you're awake," I said.

"Obviously. I was watching you." Her voice was soft, hushed. I saw then that her hands were clasped together on the pillow.

I searched for something to say. "How did you know I was dreaming?"

"You were mumbling. Talking to yourself about Annie."

That was a revelation and it left me wondering. How would a woman like Susan react to sleeping with a man who dreamed about his lost love? Would she be offended? I said, "Really? What did I say?"

"I couldn't make out most of it. But I caught the name, Annie. Did anyone else tell you that you dream about her?"

"There never was anyone else." I sat up and looked at my watch. It was only three o'clock. "I'm sorry if I woke you. Was that why you're awake? Me mumbling in my sleep?"

The moonlight showed me she was smiling, clearly not slighted by my behaviour. "No. I had to go to the bathroom. And don't be sorry. I understand why you were dreaming."

"The grief you spoke about? Is that it?"

"I was right, wasn't I?"

I wasn't prepared to answer that, so I said, "As we're awake, let's *do* something good instead of just talking." And it was good, until another gunshot echoed through the street outside. Closer this time, but just the one shot.

**

After breakfast I called a taxi and dropped Susan off outside her flat. I was sorry to see her get out of the cab and I stepped out behind her, searching for something appropriate to say. But my mind went blank.

"I'll see you in prison," she said before she gave me a passionate kiss in the middle of the pavement. I think the cabbie might have got a kick out of it.

Then I directed the taxi to Martin's house. To begin with, Martin was far more composed than either Sorcha or Will when I last interviewed them. I began to wonder if he was emotionally the strongest of the three. I was wrong. His inner anxieties emerged soon after we sat down in his front parlour room.

"This is not going to be easy for me," he said as we began to talk. "I've never discussed this part of it in any depth before, not even with Emily."

"Take it in your own good time, Martin. Don't rush it." I took out my scribble pad and prepared to take notes.

**

Friday 21st July 1972
1440 BST

The Crumlin Road was sealed off. Armed soldiers and police held back anyone who tried to get beyond the barricade. The pot of trouble here was ready to boil over, but a more immediate problem loomed heavily in Martin's mind.

Emily was right. He had been too quick to turn his back on Sorcha, and now he regretted it. He should have given her more opportunity to talk, a chance to tell him exactly what she was mixed up in. Maybe… just maybe… he had

227

misjudged the whole situation. Maybe, as Emily said, she was not as guilty as he had imagined. He wouldn't know unless he found her and talked to her. But where would he find her? He didn't know exactly where she lived, but he did know that she had some connection with that dirty little hotel in the Oldpark Road. The people there might know how to contact her.

He stood at the Oldpark Road junction with the Crumlin Road, at the rear of a group of Republican locals from the Ardoyne; an aggressive assembly hurling insults at the troops and the police. The atmosphere was tense. He peered between the figures to the front of the gathering. Farther along that road a single car was parked alongside the houses of the Crumlin Road Prison warders, close by the Star Taxi premises. That one vehicle seemed to be the centre of attention. Armed soldiers and uniformed policemen were trying to herd the mob away from the vicinity. Could this be another car bomb? Or a hoax? The locals continued shouting obscene insults at the men who had the job of dealing with it. A small band of teenage boys began throwing bricks at them.

A cry of, "Go home, English!" came from the front of the mob. Others took up the chant, stabbing their fists at the troops.

Martin turned away in disgust and walked along Oldpark Road towards the Green Hills Hotel. He glanced from side to side as he walked, hoping he was not attracting attention. At one point he looked up and saw movement at an open window. The barrel of a rifle slid into view. It was not aimed at him so he walked on.

Away from the immediate vicinity of the Crumlin Road altercation, the atmosphere was marginally quieter, but the tension persisted. Hardened women in wrap-around pinafores stood on their doorsteps, watching and waiting. Sullen-faced youths lounged against the brick walls, eyeing Martin warily. Whatever they were smoking, it wasn't nicotine. The murals and graffiti looked down on the morbid scene and gave it nothing but added hostility.

Martin was at the hotel door when the car bomb exploded in the Crumlin Road. The sudden blast of noise echoed between the houses, smoke billowed past the end of the road, and a solid wall of air pushed Martin through the door. He landed on the bare wooden stairs. He was deafened for a few seconds but unhurt. After a moment of confusion, he stood up, dusted his hands together and looked out into the street. The foul chants had given way to screams of terror. People were running now, running away from the Crumlin Road. Many of them raced down Oldpark Road. Was anyone hurt? There was no way of telling.

There was nothing he could do to help. Besides, he figured, this lot deserved all they got. Satisfied he was right, Martin climbed the stairs to the first floor. The same old lady was there, standing by a broken window, staring out. She turned to face him. Her face was ashen. For the moment he couldn't recall her name.

"Did youse see it?" she said. "The bomb. Did youse see where it was?"

"Around the corner," he said. "In the Crumlin Road, by the taxi rank."

"Was anyone killed?"

"No idea."

"One o' theirs, or one o' ours?"

"No idea." He knew what she meant; was it an IRA or UVF bomb? But he wasn't going to get drawn into that. "I came looking for Sorcha. She was here this morning."

"Ain't seen her since then." The woman peered at Martin with a suspicious look. She still carried an odious smell. "She said youse was her cousin, so she did."

"Yes."

"Ain't heard of youse before." She stepped closer. "Where're youse from?"

"Not far from here. Do you have any idea where I might find Sorcha? I need to make sure she's safe in view of these bombs."

"She can look after herself," the woman said dismissively.

229

"You don't know where I should look?"

"If she's any sense she'll be at home in Mafeking Street with her sister."

Mafeking Street? So that was where she lived.

Martin felt a sudden surge of relief. It was only partially dulled when a rattle of gunfire sounded nearby, just as he turned back towards the stairs.

He called to the woman. "You're probably right. I would have gone there first, but there was a barricade and I couldn't get through it. I'll try again."

Lies, all lies, he thought, but it didn't matter because he now knew where to look for Sorcha. He hurried down the stairs before the woman could ask any more awkward questions.

Outside, people were milling around, confused, looking lost. A hooded man with a gun raced away down the street. A phalanx of locals closed around him, hiding him. Martin stopped to gaze at the scene. He couldn't see the remains of the bomb, but smoke had drifted into Oldpark Road. Looking up, he saw a huge pall of blackness rise above the nearby buildings. An army Saracen vehicle was parked at the junction with the Crumlin Road, and soldiers were shepherding people away from the immediate danger. A fire vehicle raced past. A gang of youths threw bricks at it. To achieve what? Who could possibly benefit from this behaviour?

A solitary word ran again and again through Martin's head. *Evil, evil, evil…*" He couldn't rid himself of the echo. It engulfed every other thought. And he wondered yet again how Sorcha was caught up in it… and how he might help her escape.

Dear God, Sorcha, I have to get you away from this.

He turned to walk away from the Crumlin Road. His path would take him farther into Nationalist territory, but he figured the locals now had more to worry them than a solitary Prod tramping through their hallowed ground. And this route would take him to Mafeking Street.

Within the next fifteen minutes he heard four more

explosions. Each time he felt a shudder run through him and he wondered if Sorcha was safe. He couldn't pinpoint the locations, but none seemed to be close to him. Not that any bomb could do more damage than was already done by earlier random assaults. Further plumes of black smoke rose up over the house roofs. He could smell the burning in the air.

He walked down one street in which every single house was derelict, burned out from a sectarian attack that probably dated back a year or two. It was an old red-brick terrace with front doors opening directly onto the pavement, except that there were no front doors; just empty openings into charred empty shells. Children were playing in one of the ruins. Where are your parents? he thought. Why haven't they taken you to safety? Wasn't that supposed to be the reaction of local mammies when the IRA planned an attack on the army? Get your own children inside first, and then bang the dustbin lids to warn others.

And where were they now? Where were the mammies who routinely taught their children to hate the Prods? And where were the daddies who spent their miserable lives in the pubs and the betting shops, drinking and gambling away their dole money because it was the only way to blot out the ugliness of their existence? Where were they when their children were left to play in these foul streets?

In the next street half, the houses were boarded up, some dilapidated, some simply abandoned because it was no longer safe to live here. It was a common story. In this case it was probably the result of a Loyalist attack, he thought. Bricks and broken paving stones littered the road. Broken glass on the pavement came from shattered windows and alcohol bottles. Two shaven-headed men lounged against a wall. They were drinking from whiskey bottles and seemed unconcerned by the explosions. Their attention turned towards Martin and one of them stepped forward.

"Who are youse? Youse don't belong here." He sounded half drunk.

"I'm looking for my girlfriend. I want to be sure she's

231

safe."

"Where does she live?"

"Mafeking Street."

"What's her name?" The man jutted his stubbly chin at Martin.

"Sorcha Mulveny," Martin replied with a false air of calm.

"Her?" The man laughed, showing rows of rotten teeth. "I know her. Youse call her your girlfriend? She's a fuckin' whore, so she is. Seen more cocks than a chicken farmer."

Martin clenched his fists. "I want to be sure she's safe."

"Safe in another man's bed, most likely. Jaysus, but she's been shagged more times than I've been pissed."

The accusation cut deep into Martin's conscience. Was it true? Had he been bedding a girl with the reputation of being a whore?

He said, "Look, I don't want any trouble. I'll carry on looking for her."

"I told youse, boy! She's a bleedin' whore. Ask Mickey Murphy. He'll tell youse, so he will. Ask him what happened after he shagged her. Ask him why Sorcha Mulveny was sent away from home. Youse just ask Mickey what he did."

"Who is Mickey Murphy?" Martin asked. His mind began to whirl with shock. Realisation seeped into his thoughts; a cruel, ugly realisation that what the man was telling him might be true.

"Mickey Murphy? Sure an' these days he's a peeler, so he is. Bleedin' traitor."

"What did he do?" Martin asked, but he knew the answer already.

"Put her up the spout, so he did."

Martin staggered back a step.

No! Not Sorcha! Surely not.

Before the first man could reply, the second man came up behind him. "You're not from round here. Where d'youse live?"

Martin struggled to regain control of his emotions. It was

time to take a risk. He gritted his teeth and replied firmly. "If you want to know more about me, ask Brian Fitzpain. You know him, do you?"

"Fitzpain?" The second man took a step back. "What's he to youse?"

"Ask him yourself." Martin pushed past both men and walked on. He didn't look back and neither of the two men tried to stop him. He didn't breathe easily until he was in the next street.

Mafeking Street was busy. A noisy mob was gathered at the junction with Ladysmith Road, building a barricade. Old furniture was dragged from nearby houses and flung onto a growing pile that stretched from one side of the road almost to the other. Just enough room was left for pedestrians and the odd vehicle to pass. Two men in black balaclava helmets stood guard with rifles, checking people in and out of the limited access. Mafeking Street was now a sealed ghetto within an outer ghetto. The residents seemed determined no one would attack this place. Martin eyed the growing barrier with puzzlement. Did someone important within the Nationalist movement live here? Or was it simply a case of local fear getting out of hand? Was paranoia now in control of the area?

Another makeshift barrier was being erected one hundred yards farther along Ladysmith Road, just beyond the junction with Rorke Street. It was another redoubt aimed at holding back any Loyalist gangs who came here with evil intent. But was it also intended to keep at bay any police or army patrols? In these streets the security forces were no longer the accepted guardians of the peace. Martin shook his head sadly. What peace was there to guard here anyway? Was this the sort of life that Sorcha endured? Was this what she meant when she said, 'we live on opposite sides of the divide'? He hadn't understood just how wide that divide really was.

He should have.

And he remembered again what the thug had said about Sorcha.

Up the spout.

Dear God, no!

He looked behind him. There was still no barrier in Ladysmith Road at the way he had come in. Not yet. Nor was there any barrier directly into Rorke Street. For the moment, he still had two possible exit routes if he needed to make a quick escape.

He walked on, keeping on the opposite side to the hooded gunmen.

No one made any move to stop him as he by-passed the Mafeking Street barricade and continued along Ladysmith Road. He wasn't going to chance his luck getting into the sealed street. Maybe he could get access to the Mulveny house via the alleyway behind it. There had to be an alleyway. All of these streets had such putrid passages between the backs of the terraces. He walked along the rubble-strewn pavement, constantly watching in case he drew undue attention to himself. A car was parked a few yards ahead, right across the alleyway entrance. It was a light blue Vauxhall Viva.

Martin crossed the road, hoping there was no one inside the vehicle. Then he stopped to consider his next move. The rear end of the car hung low, a sure sign the boot was heavily laden. With a bomb, maybe? While he studied the vehicle, the front door of the next house opened, and three men came out.

One was Fitzpain. Martin recognized him instantly. He carried an AK47 rifle.

The IRA man walked straight to the car and pulled open the driver's door. Then he paused and looked towards Martin. The other two men crowded up beside him. One wore a livid scar on his cheek.

It was Fitzpain who spoke to Martin. "I've seen youse before, and youse don't belong round here. Youse was at the hotel this mornin'. Who the hell *are* youse?"

Martin tried his best to disguise the shiver that ran through him. "I'm looking for my cousin, Sorcha Mulveny."

"Cousin? I know all Sorcha's cousins and youse ain't one

o' them."

Martin clenched his hands tight. This was getting more dangerous than he had expected. "Do you know where I can find her?"

"If I did I wouldn't be tellin' youse. I got this bad feelin' about youse, boy." He turned to the man behind him, the brute with the livid scar. "Reckon we should rough him up a bit, Finn? Find out who he really is. Eh?"

"Could be a Prod, Brian."

Fitzpain faced up to Martin again. "Are you, boy? Are you a filthy black Prod spyin' on us?"

"There's been rumours about Sorcha, Brian," the man called Finn said. "Rumours about her droppin' her knickers for a Prod. Are youse thinkin' what I'm thinkin'?"

"If this boy is a Prod and he's been seein' Sorcha Mulveny, I reckon they both got somethin' comin' to them."

"She could've been passin' on information to the Prods, Brian. Or the Brits."

"Youse could be right there, Finn. We all know there's traitors passin' on information for money. If ye're right... Last night I cut off a boy's dick because of what he did to a poor wee Catholic girl. I got this feelin' I might do the same to this one. And as for Sorcha, she knows what happens to anyone who grasses on us."

"You're wrong," Martin protested, but he knew he was already onto a loser.

Fitzpain scowled at him. "We eliminate anyone who passes information to our enemies. Is that what Sorcha was doing? Who was the information goin' to? The Brits or the RUC? Were youse the Proddy contact passin' it on?"

"No!"

"Well, I don't believe youse, and we ain't takin' any chances."

"What about Sorcha, Brian?" Finn, the thug with the scar, glowered at Martin.

"If she's been grassin' on us I'll kill her, so I will."

Martin trembled at the anger in Fitzpain's voice. It left no doubt that he would act upon his words. Killing was this man's game and even Sorcha was not protected from it.

"There's trouble, Brian." Finn suddenly grabbed Fitzpain's arm and pulled him round to see an army Saracen vehicle rounding the corner at the unguarded end of Ladysmith Road. Armed and armoured soldiers strode purposefully alongside it.

"Shite!" Fitzpain dropped to one knee and aimed his AK47 towards the oncoming patrol. He let off a single round before two shots were fired in return. Both scraped the road alongside the car.

Martin dropped to the ground and clasped his hands over his head. It was no more than an instinctive reaction to the danger. He saw the IRA men bundle themselves into the car and drive off. Two more army shots followed them, but the car was out of sight around the corner into Rorke Street in seconds. Martin continued to lie flat on his front, his hands still pressed tight into his skull, hoping no one would mistake him for a terrorist.

"Are you armed?"

He glanced up. A figure in combat uniform stood over him. An army SLR was aimed at his head.

"No."

"Stand up slowly with your arms outstretched. Don't make any sudden moves or we will shoot."

Relief flooded through Martin as he stood up. "I'm glad you came when you did. Those men were about to kill me."

"Why?"

The soldier was an older man, an officer, Martin noted. He registered the commanding tone of voice officers used towards their troops. If he joined the British army, he would expect to serve under an officer like this one.

Martin kept his hands in clear view. "They're IRA gunmen and I'm a Protestant. Can you think of a better reason for them to want to kill me?"

"You're not from round here?"

"No." He scanned around. The streets were empty apart from himself and the army. The residents and the armed men had retreated into the houses. But how many hidden rifles were even now trained upon them?

"It seems like you've been extremely foolish to stray into this territory. I'm going to get one of my men to check you for hidden weapons. Don't do anything sudden or my finger might slip on the trigger." The soldier nodded towards his self-loading rifle and then beckoned to his patrol.

Another soldier stepped forward from behind the Saracen, now parked alongside the pavement a few feet away. This was a younger man who walked steadily and cautiously up to Martin, constantly looking from side to side. He handed his rifle to the senior man and began frisking Martin.

"Are you all right, mate?" He spoke casually with a southern counties English accent.

"Sort of. No real harm done." Martin began to relax. Being frisked was nothing to worry about when you'd been on the verge of losing your life.

"Who were those guys?" the young soldier asked.

It was the same interrogation all over again, but Martin went along with it. In a strange way, he was glad of the conversation. It was reassuring.

"A couple of IRA hoodlums," he said. "They were about to take me apart, bit by bit. Thanks for scaring them off."

"Why were they attacking you?"

"Wrong religion. It accounts for more killings round here than you'd imagine."

The soldier nodded in understanding. "I've learned about it since I came here. Sounds like you're in the wrong part of town, mate."

"I reckon you're right."

"Why are you here?"

"Trying to get away from the bombs. Took a wrong turn."

"You can put your hands down now." The frisking was finished.

Martin sighed, lowered his arms and dusted his hands together. The older man stepped forward and returned the young soldier's rifle. He faced Martin square on, his sharp eyes never losing focus.

"My advice to you is to get out of here right now."

"Good advice. Thanks again for your help."

"Watch your back." The senior soldier gestured to the rest of his patrol and they moved off in unison towards Rorke Street, the Saracen trundling along beside them.

Martin watched until they rounded the same corner as Fitzpain's car.

What to do now? Common sense told him to do as the army guys suggested: get out of here, and fast. But that would not help him find Sorcha. And he was now more than ever determined to find her before she was killed by Fitzpain. Forget common sense, he was going to do what his heart told him. He'd come this far, and he wasn't going to give up now. Despite the shock of the accusations those drunken thugs made about Sorcha, he was going to find her, one way or another.

When the army patrol was out of sight, the houses began to disgorge residents and gunmen alike. Work continued on the barricades as if it had never been interrupted.

"What was them army bastards sayin' to youse?" A young acne-faced man armed with an Armalite approached Martin. He looked nervous, as if he was new to this sort of action.

"Asking me about Brian Fitzpain," Martin replied. "I told them nothing. Told them I never heard of the man."

"Youse know Brian?"

"Of course I do. He's a friend of my cousin, Sorcha Mulveny. You know where Sorcha is, do you?"

"Dunno. At home if she's any sense."

"I'll go and see."

"You don't live here, do youse?" The voice carried a note of suspicion.

"Visiting my aunt, Mrs Mulveny. Is this the right street?"

"Down there, number twenty-three. Tell her to stay indoors until them bombs is finished." Apparently reassured, the young gunman walked on by. He paused a few yards farther along the street, looked back at Martin, and then continued as if his interest in the stranger had waned. He would, Martin thought, make a poor soldier. Not nearly inquisitive enough. At least he had served a useful purpose in showing the local residents that the stranger in their street had been checked out.

Martin cast around to make sure no one else had any interest in him before he turned into the filthy alley at the rear of Mafeking Street. On each side, the old brick walls were studded with wooden gates which gave access to the small back yards at the rear of the houses. Which gate would give him access to number 23?

A group of small children had been playing a few yards away. They looked to be no more than seven or eight years old and were scruffily dressed. Yet more kids who had not been drawn back indoors by their mammies. Their game ceased when they turned to look at him; suspicious looks that were learned early in life by kids around here.

Martin called to them. "Can you tell me where the Mulveny family live?"

A pug-nosed child pointed to a green gate.

"Thank you." Martin opened the creaky gate and walked into a tiny yard littered with scattered rubbish, a rusty bicycle and a dustbin lying on its side. The lid was missing. He rapped loudly on the back door of the house.

An older woman opened the door, yawned and peered out. Was she older than her time, Martin wondered, or had she been on the booze already today? Behind her was a typical terrace kitchen, tiny and untidy. A rancid smell escaped through the open door.

"What d'youse want?"

"I'm looking for Sorcha Mulveny."

The woman adopted the same suspicious look as the children in the alley. It seemed to be a uniform mask. "Why? Who the hell are youse?"

"A friend. Is she here?"

"What's yer name?"

"Martin."

"Piss off. She ain't 'ere." She slammed the door shut.

Martin heard the sound of bolt being rammed home inside. He stood looking at the door for a few moments. Who was that woman? Sorcha's mother? He reeled at the thought of it. Was it worth trying again to speak to the woman? Probably not.

He walked back out into the rear alleyway. If this was the sort of life Sorcha lived, if these were the people she mixed with, it was no wonder she had been caught up amongst unsavoury characters like Fitzpain. He shivered at the thought of what she might have endured here. Then he remembered once more the insinuations about Sorcha's past, and he shivered.

Up the spout. Pregnant.

Was it true? If it was, what did she do about it?

He shivered again and tried to calm his nerves.

He could take her away from this appalling place. Take her to England, give her a decent life. They could have nothing like this across the water, he was sure. Yes, they had run-down towns like the one in Coronation Street, but nothing like this. His determination to help the girl mounted up within him.

Whatever she had done wrong, he had to help her.

He hurried back into Ladysmith Road. Two men in balaclava helmets stood at the end of Mafeking Street. A teenage girl was chatting to them. Martin walked swiftly away from them, not daring to look back in case he appeared to be suspicious… which he was. He breathed a sigh of relief as he turned into Rorke Street… where two men grabbed him and pushed him up against a house wall. Martin recognised them immediately. Not the army patrol and not Fitzpain. They were now likely to be well out of the area. These two were 'Mad Mac' McKinnon and 'Bad Boy' Blair. There could hardly be a resident of any part of Belfast who had not seen their faces in the newspapers or on local television news broadcasts. There could be few who did not fear them.

"Ya's got one chance to get away from here alive." Mad Mac thrust his face into Martin's. "Tell us where to find the

Mulvenys and ya goes free. Otherwise…"

"I don't live round here," Martin gasped. "How the hell should I know where they live?"

"Ya's a filthy taig."

"No. I'm a Protestant. A couple of IRA thugs picked me up, but I got away."

Mad Mac didn't seem convinced. "Prove it. Prove ya's not a Catholic."

Martin thought quickly. "Look in my pocket. The left-hand pocket in my jacket."

Mad Mac KcKinnon fumbled in the pocket and pulled out a small envelope. He passed it back to his accomplice. "What is it, Georgie?"

Blair read the inscription on the envelope, slowly and deliberately, as if reading was not his strong suit. "'Tis a church collection envelope. The Reverend Ian's church."

"Damn!" Mad Mac released his hold on Martin. "Get the hell out of here, boy! And if anyone asks, ya never saw us, right?"

"Right." Martin hurried away, once again not daring to look back. It was the first time felt glad to have had one of his aunt's collection envelopes in his pocket.

***

January 1981

"You must have been scared out of your mind, Martin," I said. "I reckon it was a sign of your courage that you carried on looking for Sorcha."

He took out a cigarette and lit up. It was the first time I had seen him smoke. His hand was steady, but his eyes turned dull. "I did what I had to do. What will your English readers think? Will they understand what counts as normal over here? They don't have bombs and riots like we have, do they?"

"They know only what they see on the television news. And that doesn't tell them everything. For them, I think the riots are the most puzzling part of it. The bombs are planted by violent terrorists, they understand that, but the riots are the work of ordinary people. They don't understand that."

"Ordinary people. You think we're ordinary over here?"

"They don't understand how people like themselves can get caught up in violence."

"But we're not like them, are we?" He drew deeply on his cigarette. "I reckon you understand that. You do, don't you? Even though you're English. You know most of the rioters are there because they're told to be there. It's as well organised as a bloody play. You understand that, don't you?"

I nodded. "Reckon I might quote you on that."

"Thought you might."

"And I'll tell you this... on Bloody Friday there were gangs of Republicans cheering every time a bomb went off. Cheering! Bombs exploded, people died, and the mob cheered. Did you know that?"

I did, but I let it pass. "Do you want to tell me more about your search for Sorcha?"

"Another time." He stood up suddenly. "You're beginning to tire me, you and your damned book. You don't scare me, but you tire me. I feel sick at heart every time I have to remember what happened. That's enough."

I took it as a blunt order to leave.

Chapter Seventeen

January 1981

I took a taxi to Armagh and met Susan in a small prison waiting room. She was dressed every bit as attractively as she had been the previous evening, and she looked every bit as alluring, but this was no time or place for a romantic conversation. The same beefy warder led us down the same pee and sweat infused corridor to the interview room where Sorcha was waiting for us.

"I'm glad youse both came," she said, standing to greet us. "Glad youse came together."

"We met in the waiting room." I decided not to get side-tracked into any discussion about Susan and me.

She seemed to take the comment at face value, and I was glad of that. She sat down and asked, "What do youse want to talk about this time?"

"I spoke to Will Foster a couple of weeks ago," I said. "He told me how he heard a young woman call out your name at the Oxford Street bus station just before the bomb exploded. Would you like to tell me what happened?"

Sorcha glanced at Susan who nodded back to her.

"Do the best you can, Sorcha," Susan said calmly.

"It was a bad experience..." she began. "I felt bad even before the bomb went off."

***

Friday 21st July 1972
1445 BST

Sorcha felt drained as she walked towards the Oxford Street bus station; physically and mentally exhausted. Her new dress was no longer as pristine as it was when she stole it. It no longer felt like an advertisement for a wealthy young socialite. Young socialite? Who was she kidding? She felt as grubby as she had this morning while wearing her own clothes; as grubby without her panties as she had felt when wearing them. Was that the fault of the dress, or a result of her melancholy and her aching head?

The road was busy now, not just cars loaded with people anxious to get out of Belfast, but ambulances and fire vehicles struggling to get to the bomb sites. Each hindered the other. The screech of sirens split the air. Army personnel carriers lumbered past, taking troops from one tragedy to another. Sorcha shrugged and walked on. The Belfast gasworks was visible in the distance ahead of her. An important part of the city's history. It was built in 1822 and its profits helped build the Belfast City Hall. There was that big gasometer close by the River Lagan. And there was that lingering hint of gas that drifted along the river like the residue of a lethal weapon from a long past war in Flanders fields. It added to the miserable atmosphere. Today, the sight of the gasworks was, she thought, utterly depressing, as gloomy as the narrow, terraced streets where the workers lived. As tired and dirty as Mafeking Street. It was a reminder of the Belfast she had grown up in, and the Belfast she now detested. She swung her gaze over the city skyline, where the smoke from so many bombs rose into the summer air and she wondered if this was what those Nazi blitzes of World War Two had been like. The dull thud of yet another distant explosion reached her, and she saw yet another cloud of smoke climb up out of the city, but she couldn't identify the location.

Her list of bomb targets was lost, but she knew that the Oxford Street bus station was on it. Frustratingly, she had no idea of the time the bomb here would be detonated. She was sure she had saved some lives at the Smithfield station, but could she now do the same here? If only she was not so

244

fatigued.

She had the station in sight when an Austin 1100 saloon car came along the road. Instead of taking the bridge across the river and out of danger, it turned down a road that led to the rear of the station. Was it the carrier of the next bomb? Probably, in which case she was already in trouble. Everyone in the vicinity was.

She walked on, increasing her pace.

She knew this station well. Buses from here served County Down and she had many times left from here to visit her mother's relatives in Ardglass, on the coast some five miles beyond Downpatrick. There was something puzzling about the families who had lived in Ardglass years ago, including her own relatives. It felt as if a million secrets were embedded in the village framework, never to be publicly aired. A million secrets, and she could only guess at the one that affected her personally.

It constantly upset her.

Other girls would know the truth about themselves by looking at their birth certificates, but not Sorcha. There was a name on her certificate that was a lie. Her mother denied it, but Sorcha was certain. Patrick Mulveny's name was there for everyone to see, but he was not her father.

Couldn't possibly be.

She continued walking.

Something was wrong here. As she came closer to the bus station, she saw that people were hurrying towards it instead of away from it. She put out a hand to a young man racing past her. "Where are you going?"

He pointed back the way he had come. "There's a bomb somewhere back there. The peelers are telling us to get clear."

"But the bomb is at the bus station," she protested. "You mustn't go that way."

"How d'youse know it's there?"

"It has to be."

"To hell with that. We've been told to get to safety inside the building." The young man hurried on towards the station. Others followed him.

Oh God! Sorcha groaned. This was what the IRA intended with those hoax calls. Victims were being driven *towards* the bomb. Confusion surrounded the area at the front of the station. Armed policemen were shepherding a noisy group of passengers into the building. At the same time, more pedestrians were arriving from other streets, intent on getting to safety inside the station.

Sorcha was one hundred yards from the building when an armoured military vehicle pulled up outside. Troops poured out and immediately began trying to clear the area. An argument broke out with the police already on the scene.

"But we have to come here!" someone shouted. "We were told to come here!"

Other voices were raised in protest as the newly-arrived troops ordered pedestrians to get away from the station as quickly as possible. The confusion intensified.

Then a voice called out, "Sorcha! Sorcha Mulveny!"

She stopped abruptly. A figure was running towards her, a young woman seemingly caught up in the melee of confusion. Sorcha gasped in instant recognition. It was Moira McShane, a school friend she hadn't seen in two or three years.

Sorcha raised a hand in recognition while Moira passed by two men. Both men turned and stared at her... and at Sorcha.

One hundred yards beyond them, at the entrance to the station, a military Land Rover pulled up and more soldiers clambered out.

Then the bomb exploded.

***

January 1981

Sorcha went suddenly silent and slumped back in her seat. Her head was bent forward, but the heaving of her shoulders indicated she was sobbing. Susan immediately went round the table and put an arm around her shoulders.

"Do you want to carry on?" she asked.

Sorcha shifted back into an upright stance. She took a deep breath, wiped at her eyes and nodded. Her voice was hoarse. "I have to. I have to get it all out now. If I don't I'll regret it later."

Susan turned to the warder. "Could you ask for a glass of water, please?"

The warder went to the door and spoke to someone outside. The water was handed in just a minute later and Sorcha downed it in one go.

"I'm all right now," she said. "Let's get on with this, shall we?"

***

Friday 21st July 1972
1450 BST

Sorcha was never sure how long she was unconscious. It could have been a few seconds. It could have been several minutes. When she came to, a man was leaning over her, filling her vision.

"Are you in any pain?" he asked as he helped her into a sitting position. He had some sort of strange accent. Welsh, she thought but she couldn't be sure.

"Must've got a bit of a whack on the head when I fell," she replied and rubbed a hand across the back of her scalp.

She looked about her, still unsure what had happened. In the background, the bus station was afire, smoke and flames pouring through the windows and the roof. People were running away from it. Police and army personnel seemed to be marshalling survivors out of the building. Some looked bloodied and confused. Panic was all around. And there was an overriding smell of burning.

"Let me take a look." The man knelt beside her and pulled aside her hair, searching her scalp. "No sign of any blood. But you may get a lump appearing in due course. Sit still for a moment while you recover from the shock."

"I'm all right now," she said and made a move to stand, but the man held her back.

"Just sit still. Sometimes a bang on the head can be more serious than it looks."

"What about my friend?" She looked around. "I saw my friend coming towards me. Just before…"

"Your friend wasn't so lucky, I'm afraid." An older man stood a little behind the kneeling one. His accent was definitely Belfast. "A big piece of flying metal hit her." He pointed to where Moira McShane's body was face-down amid a pool of blood. The back of her skull was shattered. Brain tissue was spilled onto the pavement.

Dear God, no!

Sorcha turned away with a sudden overwhelming need to retch. The smell of the vomit was even stronger than the smell of burning. She wiped a hand across her mouth, and then vomited again. Several minutes passed before she felt able to speak.

"Is she dead?" It occurred to her only after she spoke that it was a foolish question.

"I'm sorry," the policeman said.

"I hadn't seen her in a long time… and now… oh God… she's dead." Sorcha felt a tear trickle down one cheek and she angrily brushed it aside. Life was so unfair.

"We will ensure her family are told," the standing man said. "But you are more important at the moment because you're alive and we want you to stay alive."

"That's why I'm going to ask you some questions," the kneeling man said. "So we can assess whether there is any brain damage. Can you tell me your name?"

"Sorcha," she said. "Sorcha Mulveny."

"That's good, Sorcha. And where do you live?"

"23 Mafeking Street."

"Excellent. My name is Will Evans, by the way. I'm a policeman."

"Police?"

A spasm of fear suddenly flamed through her. The last

thing she wanted now was to be interrogated by the police. She tried again to get to her feet. This time the man didn't stop her. What was his name? Evans? He seemed nice enough, but he was a Belfast peeler. No Catholic could trust a Belfast peeler.

"How do you feel now you are on your feet?" he asked, standing close beside her.

"I'm all right."

She wasn't. Her head ached and her vision was blurred for a few seconds. Her stomach felt queasy and she wondered if she was going to vomit again.

The older man seemed to see through her assurances. He put out a hand to support her. "I'll tell you what we're going to do now, Miss Mulveny. My colleague, Will Evans, is going to take you somewhere safe while I see what help I can give to the other victims."

"I'm all right," she protested.

But the older man was insistent. "I don't like the way you have been swaying on your feet. I'd like to be sure you're not suffering from concussion. We'll get a medic to look at you as soon as we can, but they're all going to be very busy in the station right now. In the meantime I prescribe ten minutes sitting down somewhere away from here, and a cup of tea if Will can arrange it. Can you do that, Will?"

"Leave it to me, boss."

As he led the girl away another bomb exploded, not at the bus station but in the direction of the ferry terminal.

***

January 1981

It was clear we had to stop the interview there. Sorcha was, once again, sobbing quietly.

"That's enough for now." The warder took Sorcha's arm and led her away. She went willingly and her shoulders still heaved as she staggered off down the adjacent corridor.

Susan gave me a sad look and nodded to the door. "We

can't do any more here. Not today. How about we find a quiet spot and talk about this?"

I readily agreed. "There's a coffee shop at the hotel. How about…?"

"Yes, we'll go back there to talk about this part of the story," she interrupted me. "Then we'll go to my place. You can stay there with me until we know that Sorcha is recovered."

"Stay at your place?" I hadn't been expecting that.

"You ought to stay here in Belfast for a while longer. Long enough to see Sorcha again. I know it's hard on her, but she needs to work through this. Get it all out of her system now, if she possibly can. It won't be easy for her."

"I'd like to know what she said to Will Evans after that bomb… and what he said to her." I went on to tell her more about Will Evans and the interviews I'd had with him at his home in Wales.

"Why don't you ask him?" Susan said. "Ask Will what happened after that particular bomb. You can use a telephone, can't you? Do it today, while this session is still fresh in your mind. Go back to the hotel to collect your luggage, and make a call from there."

She was right, of course. In the taxi back to Belfast I told her more of the detail I'd already amassed about the various people mixed up in the Bloody Friday bombings. She listened intently. When we got back to the hotel bedroom, I telephoned Will Evans. Susan sat on the bed beside me, one arm about my waist.

"I'm in Belfast," I told Will and I've been interviewing Sorcha Mulveny."

"Again?" It was only a mild expression of surprise. He knew well enough that my enquiries were on-going.

"Yes, again. She told me about the bomb at the Oxford Street Bus Station. She says you took her away for a cup of tea. Was that a ploy to get her to talk?"

"Of course."

"What did she tell you? I need to know, Will."

21st July 1972
1500 BST

Will understood perfectly what McIlroy wanted him to do.

In a way it was a stroke of luck. Gruesome luck, but still luck. The very same person they needed to interview, and she had been delivered right into their hands. He led her round a corner to a small Chinese Restaurant, the only suitable place he could find. It was empty, but the windows were intact, and the door was open, so he ushered Sorcha Mulveny inside. The room was small, with no more than half a dozen dining tables, and it smelt strongly of curry. Will hoped the smell would not make the girl gag.

A Chinese man dressed as a waiter approached them. He looked frightened, as if the horrors of Belfast outweighed any horrors he might have seen in his own country. He waved his hands at Will and shouted, "No. No. We're closed." His voice was heavily accented.

Will showed his warrant card. "Police. And you are open. Two cups of tea. Hot and sweet. Now!"

The fear in the man's face intensified, but he backed off. Without another word, he went away to the kitchen. Will led the girl to a table well away from the front window. Although it was still intact another blast could so easily shatter it. He waited until the girl was seated before he sat opposite her.

"A cup of hot tea will work wonders," he said.

"A whiskey would work better," she replied.

"I don't think so, Sorcha. I want you stone cold sober because I have some bad news for you." He kept his voice calm. He didn't want her to panic.

She gestured to the window. "You think what's happening out there isn't bad enough? How can you have any more bad news than that?"

"A different sort of bad news."

"Go on."

"We would have come looking for you if you hadn't turned up here... because of your sister," he said.

This wasn't the way a family member was supposed to be told bad news, but nothing today was as it supposed to be. There should be a female officer here. There should be someone else to back him up. But there wasn't. It was right that DCI McIlroy went to help the victims of the bus station bomb. That was the main priority. Will now had to tackle this other matter as best he could, and the girl needed to know the truth because she could be the next on the murderer's list.

Dammit, there was no one else here to help him.

"Bridie?" She frowned.

He tried to capture her gaze. "Yes, Bridie. I'm sorry to tell you she's been killed."

She gaped at him for two full seconds and then she cried out, "Oh, God! A bomb! She's been killed by a bomb!" She half rose from her seat.

Will put out a hand to settle her back down again. "No. Not a bomb."

"What then?"

"I'm sorry to tell you that your sister has been murdered."

She visibly shivered and then a strange expression crept over the girl's face. Her pale skin grew paler. Her eyes became dilated and unfocussed. He mouth hung open but no more words emerged.

Will continued speaking slowly. "My boss and I were at the York Road railway station not long ago when Bridie's body was found in an alley nearby. This is not going to be easy for you, Sorcha. She had been stabbed."

"No. It can't be her. It just can't. How do you know it was her?"

"There were letters in her handbag that helped us identify her. Bridie Mulveny of Mafeking Street. I'm very sorry." He said nothing about the illiterate warning. She didn't need to know about that.

"God help us all," she whispered.

"I'm sorry," he repeated.

In the silence that followed, the Chinese waiter came back with two cups of tea and placed them on the table. He still looked to be in fear of his life. Will thanked him, handed him a pound note and told him to keep the change. Outside, a fire vehicle raced past the restaurant, its siren blaring. The noise reverberated inside the room.

When the waiter had gone back into the kitchen, Will pushed one of the cups closer to the girl. "Drink this, Sorcha. Then I want you to think carefully and tell me if you know of anyone who would want to kill your sister."

She sipped at the cup. Her hands were trembling and some of the tea spilled onto the table. Her voice was cracked and hollow. "It must have been a Loyalist gang. You know what they're like. They'd kill any Catholic, given half a chance. Especially on a day like this. Yes, it would have to be the work of the Prods."

"Any one of them in particular?" Will asked.

"Any one of them would do it," she said. "You know that. People like Mad Mac McKinnon or Bad Boy Blair. You're a policeman. You must know them all. There are so many of them making threats against us Catholics."

"You're right, of course. And we shall have to pull them in and question them. But was there anyone else who might want to kill Bridie? This is important, Sorcha, in case the same person tries to kill you or your mother. Do you know any Republican terrorists who might want to do this?"

"No. No one like that." She looked away then, and Will saw immediately that she was afraid to give him a straight answer.

"Have you heard of a man called Brian Fitzpain?" he asked.

She blinked, and then nodded, still avoiding his gaze. "We've all heard of him, so we have."

"Do you know him?"

"Why do youse ask?"

He didn't answer the question. Instead he asked, "What about Seamus Codd? Do you know him?"

253

"Jimmy Fish?" She turned her head back and gave him a querying look.

"Yes, Jimmy Fish."

"Little runt. They say he's a police informer. He deserved to get killed."

Will stared at her. "How did you know he was killed?"

She looked away again, suddenly caught off guard. "Dunno… someone must have told me."

"Who?"

"Can't remember." She sat staring straight ahead. "Best thing for him."

"All right. Let's go back to Brian Fitzpain, shall we? He's known to your family, isn't he?"

"Youse think so?"

"We know so, Sorcha." Just a few words of insistence, but they worked. She blinked again and looked down at the floor.

"Youse got a fag?" she asked. "I don't normally smoke, but… this news… youse know."

"Wait here." Will found the waiter and bought a packet of filter tips and a box of matches. He gave them to the girl. "Take your time. Do you want another cup of tea?"

"Hell no. Just need to calm me nerves." She lit up with shaking hands.

"Tell me about Brian Fitzpain. What's his connection with your family?"

She blew out a long trail of smoke. "Why d'youse want to know?"

"We'll need to question anyone in close contact with you, including Fitzpain. He may have information that could lead us to the killer."

The girl took a few seconds to think of a reply. "Me mammy and Brian grew up together in Ardglass. But I suppose youse know that already. Youse seem to know a lot already. When was Bridie killed?"

"We don't know. She was found about half an hour or more ago."

"And yet you already know about me and Brian

Fitzpain?" This time she stared into his eyes, visibly demanding some sort of explanation.

Will kept his cool. He'd enough experience of questioning people. "We've been trying to piece together what happened. It's our job. Tell me more about Fitzpain and your mother. Were they close, do you think, in their younger days?"

She took another deep draw on the cigarette. "Lived in the same street. Went to the same school. Played together as kids. Youse probably didn't know that, did youse?"

Will ignored the taunt. "Anything else?"

She started to gabble then, as if her inner tension was trying to ease itself with a rush of words. "The usual stuff, so mammy once told me. Went to the Gaelic football in Dublin together. Brian's a great one for the Gaelic football, so he is. Drank in the same pubs. Acted together in the school plays. Always in and out of each other's houses."

"They acted together?" A memory was jolted back into Will's mind.

"He'd have to be a good actor."

"Maybe he is."

"Youse suspect him, don't youse?" the girl said. A note of sour accusation had crept into her voice.

"No one is beyond suspicion at the moment."

The girl became angry then. She stabbed the forefinger of her free hand onto the table. "Youse can forget about Brian. He'd never lay a finger on any of us. I know he wouldn't."

"Because he was close to your mother?"

"Because..."

"Yes?" Will's interest intensified. This could be vital. Suspicions were beginning to solidify. "Tell me what Brian Fitzpain really means to you, Sorcha. He means something special, doesn't he?"

"I think…" She drew heavily on the cigarette. "No… not think… I'm certain he's me real daddy. Godsakes, I don't know why I'm tellin' youse this. Forget it. It's not important."

"You have evidence of what you say?"

255

"They wrote Pat Mulveny on me birth certificate. But I think t'was Brian."

"So why do you think that?"

"I need a pee," she said suddenly. She stubbed out her cigarette in the saucer and stood up.

Will pointed to a 'toilets' sign on a door. "Through there."

She was gone only a few moments before McIlroy came into the restaurant. He sniffed at the curried air, went to the table and sat down. "Thought I'd find you here, Will. Where's the girl?"

"She needed to go to the toilet."

"Fair enough. You've told her about her sister?"

"Yes."

"How did she take it?"

"How do you think?"

"You've been questioning her?"

"Yes." Will looked down at his teacup. He hadn't even started drinking it. It would be cold by now. "She's been somewhat evasive, but I did pick up that her mother and Fitzpain were close. Went to the same school. Acted in school plays."

"Really?" McIlroy looked surprised.

"Could have given him the ability to lie convincingly."

"Or he might just be a born liar."

"There's something else," Will said. "She knew Jimmy Fish had been killed. Claimed someone told her, but she wouldn't say who."

"Fitzpain?"

"That's my guess, boss."

"Looks like she's caught up in this business more than we thought. And here's something you'll want to know. She thinks Fitzpain is her real father."

"Really? Why?"

"We never got round to that before she went off to the toilet."

"Pity."

It was important information, Will thought, but somehow

it didn't ring true. Something was wrong with Sorcha Mulveny's assertion, and he couldn't pinpoint why. He needed time to think about it.

"What are things like at the bus station, boss?" he asked.

"Horrific. The building is ablaze. I'm sorry to tell you this, but some of your fellow countrymen, a couple of Welsh Guardsmen, were in the Land Rover which pulled up just before the bomb exploded. Two of them died instantly."

Will shrugged. Was he getting complacent in the face of all this killing? "They wouldn't have been the only casualties."

"No. I saw some terrible things in that place, Will." McIlroy clasped his hands together on the table. "Bits of bodies all over the shop. D'you know, there was a six-foot high wrought-iron railing at the back of the building. Two men were blown through it. Their bodies were torn apart through the bars. Just torn into shreds. I saw the flesh that was left splattered on the metal."

"Dear God! So they didn't get everyone away in time?"

"No. Some of them were heading into the station because they'd been told there was a bomb in the next street. The police were herding them into the building because they thought they'd be safe there."

"Hoaxes. Jimmy Fish was right. We've been taken for fools."

McIlroy went on, grimacing as he spoke. "A bus driver was killed. His body was left with no head or arms. I saw it. I knew it was a driver because I was able to make out bits of his Ulsterbus uniform. Grey serge with an enamel badge."

Will frowned. "I don't need to hear any more, boss. You want a cup of tea?"

McIlroy shook his head and looked around. "That girl should have come back by now. Unless she needed more than just a quick pee."

"Or…" Will had a sudden premonition.

McIlroy stood up as the obvious answer occurred to him. "… or you may have been the victim of the oldest trick in the book."

They both went through the door marked 'toilets'. It led to a long corridor. At the far end an outside door hung open. Will yanked open an inside door immediately beside him, marked 'ladies'.

There was no sign of Sorcha Mulveny.

"Damn! Where the hell would she go?" Will said.

McIlroy drew a deep breath and patted Will's shoulder. "Don't get frustrated. At a guess, she'd head for the most obvious place; Mafeking Street. With a bit of luck, she might be safe there amongst her own kind."

"You think we should go after her?"

"After what happened to us last time? No, we don't go back there without an army escort. Too dangerous. We'll head back to base and get some updates on what's happening. I think we both need something to calm us down, and I don't mean a cup of straight tea."

"A McIlroy standard?"

"Right."

***

January 1981

Will stopped abruptly at that point in his account. I heard Milly's voice in the background. They seemed to be arguing. Eventually, he came back to me and said, "Sorry about that. Milly is worried about me talking to you."

"Can I speak to her, Will?"

"Why?"

"It may help if she tells me what she saw that day. In her own words."

"I doubt it. She wants you out of my hair."

"Tell her I'll get out of *her* hair when I have the full story of what happened that day. Give her the phone, will you?"

"If you say so."

I put a hand over the mouthpiece and spoke to Susan. "Will never really got over his part in what happened that day. The trauma effect. You'll understand that. That's why

258

Milly is against me speaking to him. I'm hoping she'll give me some better insight into things. A better insight into how much he suffered emotionally."

Susan pulled her arm tighter around me.

A woman's voice came down the telephone line. It was Milly. "If I talk to you, will you put an end to all this questioning?"

"I'll put an end to it when I have the full story," I said. "How did that Friday affect you, Milly?"

"Badly."

"Why don't you tell me about it?"

"Now?"

"Yes, now."

I was taking a chance, but it worked.

***

21st July 1972
1450 BST

Milly was halfway to the Liverpool Ferry Terminal before she regretted leaving home. She started the journey with good reason: telephone calls to the ferry line were not being answered and Milly was determined to get the family rebooked on tomorrow's sailing. Well, if she couldn't phone them she would visit them. It wasn't far to drive, so she bundled the children in the car and set off... and quickly regretted it.

The city roads were in chaos, busier than she had ever seen them, making the journey frustrating as well as unsafe. Black smoke drifted ominously across the skyline while the shrill sound of fire and police sirens filled the air. She had heard the explosions, but she hadn't realised the consequences would be as bad as this. The traffic was slow moving, sometimes down to a snail's crawl, and drivers were impatient. Horns were being blared at every stoppage.

The girls were arguing in the back of the car, but Milly soldiered on. One way or another, she was determined to get that new booking. And she was determined it would be for all the family, including Will.

Privately, she understood Will's willingness to continue working in Belfast. It gave him a sense of satisfaction to be doing a job few other police officers could, or would tackle. The RUC was, as someone once said, a force like no other police force in Europe. It faced greater dangers and it handled far more crimes than any other. And it suffered more casualties than any other. Will lived his working life on adrenalin and he loved it. It was like a drug. He was addicted to it.

But it had to stop.

If the killing didn't stop – and it seemed highly unlikely – then Will's employment with the RUC would have to stop. She was determined on that because she saw no other option. Northern Ireland was in the grip of a children's gang mentality, but with adult mobs replacing the children. The same childish thinking, but with guns and bombs instead of sticks and stones. Funerals instead of Elastoplast. The immaturity and ignorance remained the same.

Anger intensified within her. They could not... must not continue living amongst this.

Maybe it was time to make one final stand... to stop using Irish customs and Irish food in the home. Maybe it was time to wean her husband back onto the sort of Welsh customs he would have known in his youth. She could begin by cutting out the Ulster fry-up, his habitual breakfast over the past ten years. That should be easy enough. She could simply replace the Irish potato farls and soda bread with Welsh laverbread. His mother had shown her how to make laverbread. She had also introduced her daughter-in-law to Welsh cakes and Welsh rarebit, although Milly had never really got down to making it. Well, this could be the moment to begin.

Anything to get him thinking seriously about returning to Wales.

She let out a long sigh of relief when she turned towards the Liverpool Ferry Terminus. The traffic was moving freely when she came in sight of the terminal. She pulled into the ferry car park, surprised that it seemed almost empty. She parked in front of a white Ford van, switched off the engine and turned towards the two girls.

"I'm going into the ferry office for a few minutes. I want you to sit here quietly until I get back. Do you hear me?"

"Yes, mummy." They replied in unison.

"No fighting or arguing?"

"No, mummy."

Two identical angelic faces beamed up at her. She knew they had no intention of keeping the peace. They never did.

Milly turned to the front again at the sound of a tap on her driver's side window. She wound it down to see a uniformed police sergeant bending to speak to her.

"You'll need to get away from here. Quickly." He pointed to a Mini parked two hundred yards away, near the Liverpool Bar. "There's a suspicious car over there and we've had a warning of a bomb."

"But no one stopped me coming in here," she said.

"We spotted you too late. Just turn around and drive back out the way you came." He stood up and tapped the car roof as a signal for her to move forward.

But she never did.

It was just a few minutes before three o'clock, and the Mini exploded. A flash, a loud boom and the car opened up, torn apart like a can of beans. Flames and black smoke belched out from it. The police sergeant staggered backwards against the blast.

"Oh, God!" In a moment of sheer panic, Milly threw her gearstick into reverse and floored the throttle. Her car raced backwards and rammed into the Ford van.

The girls screamed.

Milly sat stunned while the screaming continued.

The police sergeant came running. "Is anyone hurt?" He pulled open one of the rear doors and reached in for the twins.

"I don't think so." Milly climbed out and helped the sergeant lift the girls to the ground. They stopped screaming and ran into the arms of their mother, hugging her tightly.

In the background, Milly heard the crackle of flames. The air was now thick with the smell of burning. But they were alive and unhurt.

"It's all right, girls," Milly told them. "No real harm done. Except to the car."

"Your husband won't like this," the policeman gestured to the car's crumpled rear end. "The van driver won't be too impressed either."

"My husband is a detective sergeant at North Castle Street," she said. "He should be used to motor accidents."

The uniformed policeman looked at her with renewed interest. "North Castle Street? One of their men was killed last night. Johnny Dunlop. You knew him?"

"Yes, I've heard of him. My husband is Will Evans."

"Will? I know him. I saw him earlier today at the York Road railway station."

"I hope he's all right."

"Amen to that Mrs Evans. I'll see if I can get word to him. Let him know what's happened here."

"You're not from North Castle Street barracks?"

"No. Oldpark. Name's Mickey Murphy. Shouldn't really be here, but I've being shunted from one emergency to another, filling in where I can. Been darting around like a blue-arse fly. You wouldn't believe how chaotic things are."

"I think I would Sergeant Murphy. I think I would." That was when she felt tears trickle down her cheeks.

***

January 1981

"And that's all you're going to get from me! Or Will." Milly's voice was emphatic. She put down the telephone, leaving me wondering whether I had got it all wrong. I hadn't been aware just how much Will's family had suffered that day. Was Milly the one with the right idea? Was I being unfair on him?

"What did she say?" Susan asked.

I leaned back on the bed and she snuggled up beside me while I recounted Milly's experience.

"Do you think I ought to back off?" I asked.

"You'll never get to the full truth behind the story if you do. Are you willing to sacrifice the book?"

"That's a bit of a poisoned cup, isn't it? I lose either way."

"That's life," she said. "But I'll help you, whichever choice you make. You do still need help, you know."

"Am I so transparent?"

"Very. But you'll be a different person if you choose to finish the book."

"I'll need to speak to Sorcha again."

"You could phone the prison in the morning… from my flat."

Chapter Eighteen

January 1981

The first time I slept with Susan was like emerging from a long period of half-life. The second time was more akin to the way it was with Annie. How such empathy could have grown between Susan and me in such a short period was way beyond my understanding, but it happened.

After breakfast the following morning I sat at the kitchen table and phoned the prison to ask about Sorcha.

"Ulster fry up." Susan set a plate of cooked breakfast in front of me when I put the phone down. "What did they say?"

"Sorcha is anxious to see me again. I've arranged permission to go over there this morning."

"Do you want me with you?"

"Always."

She ran her hands through my hair. "Full marks for the right answer. Now eat up your breakfast and show me that my cooking is good enough for you."

***

We arrived at the prison on the dot of ten o'clock. It was raining; the sort of cold, sleety rain that counted for normal in Belfast. Susan hung onto my arm as we hurried into the building. Sorcha was waiting for us, but the earlier air of determination had gone from her now. She looked drawn and tired. Her voice was muted.

"I had to see youse again as soon as possible. If I put it off, I think I would have given up."

"I sat down opposite her, with Susan beside me. "How do you feel now, Sorcha?"

"Shitty."

I looked at the beefy warder. "Could we have a glass of water for Miss Mulveny. She may need it once we get going."

Sorcha smiled weakly at the point. "Youse think of everything, don't youse?"

"I want you to be comfortable, Sorcha. Why don't you begin by telling me your reaction to hearing that Bridie had been killed?"

"It hit me badly, so it did."

"Take your time and tell me."

***

21st July 1972
1530 BST

She had not cried when the peeler told her Bridie was dead. Most girls would have screamed and burst into tears, but not Sorcha. She had kept some outer semblance of control despite the shivering feeling that ran inside her. Despite the peeler's questions.

But it was all an act.

Inside, she was falling apart. Inside, her mental capacity was dying. She couldn't take much more. Only sheer bloody-mindedness kept her going, forcing her to return to the family home.

She had no idea who killed Bridie, or why. The peeler didn't tell her. But she was going to find out, one way or another. She and Bridie never had been close. Sometimes they did not seem to be like sisters. It felt as if they came from different families. Or, at the very least, different fathers. That was something she was able to rationalise because she thought she knew the identity of her own father. If she was right, he was not Bridie's father. And yet, despite the differences between them, she had enough compassion inside her to be sickened by this particular killing. Her sister or half-sister, it didn't matter which. In the meantime, she had to get back to her mammy and comfort her.

She was stopped two hundred yards from a garage in Donegall Street, where a uniformed policeman ordered her to turn back. She was arguing with him when a bomb exploded in a car parked on the garage premises. The blast echoed along the street. Smoke and flames billowed from the building. Sorcha was mentally stunned for a few seconds, but she quickly recovered. She was unhurt and still on her feet as she watched the debris from the building tumble into the street. Firemen raced forward to tackle the flames. Armed soldiers stood nearby to guard them. Where else in these islands would firemen need to be protected from gunmen and rioters? Was the whole world mad? Or just this tiny patch of land called Ulster?

Another small part of her nerve crumbled to dust.

She turned away and hurried back the way she had come. She had no wish to see the effect of any more explosions. She found another route home.

Mafeking Street looked different as she approached it from along Ladysmith Road. It was the new barricade that made the street look impregnable at first glance. Her mental processes were a little more in control by then; she was able to think a little more coherently. She saw that the entrance to the back alley, another twenty yards farther along, was still wide open. The idiots! What was the point of barricading the front of the houses when they hadn't had the sense to protect the alley?

She marched straight up to one of the two young gunmen guarding the barricade. Both wore balaclava helmets and both carried rifles, but that didn't stop her recognising the two Docherty teenagers from across the road. They were not alone. Coleen McTurk had been chatting with them: a fifteen-year-old wearing a flowery dress designed to hide the fact she was pregnant. She would be sent away to be put into the care of nuns any day now. Care? There was no 'care' involved. Sorcha knew that well enough. What happened to her would be cruel and painful, harsh punishment rather than compassion. Her baby would be taken away, whether she wanted it or not. Other people had already decided that.

Sorcha shuddered at a painful memory... a memory of what happened to her.

Coleen had the boys' full attention, probably because one of them was the likely father of the unborn child. In all probability, both had bedded her at some time or other. It was what happened in these miserable streets. It relieved the tedium, nothing more than that, and the follow-up was inevitably bad news. The shame and the condemnation. Yet another child taken away from its mother and given up for adoption. Sorcha understood. She had lived with the consequences and the unending mental turmoil. Even now, she lived with it.

She picked on the weediest of the two young men. "Youse're a pair of eejits, Tommy Docherty! What are youse?"

"What d'youse mean, Sorcha?" The boy's voice was unusually squeaky.

"That!" She pointed to the unguarded alleyway. "Why ain't youse got someone standing guard on the alley. Any Prod who wanted to plant a bomb could get down there."

"We'd see them," the boy protested.

"You wouldn't. Youse were payin' attention to Coleen. Neither of youse was watching who might come up behind youse from Rorke Street. Go and find someone to guard the alley, and do it now. Eejits!"

She brushed past them and strode through the narrow access into Mafeking Street. It looked almost empty. Likely the children had now been taken indoors, a sure sign that trouble was expected. How many times had she heard the mammies with their warning, "Get the children inside!" before any shooting began? Inevitably, some children would get forgotten, usually because they were playing in the alleys, but most would be gathered up.

She marched on down to number 23 and suddenly

realised she had no door key. She had left it in her coat pocket: the coat she gave away to that other girl in Anderson and McCauleys. Giving herself a mild rebuke, she rattled the doorknob. There was no answer.

She tried again.

Still no answer.

Shite! Her mother should have got back from Ardglass well before now. What was she doing away from the house at a time like this? Well, at least Edna McRostie next door would have the spare key. She turned to number 21 and knocked on the door.

Old Edna poked her head out, looked up and down the street and then focussed on Sorcha. "What the hell are youse wearin', girl? Ain't seen youse dressed like that before. Youse look like a Proddy whore, so youse do."

Sorcha ignored the comment. "I need our spare key, Edna. Me mammy ain't answerin' the door."

The old woman pulled a key from a nail in the adjacent wall. "She came home earlier. Saw her, so I did. That was before two peelers came to the house."

"Peelers? What did they want?"

"Damned if I know."

"Bastards!"

Sorcha took the key and let herself in to number 23.

"Mammy! Are youse there?"

There was no reply, so she hurried on through to the kitchen. And stopped dead when she saw her mother. She was blood-splattered and lying on her back with a knife in her chest.

This time Sorcha did scream.

"OH GOD! NO!"

And she wept. Just stood there and wept uncontrollably. She couldn't help it. Then her weeping turned to screaming. She was still screaming when she ran out into the tiny back yard where the gate into the alley was ajar. Huge gasping cries wracked her whole body as she leaned against a brick wall and allowed the full force of her anguish to pour out.

She shouted, "NO! NO! NO!" And she went on crying as

she had never cried before.

"What the hell's the matter, Sorcha?" It was little Tommy Docherty who came in through the open gate, still brandishing his rifle. "I heard youse cryin', so I did."

"SHE'S DEAD!" She screamed at him. Then her voice retracted into sobbing. "I just… just can't… can't take any more."

She struggled to say what she felt inside, but the words refused to come to her. Tears streamed down her cheeks as she pointed to the open kitchen door.

The boy went in and came out again quickly. He pulled off his helmet and gagged.

"Oh shite!" he cried. Then he vomited.

Sorcha clasped her arms about her waist and forced herself to breath long and deep. Slowly, her weeping abated. Slowly, her thoughts began to focus.

"Fat lot of use youse were, Tommy Docherty," she snapped, her voice finally coming under control. "Youse must have let the Loyalist bastards in."

Docherty's face was white and filled with alarm. "It's all right, Sorcha. I'll go and get the boys. They'll know what to do. The boys'll know." He hurried away, dragging his weapon behind him. A little lost child.

Sorcha didn't wait for him to return before she stumbled out into the alley. She stood for a moment in the spot where Fitzpain had cut off the Protestant boy's penis. In a moment of sudden panic, she saw it again. The vision was as clear as if it was happening right in front of her. There was the boy, and there was Fitzpain cutting him apart with his kitchen knife. And… good God! There was the peeler with the same knife in his chest. And there was Jimmy Fish clasping his little black beret to his chest. And… in the middle of the vision… there was her mammy, dead on the kitchen floor.

Their ghosts rose up in unison and pointed at her, shouting at her. "It was you, Sorcha! You did this to us!"

The raucous voices rang in her ears.

"NO!" She put her hands to her face and turned away, and she saw Bridie standing apart and stabbing a fat finger at her. "It was youse, Sorcha! Youse betrayed us!"

"STOP IT! STOP IT!"

She ran, wavering from side to side as she raced along the alley, not seeing where she was going, just running.

Then she stumbled.

She fell sideways and scraped down the rough brick wall, tearing her dress. A ripping sound reached her ears as she fell, face-down, onto the cobbles. She lay, stunned for a while, she had no idea how long. When she sat up, she looked back along the alley. No one was in sight. No one was following her. Where the hell were the IRA boys when you needed them?

She looked down at her chest. The front of her dress was in tatters, shredded and revealing her breasts.

Slowly, registering pain in her arms and legs, she rose to her feet. Confusion filled her head, like a giant fog which obliterated every attempt at rational thought.

She staggered on along the alley, clutching her torn dress to her chest. Minutes passed, or was it hours? Where was she now? She wasn't sure. Out here in the busy streets, people ran along the pavements. Some were shouting, some crying. Cars filled the roads, bumper to bumper. But no one seemed to notice her. She walked along various alleys and roads she did not recognise.

Until she came to a church.

She knew then where she was. It was the Catholic Church of Saint Winifred. The church of Father O'Hanlon, the priest she despised because of his bigotry and hypocrisy. The priest who buggered little boys and got away with it.

The priest's house was alongside the church building. Could she get help here? Unlikely, but there was nowhere else she could think of. So she climbed the few steps to the front door and rang the bell. It was opened by the parish priest, an obese figure with thick lips, flabby cheeks and a gaping mouth.

He stared at her. "You? Sorcha Mulveny? What the hell are you doing here?"

She spoke in a tiny voice. "Please help me, Father." No

270

matter how hard she tried, she could not bring herself to speak with confidence.

The priest took on a sneering tone. "Help you? Just look at you, girl. What do you think you look like?"

"Please. I need help."

"Well, you won't get it here. It'd be a sin for me to let the likes of you into my church. I know all about you, girl. I know all about your vile, sexual sins. Your mother told me all about it. And I know what blasphemy you've been spouting. The wicked things you've said about holy mother church. You're a sinner and you'll go to hell for it. Now get away from here."

"Please…" she begged.

"Go away!"

He turned and slammed the door behind him.

Sorcha sat down on the top step and lowered her head into her arms. He was right. She was a sinner, doomed to go to hell. Just like all those Protestants. There was no more weeping in her now, just an aching emptiness. An emptiness that seemed to be drawing her towards the flames where the devil awaited her.

Yet another bomb exploded not far away. The boom of the explosion reverberated around inside her head. She looked up and saw yet more black smoke rising above the roof tops. Would it never end?

"No more," she whispered. "Please, no more."

She could not stay here at the church, so she struggled to her feet and walked on, clasping the rags of her dress close to her. People stared at her as they hurried past, but no one spoke to her, no one seemed to care. With so many bombs destroying their city, how could they have any time for the likes of Sorcha Mulveny?

She came to a row of shops. Most were closed but one remained open. It was a cancer charity shop with used clothes on display. Sorcha leaned against the window. Weariness was all she felt now. Deep, empty weariness. She pressed her face against the glass and stared at the clothes on the other side. Then she saw a woman staring back at

271

her. An old woman in a bright flowery dress. She had snowy white hair.

Moments later, the woman was at the shop door, beckoning to her. "What on earth happened to you? Was it a bomb?"

Sorcha lumbered towards her. She forced her voice back to its normal volume. "Me mammy and me sister," she mumbled.

"What happened to them?" The old woman put an arm around Sorcha's shoulders and shepherded her into the shop. There was no one else inside. Who would be buying used clothes on a day like this?

"They're dead."

"Oh, you poor thing. And just look at the state of you." She helped Sorcha into a chair. "Sit here while I get you a glass of water." She hurried away into a back room.

Sorcha slumped down. The chair was hard, but the atmosphere was warm. Not cold and unwelcoming like Father O'Hanlon's church, but warm like a place of peace. And, dear God, she needed peace.

The old lady came back with a filled glass and placed it into Sorcha's hands. "Drink this. Then you can tell me what happened." She pulled up another chair and sat beside her.

Sorcha drank greedily. She hadn't realised just how thirsty she was.

"Thank you," she said.

"Your dress is a mess," the old lady replied. "Tell me your name."

"Sorcha."

"Ah. A Catholic name, but it's of no consequence. People of all faiths have been suffering today. We're Salvation Army, my husband and me, but we believe we're here to help anyone who needs us. You do need help, don't you, Sorcha."

She nodded.

"Good. You can call me Sophie. Tell me what happened to you."

"I saw me mammy. It was after she died. It was…" The

tears came again then, torrents rolling down both cheeks. She couldn't find any way of halting it. Neither could she find a way of describing how she felt when she saw her mammy dead on the floor.

Sophie took her hand and held it patiently, saying nothing because there was nothing that could be said. She waited until Sorcha's tears began to abate before she finally spoke again. "You can't go around in that dress any longer. It's so badly torn. Why, it's not even covering your modesty. Let's see if we can find something else that will fit you."

"I've no money," Sorcha said, wiping at her face. "I can't afford…"

"No matter." The old lady helped her to her feet. "Who would ask for money at a time like this? Come into the back room and take off those rags while I see if I can find something your size."

The back room was small and untidy. Boxes of used clothes were stacked against a wall. Sorcha took off the dress and waited. What did it matter that she was naked? Naked in the sight of God? Or had God abandoned her? She hung her head in desperation. What did anything matter any longer?

Sophie came back with a skirt, a woollen jersey and a set of underwear. "I think this will be about your size… oh, my, you've been bleeding. Just look." She set down the clothes on a chair and put out a hand to where blood had been tricking down Sorcha's chest.

"I hadn't noticed." Sorcha said.

"Wait until I get a cloth and some warm water to clean you up." Sophie hurried away again.

Sorcha picked up the clothes and saw that they were almost new. Someone had given them to charity after very little use. And they were being donated to her at no cost. It hit her then that this lady, Sophie, was showing her the sort of kindness she had rarely, if ever, experienced in her own home. When did Bridie show her such compassion? When did her poor dead mammy show such love?

The truth of it hit her hard and she began to weep again.

January 1981

The cold, sleety rain was heavier when Susan and I took a taxi back to her flat. We both knew that I had to give Sorcha some free space before I interviewed her again, and we both knew that meant me retreating back to England for a while. Neither of us was keen on the parting; we were getting too close to one another. It was possible, however, that we also needed space while we thought about where our relationship was going.

"What will you do about your investigations now?" Susan asked me that evening as we prepared for bed.

I silently considered my reply before I said, "It's a toss-up whether I speak to Will Evans again, or Martin Foster. Will is going to be the difficult one, but I really do want to hear more about what he and McIlroy did next. I want to know their thinking about how the evidence was stacking up against Fitzpain and Sorcha. Only Will Evans can tell me that."

"Why don't you drive up to Wales and tackle Will? Let me go and talk to Martin." Susan suggested. "He said he was getting tired of you – that's what you told me – so let me have a word or two with him. I can say I'm working as your researcher and I can take some detailed notes – I'm used to that – and report it all back to you."

It was a sensible suggestion, but I had one objection. "That would remove my excuse for coming over here to see you again."

"It would also give me an excuse to fly over to England and visit you."

Chapter Nineteen

January 1981

My flat felt lonely when I got home. I had to admit to myself that it wasn't Annie I was now missing, it was Susan. Was that a step forward or a step backwards into the abyss? Was the new relationship happening too quickly? I couldn't answer the question and it bothered me.

After a few days I phoned Will Evans and arranged to meet him at a pub in Llandudno. He was reluctant at first, but I told him I was now near the end of my research and would soon be out of his hair.

"Just a little farther to go, Will, and then you can tell Milly you've seen the last of me."

That seemed to clinch the matter.

It was raining when I drove into Wales, but it felt like soft Welsh rain, not the hard sleety rain of Northern Ireland. Or was that my imagination playing havoc with reality? The first thing I did when Will arrived at the pub was to buy him a double whiskey. An Irish whiskey. Then I settled back to hear about the next stage in his investigations.

***

21st July 1972
1540 BST

They returned to their base because they knew there was little they could now do out there in the city. They would likely be a hindrance in the face of the army's attempts to bring some sort of order to the chaos.

"When we get back we'll regroup our senses, Will," McIlroy said. "And I'll bring our beloved leader up to date with our murder enquiries."

Chaos filled the RUC barracks at North Castle Street. The sound of raised voices hit Will and McIlroy the moment they entered. Will caught the arm of Maisie O'Hare, the young WPC, and asked her to get them cups of tea.

"No chance, sir," she replied with a look of disdain. "Sorry. Far too busy."

"Is that because I rebuffed you earlier, in the canteen?"

"No. It's because I really am far too busy." Then she smiled at him with an undertone of malice. "Next time you refuse me I shall pour your tea all over you."

"Get the tea yourself, Will," his boss said. He gave the girl a sour look before he headed off in the direction of the superintendent's office. "Remember that mine's a McIlroy standard."

Will nodded in understanding. 'McIlroy standard' was milk and two sugars from the canteen, with more than a dash of whiskey from his office drawer. It was a variation on the 'NATO Standard' tea he had discovered in his RAF days. Basically the same, but with the addition of the whiskey.

Will had just brought the two mugs of tea down from the canteen to their office and was adding the alcohol when his boss returned with a wry expression.

"Our beloved leader is getting his knickers in a twist again." He grabbed at one of the mugs and slumped down in the chair behind his desk. He sipped at the drink with a thoughtful expression written large across his face.

"Because of the bombs?" Will pulled out a stack of forms to write up his latest report.

"Mostly. We've lost another man, Will. Two uniformed men were sent out to Mafeking Street to speak to Barbara Mulveny about her daughter, the woman that was killed. They never got anywhere near the street, and only man one made it back alive. The other was killed by a Republican mob."

"Shot?" Will looked up.

"No. Beaten up. Torn apart as if he'd been savaged by a pack of wolves."

"Shit! Who was he?"

"A youngster. Constable Damian O'Sullivan."

"I know the one. Too young to be killed. They should have sent out some older and tougher guys."

The B Specials would have handled it better and come out alive!

McIlroy shook his head sadly. "The tough guys are dealing with the bombs. Anyway, it's too late now."

"And what about the older Mulveny woman?"

"No idea. I assume she still hasn't been told her daughter is dead."

"Wouldn't want to be the next one who tried to reach her."

A few minutes of silence followed before the office door opened and Sergeant McRee called to McIlroy.

"Superintendent Boyle asked to see you again, sir."

"What? Again? I've just seen him. Did he say what he wants now?"

"No, sir. Just said to tell you to go along to his office. And bring your sergeant with you."

McIlroy drained his reinforced tea. "Come along, Will. Let's find out what our glorious leader wants now."

When they entered his office, Boyle was studying a sheet of paper. He indicated them to wait until he had finished reading it. Then he looked up.

"A girl was shot in that riot at the end of the street," he said.

"We know," McIlroy replied. "We interviewed a man earlier. He witnessed it. Do we know who the girl is... was?"

"Not yet, but this is a copy of a piece of paper that was found in her pocket. It's only just been passed on to me." Boyle pushed the paper across his desk. "It seems to be a list of all the bomb targets. This has gone right to the top. The Chief Constable is studying a copy of this right now, and so is the Assistant Chief Constable. They're both asking why it wasn't sent up the line earlier."

"Because it wasn't found earlier, I guess."

"Don't be facetious, McIlroy. That girl was one of them, one of the IRA bombers. She must've been. I've sent forensics over to the mortuary to see what they can make of her. There should be some forensic evidence."

"Maybe." McIlroy didn't seem convinced.

"She had to be involved."

"Or... maybe she was killed because she was thought to be involved. She was wearing someone else's clothes."

Boyle frowned. "Really? Why was that?"

"We don't know, but our witness recognised the clothes and they didn't belong to the girl who was shot. We know who they did belong to: a girl called Sorcha Mulveny. It's possible the Mulveny girl might have originally had the list."

Boyle let out a long breath. "I'm not happy with this, McIlroy, and neither is the Chief Constable. This is valuable evidence and we didn't pick it up soon enough. What about this Mulveny girl? Where is she?"

"We don't know. We're still working on it."

"Well, get back to it and make sure I'm informed as soon as you find her. And find out what the hell is going on."

"And the bombs?"

"I've better men than you dealing with the bombs."

McIlroy nodded towards the sheet of paper. "Well, good luck to them. At least you now know all the bomb locations."

"Too bloody late. Too bloody late!"

Back in their own office, Will and McIlroy refilled their mugs. No tea this time, just the whiskey. They needed it. Loose ends were the bane of a detective's life and they had too many. They created a fog.

McIlroy set down the paper on his desk and studied it. "Let's see if we can make any sense of this, Will. This list of bomb locations was found on a girl who was wearing Sorcha Mulveny's clothes, but it seems she wasn't Sorcha

Mulveny. And someone shot her."

"Thinking she was Sorcha Mulveny?"

"Most likely. Then the other Mulveny girl, Bridie, was murdered and a threatening note was left nearby."

"An illiterate note."

"Yes, totally illiterate, but that note threatened Sorcha. So, whoever wrote it thought she was still alive."

"Maybe they discovered they'd shot the wrong girl?"

"Seems possible. And now they have it in for the rest of the family, including the mother."

"Why? If only we knew why?"

McIlroy put down the paper and flexed his fingers. "You know what I think? I reckon Sorcha Mulveny was involved in the death of that Protestant lad who had his dick cut off in that alley behind Mafeking Street. Behind the Mulveny's house. The Loyalist gangs would want revenge for that, and they'd have ways of finding out who did it."

"You don't really think Sorcha Mulveny did it?"

"No, it's unlikely to have been her. It had to be Fitzpain. But the Mulveny girl must have been involved in it in some way, and it would be easier to kill the accomplice than to kill Fitzpain himself. He's got too many thugs to protect him."

Will understood the reasoning. "You think Fitzpain actually killed the lad, and the girl helped in some way? And that's why Loyalists went looking for her?"

"Right. A case of Protestant revenge." McIlroy took a gulp from his mug and leaned back. "Now let's look at the killing of Johnny Dunlop. He was a bloody fool to go walking through a Nationalist area, even if he wasn't in uniform. Jimmy Fish found out who killed him and tried to tell us who did it. A sort of relation, he said."

"Fitzpain again?"

"Maybe. Let's assume for the moment that it was him. And let's assume that Jimmy was killed because he tipped us the nod."

"And he was killed by…?"

"That's what we still have to discover. And something

279

has just occurred to me. Let's look again at that character description on Fitzpain, and compare it with that arrest report. There's something there …"

The phone rang, interrupting their deliberations. McIlroy picked it up, listened for a few seconds and then said, "Yes, he's here. A call for you Will. From Sergeant Murphy at Oldpark."

Will crossed the room and took the receiver.

The voice at the other end was clear and calm. "Will? It's Mickey Murphy. Look I don't want to worry you, but I saw your wife at the Liverpool ferry terminal this afternoon. She went there to rebook some ferry tickets, so she said. Got caught up in a bomb scare."

Will shuddered. The stupid woman. She should have stayed at home.

"She's okay?" he asked.

"She's not hurt. Not physically. Neither are the kids, but there was a car bomb explosion. Milly wasn't hurt by it, but she tried to escape and made a bit of a mess of your own car. Smashed it into a van. I saw it happen."

"Oh, God, no! Where is she now?"

"On her way home. I twisted the arm of one of our reservists. He's taking all of them home; Milly and the kids. The car is still down at the docks. It'll need to be towed away."

"Thanks for letting me know, Mickey."

Will had confidence in Mickey Murphy. They were Catholics together in the RUC; men who looked out for one another. Will Evans, Johnny Dunlop and Mickey Murphy; a small tight-knit group within a larger, looser group. And their little group was regarded as traitorous by the IRA.

"Anything else I can do to help, Will?" Murphy asked.

"Not really." Then a thought came to him. "Wait a moment though. You grew up in Ladysmith Road, didn't you, Mickey?"

Murphy allowed a few seconds to lapse before he replied. "Past history, Will. All behind me now."

"Did you know a family called Mulveny?"

"The Mulvenys? Yes, they lived in Mafeking Street." His voice was hesitant now, as if he was holding back on something.

"What about Sorcha Mulveny? What can you tell me about her?"

A few more seconds lapsed. "Sorcha? Lovely girl. I saw her earlier today, in Anderson and McCauleys. She was being accosted by that Loyalist thug, Mad Mac McKinnon. I had to send him on his way."

"He was threatening her?"

"As far as you can threaten anyone in the restaurant at Anderson and McCauleys. But I intervened and she was okay when I last saw her. She was leaving the place on her own."

"You haven't seen or spoken to her since?"

"No. She left before we could really get talking. As for me… well, too busy with other things. It's not all sunshine and light in Belfast right now. I've been acting like a one-man flying squad, shuttling around between various bomb locations, sending updates back to base. Doing my bit to help."

"You and me, Mickey."

"What's the problem with Sorcha?"

"Her name came up in one of our investigations. I can't go into detail, but we need to speak to her."

"I'll let you know if I hear anything."

"Okay. Thanks, Mickey."

Will put down the phone. He turned to where McIlroy was studying two sheets of paper. A deep frown was paste across his face.

"Reckon you were right, boss," Will said. "Mickey Murphy saw Sorcha Mulveny earlier in Anderson and McCauleys. She was being threatened by Mad Mac McKinnon. It's the Loyalists who are after her."

McIlroy looked up. "Mad Mac? That seems to confirm what we thought. Clever girl, that Sorcha Mulveny. Looks like she swapped clothes with someone else to put McKinnon off the scent."

"And the other girl was killed. That wasn't so clever."

"You're right. And the Loyalists will still be looking for her."

"And if they find her…"

"She's dead meat."

"So where do we look now?"

McIlroy leapt to his feet. "Where we should have looked right at the start. If she isn't at her own home, sooner or later she'll be go to Fitzpain's place. We should try there."

"Whooa, boss." Will raised a hand in protest. "Give me just a couple of minutes first. Milly had some trouble down at the ferry terminal. Damaged our car. I need to phone her to find out if she's all right. And I need to get a garage to recover the car."

"She should have stayed at home."

"You try telling her that."

McIlroy sat down again. "Okay, but before you do that, Will, take a look at this." McIlroy gestured to the two sheets of paper on his desk. "This is the character outline on Fitzpain. I've just taken it from the file we got from Boyle. And this…" He fingered the other page. "… this is the report on Fitzpain's arrest. It includes the two women the uniforms found at that hotel. Have a look at what it says about the Mulveny girl and tell me if anything stands out."

Will picked up both pages and looked at them. "Specifically, what should I be looking for."

"The dates."

"I don't see it."

"The girl thinks Fitzpain is her real father. That's what she told you in that Chinese Restaurant. Yes?"

"Yes."

McIlroy stabbed at finger at each page. "Well, now look here… and here."

"Oh, yes! I see what you mean. It's not what she thinks, is it?"

***

282

January 1981

"What did you see, Will?" I asked.
   He told me and it all made sense.

Chapter Twenty

November 1981

Susan flew over to London one afternoon towards the end of the month and I met her at Heathrow. I drove her back to my flat in Wimbledon and we went straight to bed. I'd been married long enough to spot when a woman is sexually eager, and I wasn't wrong.

Afterwards, we both slept for an hour.

Susan was the first to wake and she eased me back into full consciousness by tickling my chin.

"Please, sir, I want some more," she cooed.

"Now?"

"Yes, now. I want some more now."

"Your name is Susan, not Oliver."

She pursed her lips. "But I want…"

"Supper can be made tastier by allowing it to simmer for an hour or so."

"I might go off the boil."

"Not you." I kissed the tip of her nose. "Are you ready to fill me in with the detail about your chat with Martin?" I was now fully awake.

"I told you the gist of it." She shifted onto her back and pulled the duvet up over her chest. "I probably got on with him better than you did. He actually sounded glad to talk to me."

"Must be your feminine charm. You said he told you how he got confirmation that Sorcha really had been pregnant some time before she met him. What those thugs told him worried him, but he doubted the truth of it until it was confirmed by the policeman."

"He said the truth of it shook him." She turned onto her side and snuggled closer. "What would you think of me if I had been…?"

"Were you?"

"Of course not. And don't ever again ask such an unkind question. But, if I had, what would you think?"

"Love should overcome problems like that. I'd still love you."

"Thank you for saying that. You've just ticked another box on your progress chart."

"Meaning?"

"You and I are getting to the point where important decisions need to be made. Do we have a future together? I've had boyfriends in the past, obviously, but they all failed in one important final test."

"Which was?"

"Would I want to spend my life with them?"

"And…?"

"In every case, I decided no. Sometimes it was because of a character flaw, and sometimes it was for a reason I couldn't quite put my finger on. I will never fully commit myself until I'm totally sure it's the right thing to do. Does that make me a difficult woman?"

"I doubt it. Would you marry me?" I stared into her eyes, daring her to give me an honest reply. I hadn't planned on asking the question, but it came out easily and I knew straightaway it was what I wanted.

"Are you asking me, or just testing the water?"

"Asking."

She thought for a few moments, chewing at her lip. "Far too early to say. But I'll put the question in my pending tray."

"When do you empty it? Your pending tray."

"When it's full."

"Please fill it. And in the meantime?"

"In the meantime… you still need to get over the loss of Annie. And I still want some more."

I gave in. She deserved more.

We continued the discussion about Martin Foster over supper.

***

21st July 1972
1545 BST

It was probably a last option, Martin thought, but he had to try it. He had visited the North Castle Street RUC barracks and learned nothing about Sorcha. He had given the police information about Sorcha, but they had offered nothing in return. Now he would try the Oldpark barracks, the closest RUC base to that dingy hotel. This time he would be careful to give nothing away until he was offered something in return.

It wasn't easy getting inside the barracks. The sangar at the main entrance was well defended, but Martin persisted until he was able to talk to the duty officer at the front desk inside the building.

"What is it you want to report?" he was asked by a uniformed sergeant who was clearly overburdened with other tasks and didn't really give a damn.

Martin replied civilly, but forcefully. "I'm not here to report anything. I'm trying to trace someone."

"Name?"

"Sorcha Mulveny."

"*Your* name, laddie. Unless you're some sort of poofter with a girl's name."

"My name is Martin…" He stopped when he felt a hand rest on his arm. He turned to see a uniformed officer looking at him intently.

"I overheard you asking about Sorcha Mulveny," the policeman said. "Is that the same Sorcha Mulveny from Mafeking Street?"

"Yes. And you are?" His hopes began to rise.

"I'm Sergeant Murphy."

The name came back to Martin in a flash. Those Loyalist

thugs had talked about someone called Mickey Murphy. A peeler, they'd said.

Ask him what happened after... after... He couldn't bring himself to face the unspoken memory of what the thug had said.

"You're not called Mickey Murphy, are you?" Martin stared at the man and his mind was suddenly filled with hastily-created images of him and Sorcha. In bed together.

Could he have got it wrong?

The sergeant nodded. "That's my name. Should I know you?"

Yes, it had to be him!

The images hit home, hard. Unbearably hard. And the thugs' insinuations; they hit even harder.

Ask him why Sorcha Mulveny was sent away from home. Youse just ask him.

"I doubt we've ever met," Martin said.

"So, what's your interest in Sorcha?"

It was warm inside the building and Martin loosened his coat. He felt a sweat form in his armpits. "Just a friend, but I think she may be in trouble. Real trouble. Do you know where I might find her?"

Sergeant Murphy frowned. "In trouble, you say? You'd better come with me to somewhere quieter where we can talk."

He led Martin to an interview room; a small cell-like room with a plain table and wooden seats either side. It smelled stale, heavy with the odour of cigarette smoke. He sat down and gestured Martin to sit opposite him.

"Now, tell me your name."

"Foster. Martin Foster."

"And how do you know Sorcha Mulveny?"

Martin shrugged. He wasn't yet ready to give away too much. "Like I said, we're good friends."

"And why do you think she may be in trouble?"

"Isn't there enough trouble in the city today?" He had not intended to say more, but the ensuing words came out without prior thought. They escaped before he could close the exit. "Earlier, I saw a girl killed in a riot. She was wearing Sorcha's clothes."

"Really? That sounds rather odd. And it begs the question; why would she be doing that?"

"I've no idea." He'd said enough, he decided. Now it was time to get some information in return. "Tell me, Sergeant, what do you know about Sorcha? You were more than just friends at one time, weren't you? Much more."

The images were still there, still hurting.

Murphy looked taken aback. "Who told you that?"

"A couple of Republican ruffians I came across while I was searching for her. They told me someone called Mickey Murphy was romantically linked to Sorcha. Not that they put it so politely, but you'll get the message."

"Romantic?"

"Sexual would be a better way of putting it. Sexual with unwanted consequences." Martin leaned forward to put extra emphasis on the second sentence.

Murphy jerked his head back. "Does that concern you?"

"Yes, it does. I love her."

Loved her and yet I walked away from her.

"I see." The sergeant stood up and strode across the room to a heavily barred window. He stared through the bars for a few moments before turning to face Martin. "Give me one good reason why I should talk about Sorcha's past to you?"

"I intend to marry her."

"Knowing what you've learned already?"

"I told you; I love her."

Murphy gave it a few more moments of thought. "All right, I'll tell you the truth, Martin. Sorcha and I were once lovers. You were not the first to fall in love with her. I was."

"When…?"

The sergeant brushed aside the rest of the question. "It was a few years ago… five years ago. She was only fifteen and I was four years older. We lived in adjacent streets. And, yes, we went to bed together once or twice. Is that such a sin when we loved one another?"

"What happened?"

"I really don't think..."

"I need to know, Sergeant."

The sergeant looked down at the floor. "All right, I'll tell you. Sorcha became pregnant. One of those stupid mistakes we Catholics make so easily because we listen to those brainwashed holy priests and we don't bloody well think for ourselves." He looked up suddenly, came back to the table and sat down, clasping his hands together. "Her mother beat her round the head and went screaming to the local priest. He arranged for her to be sent away to a Magdalene laundry where she had a very rough time. Rough? God help us, the cruelty of the nuns was unforgiveable. And they're supposed to be Christians!"

Martin felt no sense of shock. He had already guessed the truth in the light of the accusations made by those thugs. It hurt to hear it from Sergeant Murphy, but hurt was not the same as shock.

"What happened to the baby?" he asked.

"The baby was forcibly taken away and Sorcha was told it died."

"Died. Oh, God. Poor Sorcha."

"It may not have been true. Probably wasn't. The child may have been adopted or sold to some rich Americans. Lies were a part of the cruelty." He shook his head sadly. "That's the freedom the IRA is fighting for, Martin. Allow the church to govern people's lives and enjoy the 'freedom' to be slaves of religion. The 'freedom' for women to be treated with animal cruelty. It has to be stopped, you know. One way or another, it has to be stopped."

"And what did you do to help Sorcha?"

"Not nearly enough, it shames me to say. I would have married her when she was old enough, but my parents intervened. They were embarrassed by what Sorcha and I did. Told me I'd disgraced the family name. They wouldn't allow us to marry, and when you live in a place like that you don't go against your parents. Not unless you want a punishment squad on your tail. Anyway, we moved away from the area soon after Sorcha came home again. Shame had a lot to do with it."

Martin nodded. "Thank you for telling me this. It helps me understand Sorcha better."

"Does it alter your feelings towards her?"

"That's something I shall have to think about."

But it won't take much thought. I love her too much.

"You still want to find her because you think she's in danger?"

"Yes. I've tried her home in Mafeking Street and she's not there. I've also tried all the hospitals, with no luck."

Murphy leaned forward. "I'm going to help you because I like you, Martin. And because I owe it to Sorcha. Find a man called Brian Fitzpain and he'll lead you to her."

"Fitzpain? I know that name. And finding him is easier said than done."

"Go to this address." Murphy wrote on a scrap of paper and slid it across the table. "This is where Fitzpain lives. He won't be there now. He'll be out on the streets directing the bombings."

"You should be out there after him."

"We've men out looking for him. So have the guys over at North Castle Street. In the meantime, it's my guess that if Sorcha is not at home she may well be at that address, or heading that way. Just be careful. It's a Nationalist area. Speak to no one else in that street, and I mean no one."

"And if she's not there?"

"Wait there for her."

***

January 1981

"You have to admire his love for her," I said. "Most men would not have been so loyal."

"But their affair was still doomed to failure, wasn't it?"

"Probably. Tell me what happened next."

***

21st July 1972
1605 BST

The street looked eerily quiet, but Martin knew there would be inquisitive eyes behind the curtains at every window. There always were in places like this. Especially on a day like this. Even in normal times, a stranger would be viewed with suspicion, and today was far from normal.

He glanced again at the slip of paper as he walked on. The next street should do it.

Then he allowed his thought to return to Mickey Murphy. Had Mickey's relationship with Sorcha been as intense as the one he had enjoyed? Did he lie on his back with Sorcha naked on top of him, thrusting and panting? Did she throw back her head and cry, "Yes, yes!" as she did when Martin ejaculated inside her? Did he enjoy wrapping his hands about her breasts and kissing her nipples? Did she suck his penis in the same way? Did she… ?

He deliberately closed his mind to more memories. Why was he torturing himself when he knew all along that Sorcha was no virgin? Was it because of the baby, the ultimate achievement of sex?

I love you, Sorcha, but this is too painful!

He turned the corner into the next street, two lines of red-brick terraced homes facing each other across a dirty road. It was the same old story; general dereliction, along with broken bricks and broken glass littering the pavement.

He started counting the house numbers.

A black car drew up alongside him and Martin glanced sideways at it. The driver wound down his window and called, "You! Get inside. Now!"

***

January 1981

"Was that Fitzpain and one of his thugs?" I asked. I had one hand curved around Susan's left breast. It felt warm and perfectly moulded. I could have left it there forever.

She put a finger firmly across my lips. "No. Why don't you just be quiet and listen to me?"

"Sorry. I love listening to you, but it's an exciting story."

"And you're being impatient. It wasn't Fitzpain."

***

21st July 1972
1610 BST

A distant bomb exploded as Martin got into the car, a black Cortina. Two men were seated in the front seats. Two plain clothes policemen. Martin recognised them instantly. They were the CID policemen from North Castle Street. The same two men who had interviewed him and told him nothing of value.

What were they called?

DCI McIlroy and DS Evans. The names came back to him suddenly.

The younger one was Welsh, he remembered that. Remembered his tell-tale Welsh accent. God alone must have known what a Welshman was doing here, working for the RUC at a time like this.

The older man, the Detective Chief Inspector, was at the wheel. He leaned back and snapped, "What the hell are you doing wandering around these streets, Martin Foster? You could be shot on sight in a place like this. Bloody nearly were."

He even remembers my name!

"I'm looking for Sorcha Mulveny. I told you that before."

"Why here, for God's sake?"

"I was told she might be at Brian Fitzpain's house. He lives here."

"Who told you that?"

"Sergeant Murphy at Oldpark police station."

The younger policeman gave his boss a knowing look.

"I'll phone him when we get back, boss. See that the hell he's playing at."

Then he turned to Martin. "How did you meet Mickey Murphy?"

"Went along to Oldpark barracks to see if they had any news of Sorcha Mulveny. It was just a wild hope, I suppose. It was pure luck I met Sergeant Murphy there."

"He knew her, I assume?"

"Oh, yes. Knew her better than you might guess," Martin muttered, avoiding the gaze of both policemen. "He gave me Fitzpain's address."

The older man interrupted at that point. "Well, we've got news for you, boy. You were seen. There are two gunmen just around the corner in the next street, hidden in a doorway. Face masks, black berets and Armalite rifles. Does that mean anything to you?"

"IRA."

"Right. If we hadn't come along you would likely be dead by now."

"I was trying not to draw attention to myself."

"Well, you failed. Miserably. Now, let's get the hell out of here while we still have our lives."

He floored his throttle and the car sped off along the road.

Martin settled back into one of the rear seats. Outside, black smoke still lingered over the city. The smell of burning still refused to die down. Away from these mean streets the roads were still clogged with vehicles heading out into the countryside, but there had been no more explosions since he got into the car. Could this be an end to the day's horrors?

Eventually, the Welshman spoke. "What did Sergeant Murphy tell you about Sorcha Mulveny?"

Martin toyed with the idea of saying nothing, but that might not endear him to the two detectives. He decided on an expurgated version of Murphy's account. "He told me about the difficult life she had, growing up in Mafeking Street. I think I understand her better now that I know more

293

about her background."

"You still count her as your girlfriend?"

"More than that. I want to give her a better life."

"In Belfast?"

"Good heavens, no. In England. I plan to join the British army and I want to take her to England with me."

"Join the army? Be very careful, Martin. Sorcha comes from a Nationalist background. She won't take kindly to living amongst British army wives. You may be creating one whole heap of trouble for both of you."

"I'll handle it."

Neither policeman responded immediately. Then McIlroy said, "Take a look behind, Will. We're being followed."

DS Evans turned in his seat. "I see it. A blue Mini. Fifty yards behind. Two men in the front. They don't look too friendly."

Martin shifted to look through the back window. Sure enough, there was the following car.

DCI McIlroy spoke calmly. "Any sign of weapons?"

"The passenger side," Evans said. "The end of a rifle barrel is just visible above the dash."

"Right. Once we get out amongst the busy traffic on the main roads we'll be caught up in the exodus and I'll have problems losing him. Get your pistol out, Will."

"Not a shooting match boss?" But the younger man took his pistol from its holster and held it in his lap.

"Wind down your window," his boss said. "I'll give you one chance to shoot out his tyres. Just one chance. Don't miss it."

He swung the car into a screaming handbrake turn at the junction at the end of the road until he was facing back on the opposite side.

"Get ready, Will."

The seconds ticked by slower now. The Cortina advanced down the road. As it came abeam the Mini, McIlroy shouted, "Now, Will! Take him!"

The Welshman raised his pistol, aimed and fired. The single shot took out the Mini's front offside tyre. The

Cortina moved on and a second shot took out the rear tyre.

Then McIlroy rammed his foot to the floor and the Cortina raced to the end of the road.

"Well done, Will."

McIlroy took the corner fast, two wheels barely keeping contact with the ground. And then they were out of sight of the Mini with not a single shot being fired in retaliation.

Martin heaved a sigh of relief. If this was police work, he was impressed, but he was also glad he was no part of it. He hoped the army would not expect him to get involved in a shooting match. All he wanted was a quiet office and one whole heap of routine paperwork.

DS Evans seemed to be similarly relieved as he put away his pistol. "Well, boss... that was an abortive attempt to find the girl, so what now?"

"There hasn't been an explosion in a while. The campaign seems to be over for the moment. We'll drop this young man somewhere safe and then we'll check on what's happening at some of the bomb locations. We may be able to help with the clear-up."

"The girl?"

"Nothing more we can do about her right now. Remind me where you live, Martin."

Martin gave him the address in Harold Street.

"We'll drop you somewhere near there." McIlroy glanced at his colleague. "Turn up the radio, Will. Let's find out where the last bomb exploded and see if we can be of any help there."

As the DCI had expected, the main routes through Belfast were far busier than usual. He navigated through it until he was driving along the upper part of the Ballysillan Road. He pulled up at the kerbside by the Eglinton Presbyterian church.

"Is this near enough to home for you, Martin?"

"Near enough. I can walk from here."

"This is Protestant territory, so you should be safe here. Promise us you won't stray back into Nationalist territory. Next time it could cost you your life."

"I'll heed your warning, Chief Inspector."

"And if you find Sorcha Mulveny I want you to phone me at North Castle Street barracks. If I'm not there, leave a message. That girl needs help."

Something in DCI McIlroy's voice told Martin it was more than help he had in mind. It was an arrest.

"I'll do that, I promise," he said. He tried to sound sincere, but he had no intention of setting up Sorcha for police custody.

"Be careful in the meantime."

"Sure."

Martin got out of the car and walked away without looking back. What now? The warnings he'd been given were sound, he knew that, but he still needed to find Sorcha.

***

January 1981

Later that morning, I studied Susan's notes while she prepared lunch for us. She stood at the cooker wearing only one of my casual shirts. From the rear she was the image of Annie, just as I remembered her in those glorious days soon after we were married. Was that good or bad?

"You did a sound job interviewing Martin," I said. "If I'd been there at the time I would have been very concerned about him."

"Too naïve by far?" she said, taking two steaks from the frying pan and shovelling them onto plates.

"He's grown up since then. So has Sorcha, in a way. I'll need to get back to her again and find out exactly where she was and what she was doing at that time."

"Back to Belfast?" Susan paused and there was a hitch in her voice. She turned to face me, a look of doubt spread across her face. "When?"

"Not straight away. I need time to bring my manuscript up to date. Can you afford to stay a week or so?"

Her look of doubt changed into a wide smile. "Try and stop me."

296

Chapter Twenty-One

February 1981

It was a bitterly cold evening when we stepped off the aircraft at Belfast's Aldergrove Airport. A chill wind blew dark rain clouds down from the north. We picked up a hire car at the airport and drove straight to Susan's flat. Our plan was to see Sorcha the following morning and Martin in the afternoon. What we did after that would depend upon how much we learned on this visit.

The rainfall increased as we drove down from the waterlogged hills into the two blighted half-cities. A sudden heavy deluge pounded on the car roof, but I had lived here long enough to know that this sort of weather had an important role to play. There would be few riots in rain like this. Belfast rioting was a fair-weather sport. The killing streets would be relatively quiet tonight. In the hospitals the surgeons would have a few moments to breathe easy. They would deserve it: they were amongst the most experienced in the world when it came to dealing with gun and bomb injuries.

The flat felt cold when we arrived, and Susan was quick to turn up the heating. She switched on the television for the late evening news. The previous week Ian Paisley had held a rally at the City Hall where he signed a covenant and announced a series of protest rallies against Margaret Thatcher's dialogue with the Irish Prime Minister, Charles Caughey. In England it was already old news, no longer worth mentioning, but here the fallout still captured the headlines. Nothing changed. We didn't bother to see the end of the broadcast.

The rain clouds had passed by the next morning, leaving a cold breeze to dry out the landscape. After breakfast we drove to the prison in Armagh where Sorcha was led into the interview room soon after we arrived.

"I've been waitin' to see youse again," she announced. "We're gettin' to an important part of the book now, ain't we?"

"We are," I assured her. "And the whole thing is beginning to come together nicely. Susan has been helping me to edit the earlier parts of the manuscript."

Sorcha eyed Susan inquisitively. "Youse two seem to be spendin' a lot of time together."

Were the signs that obvious? Susan glanced away and her cheeks reddened.

I looked down at my notebook as I replied. "I appreciate Susan's analysis of the story you've been telling us, Sorcha. She seems to see deeper into people's feelings and emotions than I do."

"Is that all there is to it?"

"We've become good friends." I hurried on, anxious not to get mired in the truth. "How about you tell us what happened to you after the bombings."

***

21st July 1972
1610 BST

She walked unsteadily. At first, thoughts that were not fully grasped floated into and out of focus. Only her hearing was fully alert, waiting for the muffled crump of yet more bombs. But for the moment, it seemed, the bombings had ceased. When her mind eventually became clearer it held no feelings of satisfaction. She had no sense of having done something positive for Belfast, or Ireland. Quite the opposite.

She breathed in the stench of burning, watched the firemen and troops damping down the flames at the

Cavehill shops, and she despaired. Two women and a boy were killed here. There was nothing more Sorcha could do now that so many bombs had either been detonated or defused. Nothing except feel misery for the innocents who had died or been injured. It should not have happened like this.

She found a church hall that had been opened up as a place of refuge for people trying to escape the terrors on the streets. It was a Protestant church in a Protestant area, but Sorcha didn't care. What the hell did any sort of religion matter now? Then again, the hall was supposed to be a place of Christian peace, so maybe she would find some small amount of comfort here. The people here were Prods, just like Martin, but the building was open to all, so she walked in.

Most of the people who had gathered inside were women and children. Many of the women were white-faced and tired. The younger children were unusually quiet, clinging to their mothers. The older ones, the teenagers, sat talking to one another in hushed tones. No one shouted or railed against the atrocities that had been committed in their city. In those surreal surroundings, no one seemed to have the energy to cry out. A young, pale-faced minister sat beside an elderly woman with a blood-stained bandage about her head. He patted her hand and spoke softly to her while she sat open-mouthed but silent.

It was the first time in years that Sorcha had been inside any church building, but it seemed to offer what she was looking for: some sort of comfort. She was in need of a lot of that. Not religious comfort; she had no time for that, so the minister had better steer clear of her. No, she needed the emotional relief that came from being out of sight of the carnage, out of sight of the dead bodies, out of sight of the crumbling buildings torn apart by the bombs. It was all still there, of course, beyond the walls of the church hall. But, for a while, she was anxious to shut her mind against the worst of it.

Pretend it wasn't happening.

Fool herself.

She accepted a cup of tea from an old lady who had been wobbling around the room on spindly legs, handing out hot drinks. Sorcha closed her eyes and sipped at the cup gingerly.

"'Tis all wrong. Such wickedness," the old lady said, but her voice was dull and not at all angry. It was the soft protest of a helpless kitten about to be drowned. How did she keep her temper when the IRA was blasting her home city to bits? Sorcha had no answer so she kept her eyes closed and simply nodded. She was past the point of conversation anyway. What could she possibly say to a Protestant lady on a day of Nationalist infamy such as this?

I'm sorry? I knew where the bombs would go off and I did little enough to stop it? I should have done more, much more, and now I'm sorry?

Is that what she should say?

No, the whole thing was now beyond any apology. Beyond hope.

When the teacup was empty, she sat for some minutes, slowly regaining a degree of resilience. She tried to drain her mind of all her recent memories, but it didn't work. The horror returned and she remembered her part in the campaign. She had been given a list of targets and ordered to make hoax phone calls to the police. She knew what was planned and she should have... *could have* done more.

Dear God, she should not have had that list. It was nothing to do with her... except that she was involved because she was too close to Fitzpain and his thugs, his Pain Men. And she was as bad as them.

That was the worst part of it all. She was as bad as them.

She looked around the church hall and saw only dull, empty faces filled with tears and sadness. Was this what the bombing campaign was all about? Turning women and children into broken wrecks? Was this how the terrorists hoped to unite Ireland?

God forgive them.

On a sudden impulse, she finally decided. She would go

to England with Martin and never again think about this day. Never again think of Belfast and Mafeking Street. She stood up, more determined than ever to find Martin and tell him of her decision.

If only she knew where he lived. It was somewhere around here. But where? She remained standing while tears began to trickle down her cheeks. Where are you, Martin? I need you, need someone to help me.

Dear God, I ned someone to help me.

***

February 1981

It was all there: the truth of how the Bloody Friday bombings affected this young woman. Raw human emotion still sat heavy with her, even within those prison walls. Susan grabbed at my arm and pulled herself closer to me. She pulled out a handkerchief and wiped at her eyes.

I put down my pen and sat back in my seat. "Why did you never talk about this before now? Why did you not explain the effect it had upon you?"

"What was the point? I did wrong and I pleaded guilty. I have to pay the price for what I did… or didn't do… and I'll be paying for it fer the rest of me life."

"But you're not a bad person, Sorcha. Had you grown up next door to me, with the sort of decent family I had to support me, you would have made a success of your life. I'm sure of it. You have it in you to be good."

She sniffed and turned her head away. "But I didn't grow up next door to youse, did I? And how would youse have turned out if youse'd grown up next door to me in Mafeking street? Can youse answer me that?"

"No. I have no answer to that." I thought about it for a few moments and then the truth hit me suddenly. I would have grown up just like her. I shivered and picked up my pen. "Let's carry on, Sorcha. Tell us the rest."

301

21ˢᵗ July 1972
1640 BST

Sorcha forced herself to walk on. She left the church hall and walked slowly along the lower end of the Ballysillan Road, close to the Crumlin Road. She still felt uncomfortable in the second-hand clothes, but at least she now looked semi-respectable.

Did Martin live somewhere around here in the Ballysillan area? Or was the house in a street off the Crumlin Road? She couldn't be sure. It would have to be a Protestant or mixed area. She'd heard him mention Harold Street, but she didn't know where to find it. This wasn't her part of the city. Besides, her thinking was still too confused because of the bombs. And even if she did find the right house, she couldn't bring herself to knock at the door and ask for Martin.

What would his aunt say?

Maybe she should just scout around for a while in the hope of seeing him in the streets. Or maybe she should walk down the Crumlin Road to that newspaper shop where he bought his aunt's paper. Take it from there. It wasn't too far to walk. Her confusion increased with every step she took.

Ballysillan was a little more Protestant than Catholic, but essentially a mixed area. It was far from the sort of segregated ghetto she had grown up in. Nevertheless, the Protestants in some parts of Ballysillan had distinctly anti-Catholic views. Most of the houses were middle-class, not posh, but better than anything she could aspire to. Could she find Martin here? She wandered down a side street leading off the main Road.

It was safe enough here, she reckoned. The Ballysillan car bomb had been discovered by British troops early this morning. It was unlikely the IRA had a back-up. Surely they didn't, she told herself. But then she saw something that caused her to draw a raw breath.

She was wrong. Very wrong.

She recognised the car instantly, a light blue Vauxhall Viva parked near a street corner. It had been stolen a week ago by Finn McKenna and the number plates changed. Fitzpain had been driving around in it since then. It was an English vehicle, he had said, and that made it perfect for use as a car bomb. One tiny bit of England would be destroyed in the explosion.

Sorcha felt her senses tighten. This was the replacement car bomb! It had to be.

Was Brian behind this one? Her thoughts tumbled. Had he been released from Castlereagh? Had he planted the car here? Was he, even now, somewhere nearby? She studied the vehicle, wondering.

She walked closer and her nerves continued to tingle. The street was empty apart from a few distant figures, too far away to recognise. No one else seemed to be taking any notice of the car. Smoke from so many bombs still lingered over the city, and the air was still tainted with the acrid smell of burning, but it was quiet here. The houses looked untouched by the day's tragedies. She studied the scene, looking for clues. Was the bomb fitted with a timer? Or was Fitzpain hiding somewhere nearby with a wired detonator? Only a close inspection would tell her, and she feared getting too near the car.

Where might the car's driver now be hiding?

She paused to scan the area. It all looked so innocuous. A small area of waste land just a few yards away was bounded by metal railings, five-foot-high and topped by arrowheads. Like the weaponry of a line of primitive warriors, Sorcha thought. Primitive weapons looking useless in the face of modern explosives. But there was no obvious hiding place in there. Nowhere for the bomber to conceal himself with a detonator.

One hundred yards farther down the road a shop door opened, an elderly man came out and stumbled away. Within a minute he had disappeared along a side road. Nothing seemed out of place or sinister... except that car.

Sorcha walked back along the road until she saw a young woman coming towards her. She was pushing a pram with one hand and holding onto a small child with the other. Sorcha stood waiting until the woman was within hearing.

"Excuse me," she asked. "D'youse know anything about that car?" She pointed to the Vauxhall.

"No." The young woman shook her head, a puzzled look on her slender face. She had long blonde hair and it swayed around her cheeks.

"It could be another bomb," Sorcha said. "We should tell someone."

The young woman smiled at her. "Oh, no. They wouldn't plant bombs up here. We've had no trouble in this street."

Sorcha held back from pointing out that a hijacked car had been driven to the shops in the Cavehill Road, which was not far away. It had been laden with explosives. The residents didn't expect that one, but people were badly injured when it blew up.

"I still think it looks suspicious," she said. She looked down at the child, a fair-haired girl no more than two years old; a pretty child who would one day become a beautiful woman like her mother. She stared back with a solemn expression. Sorcha clenched her fists. How could anyone put the life of such a child at risk? How could anyone kill an innocent like this?

"You're not from round here," the young woman said, drawing back Sorcha's attention.

"No. I'm visiting a friend." She turned to look again at the car. "I'd stay clear of that vehicle if I were youse. Just in case. I don't like the look of it."

The woman smiled and made to move on. "I'm sure you're worrying unnecessarily. Look, I have to get home to feed the baby." As if in agreement, a small gurgle came from out of the pram.

"Please be careful." Sorcha spoke quietly, knowing she had no real proof there was anything dangerous in this road. All she had was a gut feeling and the knowledge of the man who had been driving that vehicle.

She watched the woman and her family go, and then she saw an army Land Rover fifty yards away, advancing slowly along an adjacent road. She could warn them. Yes, she could ask them to inspect the Vauxhall. They would know what to do. She hurried towards the Land Rover until she was out of sight of the suspect vehicle.

And then the bomb went off.

Although she was now in the adjacent street, the blast blew her forward onto the ground. She rolled off the pavement onto the road. The noise deafened her for a minute as she struggled to get back to her feet. She wiped a hand across her face and then saw that the Land Rover was still heading towards her. She stood in its path, not sure what to do, her head aching and her thoughts confused. A soldier jumped from the moving vehicle and pulled her off the road.

"Are you hurt?"

"I'm not sure… I don't think so."

"Stay here!" he shouted at her. "Someone will come to help you shortly."

How did he know that? He was just giving her platitudes. She tried to speak to him, but he was already walking away. She watched the Land Rover turn into the bombed street, the soldier sheltering behind it. Then she stumbled after them. Her senses were returning now, remembering the young woman and her children. As she came in sight of the devastation, she saw people coming from their houses. Shocked and stumbling, they came from out of homes with shattered windows and doors. The soldier shouted at them to stay clear.

The Land Rover had stopped well back from the blazing remains of the Vauxhall, but Sorcha ran past it, on down the road to where the burning car was belching smoke and flames into the air. People called out to her to stop, but she ignored them. And then the horror became clear to her and she came to a halt.

Her face felt hot, not just because of the flames. Her heart pounded.

The pram was a smashed ruin blown farther along the street. There was no sign of the baby. The young woman... oh dear God... she had been blown off her feet and was impaled upon the railings. The arrowheads pierced her back, her arms fell limply to her sides, and her sightless face stared up at the smoky sky. Her hair was clogged with blood which dripped down her face, down her clothes, pooling on the pavement. And there was the child... she saw it now... the small child was no more than a bloody mess on the road a few yards away.

A mere child for God's sake!

Sorcha clasped her hands to her face and screamed.

"OH GOD! NO!"

And she caught again an image of her mother, dead on the kitchen floor.

God, help me! I can't take any more!

Someone came running behind her. A hand gripped her arm. It was the same soldier.

"Keep well away from it, Miss."

She swung round to face him. Tried to tell him what had happened when she spoke to the young woman, but the words would not come. Just a noise. It was a loud screaming noise, her own loud screaming. She pounded her fists into the soldier's chest, anger and despair filling her head. Then she pushed him away and vomited onto the pavement.

***

February 1981

Sorcha slumped forward, cradling her head in her arms. Her words tailed off, replaced by a deep sobbing sound. Her shoulders heaved.

"Enough!" Susan stood up suddenly, rounded the table and clasped her arms about the young woman. "That's enough. She can't take any more today."

"I must!" Sorcha sat up abruptly and pushed Susan aside.

306

"I must finish this now. Right now. I don't want to have to come back to it later."

"But it's tearing you apart, Sorcha!"

"That's why I have to do this. I need to feel the pain!"

***

21st July 1972
1710 BST

She sat on a hard wooden chair and sipped at a cup of hot tea. The soldier had taken her back to the same church hall and asked the people there to look after her. She had stopped screaming now, but tears still flooded down her cheeks. Her hands shook and the teacup rattled as she set it back onto its saucer and put it down on a table beside her.

Her thoughts were more coherent now. Mostly, they were thoughts about the dead woman and the child, but she found time also to think about herself. There was no possible future for her in Belfast now. How could there be? If she was anyone else, Brian Fitzpain would find her, and he would want to kill her because she was a traitor... someone who had slept with the enemy. But he wouldn't do it because she wasn't anyone else. She knew who Brian was, and she had smoothed the way for herself and Martin to escape to England.

But what would Martin do if he found out what terrible things she had done? Could she hide that from him? Hide it for the rest of their lives?

More memories fought their way back into her head.

Memories of last night when the peeler died. Dear God, why did it have to happen?

A voice suddenly cut into her thoughts. "Sorcha? What are you doing here?"

She looked up at a figure hurrying across the hall towards her.

It was him... it was Martin!

She leapt to her feet, spilling the tea, and clasped her

arms about him. "I was looking for youse. But I didn't know where to find youse. I searched everywhere."

"And I was searching for you," he said.

"Oh, God, Martin. Hold me. Please hold me." And she wept across his shoulder as he wrapped his arms about her.

"I saw the aftermath of the Ballysillan bomb," he said, speaking hesitantly. "I was looking for you and I saw what the bomb did. I saw the dead bodies. And I saw what happened when other bombs exploded. Dear God, I saw it!"

Sorcha sighed deeply. Certainty filled her mind now. If ever there was a reason to get away from Belfast, this was it. She pulled herself back from Martin's grasp and saw then that his eyes were also filled with tears.

She gestured to the door. "Let's go somewhere else."

"Anywhere?"

She wiped at her eyes. "Yes. Anywhere away from here."

He led her from the church hall. Outside, two heavily-armed RUC officers were talking to an army officer. Unlike other soldiers, this one was not wearing full military combat kit. He could have been dressed for a parade ground. One of the policemen turned towards Martin and Sorcha.

And that was when she saw her nemesis.

Fitzpain was across the road, slouched against the side of a white van, watching and smoking. He had seen her; that was obvious. He had seen her with Martin. What was he doing here? Had he come looking for her? Whatever his intentions, he made no attempt to approach her, but he didn't need to. The look on his face told her what was in his mind.

"It's him! It's Fitzpain," Martin said, nodding in Fitzpain's direction. "I saw him earlier when I was looking for you in Mafeking Street."

"What happened?" she asked.

"He guessed I wasn't a Catholic and he would have killed me, but the army came along just in time. Saved my bacon, they did."

Sorcha didn't trust herself to reply straight away. She knew they were in dire trouble. Right now, Fitzpain would want to kill Martin… and her… but they had just one chance to stay alive. When she got him alone… when she was able to talk to him and explain what she had done for him. When Maggie confirmed what she said. Yes, that was important. Maggie had to confirm it, regardless of the truth. Then Brian would look well on her. She was confident he would let her and Martin leave Belfast and never come after them. Never send the Pain Men after either of them.

Besides, she knew who he really was.

He could never do any real harm to her.

She clasped Martin's arm tightly. "We can't stay here, Martin. We must get out of the city."

"Something wrong, Miss?" One of the peelers took a step towards her.

"No. I'm all right."

But the peeler didn't look convinced. He followed her gaze to the man across the road. "You know that man?"

"No. I…"

"I know him." It was the second peeler. He jabbed a finger at the lurking figure. "That's Fitzpain, the Provo man. There's word out for us to keep an eye open for him. What's he mean to you, Miss?"

"Nothing." She avoided his gaze. "He means nothing to me."

"Really?" The peeler didn't look convinced. "Let's have a word with him." He stepped off the pavement towards Fitzpain, but he wasn't quick enough. Fitzpain threw down his cigarette and leapt into the van. Within seconds, the engine roared into life and the vehicle raced away down the street.

"Did you get the number?" the army officer called out.

"I got it," The nearer of the two peelers replied. "Someone will want to question that man."

Martin eased Sorcha away from the two policemen, pressed himself tight beside her and spoke quietly. "You're lying, Sorcha. Fitzpain was the man who came to that hotel in the Oldpark Road. You made me leave the place because of him. You do know him, so don't deny it. What does he

309

really mean to you?"

She pushed him further away from the two policemen before replying. "He's an IRA killer, Martin, and he's found out about us. He knows we've been sleeping together, so he does."

"How did he find out?"

"I don't know, but it doesn't matter. I've tried to put things right. I just need to speak to him alone."

Martin looked puzzled. "What's going on, Sorcha? Tell me."

Sorcha struggled for a reply that would not immediately incriminate her. She looked away as she replied. "I will one day, I promise to tell youse everything." But, deep down, she knew there were things he must never find out. Never.

Martin' puzzled expression deepened. "And this man, Fitzpain? He's pissed off about us sleeping together, is that it?"

"He's a psychopath. A mad psychopath. He hates all Prods, especially Prods who go to bed with Catholic girls. In normal circumstances he would kill us. Both of us. But he won't because of what I've done. I promise youse, I've tried to put things right for us."

***

Friday 21st July 1972
1725 BST

They walked hand-in-hand looking for an easy way out of the city, just as so many other people wanted a way out. But there was no easy way. Motorists, caught up in the exodus, were offering people lifts, but they were careful to check on the passengers' identity first.

"How are youse? And what's your name then? Sorcha? And what school did youse go to?"

The same old story.

Martin and Sorcha were refused a lift because she had a Catholic name.

"We live in a medieval society here," she said as yet another car moved off without them. "We've never grown up enough to fit in with the twentieth century. There's no hope for us, is there?"

Martin said nothing, but she understood. What could he possibly say to her? They walked on in silence, with the truth of that day rattling round inside her head. The truth of her own involvement in murder. Last night she had seen a rapist die. Before that, she had seen a peeler die. And then… this morning… she had seen Jimmy Fish die. With Brian banged up at Castlereagh, it should have been his thugs, McKenna and Maginnis who carried out Jimmy Fish's execution, but there was no way of contacting them.

He had grassed on Brian, and Brian had insisted that the runt had to pay. She remembered Fitzpain's expression as the peelers led him away from the hotel. Both Maggie and Sorcha had picked up the message. Fish had to die. Sorcha remembered the glint of anger in Maggie's eyes as she demanded that Sorcha should go with her to the café he regularly visited. She remembered the initial silence as they entered the café and the look of surprise Jimmy Fish gave them. He must have guessed why they were there because he gasped and muttered a comment about the pair of them coming for him.

"Oh Maggie! Fitzpain's revenge, is it?"

Sorcha remembered the look in the runt's face as the old lady drew out her long sharp sewing scissors. "No, I'll do it, Maggie," she said. Then she remembered what happened to the peeler and she doubted, even then, that she would have the courage to kill Jimmy Fish.

Maggie shook her head fiercely. "Youse think I haven't the strength to avenge my Brian? Youse just watch me!" She threw herself at Jimmy Fish with a sudden move that caught him unawares, and the scissors were thrust into the man's chest.

Sorcha choked. It was like the killing of the peeler all over again. The blood, the look of shock in the man's face, the horror of it all. He slid to the floor with blood bubbling

311

from the wound.

Maggie hurriedly pulled out a clear plastic bag from her pocket and dumped it on the table. It contained thirty sixpenny coins. "Now let's get out of here." She seemed quite unperturbed by what she had done as she led the way out of the café.

Sorcha followed her, pulling the door to behind her. She caught up with the old lady, her mind working fast, trying to come to a decision. Her thoughts were coming together even as she spoke. She gabbled as they walked. "Tell Brian it was me, Maggie. Tell him I did the killing."

"Why?"

"I have my reasons. Just tell him. I want him to think it was me who did it."

Of course she would never have had the guts to do it. She knew that, but if Brian thought she had been the one to take revenge on Jimmy Fish... if he thought she had done this for him… it might just help Martin and herself. He might then look favourably on her. It could be their ticket to get herself and Martin safely out of Northern Ireland with no IRA assassins coming after them. Yes, Brian would understand if he thought she had taken revenge for Jimmy's Fish's betrayal.

She felt her body shaking as they hurried down the street. They were brutal murders: the peeler, the rapist, and now Jimmy Fish. This one was no easier to stomach. If anything, it was worse because she actually liked the poor wee bastard. There was something about him… she didn't know what it was… something of a connection between them. Was it because they had both acted outside the Law? Or was it something else?

Now the killing had to stop. *Dear God, it had to stop!*

***

February 1981

"You were innocent of that particular crime, Sorcha," I said.

"You didn't kill Jimmy Fish."

She shook her head fiercely. "I *wasn't* innocent, you should know that. I was there when it happened, so I was an accomplice. In law, I was guilty."

She was right, of course, but I still felt for her. Such emotions are not so easily overcome. I tried to justify my stance by a futile assertion. "Maggie carried out the murder! She should be brought to justice."

"Too late. She died three years ago. She's buried in Milltown cemetery."

I understood. Milltown in the Ballymurphy area was where most Belfast Republicans were buried.

"She knew the truth and she never spoke out," I said. I felt a sudden moment of anger with Sorcha because she continued to take full blame for the killing. I was, of course, making a serious mistake. A mistake no journalist should make. I was allowing myself to get too close to the subject, too close to the central character in my book.

Sorcha, however, seemed unconcerned by her own fate. "And incriminate herself? Of course she kept her mouth shut. And I had to make Brian think I did it. You can understand that, can't you?"

"But it wasn't just a case of convincing Fitzpain, was it? In court, you took the full blame for the killing of Jimmy Fish. You confessed to the world at large."

"I had to." She's voice took on a firmer tone. "Don't you see? It was because I needed to take responsibility... take the blame on meself because of all those *other* killings. Not just the Proddy rapist, or the peeler, or Jimmy Fish. It was all the others who died that day. I was part of the problem, you see. I was there with a list of where the bombs would go off, and I should have gone to the police. They were fooled by hoax phone calls and I could have shown them where the bombs actually were. I could have saved lives. But I didn't. And people died. I was as guilty as the rest of them and I had to make myself pay the price."

"The police got the list anyway," I said.

"Too late. People had died by then."

"You shouldn't be here in prison for something you didn't actually do," I said, although I knew I was wrong. She *was* an accomplice to the killing of Jimmy Fish.

She gritted her teeth and glared at me as if she was exasperated by my foolish argument. "What I didn't do was to give the peelers that list before the bombing began. I could have put a stop to it right at the start, but I didn't. That's what I didn't do. That's why I've been here these past eight years. Because people died as a result of what I didn't do."

When Sorcha finally stopped speaking, Susan looked straight at me and shook her head sadly. "The poor girl. She can't take much more of this."

"I can see that." There was, of course, more to be discussed, like what actually happened the night Constable Dunlop was killed, but I held back from further questioning. This wasn't the right time.

I spoke just once more to Sorcha as the warder helped her up from her seat. "Did anyone involved with the bombing see you and Martin leaving the city?"

She looked puzzled for a few seconds, as if her brain was now running in slow motion. Then she said, "Only Finn McKenna. We managed to get a lift eventually, but only for a short distance. The driver wasn't going any farther when he dropped us off in a lay-by. McKenna was parked nearby, and he probably saw us. We dashed across the road into a pub when we realised it was him, but he must have seen us. Yes, he must have."

"And he would have told Fitzpain?"

"I suppose so."

"So Fitzpain must have discovered where you were… I see… well, thank you, Sorcha. That's all I needed to know for now."

She turned to walk away, then paused and said, "Youse're seeing Martin?"

"Yes."

She looked back at me, her eyes wet with tears. "Tell him I loved him and I'm sorry it worked out so badly for us. Tell

314

him I'm sorry for what I did. Tell him 'tis best this way."

"Best this way? What do you mean, Sorcha?"

"Just tell him. 'Tis best this way."

Her head hung low as she shambled away.

Chapter Twenty-Two

February 1981

The end of the story was coming into sight and I was anxious to get to the final truth of what really happened that day. I telephoned Will Evans as soon as we got back to Susan's flat. It was close on mid-day and I hoped he would be at home. I was lucky.

"Not you again!" His opening remark wasn't helpful.

"Yes, it's me again, Will. I'm in Belfast and I've been talking to Sorcha. She's told me how she found Martin Foster after the bombing, and how they tried to make their way out of the city."

"They didn't get far. Went into a pub on the Downpatrick Road."

"That's where you found them: you and McIlroy? Yes?"

"Yes. We'd pretty much sewn up the matter before we tracked Fitzpain to the pub. Foster and the Mulveny girl were already there."

"Tell me all about it and I won't bother you again."

The sound of a deep sight echoed down the line "That's a promise?"

"Yes, a promise."

***

21st July 1972
1650 BST

Will was tired, in need of rest. They all were.

The city was in a state of utter chaos and panic. Army

and police roadblocks had sprung up wherever another bomb was reported. Some of the reports had turned out to be true, others were deliberate distractions. Uniformed men in military vehicles, police cars and ambulances by-passed the blocks where they could, but everyone else was held at bay. The traffic on Dee Street and on the Sydenham by-pass road was backed up in both directions. On the verges, the roads were lined with pedestrians who had escaped the city centre and were now desperate for someone... anyone... to drive them away from Belfast.

Was this, Will wondered, what Europe was like in the Second World War? Displaced people trying to escape enemy bomb after enemy bomb? Adults in fear of their lives, children screaming in terror? Was this a rerun of what came about as a result of Nazi hatred? Was the Provisional IRA now doing to Belfast what Hitler and his Nazis did to the countries they overran?

He sat in the police car and waited anxiously for news of another attack, only half listening to the constant chatter on the radio. But there was no news of any more bombs. The terror campaign seemed to have come to a halt... for the moment, but the after-effects continued.

DCI McIlroy had parked the car in a street of redbrick terraced houses, within sight of the towering Harland and Woolf shipyard cranes. He had ordered Will to stay with it while he walked towards the Dee Street road bridge, where the army was dealing with another possible bomb. Or was it yet another hoax? Will opened the window and scanned up and down the street. Anxious locals peered from behind curtained windows, eyeing the car warily, maybe wondering whether it would blow up in their faces. On balance, Will decided, they would do nothing as long as he stayed with the vehicle. The Provisional IRA was not noted for producing suicide bombers.

Blow up innocent people, but not yourself.

So he sat tight.

McIlroy was gone only a few minutes when a distant crump announced an explosion, at least a mile away. The chatter on the police radio halted for a moment before a positive voice announced the latest bomb had exploded in the Ballysillan area. Then the chaotic babble resumed.

Ten minutes passed and the local interest in the police car waned. The street residents were no longer keeping an eye on it. It hadn't blown up, so maybe they had decided it was innocent enough.

When his boss came hurrying back, Will leaned out from the car window to call to him. "That last one was near the Ballysillan Road!"

McIlroy said nothing until he was back in the driver's seat. "There's nothing we can do to help. Let's hope that young man, Martin Foster, was nowhere near it. Anyway, we're no longer needed here. They found this one in time and they've already defused it."

"Good for them. What now, boss?"

McIlroy breathed deeply and closed his eyes for a few seconds. When he opened them, Will saw that they were bloodshot. He had not realised the DCI was taking the stress so badly. Maybe age was against him. Maybe he had underlying health problems which Will knew nothing about. Or, was this an outcome of his marital problems? Whatever the reason, DCI McIlroy seemed to be reaching a crisis point.

"Let's not get into a panic, Will," he said, his voice wavering. "Let's just sit tight for a few minutes while we work out where we could be most needed."

"Should we call in?"

"No. They're still overloaded with calls."

"Fair enough." Will swivelled in his seat to face his boss. He wished there was somewhere nearby he could grab a cup of tea. They both needed it. Or something stronger, like a McIlroy standard.

He said, "I've been thinking, boss. Remember that message we got from Jimmy Fish about barking up the wrong tree. That's what he's supposed to have said. We were barking up the wrong tree."

"Funny you should say that. I've been pondering over

318

that as well." McIlroy's hand shook as he pulled out a cigarette and lit up. "And do you know what I reckon? I reckon Jimmy was right. He gave us a sound tip-off and we misread it completely. Utterly and completely. Remember how he said it was a relative of his who killed Johnny Dunlop? Remember that?" He drew deeply on the cigarette and blew out the smoke in one long cloud that buffeted against the inside of the windscreen.

"A *sort of* relative," Will said. "Not a relative. A sort of relative. What did he mean by that, do you think?"

"And he said I should do some digging, didn't he? He wanted me to look beyond the obvious, and I think I know now what he was getting at." The DCI blew out another cloud of smoke and waved a hand to clear the air. "We assumed he was sending us a message about Fitzpain. But… what if it wasn't him? What if someone else killed Johnny Dunlop and that's what Jimmy wanted to tell us? Not a relative, but a *sort of* relative. Fitzpain is a cousin of his. Jimmy wouldn't call him a sort of relative, would he? He'd simply say 'a relative'. And there's something else. Sorcha Mulveny was at that hotel when the uniforms went in to get Fitzpain. So what if..."

"The uniforms questioned her, but they didn't think she was involved," Will interrupted. "What exactly do you think Jimmy meant by a sort of relative?"

"Isn't it obvious? Sorcha Mulvnery thinks Fitzpain is her father. Maybe Jimmy Fish had the same idea. Maybe Jimmy also thought Sorcha is Fitzpain's bastard child. Jimmy was a cousin of Fitzpain. I figure that might make her a 'sort of relative' in his mind."

"Related by blood, but not the offspring of any formal marriage."

"And we now know they were both wrong about Fitzpain, don't we? There is no way he could be her father. The proof is there in black and white."

Will cast his mind back to the report on Fitzpain's arrest. It stated that the girl was aged twenty, so she must have been born in nineteen-fifty-two. But the character report on

Fitzpain clearly showed he was in gaol from February fifty one to February fifty three. He couldn't possibly be Sorcha's father.

"Gaol was some sort of occupational hazard for the Fitzpains... and the Codds," McIlroy said with an air of reflection. "Jimmy Fish went down for theft some while after Fitzpain. Caught stealing whiskey from a pub. He only got twelve months for it. Should have got longer if it was ever going to teach him a lesson. One thing is for sure though. Fitzpain got two years for his misdeeds and he was not around when the Mulveny woman conceived that child."

"Who's going to tell Sorcha that?" Will said.

"There was something else in that character report, Will. Something interesting on the front page. Remember? Fitzpain was once accused of raping a married woman. It was a long time ago though. Can you see what else I'm getting at?"

"You think he raped Barbara Mulverny."

"It's only conjecture, Will, but it's a possibility."

Will thought for a moment. "What if it wasn't rape, boss? Sorcha Mulveny told me those two grew up together, Fitzpain and the Mulveny woman. They were close, those two. What if the charge of rape was made as a way of hiding the fact the woman was having an affair with someone... probably Fitzpain. She was married at the time, remember? And the accusation was later dropped. If Sorcha Mulveny knows about that... and she probably does... that could be why she thinks... wrongly... that she was the outcome. And, as you said, Jimmy Fish may well have thought the same."

McIlroy took another draw on his cigarette, it was burning down fast. "That would explain why Jimmy sent the uniforms to that hotel. It was because of *her*, not Fitzpain. It would mean Jimmy was telling us that she was the one who killed Johnny Dunlop; the girl he thought to be Fitzpain's bastard child."

"But Jimmy Fish would know that Fitzpain couldn't

possibly be her father, just as we know it."

"I don't think so, Will. Jimmy Fish was banged up for theft some while after Fitzpain went down. He would have known that Fitzpain and Barbara Mulveny had a thing going between them, but he would have been in gaol when Sorcha Mulveny was born. He probably never knew the child's date of birth. I reckon he never worked out the truth about the parentage."

"Which was?"

"God knows, but she's close to Fitzpain, even if she's not his daughter. I reckon she must have known Jimmy Fish was the informer. I don't know how, but I'm certain she must have known. The more I think about it, the more I reckon she was somehow involved in Jimmy's murder."

"Okay, boss, I'll buy that as a possibility. But, assuming Jimmy Fish was right, why would she kill Johnny Dunlop?"

"Maybe Johnny knew something about her," McIlroy said.

"Caught her with her pants down... figuratively speaking."

McIlvoy laughed, a hard, cold laugh. "Caught her up to no good? Or maybe he saw something he wasn't meant to see while he was walking home that night."

"Possibly, but that's only conjecture."

"True enough." McIlvoy screwed up his face as he sought to recall what he knew. He opened his side window to flick his cigarette ash out into the bomb-smoked air. "But she is close to Fitzpain, we know that."

"Sounds like they're a right den of thieves," Will said.

"And there's something else we need to sort out. Do you remember what the café owner told us? She said Jimmy Fish's last words were, 'Not you too.' Do you recall that?"

"Yes? But he wouldn't have said 'you'. He would have said ye. That's the way he spoke."

"All right. He would have used the word 'ye'. But let's assume for a moment that he didn't say, 'Not ye too', spelt T... O... O. Let's suppose he said, 'Not ye two.' Spelt T... W... O. Remember how she said it didn't sound right.

Maybe that was because the emphasis was wrong. If he said 'Not ye too' the stress would have been on the last word. If he said 'not ye two' the stress would have been on 'ye'. Is that why it sounded wrong?"

"I'll buy that idea."

"So... let's suppose two people came to kill him that day."

"Fitzpain and the girl? Is that what you're saying, boss?"

"No. Why would Fitzpain take the Mulveny girl with him? Unlikely, I think. He could kill Jimmy Fish without any help from her. And then there's the knife. If Fitzpain killed the boy in the alley, he used a serrated knife. Jimmy Fish was killed with something sharp but straight."

"Maybe the girl brought the weapon."

"Maybe, Will. But who was with her? The café owner thinks she may have heard the name Fitzpain."

"Not Brian Fitzpain. So, is there another member of that clan? Another Fitzpain?" Will eased himself in his seat. "We need to find the girl again, boss. And not just for her own protection."

"If only we knew where she is. The uniforms are too busy right now to go looking for her, so maybe we should make a few more enquiries of our own."

"If we're right, boss, we need to get her into an interview room. If she talks, she could bring down the whole damn family, as well as a few IRA bombers. It could be the only way she'd avoid a long stretch behind bars."

McIlroy frowned. "But if she's that loose with her tongue, Fitzpain would want to wipe her out first." He ran his free hand across his forehead. His bloodshot eyes blinked. "In his warped mind, it could be just what he would do. God, what a bloody mess."

"Would he really kill her?"

"In my view, yes. Without a moment's hesitation." McIlroy threw out his cigarette and started the engine. "We'd better try to find the girl first."

"Where?"

"We could try that hotel. The one where the uniforms

went to find Fitzpain. She was there this morning, wasn't she?"

"Worth a try, boss. It's in Oldpark Road. D'you think the Oldpark boys will object to us nosing in on their patch?"

"We won't tell them. Agreed?"

"Agreed."

"Sometimes, Will, it pays to be sneaky."

As the car eased back through the narrow, terrace-lined streets, Will asked, "What might Johnny Dunlop have come across last night?"

"Discover that and we wrap up the whole miserable business, I reckon."

"I wonder if…" Will stopped when he heard their callsign on the police radio. He picked up the microphone and called back.

The radio voice was calm but firm. "IRA suspect named as Brian Fitzpain has been seen in a white Ford Transit van leaving the Ballysillan area. All cars are instructed to intercept if seen. The registration is…"

McIlroy interrupted the transmission by turning down the volume. "Let the other guys catch him. I rather fancy this trip to Oldpark will be more productive. Call in and tell the guys at base that we're on a CID job."

With so many roads closed by police and army blockades it took them half an hour to reach the Oldpark Road. McIlroy parked outside the hotel. Furtive figures lurked nearby, but the road seemed to have gone quiet now that the bombing had apparently ended.

"Siesta time?" Will queried.

"Hiding behind the curtains time, more likely. Let me do the talking, Will. I'll give you a nod if I want you to take over."

They climbed the stairs to the reception area where a white-haired, elderly lady was busily knitting. She looked up and glowered at them, as if she was astute enough to smell a policeman on first sight.

McIlroy held up his warrant card. "Police. We're looking for a girl called Sorcha Mulveny. Has she been here?"

"Never heard of her." The old lady carried on knitting as if the interference was no more important than the buzzing of a summer fly.

McIlroy stood beside her and leaned close. "Your name, madam?"

"None of your business."

"What a pity. I shall have to call in the heavy mob. They can be very persuasive."

The woman glared at him and then pointed to a small notice sitting on the reception desk. "What the hell does that say? Youse can read, can't youse?"

McIlroy peered at it. "Buggered if I can read it, it's that small. What does it say, Will?"

Will crossed the room and picked up a small card. "It says Duty Manager…" He glanced at the lady. "That's a bit posh for a place like this, isn't it? Rather like a public bog having a Chief Executive. Duty Manager, my foot!" He laughed before he read on. "Duty Manager: Margaret Fitzpain… Oh, my God, boss. Another Fitzpain."

"You're a Fitzpain?" McIlroy chuckled coldly as he faced the old lady. "Any relation to Brian Fitzpain."

"So what?"

"Answer the question!"

"His mother," she mumbled.

"Well, well, he actually has a mother." He stopped suddenly and picked up the woman's knitting bag. "And what have we got here?"

Will moved back to stand beside his boss while McIlroy pulled out a pair of scissors from the bag.

"Look at this, Will. Scissors with traces of blood on the blades. Didn't make a very good job of cleaning them, did she?" He stared down at the woman. "Today a man called Seamus Codd was murdered. Stabbed through the heart. We have reason to believe he was known to you and your son, Brian Fitzpain."

"Dirty little informer, so he was."

Will tapped McIlroy on the shoulder. "Remember what the café owner said. Not you two, and the name Fitzpain."

"You think...?"

"Two women... Sorcha Mulveny and Margaret Fitzpain."

"It figures. Brian Fitzpain was carted off to Castleragh and the two women took revenge on Jimmy Fish."

The old lady made a grab at the scissors, but McIlroy pushed her hand away. "Is that how it was? Was the Mulveny girl with you when you went to find Seamus Codd?"

"He deserved all he got, so he did."

"And the Mulveny girl?"

"She'll get what's comin' to her when my Brian catches up with her."

"Why?"

"Because she's been sleepin' with a Prod. That's why."

"That's all? It's no crime in our book."

"She told the Proddy bastard all about us. She's a traitor."

"Did she kill Seamus Codd?"

The old lady nodded but said nothing.

"Bingo. We've got her, Will." McIlroy pushed Will towards the stairs. "Get back to the car and call in. See if they've managed to trace that white van. Quickly now. We need to find that girl before Fitzpain does."

"Should we follow the chase?"

"Shortly. First, we'll arrest this old woman and take her back to the barracks. She was in on the killing of Jimmy Fish. We can get an update on the situation from there. Then we'll get out on the road after that white van. By then, the uniform guys should be able to tell us where it's going."

"Hope we're in time, boss. Hope we get to the girl before Fitzpain does."

"Don't be too sentimental about her. She's far from innocent in all of this, remember."

***

February 1981

"At that point we had the girl firmly in our sights for the

murder of Jimmy Fish." Will's voice went suddenly hoarse along the telephone line, as if he was trying to come to terms with a crucial mistake. "Fish was pointing the finger at *her*, not Fitzpain. We'd got it wrong."

"A simple mistake," I said. "But she didn't kill Jimmy Fish. Maggie Fitzpain did."

Will went silent for a few seconds. Then he said, "But the Mulveny girl confessed in court. That's why she's banged up in gaol."

I took a few minutes to explain what really happened.

Will listened patiently before he said, "She took it all on herself? What a hell of a thing to do. But we still had to find her. And quickly. We knew then that Fitzpain would show her no quarter if he got to her first."

***

21st July 1972
1740 BST

They saw their target driving along the Downpatrick Road.

"There it is!" McIlroy raced the black Cortina past the white van without slowing. "Watch as we go past, Will. Tell me if you see anyone inside the van."

"Just one person," Will said. "And it's Fitzpain. He's smoking and staring straight ahead. Hasn't spotted us. Probably thinks he's got away scot free."

"He'll soon discover the truth."

A mile farther on, McIlroy spotted a police car on a patch of muddy ground by a field gate. He pulled in the Cortina behind it and wound down his side window. A uniformed policeman darted out from behind a hedge.

"What are you waiting here for?" McIlroy asked. "Fitzpain's van is a short way behind us. It's heading this way."

"We know, sir. We got the message ten minutes ago." The policeman spoke quickly, his gaze darting between McIlroy and the road. "One of his accomplices has been seen in this area recently. McKenna, we think. We reckon they may be meeting up with others."

"You're going to stop Fitzpain?"

"Not immediately, sir. We're waiting to see if he makes contact with the rest of their gang. If he does, we'll be able to pick up several of the bombers."

"Fair enough, but save Fitzpain for me. I want words with him, and this time I might just get a little bit more determined than last time."

***

February 1981

That was as much as Will Evans was willing to tell me. He said he had to go out to work, but I suspect Milly was in the background, urging him to cut short the call. I wasn't too concerned. He had told me as much as I expected to get from him.

"No more calls and no more interviews," he said before he rang off. "You promised."

"I can get the rest of the story from Sorcha or Martin Foster. You'll hear no more from me until the book is ready for publication," I told him. "You have my word."

Chapter Twenty-Three

February 1981

Susan and I said little as we drove to Martin's house. I had a general idea how the end of that day panned out for Sorcha. I had been there at the trial and I had read all the newspaper reports, but I was anxious to get Martin's angle on it. There was, I knew, a lot of detail missing from the pages of the national and local press.

Martin was at home, waiting for us. He ushered us into the parlour room and shut the door behind him. His wife, Emily, was cut off from whatever he had to tell us. Maybe that was a bad sign; maybe he should have involved her more deeply in the story. For the moment, however, I was simply anxious to hear how the end game played out.

I introduced Susan and explained how she was helping me to put together a cohesive story of what happened on Bloody Friday. "Susan is a counsellor. She has a real insight into the way people behave and that's helping me as I write about the events of Bloody Friday. Especially when I talk to Sorcha."

"You've seen Sorcha again?" he said.

"Yes. We both went to see her this morning. She asked me to tell you she's sorry it worked out badly for you. She loved you, Martin. She still does."

He gestured us to sit down on a small two-seat sofa while he sat in a seat facing us. His voice was hesitant as he spoke. "I wanted her to come away with me to England. Away from... from all that's bad about Belfast."

"Walking away might not have solved anything, Martin." Susan leaned towards him. "Sorcha's problems needed more than that. I've done a lot of counselling with people affected by the Troubles and I've seen too many who thought they could escape it by simply walking away. It doesn't always work."

Martin gritted his teeth, His moustache quivered. "You mean... you can take the girl out of Belfast..."

"... but you can't take Belfast out of the girl. Something like that." Susan nodded, knowingly. "Sorcha was a victim of the extreme cruelty of her environment. Maybe... if she'd come from a real family with two parents who cared about her... maybe if she'd grown up in a place where people didn't hate each other so much... maybe then it would have worked out well for the two of you. But Sorcha had no loving, caring family to help her and guide her, and she grew up in an atmosphere of bigotry and hatred. She had a baby taken from her in one of those appallingly cruel Magdalene Laundries. She was guided by people who were themselves a product of Ulster's bigotry and hatred."

Martin clasped his hands together and asked, "What happens when they leave Northern Ireland? The ones who just walk away."

"The lucky ones survive and move on."

"And the others?"

"Many of them are lost in a world they don't know or understand because it's so much at odds with the way they grew up. Many of them give up and come back here to Belfast because they feel more comfortable in the world they know... cruel and heartless though it is."

"We could have made it work," he said assertively.

"But the odds would have been against you." Susan sat back in the seat and glanced at me, seemingly looking for support. "She confessed to two murders, but we now know that one of those confessions was false. She did not kill Seamus Codd. We're still not sure about the other murder."

"You've told the police she didn't do that one?" Martin asked.

"Not yet," I said, "but I will when I have the full story."

Martin clasped his hands in front of him, almost like a

penitent. "I still feel sorry for her. But what can I do?"

"Nothing, Martin. You now have a good wife and a nice family. You have a future. Sorcha has nothing. She said something rather sad when we last saw her. She said to tell you it's best this way."

"I wish I could believe that," he said.

"Think about it, Martin. But first, tell us what happened when Fitzpain finally caught up with you."

***

21st July 1972
1745 BST

They eventually managed to get a lift out of the city. The driver wasn't going far and he dropped them off in a lay-by on the Downpatrick Road.

But their troubles were not yet over.

"Look, Martin! It's McKenna!" Sorcha grabbed his elbow and pointed to a car farther along the lay-by. The driver leaned against the side of the vehicle. "He's waiting for something… or someone. Do you think he's seen us?"

"I don't know." Martin scanned around the area. He pointed across the road. "There's a pub, over there. If he has seen us, he won't dare confront us in front of other people. Let's get over there quickly."

The smell of burning and the silence were overwhelming, even this far out of Belfast. Martin wished they could be farther away, but at least they were clear of the immediate danger within the city. And McKenna did not come chasing after them.

The pub was one of the few still open. The smell was the worst part of it, lingering in the air even inside the bar. He and Sorcha sat at a window seat, staring out to where thick clouds of smoke lay malignantly over the city. They gulped at their beers and they said nothing. What was there left to say? A dozen others sat at adjacent tales, but no one spoke. They too stared out the windows at the smoke clouds hovering over Belfast. Grey faces and pale faces watched the city's agony. When had they ever experienced anything like this?

"One day…" Martin began.

"Yes?"

"One day there will be peace in Ireland, but today has set it back by fifty years at least."

Sorcha sniffed and said nothing. What could she say?

"I met Mickey Murphy earlier today," Martin went on. It had to come out sooner or later. Better get it out in the open now.

A look of alarm spread rapidly across her face. "How come?"

"I saw a girl wearing your clothes killed in a riot. Why was she wearing your clothes?"

She told him.

He thought about it and then he said, "She died because she was in your clothes."

"I never intended that."

"Of course you didn't. But it happened. The Loyalists were after you, not her."

"I'm sorry."

"I went to Oldpark police station to ask if anyone knew what happened to you. That's where I met your friend, Mickey. He's a peeler based at Oldfield Park."

"And what did he tell you?" A worried expression passed across her face.

"He told me all about you. Him and you. He told me what happened. How you got pregnant and you were sent away to a Magdalene Laundry. He told me that your baby may have died."

"Died, or was sold. Do youse hate me because of that?"

"No. I don't!" He shook his head fiercely. "I love you."

"Youse'll forgive me?"

"No need to forgive anything. You've suffered enough." It was, Martin thought, all he could say for the moment. Maybe, in days, weeks or years to come, they would talk more about it. They would have to. But not now. Now was a time for facing up to the atrocities of today, not the suffering of yesterday.

He switched his attention back into the room when the barman turned on a television. It was a wall-mounted set in one corner of the room, and they were just in time for the six o'clock news. The sound was turned off but that didn't matter. The black-and-white images were too graphic to need explanation. He focussed on film of mutilated bodies being shovelled into plastic bags at the Oxford Street bus station. Images of buildings blown apart. Images of shoppers looking distraught beyond understanding. And he felt shame. Shame that people from his own city could do such things. Shame that Northern Ireland had become famous for such horrors. Shame because these pictures would, right now, be beaming around the world and people in civilised lands would be looking at them and shaking their heads in disbelief at the barbarity of it.

Someone shouted, "For God's sake switch it off! Haven't we had enough of it today?"

No one objected when the barman complied.

The silence returned.

When they had finished their first drinks, Martin went to the bar and ordered more. The barman served him mutely, hardly daring to look up. His hands were shaking as he pulled at the beer pump.

Martin broke the silence when he sat down again, as close alongside Sorcha as the seats would allow. "What are we going to do now?" he asked. He wasn't too sure what sort of answer he was expecting, but he knew they had to talk about their immediate plans. The time for avoiding that was past.

She shook her head and wiped a stray wisp of hair from her face. "I don't know. I don't know... what to do... what to say." Tears trickled down her cheeks. She wiped at them angrily.

"This bombing campaign is the work of your murderous IRA friends. You realise that?" He deliberately injected a tone of accusation into his voice. This wasn't about an unwanted pregnancy, a lost baby, this was about murder. He knew he should not be accusing her, but he had to let out his anger towards someone. She was just unlucky to be in the firing line.

"Who said they're friends of mine?" she snapped back.

He tried to sound logical in his reply. "You did, in as many words. Anyway, why should the police be after you unless you're mixed up with the Provos?"

"You think they're after me?"

"I know they are."

She came back at him more firmly than he expected, as if she resented the accusation. Maybe she was right. "Because they think I'm mixed up with the IRA? Is that it? Youse just don't understand. We're all mixed up with them on our side of the line. 'Tis they who rule us, not the British state. When they give us orders, we do as we're told. There's no other option."

"You could have walked away." It was the only response he could bring to mind, but he knew it was a weak argument. Sorcha was right. No one argued when faced with an Armalite or a blood-soaked Black and Decker drill.

"Walk away? Bullshit, Martin! Youse don't know what it's like living in a Nationalist area. All that hatred and violence. Youse don't just walk away from it. They won't let youse walk away. I wanted to put an end to it even before I met youse. And I would have too."

"Put an end to it?" he queried. What the hell did she mean?

She stared down into her beer. "Do youse remember the day we first met?"

He nodded. Of course he did. Never forgot it, never would. "You fell as you were leaving the shop."

"I was going to kill myself." She lowered her voice. "I'd got enough pills to do it. And I would have done it."

He jerked back in his seat. "Kill yourself? You mean... suicide?"

She nodded and her hair fell forward across her eyes. "I'd bought some new clothes so that I'd look smart when they found me. Can youse believe that? I wanted to look good at the end. Wanted them to see me looking better dead than I ever looked alive. I wanted to die looking clean and decent. I must have been out of my mind." She glanced up quickly and then slowly lowered her head again.

He shook his head in disbelief. "Why? Why kill yourself."

"Because it would be so easy. You don't have to explain anything to anybody when you're dead. You just do it and that's the end of it all. It's gone. It's done."

"The end of what?"

"I told youse." She looked up again and this time she stared into his eyes. They glistened with incipient tears. "It was because of all the hatred and the violence and the killing. Day after day, week after week. And it was because of me. I was leading a shitty life and I had no future to speak of and I couldn't get out of it. No way. I'd had more than I could stand and I just wanted to end it all. The easy way. In years to come we're gonna have a whole generation living on Valium and I don't wanna be a part of it."

"Easy? You said the easy way?" he queried."

"Youse'd need to live my life to understand."

"But you didn't go through with it."

"No. That was because of youse, Martin." She stabbed a forefinger at him. "I fell in love with youse and that made all the difference. I put away the pills because I loved youse and wanted to be with youse."

He went silent for a few seconds, struggling to understand. He visualised the good times they'd had together, in bed and out of it. Then he focussed on the feelings he had towards her, feelings he still had despite everything. It was love, of course it was; the purest sort of love. Not just sex. It was far more than that. How could he possibly deny it?

He mellowed his voice when he asked, "What about your Republican friends? You didn't part company with them, did you?"

She shook her head. "I tried, but they wouldn't let go of

me. I tried ignoring them, tried telling them to leave me alone. But they wouldn't. They said I had to do as I was told or I would end up like all the others who turned against the cause. Dead."

"They threatened to kill you?"

She nodded silently.

"That man, the one called Fitzpain?"

"No, not him. He might hate me, but I don't think he could ever bring himself to kill me. Not him. He couldn't... just couldn't."

"But others would."

"Except that Brian will stop them once he knows what I've done." She drew a deep breath. "I have to speak to him again. I have to be certain we can get away without being followed. I'm sure I can convince him."

"How?"

"I have it all in hand, Martin. Trust me."

"There's no way you can stay here. Not now. You realise that, don't you?"

"Yes."

"You'll go with me?"

"Do you still want me?"

"Of course I still want you. I love you. I want to marry you, dammit!" There, he had said it. He had not planned on saying it, not here, but the words had come out, so there could be no going back now.

She put a hand to her mouth. Her eyes were dilated. Was that shock? "Marry youse? But youse don't know what I'm like. What I'm really like." There was something in her voice that hinted at reasons why she could never marry him, but whatever it was remained unspoken.

"I'm finding out, Sorcha. Now that I've spoken to Mickey Murphy, I've discovered a lot that I didn't understand. Give me time to find out the rest of it." He clasped an arm about her shoulders. "I know what you're like when I'm with you. As for what's in your past, that will only matter if we stay here. Let's get out of Belfast, Sorcha Let's... let's... let's get the hell out of here."

335

A small grin crept across her face, causing a tremble in her lips. She leaned forward and kissed him. "I'll try to be worthy of youse."

"How?"

"In future I'll try to say 'you' instead of 'youse'. Would that do as a starter?"

"For the time being." He laughed and rose to his feet. "Look, we can't stay here all night. We could get a bus or taxi, if they any of them are still running. Get out of town and find a hotel for the night; somewhere well away from all this."

"And tomorrow?"

"We'll fly over to England." He paused to think. "I'll have to say goodbye to Aunt Judy, but I don't think she'll mind. She might even be glad to see the back of me."

"It doesn't matter." She squeezed his hand. "I've done somethin' to help us get away. We'll have a new life, and it's going to be better than this, Martin. Better than this."

"What have you done, Sorcha?" He frowned.

"'Tis not so much what I've done, but what I've said I've done. I'll tell youse all about it some other time. Be patient. I'll tell youse soon enough."

He shrugged and clasped her hand tightly as they walked towards the door. After such a frightening day of disaster, a feeling of relief began to invade his mind. His mind was made up. He was leaving and Sorcha was willing to go with him. She hadn't actually said she would marry him, but he took it as a foregone conclusion. The darkness of the past twelve hours was lifting.

Then everything changed.

He saw the gunman the moment he stepped outside the pub. It was Fitzpain and he was carrying a pistol! What the hell was he up to? The Provo man stood at the opposite side of the car park, leaning against a white van. He jerked upright when he saw Martin and Sorcha appear.

"Get back inside!" Martin grabbed Sorcha's arm and drew her backwards so hard she stumbled and fell. She struggled to regain her feet.

336

Fitzpain had his arm raised now, aiming along the barrel of his pistol.

"Inside!" Martin roared, but it was too late.

Martin felt a tremor run through him. "It's him! Fitzpain! The mad psychopath. The one who nearly killed me at Mafeking Street."

Sorcha turned and put her hands against his chest. "'Tis all right, Martin. He won't hurt me. He couldn't ever hurt me."

"But he's got a gun, Sorcha. Get inside now. Quickly."

A determined look rippled across her face. "Leave this to me. I know how to handle him."

"What does he want from us?"

"Never mind. You go back inside, but just leave Brian to me."

She turned and began to walk towards the gunman.

"Oh God, Sorcha, no!" Martin's heart thumped heavily inside his chest as he went after her, following a few steps behind. How could he do anything but follow her? The girl he loved was putting herself in danger.

"Put your gun away, Brian," she called out as she came close to Fitzpain. "There's only us here. No peelers."

"That's the Prod youse been sleepin' with!" Fitzpain gestured towards Martin. "Don't deny it, Sorcha. Ye're a turncoat. Grassed on me with a Prod, so youse did! Grassed on me! I saw youse with them peelers. Saw one o' them point the finger at me. I saw it! And youse was there. Youse grassed on me."

"No, Brian. I'd never do that. It was Jimmy Fish who grassed on you, not me. It was me who did for him. Didn't Maggie tell youse? She was there. We both went to find him and I killed him."

"Maggie, youse say? I ain't seen Maggie since this mornin'."

"'Tis true. I did it for youse, Brian. For youse!"

"Why?"

"'Cos I know who youse are. I know what youse meant to me mammy."

"Yer mammy?" A frown filled his face. "What d'youse mean?"

Martin watched in fear as she continued forward at a slow pace, her arms by her side. "I was born more than a year after Pat Mulveny walked out on mammy. He wasn't me daddy. Couldn't have been." She was close up to him now and slowed to a halt. "It was youse, wasn't it? You're me daddy, ain't youse? That's why youse'd never kill me."

Fitzpain gave her a look that was a mixture of contempt and anger. "Stupid bitch! What're youse talkin' about? Course I ain't yer daddy."

She took a step backwards. "But I thought…"

"I was in gaol when yer mammy got pregnant with youse. Banged up in Crumlin Road Gaol, so I was, from fifty-one to fifty-three."

She gasped. "Youse were… Jeezuz!" She turned away from him then, her mouth agape as she faced Martin. "I thought… I honestly thought…"

"Youse want to know the truth, girl?" Fitzpain waved his pistol. "While I was banged up in gaol, yer mammy took in a lodger to pay the rent, and he spent his nights in her bed. Made her pregnant, so he did. Know who that was, girl? Do youse? 'Twas Jimmy Fish. He was yer real daddy!"

She turned to face him again. "No." The single word slipped from her lips in a soft hush of breath, almost like a prayer. "Not…"

"Yes, him! He never knew the truth of it, the poor sod. He thought I was yer daddy. But it was him fer sure, yer mammy told me so. And, youse know what? He was an informer, right enough, but he grassed on youse when youse were at the hotel, not me!"

"No! The peelers came fer youse."

"The peelers got it all wrong. But it was Jimmy Fish who sent them there. We saw him outside the hotel, didn't we? We all thought he sent the peelers to pick up me. But he didn't. He sent them there to pick up his illegitimate daughter. The dirty little rat." He let out a long, exasperate sigh. "Ironic wasn't it? He squealed on his own child, even

338

if he didn't know it, and youse're tellin' me youse killed him! Stupid bitch!"

"Why would Jimmy Fish grass on me?" she said. Her voice trembled with emotion.

"Because he needed the money. Up to his ears in gambling debts, he was. And the peelers paid him to grass on anyone worth the money. He phoned them and told them where to find youse at the hotel, but he didn't know I was on me way there."

"He really was me daddy?"

"True enough."

"I didn't know..."

"Neither did he. He was a thief, caught by the peelers and banged up in gaol before yer mammy discovered she was pregnant by him."

"I thought..." she mumbled. "I thought he squealed on youse. And I thought youse would want me to kill him because of it. Thought youse would let me go away from Belfast if I did that. Thought you'd let me go and never come after me."

Fitzpain gave her a sour look. "I'm not *yer* daddy, Sorcha. No way. But I'll tell youse the truth, girl. I was Bridie's real daddy. That was why Pat Mulveny walked out on yer mammy. Because I shagged her and made her pregnant."

"Bridie!" A look of anger erupted across her face. "You... you bastard, Brian Fitzpain!"

"Aye, t'was me. And them UVF guys killed Bridie, so they did. Killed my child. The dirty bastards. Filthy Prods, just like the bastard youse been sleepin' with. Youse're as bad as them, Sorcha. Youse deserve all that's comin' to youse."

Martin stared into the IRA man's face. Despite the danger he felt no fear of him. His only concern now was for Sorcha. She stood stock still in front of him, saying nothing, as if further words were trapped inside her, unable to break free.

On a sudden impulse, Martin grabbed at her shoulders.

This had gone far enough. He had to stop it now. "Come back inside, Sorcha. Please, come inside now."

But she made no effort to move, rooted to the tarmac as the implications sank deeper into her brain. Then she turned to him and muttered, "Oh, Martin. I'm sorry. I thought it would help us if Brian thought...I thought it would help us get away without his men comin' after us. I thought..."

A single gunshot cut off her words. She clutched at her right elbow as she slumped forward in his arms. Blood oozed from around the wound. Behind her, Fitzpain was scowling, his pistol still pointed at her. "She'd be better off dead," he said, aiming his weapon for a second shot.

"No, Sorcha! No!" Martin clasped her tight to him.

He was only vaguely aware of a black saloon racing into the car park, screeching to a halt just a few yards from the gunman. It swerved through ninety degrees so that the passenger side was closest to Fitzpain. Martin gasped in astonishment. It was them! The two peelers who'd saved him this very afternoon: Evans and McIlroy. He recognised the car before he recognised the occupants.

The younger policeman, Evans, leapt from the vehicle with his pistol firmly held and supported in his outstretched hands. He dropped onto one knee and aimed at the killer. He was in a perfect position to shoot.

Fitzpain glared at him.

Evans shouted, "Put the gun down!"

Martin spotted the other peeler, McIlroy, exiting the car on the opposite side. He took cover on his side of the vehicle. Evans was still in the better position to shoot.

"Fuck off, peelers!" Fitzpain roared. Then he lunged forward and grabbed at Sorcha.

Martin tried to hold on to her but Fitzpain was the stronger man. He ripped her from Martin's grasp and swung the girl round to shield him from the two policemen.

And then something happened to the younger policeman, something unexpected. He jabbed a hand to his head and lowered his gun. He seemed to be in a daze. Or was he blacking out? It was difficult to tell.

McIlroy shouted at him. "Shoot, man! Shoot!"

But Evans was in trouble. He still had the perfect line, but he was seemingly unable to aim his pistol. Something was seriously wrong with him. His gun dropped from his hand and he collapsed to the ground.

Martin turned his attention to Fitzpain. Why hadn't the IRA man fired at Evans? Why had he wasted a few precious seconds? Then he understood. The man was afraid because Evans was now unarmed. Fitzpain was used to shooting at armed policemen from within the cover of a mob. He was so used to having others surround him and protect him. But it wasn't so easy when you killed an unarmed peeler in the sight of so many witnesses. Too many witnesses.

But the other peeler was still armed. He stood up to get a better aim and moved out of cover.

Still using Sorcha as a shield, the IRA man swung his gun towards the police car. Then he fired. Twice. The first shot went wild. The second caused McIlroy to cry out in pain. Martin saw the older policeman crumple to the ground, clutching his groin.

In that same moment, he heard McIlroy shout, "Take him, Will! Take him!"

Evans seemed to be recovering, he was staggering to his feet, reaching out for his fallen pistol.

Again, McIlroy shouted. "Do it, man! You have the best line of shot. Take him now!"

Fitzpain fired a third time and, in that moment, Sorcha dragged herself free.

But Evans was hit. He was stumbling when he finally pulled his trigger.

Just the one shot.

And that was when Fitzpain cried out and fell.

He would have been dead before he hit the ground.

***

February 1981

I left Martin's house confident I now had most of the story.
Not just the facts of the bombings, but the effect it had on
three people who were out there on the streets at the time:
Sorcha, Will and Martin. It was almost enough for me to
complete my manuscript. Almost enough. All I needed now
was to find out more about the killing of the Police
Constable Dunlop. What exactly happened that night?
Despite the way my story was coming together, I felt no
sense of satisfaction as I walked away from the house. How
can there ever be satisfaction in other people's suffering?

There was a call waiting for us on Susan's answerphone
when we got back to her flat. It was the prison's deputy
governor asking us to come and see her. She wouldn't tell
us why, only that it concerned Sorcha Mulveny. Susan and I
drove to the prison straight away. On arrival we were shown
into an office on the first floor.

The deputy governor was a smartly-dressed woman with
a commanding presence. A middle-aged clergyman, grey-
haired and wearing a grey suit, stood beside her. She
indicated seats for us before she and the clergyman sat
down.

"This is the Reverend Mayfair, the prison chaplain. I've
asked him to be here because we have some bad news for
you." She spoke in a solemn voice, the sort of voice the
chaplain might have used at a funeral. Instinctively, I braced
myself for what was to come next. "Miss Mulveny died
earlier today. She committed suicide in her cell."

In the pregnant silence that followed, Susan grabbed at
my hand. It took a moment or two before I was able to ask,
"How?"

"She hanged herself."

"Oh God."

The woman looked at me with the expression of someone
who had been through this act before. Any semblance of
sympathy was clearly an act. She picked up a notepad from
her desk and studied it for a few seconds. "I see that you

had a number of interviews with Miss Mulveny. I need to ask you if she gave any indication that she had such a thing in mind."

"No. No indication at all."

"Never?"

"Never." That was not true, of course, because Sorcha had told me how she considered suicide years ago, before she met Martin. I didn't intend the lie, it was just an automatic reaction to the news, an attempt to protect Sorcha's memory.

"Is there anything she did say that stands out in your mind?"

"What sort of thing?"

"Anything that may throw some light on her state of mind."

"No. Nothing." Then I remembered then Sorcha's final words to us. *'Tis best this way.* But, once again, I held back with the truth. I wasn't going to get mired in words that might be turned against Sorcha's memory. She didn't deserve that. She was, after all, the ultimate victim.

"She talked about a brutal killing before she died," The deputy governor said. "She asked to see the prison chaplain and she told him about her part in it. In view of your involvement with Miss Mulveny, I think you may want to hear this."

Without waiting for any comment from either Susan or myself, the Reverend Mayfair leaned forward. "She confessed to the murder at the trial, but she never revealed what actually happened... until now. She was in tears by the time she had finished telling me."

"Are you allowed to tell us about it?" I asked, aware that my voice was shallow and hoarse.

He smiled grimly. "Yes. This was not a Catholic confession. And I am not a priest, just a Presbyterian minister. More to the point, she actually asked me to tell you what happened to that young policeman, Constable Dunlop. She wanted you to know, but she didn't want to tell you yourself."

***

Thursday 20th July 1972
2345 BST

She had been with Fitzpain on a street corner in the Ardoyne. He had a fistful of the bomb target lists, sealed inside envelopes. It was information to be shared with other Provo thugs, the ones who would give the hoax warnings. Beneath a streetlamp, one of the few lamps still working, he handed one envelope to Sorcha with a demand that she call the police with false information once the campaign started. He gave her the telephone code word, *Phoenix*, telling her she had to make sure the peelers never knew which way to turn.

And then the lone peeler came walking along the street.

Fitzpain was first to spot him. "D'youse see that bastard across the street, Sorcha, the one watchin' us?"

Sorcha glanced around. Sure enough, there was a solitary man standing just one hundred yards away, staring at them.

"D'youse know who he is?" she asked.

Fitzpain nodded. "A traitor called Dunlop. A Catholic who joined the RUC pigs. We've got his picture in the Provo files. We'll get him one of these days, the bastard."

"Not now."

"No. He'll be armed."

"Why's he starin' at us?"

"Because he's recognised me, that's fer sure. I'll bet he's wonderin' what we're doin' here."

"Let's walk away," she suggested.

"Just walk easy, Sorcha. The chances are he doesn't know youse, so don't make any sudden moves."

They were fifty yards farther along the street when Sorcha turned to look back. The peeler was beneath the same streetlamp, bent over and picking up something.

"He's found something, Brian," she said. "It's an envelope. Shite! Youse must have dropped one of them. If he reads that we're done for."

344

Fitzpain paused in mid stride, but he kept looking ahead. He didn't even bother to check whether had had lost one of the envelopes. He just stared ahead. His voice held a hint of alarm.

"Don't panic. Tell me what he's doin'."

"He's openin' the envelope. Dear God, he'll be readin' the list. What'll we do now?"

"Shite! There's only one thing we can do." Fitzpain pulled his serrated kitchen knife from inside his coat. "And 'tis youse who'll have to do it, girl. He knows me, that's why he was starin' at us in the first place, but I figure he doesn't know youse though."

"Youse want me to kill him?"

"Of course I want youse to kill him! Now, Sorcha. Now, before it's too late."

"No! I'm not a murderer, damn you!"

"'Tis time youse started."

"No! I don't want to."

He gritted his teeth and thrust his face up against hers. "Do it! Do it or we're both gonna land up in gaol. Is that what youse wants?"

She took the knife gingerly, her heart thumping. She had done many wicked things in her life, but she had never killed a man. Not then. "I can't..." she mumbled.

"Do it! Hold the knife behind yer back and just walk up to him. Smile at him like ye're offerin' him a quick dip in yer knickers for a few quid. There's enough whores around here, and he'll know that. He'll likely not know what ye're really up to until 'tis too late."

Sorcha would have held back, argued with Fitzpain, but he was already walking away. Within seconds he had rounded a corner and was out of sight. Sorcha was left with no other option than to do as he said. God help her, she hated the thought of it, but she had to do it.

She began to walk back towards the peeler.

It all happened quicker than she expected. He gazed at her with a puzzled expression and never gave a sign of comprehension until she brought the knife into view at the last moment. She stared into his face and tensed herself for the one fatal act that would make her a killer.

But she couldn't do it.

She held the knife close to his chest, but she couldn't bring herself to make that final thrust. She continued to stare into his face, and he stared back as if mesmerised. An intense expression filled his eyes, an expression of fear. He knew he was about to die, and he wasn't ready for it.

And still she hesitated.

"Do it!" The voice bellowed close behind her. It was Fitzpain's voice. Deep and demanding. "Do it, Sorcha!"

She had not heard him approach, but she felt his hands clasp about hers: hard, beefy hands, that crushed her slender fingers in a tight grip. Before she could react, he forced the knife forward, deep into the peeler's chest. The peeler still held the envelope as he fell to the pavement with the knife lodged in him. She stared down at him and gulped back a cry of alarm.

Dear God, she was now a murderer!

She turned to face Fitzpain. "Why?"

"Because you would have let him get away, damn you!"

She shivered. He had made the final move, but she was the one who held the knife. She tried to focus on the weapon rammed into the peeler's chest, but her gaze was hazy now. Dear God, what had she done? The guilt was as much hers as his. She had been guilty of so many wicked things in her life, but she had never actually killed anyone. Now she was as bad as Brian Fitzpain and his men.

It was Fitzpain who leaned over the body and grabbed the bomb list. He also grabbed the knife, wrenching it from the man's chest with a sudden twist. Bile rose in her throat as he casually wiped it on his sleeve.

She turned and ran, but her nerve finally failed her at the street corner. She came to a sudden halt, bent double and vomited into the gutter. She had no remaining coherent thoughts in her head when she hurried on. The impact of what she had just done was too much to live with. She couldn't have done it, surely not! It wasn't her racing away from the scene. It was some other person pretending to be her. How could she possibly be a murderer?

When she reached Fitzpain's dingy backstreet house, she began to recover her senses and she knew then what it felt like to kill a man. What it really felt like in the cold light of understanding. It was Brian's knife, Brian's orders, Brian's strength forcing her to thrust the knife forward. But her hand was on the handle as the blade sank into the peeler's chest. And she hated herself for it.

Brian Fitzpain was no help; but how could she expect help from a man for whom killing was just another job? She stripped off her bloodied clothes and used his bath to wash the stains from her skin, soaking in the warm water while her thoughts spun dizzily. The only useful thing Fitzpain did that night was to persuade a local prostitute to give her some clean clothes on promise of later payment. Worn and faded jeans that later became splashed with the blood of the rapist who lost his dick in the back alley.

She was sitting in Brian's small sitting room, drinking whiskey to dull the ache in her head when an IRA runner brought a message: a twelve-year-old girl had been raped and the rapist had to be punished. That was when Fitzpain ordered her to confirm the boy's crime before he was executed.

Hadn't she been through enough that night!

But she did as he ordered. She set up the rapist for a revenge killing.

Would the butchery never end?

***

February 1981

"She didn't do it," I said. "She confessed to it, and everyone believed it was her. But it wasn't her at all. She didn't kill the policeman."

The chaplain let out a long sigh. "Her hands were on the knife. She felt the horror of it as much as if she had done it all by herself. That was partly why she pleaded guilty."

"Not because she was protecting someone?"

"That was only one part of it. More importantly, it was her feelings of guilt. It all went back to that list of the bomb locations. She could have taken it to the police and saved lives. She could have, but she didn't, and that sat heavily on her mind. That was her real guilt. Had she taken the list to the police other people's lives would have been saved, but her own life would have been sacrificed. The IRA would have got to her, even in prison. They had ways and they would have tortured her and killed her. She thought about it in the first few days of her trial and the guilty feelings became too much for her. That was why she made the decision to confess to something she didn't do. It was her act of atonement."

"You mean she wanted to ease her conscience. Make amends for all the people who died that day." I struggled to imagine the mental anguish she must have suffered. A young woman who needed help, not prison.

The chaplain nodded. "Yes. People died. And Sorcha told herself they died because of her. She couldn't cope with the feelings of guilt, so she made the false confession, knowing she would be locked up here for a long time. She hoped that her gaol sentence would... as you said... ease her conscience."

"Do you think she found peace after telling you this?" I asked.

"I don't know, and that's the truth." Reverend Mayfair sat back in his seat and gave me a sad expression. "The only person who knows the answer to that is now dead."

"God rest her soul," I whispered.

Susan reached across to grasp my hand. "That's the end of it," she said. "No more investigation, no more interviews. It has to end here."

She was partly right of course. There would be no more interviews with Sorcha. The book would be her epitaph.

"I shall miss talking to her," I said as Susan and I walked away from the deputy governor's office. "I'd grown to like her, for all that she did."

"Talk to me instead." Susan's voice went hushed. She drew a deep breath before she added, "I've emptied my pending tray."

I felt a shiver of anticipation run through me. Why was she telling me now, at this solemn time? Did this mean she wanted to cheer me up, or let me down?

I hesitated and said, "And?"

"The answer is yes."

"Yes?" There were tears in my eyes and I was unable to reply. It was as if the ghost of Annie was easing itself back into my life. A good ghost, a friendly ghost. Not Annie herself, of course, but a ghost that was encouraging someone who would be every bit as good for me.

Chapter Twenty-Four

October 1981

The summer was long gone, and autumn was already handing over to early winter weather. It had been a busy year getting the book ready for publication. In the middle of that, Susan and I were married at a quiet register office ceremony in Belfast. After that we made plans to sell Susan's flat in Ireland and my flat in Wimbledon. We would start a new life together in a new place, but we were not too sure where. The decision was put on hold because I had to earn a living to support her and that meant finishing the book. In the meantime, we lived in Wimbledon.

We decided to make one last foray up to North Wales shortly after I finished reading a proof edition. It wasn't quite ready for publication because the publishers were keen for me to find out more about what happened in the aftermath. In fact, they wanted another chapter. I wasn't so keen, but publication of the book depended upon it, so I phoned Will Evans, apologised for breaking my promise, and asked him for that one last chat. I called it a chat rather than an interview as a way of lessening the impact. I felt guilty about it, but I was under pressure from my editor.

Will said he would think about it, but his initial reaction was that he wanted no more to do with my book. However, he called back an hour later with a compromise. "I won't talk to you again," he said. "But Milly will."

That surprised me.

"Don't come to the house," he said. "We don't want the girls to see you. We're proud of them, but any talk of Belfast still affects them. They clam up and go silent for days."

"Where can we meet your wife, Will?"

"There's a coffee shop at the end of our road. You can't miss it. She says she'll be there at eleven in the morning next Monday. Can you make that?"

"Yes, certainly." It was three days away, but we could wait.

In the event, Milly was there waiting for me and Susan when we arrived just a few minutes before eleven. She was smartly dressed in a cream suit, as if she was attending an important meeting, and she had a cup of coffee on the table in front of her. While I was introducing Susan, my attention was drawn to her glasses. I had never before seen her with glasses.

She must have seen me focus on her face because she said, "The glasses are new. My eyesight is going downhill. Our doctor says it's because of my high blood pressure. Hypertension, you see. It affects the blood vessels."

"I'm sorry," I said. "You suffer with…"

"With my nerves."

That was an honest admission I wasn't expecting. Now I began to see the truth behind Will's rash assertion that Milly was the strong one. He was wrong. She was just as badly affected as the rest of her family, but she had covered her tracks well.

"I'm sorry," I said.

"I blame it on the after-effects of Belfast. Will says I'm wrong, but he can't even see the full extent of the damage it's caused him. So what would he know?"

"And your doctor?"

"Says he wants more tests. In the meantime he's got me on these pills."

I ordered two more coffees and Susan and I sat opposite her.

After a few pleasantries, I said, "I appreciate you seeing us, Mrs Evans. I realise this won't be easy for you."

"I'm doing this for Will's sake." She took off her glasses and wiped a hand across her brow. "He still has nightmares

351

about Northern Ireland. So do our girls. Eight years since we left, and they're young ladies now, but they're still affected. You won't understand that, of course."

I looked sideways at Susan, wondering if she wanted to comment, but she silently shook her head.

"What are you willing to tell me, Mrs Evans?" I asked. Because, sure as fate, there was something she wanted me to know.

"I want you to know the reason why Will finally gave in and agreed to leave Belfast."

***

21st July 1972
2130 BST

The hospital ward was full. Eight beds each held a victim of the bombings; a victim who had survived, but not intact. A young nurse was pulling the curtains around a bed where an old man lay groaning. An older nurse was checking the pulse rate of a younger man with both arms in plaster. A doctor stood at the end of another bed, silently examining a chart. This patient seemed to have no legs.

Milly Foster held the hands of the twins as she picked her way quietly to the end bed where Will lay. His right shoulder was heavily bandaged and his right arm was cased in plaster. He tried to smile at her as she approached, but the left side of his face was paralysed. It gave him an ugly appearance.

"They told me you're going to live, damn you," she whispered, hoping the girls would not hear. They stood in the background looking bemused, unused to the atmosphere of a busy hospital. Milly bent and kissed Will, belatedly wondering if that had been a silly thing to say. Of course he was going to live. They were both going to live, but it would never be the same again. Their lives would have to change.

"It'll take more than a mad gunman to get rid of me,

love." He whispered with words that were slurred.

She wiped a tear from her cheek. "I've been talking to the doctor. It wasn't just about the gunshot. Right at the end you had a stroke. That's why you collapsed." She stared at his lopsided face and wondered how much of it would repair itself. No one could tell her.

"They did a brain scan," he said.

"I know. You should have seen the doctor long ago, after that blow on the head. You should have had it investigated then. It might not have come to this."

"You're right, Milly." He turned his head away and beckoned the girls closer with his good hand. "Come here my pretty ones."

"You must be very careful not to hurt daddy," Milly said as she sat the two girls on the side of the bed and pulled up a chair for herself.

Patsy asked, "Mummy, why is daddy all bandaged up?"

"He had an accident at work, Sweetheart."

"Why is he making that funny face and why is he talking funny?"

"His mouth is a bit sore."

"Is he going to get better?"

"Of course he will. If he doesn't, I shall…"

"Yes, mummy?"

"Never mind what I shall do to him." She leaned closer to Will. "I heard that the girl… she'll probably go to gaol."

He nodded. "But she lived. Too many other people didn't make it today."

"And the IRA man who shot you?"

"He didn't make it."

"Thank God for that."

"It was the first time I ever killed a man, Milly."

She put a finger to her lips. "Not in front of the children…" she said, seeing the wide-eyed look in their faces.

"Sorry." He quickly changed the subject. "Reckon we'll have to put off the holiday until I get out of here. We'll have a holiday in Wales then."

She shook her head, firm resolve forcing her to say what she needed to say. "No, Will. Not just a holiday. Your life is going to be very different from now on. It has to be. And I want a new way of life as well. A life without fear for me and the children. I can't take any more of this and neither can the girls."

A look of understanding crept into his eyes, as if he was taking on a new perception of what he had been through. He said, "I'm sorry, Milly."

"Sorry for what?" she said, suddenly wondering if all her hopes were about to be crushed.

"Sorry for everything. Earlier today DCI McIlroy said something important to me. He said, 'If you do wrong, don't say sorry to a priest, say sorry to the person you hurt.'" He reached out his hand and she saw that it was still bloodied. He squeezed her fingers between his. "Milly, I'm sorry for all the hurt I've caused you. I was wrong; we do need to get away from here. For all our sakes: you, me and the girls."

It was what she had been longing to hear for a long time, but she held back from saying so.

"Do you think you could live in Wales?" She asked.

"Why not? My ancestors did. Reckon I'm up for it."

"Finally?"

"Finally."

"Promise?"

"I promise."

"Thank God for that, Will."

***

October 1981

That was the last time I saw Milly Evans, but not the last time I spoke to her. She telephoned me two weeks later. She sounded like she's been crying.

"I want you to know what Northern Ireland has done to our lives," she said in a rasping hoarse voice. "I want you to

354

know so you can put it in your book; a warning to other people. Make them understand what they've done. What they're still doing!"

"What is it, Milly?" I asked. "Is it Will? Has he..."

"It's Patsy," she said. "She's in hospital. Will is there with her. They say she'll live, thank God."

"What happened, Milly?"

A deep sigh echoed down the line. "One of my cousin's boys came over on a visit from Belfast. He was only a lad when we lived there. A big brute he is now. Had too much to drink and started on at Will because of his time in the RUC. Told Will he was a traitor and he was responsible for the trouble in Belfast. Shouting at him, he was. Shouting and bellowing. Patsy saw it all and it brought everything back to her. All the bombing and killing; it brought it all back. Sent her into hysterics. She couldn't cope with it. That night she got hold of some pills and tried to take her own life."

"Oh, God, Milly! I'm so sorry."

"Put it in your book, damn you! Tell them what it's really like. Tell them what it's done to the children. Tell them because they still don't understand!"

She rang off, but her words stayed with me. *They still don't understand.*

I sent Will a proof copy of the book before it was published in case he wanted me to delete anything. In the event I didn't hear from him until a year later when I received a picture postcard from the Canary Islands. I assumed the family were on holiday. It said simply, *Hated the book.*

I understood exactly what he meant.

POSTSCRIPT TO THE SECOND EDITION

Tom McIlroy no longer lived in Belfast, but I was able to make contact with him indirectly through the Retired Police Officers Association. When the first edition of the book was edited and ready for publication, I sent him a typed copy of the manuscript and asked for his agreement for the things I wrote about him. He said it was all pretty accurate, especially the description of his wife. Publication went ahead with no changes and I sent him a hardback copy. Two weeks later I received a long letter from him. He gave me an address in Fermanagh and a telephone number, so I called him. We had a long and interesting conversation.

This is what he told me:

***

Four weeks after he was shot in the groin, DCI Thomas McIlroy attended the opening of the trial of 'Mad Mac' McKinnon. The evidence was strong, especially his inky fingerprints on the threatening note left beside the body at York Road Railway Station. There was every expectation he would go down for the murders of both Bridie and Barbara Mulveny. His accomplice, Blair, was charged with conspiracy to murder. He had a very weak defence and was destined for a lengthy spell in prison.

McIlroy left the trial in a happier frame of mind.

Three days later McIlroy set out to speak to Detective Superintendent Boyle at North Castle Street. On the way he called in to see Will and Milly Evans. They were busy packing up their belongings, hindered by the twins playing on the lounge floor. Will's face was still lopsided, and would be for a long time to come, but his arm was healing well and he seemed in good spirits.

Milly had a cheerful smile for the DCI.

"You look happy," he said to her and he gave her a peck on the cheek.

"And you still look like you're suffering," she replied, indicating his prominent limp.

"Another operation next week. They know what's wrong, but putting it right isn't proving too easy. When do you leave?"

"In two days. Will starts work in Wales next week; a desk job at a rural police station where the worst crime they have is tourists dropping litter."

"No bombs?"

"God forbid."

"I hope you'll both be happy."

"We are already." Her continuing smile indicated the truth of it.

Will led him into the kitchen while Milly carried on with the packing, surrounded by cardboard boxes. He closed the door to keep out the sound of the two girls at play.

Will gestured to a chair at the kitchen table and switched on the kettle. "How are things at home, Tom? How are things with your wife?" He no longer called him, boss. No longer needed to.

McIlroy eased himself into the seat and noted a whiskey bottle nearby. Was it there to fortify the coffee?

"According to her lawyer, she still wants a divorce. Still won't believe me when I tell her what actually happened. You know what it was all about, do you?"

"I can guess. Maisie O'Hare, wasn't it? You know, when I was in the canteen earlier, on the day of the bombs, she made a pass at me."

"You refused, I hope."

"Of course. But that was when she made an accusation against you. She said that was why your wife walked out on you."

"And you believed her?"

"Frankly, no. I don't believe it then and I don't believe it now."

"Thank you for that." McIlroy replied. His educated Belfast accent was softly spoken now. "Do you really think a young woman like that would want sex with an old duffer like me? Old enough to be her father. Of course she wouldn't. But, like all stories, Will, there is an element of truth in it."

"Do you want to tell me?" Will poured out the coffee, added the whiskey and handed McIlroy a mug.

He took it with a grin.

"It was all because the job was getting on top of me, Will. Just like it was getting on top of all of us. One night I got absolutely pissed at a party. Drowning out the reality of life in CID. Maisie was there and she took me away and put me to bed at her flat. I was so plastered I knew nothing about it until the next day when I woke up with a splitting headache. I was in her bed, but I was still fully dressed, dammit. It would all have ended there if the vindictive bitch hadn't told my missus that I slept with her."

"But nothing happened between you and Maisie?"

"Nothing. I wasn't capable of it, even if I'd wanted to."

"So, what will you do now?"

"The wife's lawyer has been on to me and I've told him she can go ahead with the divorce. What's the point of contesting it if she refuses to believe me?"

"And then?"

"Then I shall divorce myself from the RUC. Just like you, Will. Just like you."

Will was not surprised. "You've another job lined up?"

"I'll go freelance. Escape to the countryside beyond Belfast and take on private jobs... make a new life for myself. When the medics have finished with me."

"The countryside? You think that will be far enough?"

"I'll give it a try. I'll aim to settle somewhere new just like you. Besides, my mum in Fermanagh is getting on in years and I feel a need to be closer to her."

"I suppose we're not the only ones who want to pull out

of Belfast. And more will follow." Will nodded towards McIlroy's groin. "And that... that's a wife-shattering thing, isn't it?"

He put on a false air of bravado because he couldn't think of any other immediate response. "That's one way of putting it. It certainly puts me out of bedtime action until they finally get things sorted." Then he quickly changed the subject. "On a happier note, I had a letter this morning from that young man, Martin Foster. He's actually got himself a job, which is good. It's in Belfast but that's his choice."

"In Belfast? He wanted to join the British army, didn't he?"

McIlroy grinned. "I talked him out of that. He came to see me a couple of times while I was in hospital and I had some fatherly chats with him. He may be naïve, but underneath he's a hell of a nice lad. I managed to persuade him to try for something better than the army. I urged him to leave Northern Ireland, but he said he wanted to stay because of a girl."

"Sorcha Mulveny?"

"I think so. I think he felt a need to be close to where she's banged up. I argued with him but he wouldn't budge, so I wrote to a pal of mine who works for an accountancy firm in Belfast, and I put in a good word for Martin. They agreed to interview him. In the letter he says they've offered him a job as a junior clerk. It means starting at the bottom of the tree, but it's a job and I have this feeling he'll soon work his way up the ladder. I hope so, anyway."

"Things would never have worked out for him with the Mulveny girl, would they?" Will said.

"Of course not. He'll not forget her easily, but in time he'll move on." He worked up a cheery smile. "We'll all move on, Will. You and Milly and the kids. Martin Foster. Even me, in my own sweet way. We'll all move on."

"Amen to that, Tom."

McIlroy finished his tea. "And now I must move on to an important meeting with Detective Superintendent Boyle."

"I hope it goes well for you." Will put down his own

coffee and shook the hand of his one-time boss. "I shall miss you. You know that, don't you?"

"Reckon I do, Will."

An hour later McIlroy limped into the North Castle Street RUC station. The ache in his groin was persistent, but he tried to look comfortable. Sergeant Billy McRee came from behind his reception desk to shake his hand and welcome him back to work.

"Glad to see you back on duty again, sir," he said.

McIlroy thanked him and asked, "Is Superintendent Boyle in his office?"

"He is that, sir."

McIlroy went straight to Boyle's office and walked in without knocking. The Detective Superintendent blinked at him in surprise but made no effort to rebuke him. Neither did he speak straight away. He remained solidly behind his desk while McIlroy took the empty seat opposite.

"You were expecting me?" McIlroy said.

Boyle nodded. "Yes. I was told you might call in today. Are you fully fit once more? Or at least fit enough to resume your duties?"

"Partially fit."

"That's good enough. We're under-manned at present."

"I said I was partially fit. I didn't say I would actually return to duty." McIlroy leaned forward and placed a document on the senior officer's desk. "This is my resignation. Signed and dated. I'm handing it to you in person so there will be no doubts about my intentions."

Boyle stared at the document, but he made no attempt to pick it up. He leaned back in his seat and scratched at his cheek. "Well, now. That is somewhat unexpected. What are your plans? What will you do now?"

"That's my business."

"Does your wife know about this?"

"I'm sure you'll tell her."

Boyle shook his head. "No. I can't do that. She's no longer with me. We had a disagreement and now she and your daughter are staying with a cousin in Lisburn. For the

360

time being."

"Really? Well, well. There's a surprise." McIlroy suppressed the urge to laugh out loud. In truth, he wasn't at all surprised. He even felt a little sympathy for his erstwhile boss.

"You didn't know?" Boyle said.

"I do now."

"I understand she plans to move back in with you. You'll take her back?"

"I'm not going to discuss my plans with you." McIlroy stood up slowly. The ache in his groin persisted. "I'll be on my way now. If you hear from my wife, do pass on my regards. I hope she finds whatever it is in life she's looking for."

"That's it? So soon." Boyle rose up from behind his desk. "You're off already."

"Into the wide blue yonder." McIlroy waved a hand as he turned and headed for the door. "I've done what I came to do. We won't meet again, which will be no loss to me."

"But you're throwing away your whole future."

"Remember what Scarlett O'Hara said." McIlroy paused by the door, one hand on the handle. "One of the best closing lines in film history. Tomorrow is another day."

He was tempted to slam the door behind him, but he didn't. He closed it quietly, politely leaving behind a world in which he had no further interest.

Fantastic Books
Great Authors

darkstroke is
an imprint of
Crooked Cat Books

- Gripping Thrillers
- Cosy Mysteries
- Dark Horror
- Fascinating Historicals
- Exciting Fantasy
- Young Adult and Children's
  Adventures
- Non-Fiction

Discover us online
www.darkstroke.com

Find us on instagram:
www.instagram.com/darkstrokebooks

Printed in Poland
by Amazon Fulfillment
Poland Sp. z o.o., Wrocław

56416648R00218